Grave Secret

Book Six of the Sidney Becker Mysteries

LINDA BERRY

Five Star Reviews from Amazon Readers

—*What would you do if you found a decomposed body in your compost pile? Ben Colby immediately called in Police Chief Sidney Becker. I have never read any of the Sidney Becker books but this one gave me enough background on the characters and town that I didn't feel lost. The characters were all very real and believable. The story grabbed my attention and kept it to the end. The story touches on several very real human conditions including loss, love, grief, greed, compassion, homelessness, and recovery. I thoroughly enjoyed it and plan to read the rest of the series.* -R.Robinson

—*Linda Berry has once again knocked it out of the park with this thrill ride! I absolutely loved this book and if you love suspense and mystery, you will too!*-LehcC00

—*While each book is part of a series, they are absolutely stand-alone novels. The characters quickly become old friends and acquaintances, people you actually care about and are interested in. One of the other things that I truly like about Ms. Berry's work is that she goes to great length to research both her plot elements and law enforcement practices. She makes a point of getting it "right", which further supports the legitimacy and believability of the characters' actions and plot. Ms. Berry is not a lazy author, and the result of her effort are books that grab and keep the readers' attention, and flow to a satisfying climax. If you like a strong female protagonist in a mystery/police procedural that does things correctly, you will enjoy any of the books in the series. I recommend reading them all!* -Rob H

—*I have read all of the Sidney Becker books, and every one has been engrossing and entertaining . Grave Secret is no exception! It's well written, and full of surprising twists and turns. Ms. Berry seamlessly interweaves complex plots with beautiful imagery and a colorful cast of original characters. I have grown to love the main characters, and am always intrigued by the new personalities introduced. I found myself thinking about the book even after the last page. I look forward to the next book in the series!* –Jaen Martine

—*I was hooked from the very beginning. I cared about the characters and felt all their emotions with them. This is the first book of the series I have read and can't wait to read the other books.* —Linda

Anyone who has lost something they
thought was theirs forever
finally comes to realize that nothing
really belongs to them.

— Paulo Coelho

Books by Linda Berry

Hidden Part 1

Hidden Part 2

Pretty Corpse

The Killing Woods

The Dead Chill

Cold Revenge

Killer Magic

The Sting of Death

Grave Secret

To learn of new releases and discounts,
add your name to Linda's mailing list:

https://www.lindaberry.net

ACKNOWLEDGMENTS

I OWE A HUGE debt of gratitude to the extraordinary editors who helped craft *Grave Secret* into a suspenseful and entertaining work of fiction.

A heartfelt thank you goes to my dear friend and trusted advisor, Rob Hall. Every bit of Rob's twenty years of experience in uniform—as a deputy sheriff, patrol cop, homicide investigator, and police chief—was drawn upon to ensure that the police protocols in *Grave Secret* were authentic.

I thank Jeanine "Smarty Pants" Pollak, my adventurous and extravagant friend, and editor extraordinaire. Jeanine's enthusiasm and sense of humor made editing this book loads of fun. Her remarkable eye for detail helped shape the story from beginning to end.

I thank my husband, Mark, for many years of solid support and encouragement, and most importantly, for all the laughter. Mark's unerring skill as editor and project manager ensured that *Grave Secret* rose to the highest professional standard.

CHAPTER ONE

DRESSED IN JEANS and a flannel jacket, Ben Colby contemplated his morning chores from the back porch of his single-story home. Fine layers of mist stretched into the woods bordering his property on the north shore of Lake Kalapuya, and everything glistened with a sheen of moisture from last night's storm. The last of the season's leaves carpeted the ground and bare branches stood stark against the pewter sky, a reminder that winter would soon be upon them. He shared his wilderness paradise with creatures of all kinds, and sometimes he saw evidence that a bear or cougar had passed through his yard. But this morning nothing marred the tranquility of the setting. No menacing predator lurked in the shadows. No needling premonition warned him of encroaching danger.

The air was cold and damp. He turned up his collar and pulled his knit hat lower over his ears, then he trudged into the tool shed. He emerged with a rake and a large plastic garbage bin. He needed to rake up the leaves and add them to the compost pile behind the shed, then split a half cord of wood. Twenty minutes later he had spread the newly collected leaves over the top of the compost heap. In the spring, the resulting mulch would enrich the soil of his garden, producing a high yield of healthy summer vegetables. He used a shovel to turn and mix the leaves into the material already decomposing. The layers of twigs that he had placed underneath the pile allowed worms and maggots to colonize the compost, and he saw with amazement that they had multiplied far beyond his expectation. An unusually strong smell of decay wafted from the mix and enveloped him.

Unexpectedly, his shovel clicked on something hard. That was odd. Compost material was spongy and moist. He turned it every two weeks and nothing hard had been in there before. Puzzled, he scraped away some of the mulch with a gloved hand and revealed what appeared to be a branch. *How did that get in there?* He reached down, grasped it, and pulled. The branch didn't give. He pulled harder. It gave. With a shocked gasp, he dropped what he held in his hand and took a frightened step backward. His heart pounded like a war drum and adrenaline charged through his system.

He stared in horror at the decomposing arm, upper torso, and head that had been yanked out of the heap. The hollow sightless eyes stared up at him. The two rows of teeth were fixed in a hideous grin. Worms and maggots squirmed away from the bright light of day.

Ben rushed across the yard, tripped on the stairs, and burst into the kitchen like a madman.

His wife was reading the paper and drinking coffee at the table. "You look like you've just seen a ghost," she exclaimed, her eyebrows lifting in surprise.

"It's worse. So much worse." He shook his head, trying to comprehend what he saw in the yard, then he grabbed his cell phone off the table and jabbed 911 with his finger.

***

Sidney peeled open an eye and glanced at the clock on the nightstand. It was 11:00 a.m. Sunday morning, her day off, though technically she never really had a day off. As Police Chief of small-town Garnerville, she was on call twenty-four seven. For another few minutes, she luxuriated in the warmth of her bed and the peaceful quiet of the house she shared with her sister. The last three weeks had been relatively uneventful. Her small department raked in the usual misdemeanors and petty crimes, but no major upheavals, leaving her Sundays blissfully free. Hopefully, today would be more of the same.

Wearing flannel pjs and the bunny slippers with big floppy ears that Selena gave her as a gag gift—which had proven to be ridiculously comfortable—she headed downstairs in search of coffee. She crossed the living room decorated in Selena's Bohemian style—overstuffed sofas, faux Tiffany lamps, a faded Asian rug—to the dining room where her sister's four cats decorated the rug and watched her with large, curious eyes. The table was set for one, and delicious aromas drifted from the kitchen where her sister stood over the stove, spatula in hand.

While Sidney was hibernating, Selena had given two yoga classes at her studio. She was still dressed in her yoga clothes, which showed off her toned figure to its best advantage. Sidney was momentarily struck by how much her younger sister resembled their mother—beautiful Scandinavian features, straight blond hair, celery green eyes—while Sidney had inherited their father's hazel eyes, wavy auburn hair and freckles. The only genetic trait the sisters shared was their lofty height of six feet.

"Morning. I heard you get up," Selena said brightly when Sidney entered the kitchen. "I'm making you breakfast."

"What's the occasion?" Sidney gazed hungrily at the cheese and mushroom omelet cooking in one pan, and the bacon sizzling in the other. Her sister was a wizard in the kitchen and everything she made was mouth-watering. "Christmas is still a month away. What are you buttering me up for?"

"My, aren't you suspicious."

"Comes with the job." Sidney filled a mug with coffee from the pot on the counter and stirred in cream and sugar.

"No ulterior motive," Selena said. "Just taking pity on you. I heard you come in at two. That's late, even for you."

Sidney sipped the dark French roast and sighed with satisfaction. "A couple of drunks got into it at Barney's, right at midnight."

"Just when you and Granger were ending your shifts. Lousy timing."

"We thought so, too. Damned inconsiderate." Granger was Selena's boyfriend and one of Sidney's three patrol officers who made up the small police force. A former Marine with combat experience, cool in a crisis, he was a good man to have on the job on Saturday nights when most brawls erupted. "We arrived just in time to see a drunk slither off a stool and do a faceplant on the floor. His loud-mouthed drinking buddy was giving the waitresses a hard time. When we asked him to call it a night, he tried to morph into Bruce Lee, and failed. He came at us with some crazy-ass martial arts moves. The waitresses were in stitches. Then he accidently tripped over the foot Granger stuck out in front of him."

Selena chuckled. "Sounds entertaining."

"It was. The waitresses clapped when we cuffed him. We peeled his friend off the floor and put him in an Uber, then deposited Badass in the drunk tank at the station."

"A night's work well done."

"Amen."

Selena's eyes sparkled and her voice got a little naughty. "Granger's coming over later."

"Lucky for you, I'll be with David. The house is yours."

"Perfect."

After nine months, Selena and Granger were still caught up in the magical romance phase of their relationship. In each other's eyes, they could do no wrong, and the erotic addiction was still going strong. Sidney could relate. After two years, the magnetic pull between her and David had only strengthened, and the engagement ring on her finger attested to a deep-rooted commitment. "What are you two lovebirds doing today, besides the obvious?"

"A whole lot of nothing. Watching movies. Eating a bucket of buttered popcorn."

Sidney glanced out the window at the overcast day. November on the western flanks of the Oregon Cascades was typically wet with storms rolling in from the coast. Today was no exception. Everything glistened with raindrops from the storm that barreled through overnight. "Good day to stay indoors."

"That's the plan." Selena slipped the omelet onto a plate, added two strips of bacon, then set it on the placemat in the dining room.

Sidney followed her to the table and took a seat. "Yum. My tastebuds thank you. My stomach thanks you. The food gods thank you."

"Bon Appetit. I've got laundry to do." Selena disappeared into the laundry room.

Smokey and Chile started rubbing against her legs under the table, meowing loudly, hoping for handouts, but Sidney ignored them. She wasted no time packing away her breakfast and washing it down with coffee, eager to drive to David's house on the lakeshore. She put her plate in the dishwasher and headed upstairs. Five minutes later, her phone buzzed as she stepped out of the shower. No doubt, it was David, wondering where she was. Wrapped in a towel, she hustled into the bedroom and grabbed her phone. Reading the screen, she felt a sharp pang of disappointment. It was her dispatcher. "What's up, Jesse?"

"Sorry to interrupt your Sunday, Chief, but we've got a dead body out by Coyote Creek. Ben Colby just called it in."

Sidney's gut tightened. Her peaceful morning instantly shattered. Ben Colby, a history teacher at the high school, lived on the other side of the lake. His property was adjacent to a wilderness area with a vast network of biking and hiking trails. Though rare, accidents did occur; a hiker fell off a cliff, or a cyclist crashed into a tree. She clicked into cop mode. "Hiker or cyclist?"

"Hard to say. The body is pretty much decomposed. Ben found it in his compost pile. Doesn't sound like an accident."

"Murder, more like it. Get everyone out there, pronto. All hands on deck." That included her three junior officers, the M.E. and the forensic tech. "I'll be there in twenty minutes."

"Copy, Chief."

A homicide was the worst possible news. A violent death rippled through the community like a flash flood, spreading fear and shattering the lives of the victim's family and friends. It also meant long stressful hours for her department and little sleep.

Sidney hastily got ready. Dressed in her uniform with her hair knotted at the back of her neck, she added her duty belt, making sure the magazine of her Glock semi-automatic contained a full load before holstering it.

She was born to be a cop. Duty and service were encoded in her DNA—passed down from her dad, who was Garnerville's Police Chief for ten years while she was growing up. Following in his footsteps, she enrolled in the academy in San Francisco, worked her way up from patrol cop to detective, then led a homicide division across the bay in Oakland for five years. When the position of police chief became available back here in her hometown, she threw her hat in the ring. She'd had her fill of the unceasing violence of a big city, witnessing every kind of human depravity, working a dozen homicide cases at any given time. She knew she was burned out, plagued by feelings of exhaustion, cynicism, and reduced effectiveness. She was hired uncontested by Garnerville's mayor and council members. The salary was nothing to brag about, and she was over-qualified for the job, but for her own mental health, she accepted. Her stress level steadily went down with her ability to cope with what was put on her plate. Aside from providing a calming police presence on a daily basis, her team closed all ten homicide cases that occurred on her watch in the last three years.

After sending a quick heartfelt apology to David by text, Sidney raced downstairs to the laundry room. The sisters used this side door to come in and out of the house from the garage and driveway. Selena was pulling clothes from the dryer and turned with wide-eyed surprise when Sidney rushed in behind her. Her gaze swept over her uniform and serious demeanor. "Uh oh. Emergency."

"Sounds like we've got a homicide on our hands. Ben Colby called it in." Sidney opened the door and a current of cold air rushed into the room. "I texted David. Told him I'd be MIA today."

"Guess that means I won't be seeing Granger, either."

"Sorry."

"Me, too."

They both knew the score. They understood firsthand the sacrifices placed upon the families of first responders. Protecting and serving the public would always come first.

***

A ceiling of lead-bottom clouds hung over the treetops, darkening the sky. The branches were stripped bare, carpeting lawns with the last of the gold and russet leaves. Sidney drove her Yukon down Main Street through historic downtown, lined with buildings dating back to the late 1800s, now trendy boutiques and eateries. Townsfolk and tourists sauntered on the streets carrying gift bags and disposable cups of coffee, oblivious to the victim found in a compost heap ten miles away. It was Sidney's job to keep them that way; worry free, feeling safe, enjoying their Sunday. Her team would work this case relentlessly until the killer was in custody.

Following a bit of static, Officer Granger Wyatt's voice came over her radio. "Hey Chief, I'm going to be delayed. A couple of dairy cows got loose from Rutenberg's farm. They were running on the highway."

"That's a catastrophe waiting to happen." Animal collisions were serious business. A few times a year, elk and deer were hit by vehicles, causing injuries or death to drivers and animals. "You need help?"

"I got flares down. Two farmers are blocking the highway with tractors. The cows are huddled together in the middle. We just need to herd them into a trailer. We're good."

"Head over when you're done."

"Copy that." He signed off.

When Sidney reached the highway, she gunned the engine and hit the strobes. The gray asphalt ribbon snaked through towering walls of dense forest. Through the tunnels between the trees, Lake Kalapuya appeared and disappeared under thinning layers of mist. After ten miles, she pulled off the highway and drove down a few narrow roads before turning into the Colby's gravel driveway. No surprise, the strobes of two parked police vehicles pulsed in front of the house. Her morning shift officers, Darnell Wood and Amanda Cruz had already arrived. Dressed in crisp blue uniforms, they stood in the yard talking to the Colbys.

Though in their fifties and graying, Ben and Amy Colby still appeared to be trim and youthful. They were both casually dressed in jeans and jackets. Sidney knew the two teachers to be friendly and outgoing, and hugely popular with students at Garnerville High. They now stood tense; anxiety written on their faces. She joined the group, and everyone exchanged a cursory greeting. "Sorry for this shocking experience," she said to the couple. "How're you holding up?"

Ben shrugged. "Trying to get over the shock."

Amy grimaced. "Me, too."

"We're going to go take a look. Could you direct us to the body, Ben?"

His expression tightened. Discovering a decomposing body in your yard was a hell of a jolt, especially to a civilian, and not one that needed to be repeated.

"No need for you to come."

Ben blew out a breath and looked relieved. "It's around back, behind the shed."

"Why don't you two wait in the house? The coroner will remove the body, but the rest of us will be here for a while. I'll come talk to you in a few minutes."

Ben nodded, put a comforting arm around his wife and guided her into the house. The officers turned as the coroner's white van pulled into the driveway. The M.E. and forensic tech climbed out dressed in field clothes. Dr. Linthrope looked like a stocky version of Albert Einstein, with a halo of wild white hair, bushy white brows, and a well-lived-in face. In his early seventies, he was a spry man with a razor-sharp intellect. Stewart Wong proceeded to pull a gurney out of the back of the van. A folded black body bag and crime kit sat on top. He was a lanky man of Chinese descent, mid-forties, with a thick crop of black hair and wire rimmed glasses. A DSLR camera hung from his neck. The two men had been recovering bodies in Linnly County for over twenty years, witnessing every possible manner of death and every stage of decomp. Steering the gurney over the grass, they joined the officers. After rudimentary pleasantries, Stewart got right down to business. "Where's the body?"

"Around the back." Sidney led the procession to the back yard. As they rounded the corner of the shed, the ripe smell of decomp reached their nostrils. Then they saw the partially buried corpse. Sidney drew in a sharp breath. It was in an active stage of putrefaction.

"Ain't a pretty sight. Don't smell too good either," Stewart said matter-of-factly. He had a gift for stating the obvious. He started snapping photos, brightening the morning with bursts of light from his flash. Without hesitation, Linthrope donned Nitrile gloves and squatted over the body. He began to carefully brush away the moist debris, exposing more of the body and releasing a stronger stench into the air. Death didn't faze them. Their unruffled demeanors brought a sense of calm to the grisly business of death.

On the other hand, no matter how many times Sidney witnessed a murder victim, she still had a gut reaction—a spurt of anger mixed with sadness, for a life cut short, for what the survivors would suffer. She hid her emotions behind a neutral expression.

Her officers were not so practiced. Their faces clearly showed revulsion, and Amanda pulled her collar over her nose to stifle the smell. Sidney hired the two when she took office three years ago. At that time, neither had ever observed a murder victim up close and personal. A small town with a tight operating budget required that law enforcement personnel have more than one area of expertise. Darnell, a young black man, had been a rookie fresh out of the academy, but he was a whiz with I.T. Amanda, a Latina, had four years of patrol experience, and more importantly, she had just completed CSI training. Their skills had been instrumental in closing the ten Garnerville homicide cases. This one, admittedly, smelled the worst.

"Amanda, why don't you start scoping out the yard? Darnell, walk into the woods bordering the property. Look for any irregularity, anything the killer may have left behind." Only too happy to get away, the two left in haste, disappearing around the shed. A lot of time had passed, and Sidney wasn't expecting them to find anything. Even if the killer had left footprints, they would have been washed out by last night's rain. But killers inadvertently left trace evidence. Even something minute could be a helpful clue.

The body was now completely unearthed.

Stewart stretched the unzipped body bag on the ground and the two men carefully placed the corpse on it, straightening the limbs. Linthrope sat back on his heels and started examining it closely. Ragged pieces of clothing clung to the boney frame, mostly stripped of flesh and internal organs. "Maggots will eat through anything to get to a meal," Linthrope said. "No telling what shape these clothes were in. Looks like it was a long black dress." Patches of hair about five inches long were still attached to the scalp. He handled the skull gently, rolling it to the left and right, no doubt looking for cause of death, fractures or bullet holes. "I see no obvious trauma to the head," he said.

Sidney squatted next to him. "Can you tell me anything, Doc? How long it was buried here?"

He glanced at her, and his glasses momentarily blinked in the light. "With the help of these worms and maggots, and the already decaying material in this compost pile, a body would reach this state in about two weeks."

"Gender?"

He pointed to the groin area. "Look at the space inside the pelvic bones. The inlet is larger in women to aid the birthing process. The skull also offers a clue. Males tend to have backward-slanting foreheads. This skull is rounder."

"So, we have a female."

"Yes, indeed. I can't tell you anything more. I need to get the remains to the lab, wash off all this debris and do an autopsy."

Maggots and worms squiggled over the corpse and Linthrope saw her wrinkle her nose. "We'll analyze DNA pulled from these little critters. See what they can tell us."

She knew the maggots would be examined to determine how many birth cycles they'd gone through, indicating how long they'd been working on the corpse, but she still found them loathsome.

"Insects are a forensic scientist's dream," Stewart added cheerfully, standing over them. His camera flash momentarily blinded her. "Years ago, when your father was police chief, he found an unidentified decomposed corpse. I compared the DNA from the maggots to the mother of a missing teenager, and we were able to confirm it was her daughter."

"I remember that case," Sidney said. "I was fifteen. The abducted girl was Emmy Tate, a cheerleader at my high school. It spooked the entire school, let alone the town. Turned out, the killer was a transient."

"Yep. He left a trail of thirteen dead women across the Pacific Northwest. He eluded the FBI, but we got him right here, in small town Garnerville."

"You did good, Stewart. My dad was proud of closing that case. It was one of the things that steered me into law enforcement."

"And here we are. Twenty years later," he said with a grin. "Standing together over a corpse. Bonding."

The moment didn't feel warm and fuzzy to Sidney, but she appreciated his enthusiasm.

"I'll sift through this compost," he said. "See what I can find."

For that, Sidney was grateful. Stewart's attention to detail was a significant asset to her investigations. Like Sidney, when working a homicide, he got an itch that couldn't be appeased until the suspect was behind bars.

"Let's get her zipped up," the doctor said. "I'll head for the morgue, get started with the post-mortem."

They both arrived in the van. "I'll get Stewart back to the lab when we're done here," she said.

They lifted the body bag onto the gurney and Linthrope wheeled it around the house and into the van. As the doctor drove away, a barking dog drew her attention to the woods across the driveway. Four hikers and two dogs were trampling through the trees toward the house, drawn by the police activity. On a hiking trail behind them, other hikers were gathering to watch. Folks had a macabre fascination with death.

"What's going on?" a bearded young man called out when they reached the driveway. "We saw the coroner's van. Someone dead?"

"Please return to the trail," Sidney said firmly. People trampling onto the Colby's property could contaminate her crime scene, destroy evidence. Luckily, she saw no cameras. Strangers snapping photos of crime scenes and posting them online was a continuing threat. It was a cruel way for relatives to discover their loved ones were injured or dead.

"Was someone murdered?" a young woman asked.

"Who died?" another asked.

"Go back. Stay on the trails," a man's commanding voice called out.

Officer Granger Wyatt had arrived, parking his truck behind her Yukon. Just in time. She needed help holding back the looky loos.

"This is private property." Sidney and Granger approached them with arms spread wide and the hikers retreated to the trail, joining the other spectators.

"Just finished herding cows. Now I'm herding people."

"That's what makes police work interesting, right? The cows are taken care of?"

He grinned. "Their race to freedom was short-lived."

"Let's get a perimeter around this yard. Keep the hoards at bay."

He was already pulling out the yellow crime scene tape from the back of his truck. The two went to work, wrapping the tape around trees until the front yard was roped off. Sidney filled Granger in on the discovery in the backyard.

"Can't say I'm sorry I missed it," he said soberly.

Of her three officers, Granger would have stomached it the best. He'd seen much worse in Afghanistan; bodies blown apart by IEDs, buddies killed. He came home haunted by ghosts. Like Sidney, he had an archive of nightmarish images vaulted in his mind.

"Let's go talk to the Colbys," Sidney said. "Take notes."

"Copy that." He whipped a pen and notepad from his breast pocket. They climbed the porch. Sidney rang the bell.

CHAPTER TWO

BEN USHERED THEM into the living room, and they seated themselves on chairs facing the couch. His features were unremarkable, except for his warm brown eyes that were responsive and approachable. Amy was a pretty woman, even with the lines of middle-age engraved on her face.

"Can I get you coffee?" she asked. "I just made a fresh pot. I need to do something normal to shake off these spooky feelings."

"Please."

"Sure."

The couple disappeared into the kitchen.

Sidney took in the trappings of their home. The living room was furnished comfortably but modestly. Photos of their two children lined the mantel, both now in college.

Ben walked in holding a tray of steaming mugs and distributed them. Amy placed a platter of homemade cookies on the table.

Seated on the couch, they faced Sidney with residual shock on their faces. Amy looked toward the window and visibly shivered. "Is it still out there?"

"No. The coroner left ten minutes ago."

"Thank god," Ben said. "There's a place in hell for whoever murdered that person. I can't believe the callousness of dumping a body in a compost heap, like a piece of trash."

"Why would someone bury a body in our yard?" Amy asked.

"We're hoping you can help us find out. Dr. Linthrope estimates it's been in there for about two weeks. Can you recall anything unusual happening back then?"

Ben sat back, his fingers tapping the armrest. "Hmm. Can't really think of anything besides the usual."

"What's the usual?"

"We hear noises at night. Animals come through. An occasional raccoon tries to get in the garbage bins, but the covers are on tight. We've never thought much about it."

"Honey, remember when I heard something that rainy night? You didn't want to go out to look?"

"Oh yeah, I forgot about that." His eyes met Sidney's. "Amy woke me up. It was raining hard. And windy. Sounded like a trash bin had fallen over. We didn't hear anything else, so I shook it off. The next morning, the trash bins weren't knocked over, but something was peculiar. The lids to the bins were mismatched. I could tell because they're different colors. I thought I must have done it. Absent-minded. But now I wonder. Maybe someone was out there …."

Granger was scribbling in his notebook.

"And knocked over the bins," Sidney said. "The tops came off. In the dark, the intruder didn't see the color difference."

He nodded. "Could've happened."

"What night was that?"

"You stayed up late that night, grading papers," Amy said.

"Hmm. That was November ninth. I gave the kids a test that day."

Granger scribbled, then looked up, waiting for more.

"What time did you hear the racket?"

"Around two," Amy said.

"Have you seen any folks around your property? Someone who may have seen your compost pile? Hikers, cyclists?"

They were quiet, thinking. They looked at each other, and her eyes widened momentarily.

"What is it, Amy?" Sidney asked.

"There was this one guy. Tell her, Ben. About the guy looking for his dog."

He puffed out a breath. "This guy came out of the woods out back while I was raking leaves. I turned and saw him standing a few feet away, watching me. Freaked me out that he got so close without me hearing him. There was something strange about him. Then he said his dog was off leash and may have run through my yard. I told him no dog had come through. He looked in every direction, then he said sorry, and walked back into the woods. He walked past the shed and must've seen the compost pile. That was the last week of October."

"What was strange about him?"

"I can't put my finger on it. The way he was watching me, I guess. Very intense."

"Can you describe him?"

"Around six feet. He wore jeans and a sweatshirt and sneakers. Athletic. Had dark hair, average features."

"Had you ever seen him before, or after?"

"Who knows?" Amy said. "There are always people hiking around here. We don't really pay attention."

"We're gone during the day, working," Ben said. "And at night we're busy, grading papers, cooking. Anyone could've come onto the property."

"Very scary to think someone was scouting around," Amy said. "Trespassing. Maybe spying on us."

"It's a good idea to have an alarm system when you're this isolated," Sidney said.

"Sounds expensive," Amy said. "We're cutting corners as it is, with the kids in college."

"Maybe a dog. Two dogs," Granger said. "They discourage would-be burglars."

"Our lab died this year. We've talked about getting another dog," Ben said. "This might be the time to do it."

"I'd feel safer." Amy looked at her husband and said adamantly, "I want every bit of that compost out of here. I won't feel settled until it's gone."

Ben frowned. Clearly, he wasn't ready to face it again, or deal with the smell.

"I can help," Granger said. "Do you have a couple of big tarps?

"Yeah, in the garage."

"When we're done here, I'll help you shovel it up. It's organic material. We'll dump it in the woods where it'll do some good."

"That would be a big help. Better to face my demons and conquer them," Ben said with a smile.

Amy also smiled her appreciation.

A little community service went a long way in helping folks shake off spooky feelings.

Taking the initiative to lend a neighbor a hand wasn't unusual for Granger. Raised on a local cattle ranch, he was used to hard work, and he had a country boy's down to earth sensibility. His family always had a menagerie of animals aside from cattle—pigs, chickens, horses, dogs—and he witnessed firsthand the cycle of life and death. All-American handsome, he was also her sister's boyfriend, which had no bearing on his professionalism. Unquestionably, Sidney was the boss.

"Please, drink your coffee. Have a cookie," Amy said, pushing the platter closer. "Chocolate chip pecan. My kids' favorite."

Sidney was still full from breakfast and they needed to get back to work, but she ate a cookie to be polite.

Granger ate a cookie in one bite, then quickly drained his cup. "So good," he said.

"Take the cookies out to the others. Just leave the empty platter on the porch."

Sidney thanked her and put her business card on the table. "If you think of anything else, please call."

"You'll let us know if you find out who did this?" Amy asked.

"You can count on it."

***

When they came out of the house, more spectators had gathered on the trail. "Granger, why don't you talk to those hikers. If they come here often, maybe someone noticed unusual behavior in the last two weeks." Sidney was grasping at straws, but one never knew what might crawl out from under a rock.

"I'm on it."

Sidney went to the back of the house. Amanda was at the opposite end of the small yard from where she started, swishing through the grass and bushes with a thatch rake. Searching the woods immediately around the house, Darnell had also gone from one end of the yard to the other.

Stewart had sifted through the pile of compost and had created a new pile in the process. His protective apparel was smeared with debris from the compost heap, especially at the knees where he'd been kneeling. She certainly had to admire his commitment to the job. The stench had dissipated somewhat, making it easier to breathe without the urge to gag.

"Find anything?" she asked him.

"Yeah," he said, frowning. "Something puzzling."

"What's that?"

He hesitated, the crease between his brows deepening.

"What is it?" she asked again.

He expelled a deep breath. "I don't want to lead the investigation down the wrong path. Let me check it out at the lab and confer with Dr. Linthrope. Compare our findings."

Sidney was now burning with curiosity. "What's the wrong path?"

"That this woman wasn't murdered."

Stewart looked dead serious, and she respected him enough to take him seriously. "Why would the body of a person who wasn't murdered end up in a compost heap?" Sidney asked. "Even if she wasn't murdered, a serious crime has been committed. Tampering with a dead body is a Class 4 felony."

"Copy that. We may not be looking for a killer, just a very special kind of nutjob."

"How soon will you confirm your theory?"

"I have a hunch Dr. Linthrope will have the answer at the morgue."

Her two officers joined them. "There's nothing that points to a trespasser, Chief," Darnell said. "Just lots of deer poop."

"I searched the front yard, too," Amanda said. "Nada. More deer poop."

"Until we get lab and postmortem results, we're at a stalemate," Sidney told them. "You two can go back to your patrols. Stewart and I will head into town."

"Curious, why are you holding a platter of cookies?" Darnell asked.

"Are they evidence?" Amanda teased.

Stewart removed his dirty gloves. "While we're out here working hard, you and Granger are all cozy inside eating cookies."

Dealing with people who were in shock wasn't exactly cozy. "Sorry. Help yourselves. Compliments of Amy."

They all grabbed a couple, leaving three on the platter.

As everyone headed to their respective vehicles, Sidney waited for Granger who was hiking back through the trees after talking to the spectators. "Anything?"

"Nope."

"Take down the crime scene tape. The Colby's lives can get back to normal."

"Then I'll help Ben shovel up that compost."

"Good man. I'm going to the morgue with Stewart."

He glanced down at the platter of cookies she was holding, and she held it out to him.

He grabbed two, shoving both into his mouth. With his cheeks bulging like a chipmunk's, he began taking down the tape.

Stewart took the last cookie. Walking next to him, she picked up the foul odor of decomp. "Owee. You're not getting into my vehicle smelling like that."

"Wasn't planning on it." He quickly stripped out of his disposable coverall and crumpled it into a ball. He pulled a trash bag from his crime kit and deposited it inside, then tied off the top. "Yeehah." He stood back grinning with his hands up, like a cowboy who had just roped the feet of a calf. He put the bag and his crime kit in the back of the truck and climbed into the passenger seat.

"Good work, Cowboy."

"Just one of my many talents."

CHAPTER THREE

SIDNEY AND STEWART entered the small community hospital, crossed the lobby to the elevator, and descended to the basement. Their footsteps sounded hollow in the sterile tiled hallway.

"Hang on a minute," Stewart said. They paused halfway to the morgue, and he unlocked the door to the lab. Most small communities had to hire CSIs and pathologists from out of town, but thanks to Dr. Linthrope's tireless quest for grant money, and generous donations from the town's deep pockets, Garnerville had a well-equipped morgue and forensic lab.

Stewart planted his crime kit at his workstation and pulled out a small evidence bag from the crime scene. "Okay, let's go see the doc."

An astringent chemical odor reached their nostrils as they pushed through one of the double doors at the end of the hall and entered the morgue. The spotless room was equipped with cold storage compartments for bodies, a cleanup and storage area, and two stainless-steel slabs in the middle of the room. One was currently occupied by the remains of Jane Doe. Good ventilation was doing a great job of sucking up the putrid odor.

Wearing green scrubs and nitrile gloves, Dr. Linthrope was bending over the corpse with a scalpel in hand. He had washed away the debris, revealing what was left of the body under the glare of bright lights. Sidney exhaled slowly. It looked like something out of a horror movie, parts of flesh and organs clinging to the skeleton. "Hey, Doc."

He stripped off his gloves and disposed of them in the hazardous waste bin. "I suspected you two would show up at any second." He nodded at the evidence bag Stewart held in his hand. "You found cotton."

"Yep." He handed the small bag to Dr. Linthrope, who put the contents on a dish and examined it under the light. "A match to what I found." He pointed to a glass container sitting on his worktable filled with cotton.

"What's going on?" Sidney asked. "What does cotton tell you?"

"It tells us that this body had been prepared for a funeral by a mortician."

Sidney blinked, taking a long moment to digest the information. *How did she get from a mortuary to a compost heap?*

"There's more. I found these inside her skull where her eyes used to be." He lifted another dish and held it out to her. Inside were two flesh-colored oval-shaped plastic caps. "A mortician inserts these caps under the lids of a deceased person to help hold their shape. They sit on the eye and secure the eyelid in place." He directed her attention to what was left of the dead woman's face. The jaws were now wide open. "A mortician uses wires on the jaws, which are tied together to securely close the mouth."

"And hers were wired?"

"Yes. I cut through the wires to open the jaws, and no surprise, I found the cotton. A mortician stuffs the mouth, throat, and nose to hold the shape and to prevent possible fluid seepage."

Sidney had no idea these procedures took place in the private chambers of a mortuary.

"The cotton I found in the compost heap are smaller plugs," Stewart said. "I suspected immediately that they had once been stuffed into her nasal passages."

"And that's why you assumed she hadn't been murdered."

"Yep. Just a body stolen from a mortuary. Or dug up from a grave."

"So, we have a stolen corpse, and possibly a grave robber?"

He grinned. The oddities of human behavior never failed to amuse Stewart. The weirder, the better. "I bet when I analyze samples from her corpse, I'll find traces of formaldehyde."

She sighed. "Well, this case has certainly taken a strange twist. We're going to have to contact all the mortuaries in the county. The more info we have about this woman, the better. Is there any way to tell her cause of death, Doc?"

His bushy white brows knitted together in a frown. "Not with what little of her remains."

"What about her age?"

"I can give you a pretty good estimate." He continued in a calm, professional tone. "Wear and tear on a body throughout a lifetime affects the skeleton. This woman had arthritis of the spine and hip joints. Also, the rib ends that join them to the sternum are thin, with sharp edges, and the rim has bony, irregular projections. These are clear indications of an older adult. I'd say she was seventy-five, eighty, or older."

"She has no fingertips left. We can't identify her with prints," Sidney said.

"I found something that may help." He reached for another dish and pulled out a locket on a silver chain. "I found this after I washed away the debris on her upper torso. It has words engraved inside." He opened it and read: "Forever yours, Forest."

"A mortician would certainly remember that. Let me take a photo." Sidney took out her cell phone and snapped a shot. "We can send this out by text to each mortuary."

***

After sending the photo to ten different mortuaries listed on the internet, and speaking to several administrators, Sidney finally got a positive response from a Ms. Solace at Beyond the Grave.

"A silver locket that resembles the one in the photo was worn by one of our clients," she said. "It was buried with her."

"How long ago?"

"Thirteen days."

"Do you remember what was engraved inside the locket?"

"No, sorry."

"What was the age of the woman it belonged to?"

"She was a lovely elderly woman. Eighty-five years old."

Sidney had found the right mortuary. "Can you give me her name?"

A long moment of hesitation followed. "What is this regarding?" A note of concern entered her voice. "Why is this a police matter?"

"Her name, please, Ms. Solace."

"Stevana Thornburg."

"We need to speak in private to your mortician," Sidney said.

"That would be me. When?"

"Now would be good."

"I'm very busy, but I can take a quick break."

Sidney read the address. Beyond the Grave was just a few blocks north of downtown in the historical district of Montford. "We'll be there in five minutes. Please have Ms. Thornburg's records available."

CHAPTER FOUR

WITH GRANGER RIDING SHOTGUN, Sidney drove to the Montford district, a neighborhood made up of grand old Victorian mansions on wooded estates. In the summer the branches of giant maple trees cast the roads in deep cool shade, but now their bony branches looked forlorn. Sidney drove past private residences, a bed and breakfast inn, and a law office. At the end of a cul-de-sac, they arrived at Beyond the Grave Funeral Home. The three-story house had a turret and steep gabled roofs, a rounded bay with stained glass windows, and decorative woodwork. It sat back from the street behind a circular driveway and was bordered on all sides by Creekside Cemetery. The cemetery was the resting place of many of Garnerville's founding residents.

"I've always loved this neighborhood," Sidney said. "I attended a few services here when this was Brad Miller's mortuary. His family lived upstairs. I knew he retired but I didn't know there was a new owner."

"Me, either. There's no crime in this neighborhood so there's no reason to come unless you're invited to a funeral."

They pulled into the driveway, climbed the stairs and crossed a large veranda, and entered. The foyer opened on both sides to spacious wood paneled rooms decorated with period furnishings. The office on the left had an ornate desk and bookshelves that held an array of funeral urns. Plush velvet chairs and a settee formed a sitting area in front of a gas fireplace that emitted a warm glow. The room on the right was lined with a dozen casket selections. Directly in front of them was a grand staircase that curved up to the next level. The overall effect was like stepping back in time. The atmosphere was peaceful, perfect for consoling grieving families.

A door opened at the end of the hall and a woman stepped out. As she emerged from the shadow into the light, Sidney's eyes widened momentarily. Granger's eyebrows lifted in surprise. The woman was a double for Morticia from the Addams Family TV show and movies—pale skin, long black hair, a form-fitting black dress that accentuated her curvy figure.

"I'm Chief Becker and this is Officer Wyatt."

She extended her hand and said in a low husky voice, "I'm Morticia Solace." The color of her long fingernails matched her blood red lipstick, completing her goth-meets-sexpot appearance.

Sidney wondered if they were interrupting some kind of costume affair, or was this the woman's normal business attire? *Was her name really Morticia Solace?* Years on the job taught Sidney to be sensitive and cautious when questioning people, especially eccentrics. They could be easily offended. Stretches of silence, or just polite conversation, often encouraged people to fill in the blanks about their lifestyles voluntarily.

"Are you having some kind of costume party?" Granger asked bluntly.

"Why do you ask?" the woman's alluring green eyes narrowed. "Are you criticizing my appearance?"

Granger's cheeks flushed red, and he looked at Sidney for help.

"Can we sit down with you for a few minutes, Ms. Solace?" Sidney asked. "What we have to share may be unsettling."

"Please, call me Morticia." They seated themselves on the velvet chairs in front of the fireplace. A file folder, brochures, and what appeared to be a photo album sat on the coffee table. "There's the file you asked for," she said.

Sidney opened it and scanned the two pages of information inside. "Mrs. Thornburg died of acute heart failure. She lived here in Montford for the last twenty years."

Granger started scribbling notes.

"Just down the street," Morticia said. "For the last two decades, Stevana was a frail invalid who lived a quiet and private life. Wheelchair bound. She never left the house. Her care worker, Bonnie Lingheimer, did everything for her. Stevana planned her entire funeral herself. I met with her several times to get all the details pinned down." She met Sidney's eyes with a steady gaze. "So why are you here? What's this unsettling news you have? Did someone complain about our practices?"

"We're not here to question your practices, but about someone tampering with a dead body."

Her brows arched and she looked at Sidney questioningly. "It's our job to tamper with dead bodies. I can assure you, everything we do here meets the highest standards, even if we're somewhat unorthodox."

"What do you mean by unorthodox?"

"The staging of the bodies …."

"Morticia, we're here because an elderly woman's remains were found on someone's private property. She was wearing the silver locket in the photo

I sent you. We have strong reason to believe it's Ms. Thornburg."

The mortician's eyes widened, and her face blanched even paler. She looked positively bloodless, which made her eyes and red mouth stand out. "That's not just unsettling, it's shocking. But it isn't Stevana. She was buried here in Creekside Cemetery. I personally oversaw her party and burial."

"Party? Do you mean a celebration of her life?"

"I mean a party. Here at Beyond the Grave, we offer nontraditional, as well as traditional memorial services. Instead of displaying a loved one in a casket, we pose the bodies in life-like scenarios. We recreate a time in a client's life that was a highpoint. Stevana wanted a cocktail party." Morticia picked up the photo album and flipped through a few pages, then handed it to Sidney. Granger looked up from his notes and leaned in to look.

The photos showed a half dozen people in evening attire conversing and holding drinks. An elderly woman was the center of attention in each shot. Her white hair was perfectly styled, she wore a black cocktail dress and a sparkly necklace, and she held a martini in one hand. The people around her changed positions and poses, yet the old woman stood as frozen as a mannequin in the same spot in every shot. Sidney realized that she was somehow propped up against the mantle.

"Holy smoke," Granger said.

"So, this is what you mean by staging a body," Sidney said. "This is Ms. Thornburg ... dead."

"Yes."

"She looks so lifelike," Granger said.

"That's my art. That's what Stevana wanted. I made her last wish come true. She was a socialite in her day, in Salem. She knew everyone who was anyone and she entertained lavishly. After her health failed, she moved here to live a quiet life. But she wanted to have one last party as a send-off, out of her wheelchair, standing, enjoying her guests. The music was by Frank Sinatra. "That's Life" and "The Way You Look Tonight" were some of the tunes on her playlist."

"Are those real diamonds on her necklace?" Sidney asked.

"Oh, yes. And that big emerald on her finger is real, too."

"They look valuable."

"Very. Thousands, I'm sure."

"Was she buried with this stuff?" Granger asked.

"Yes. That was her wish. They're secured to her body with glue and stitching."

"I see a big motive for stealing her body, Chief," Granger said.

"I agree. Someone wanted to get to that jewelry. And they couldn't just lift it off."

Morticia looked miffed. "That's absurd."

"The jewelry was missing when we found her, except for the locket, which was probably hidden beneath her dress. True?"

She nodded. "Yes, but ...."

Sidney cut her off. "Who are the people in these photos?"

"They're pros. Local performers. I hire them as extras if the deceased has no family. And of course, there was Gordon, Bonnie, and I."

Granger was furiously taking notes.

"We're going to need names and contact information for each of these extras."

"Of course. But you're wasting your time. None of them is a thief. I've used the same folks many times. It's not uncommon for our clients to be buried with valuables. Nothing has ever been stolen."

Morticia looked young, mid to late twenties, and Sidney suspected that she was inexperienced and naive. "You can't be entirely sure of that, can you? How long have you been in this business, Morticia?"

"My entire life. My dad ran this funeral home for thirty years before I took over. Never had a single incident."

"Your dad was Brad Miller?"

"Yes. I grew up in this house. My birth name is Brenda Miller. Morticia is my working name. We lived on the third floor. I still do, but mom and dad are gone."

"I'm sorry," Sidney said gently. "I greatly respected your parents. I didn't know they died."

"No, they're fine. They live in Florida. I grew up working right alongside Dad." As she spoke, her voice took on energy and her eyes sparkled with passion. "I was always fascinated by death. I love being a mortician. It's rewarding. I provide support and care during a time when people need it most, but I saw that for some families, something was missing. People wanted more than to see their loved one lying in a coffin. They didn't want that to be their last memory. When I was twenty, I went to work in New Orleans to learn body staging. It's very popular there. When Dad retired, he asked if I wanted to keep the business going. I said yes, of course. I came home and took over two years ago. Now I provide services for a select clientele."

Sidney and Granger leafed through the album. There were dozens of staged scenarios, most from her time in Louisiana. A dead man posed on a Harley wore his bike club gear and sunglasses, a fireman in full uniform held a wrapped bundle like a baby in his arms, a man sitting over a chess board held a chess piece, a woman in her running clothes held a water bottle. Admittedly, Morticia's services were creative and more upbeat than a typical funeral, if somewhat macabre, and no doubt came with a hefty price tag. Now Sidney understood why she dressed like Morticia. Her work was very theatrical.

"Back to Mrs. Thornburg," Sidney said, looking up from the album. "Tell us exactly what happened to her body after the party."

"My assistant, Gordon Ortega, and I laid her in her designated casket. She wanted the violet exterior with pink silk lining inside. See for yourself. Turn to the last page."

Sidney turned to the photo of the deceased woman in the described coffin; eyes closed, hands folded across her chest, still wearing the necklace and ring.

"Then we closed the coffin," Morticia continued. "Once closed, a locking mechanism draws the lid onto the base and the gasket forms a seal. We left it in our viewing room overnight and Stevana was buried first thing the next morning. Pastor John conducted the service at the gravesite."

"Who attended?"

"Only Bonnie, Gordon, and myself. And of course, the pastor."

"Was there any evidence the casket was reopened in the viewing room without your knowledge?"

"No. The casket was closed using a hexagonal lock. These types of locks are on our more expensive caskets. They physically hold the lid in place and can only be reopened by a special key."

"Who had access to the key?"

"Gordon and me."

"No one else?"

"I put the key in my desk drawer. And that was also locked." She stared at her hands for a long moment and a troubled expression came over her face.

"What is it?"

"Oh dear. I remember Gordon distracted me by calling me into the viewing room." Her voice was low and tense. "And then I went upstairs and went to bed. Oddly, I woke up around 1:00, thinking about the key, and that I may have forgotten to lock the drawer. So, I went down to check. The key was on my desk, not in the drawer. That gave me an uncomfortable feeling. I locked the drawer, and checked the casket, just as a precaution. It was locked. Then I went back to bed."

"What time did the party end?"

"Around 10:00 p.m."

"So, there was a window of about three hours where someone could have gotten that key."

"It's possible."

"Ms. Thornburg's body was most likely taken from here, not from her gravesite," Sidney said.

"I know it wasn't from her gravesite. I've changed the flowers on her grave two times since the burial. Nothing has been disturbed. I would have noticed. We're very meticulous." Her eyes suddenly watered and her voice vibrated with emotion. "We've never had trouble here before. Now someone stole poor Stevana. It's all my fault. Dad will be in shock. He told me to get an alarm, but I just never got around to it. It's scary to think that someone may have broken in while I was asleep upstairs."

"We need to do a thorough investigation," Sidney said. "If someone broke in, this wasn't your fault."

"Thank you for that." She wiped her eyes with her fingertips. "The horrible thing is, I think someone else was buried in her casket."

Sidney's eyes narrowed. "What makes you think that?"

"We would have noticed if it was lighter. And when we lifted it to put it on the gurney, one corner slipped from my hands. I heard what I thought was a body thud to one side."

"We need to see what's in that casket. First, I need to verify that Mrs. Thornburg's DNA is a match to the remains we found. Do you have anything that may have her DNA on it?"

"Sorry, no. But I'm sure there's plenty to be found in her mansion. Bonnie still lives there. She's executor of the property."

Granger looked up from his notes and asked with a hint of suspicion, "She made her caretaker her executor?"

"Yes. Bonnie was with her for twenty years. She's like family. Stevana left her enough to take care of her cats."

"Just a couple more questions, Morticia. What's the pastor's last name and which church is he associated with?" Sidney asked.

"Pastor John Bowers, at Wellspring Community."

"Pastor Bowers. I've met him several times at town functions." The church was on the street bordering the rear side of the cemetery. "He runs the soup kitchen."

"Yes. He's very involved with helping the poor and homeless."

"When can we speak to your assistant?"

"Gordon will be here in a couple of hours. We're working on a new staging."

Sidney looked at her watch. It was 2:00 p.m. "We'll be back after 4:00. I'm going to need that contact list of the extras you used for Stevana's party."

"Certainly." While Morticia sat at her desk tapping her keyboard, Sidney took pictures of Stevana's necklace and ring.

Morticia printed the list of four names and handed it to Sidney. "Here you go, Chief Becker. They can be reached through their manager, Ed Horton."

***

"Do you believe her story about the key and the unlocked drawer, Chief?" Granger asked when they were seated in the Yukon. "Sounds bogus to me. Who deliberately buries extremely valuable jewelry in a coffin? The temptation would be too great to steal it."

"We have no shortage of suspects, Granger. Morticia and everyone on that list is a suspect. But she had no reason to steal the body. She and Gordon were in the best position to just take the jewelry, then bury Stevana in Creekside Cemetery and hide the crime forever. Whoever took the body could have buried it in the woods where no one would ever find it. But by stashing it on private property, its discovery was inevitable, and it brought the theft directly to our attention."

"You think whoever put it there wanted it be found?"

"Or else they didn't care. We can't bring charges against anyone without compelling evidence. We need to talk to everyone on that list and start piecing together what happened before and after the party."

Sidney's phone pinged and she put it on speaker so Granger could hear. "What's up, Stewart? Did you find formaldehyde in Stevana's remains?"

"I did, as expected. But I also found something far more interesting. Taxine alkaloids."

"Which are what?"

"Taxines are the ingredients found in the common yew tree, Taxus brevifolia."

"What relevance does that have to our case?"

"Taxine alkaloids are absorbed quickly from the intestine. In high enough quantities they can cause death due to general cardiac failure, cardiac arrest, or respiratory failure."

"And she had a high concentration?"

"Exceedingly. It could have built up over a period of time."

A hollow feeling gnawed at Sidney's stomach. *They had a homicide on their hands after all.* "Stevana Thornburg died of acute heart failure, but it wasn't a natural death. It was induced by taxine poisoning?"

"No question, Chief."

"How would you get the poison out of the plant?"

"Easiest way is to just boil the yew tree needles. Then someone added it to her food or beverages."

Sidney thanked him and disconnected.

"Holy hell. That poor old lady was murdered." Granger had an angry edge to his voice. "Who kills an old lady?"

They were both silent for a moment, working through their emotions.

"Bonnie Lingheimer's at the top of the list," Granger said. "She took care of Stevana and could easily have slipped her the poison. As executor, she has a lot to gain."

"True, but let's hold back judgment until we have all the facts," Sidney said.

"So, we're going to go talk to her?"

"Yeah, but not without a warrant. This case just got deadly serious. In addition to getting Stevana's DNA sample, we need to search the house for the source of the poison. An executor's duty is to carry out the wishes of the deceased. Instructions are clearly spelled out in the will or trust documents. We need to review those documents to see if Bonnie is upholding her end of the deal."

Sidney wasted no time calling Judge Whitmore, who was generally very responsive to her requests. They spoke for several minutes as she explained the circumstances and laid out the details. The judge agreed to have the warrant ready in an hour. Sidney ended the call and heard Granger's stomach growl, loudly. "You hungry?"

"You have to ask?"

No, she didn't have to ask. Granger was always hungry, and he never turned down an opportunity to eat. He carried a lot on his shoulders. In addition to being a gym rat, he worked hard on the family ranch. His father suffered from Parkinson's, and as the disease progressed over the years, Granger took on most of the chores. Then he reported for police duty. It seemed he burned fuel as fast as he consumed it.

"Let's grab a bite at Pickles Deli." Sidney started the engine and pulled out of the driveway, and her mouth started to water. The sandwiches at Pickles were two inches thick, packed with hickory smoked ham and melted Swiss cheese on rye, and the Kosher dill pickles were the best this side of the Cascades. And they came with a side order of crispy sweet potato fries.

Tugging her thoughts away from food, she said, "Call Amanda and Darnell. We're going to need help searching the premises. Tell them what we're looking for, and why."

"Copy that."

CHAPTER FIVE

NEITHER SHE NOR GRANGER wasted a second peeling back wrappers and devouring their sandwiches in record time. As patrol cops, they never knew when they might be called to an emergency, so eating while they had the chance was a survival instinct. For several minutes, they chewed, sipped, crunched, and used napkins liberally to catch the dripping secret sauce. After the last sip of soda was sucked through their straws, they drove back to the Montford neighborhood and found Stevana's rambling old gray mansion. Set back from the street in a tangle of oak trees, it stood out starkly from the surrounding mansions, and not in a good way. The landscaping was wildly overgrown, and a thick carpet of dead brown leaves covered the entire property. An imposing turret on the roof was half veiled in mist, every window on the second story was shuttered, and the whole structure was in dire need of paint. "Not what I was expecting. Doesn't look like it was kept up very well."

"That's an understatement," Granger said. "It looks haunted. I see bats circling the belfry."

"That's a turret. And I'm pretty sure those are pigeons."

"Whatever. It still looks haunted."

Sidney had to admit, something about the place felt dark and sinister. "Amanda and Darnell should be here momentarily. Let's go meet Bonnie Lingheimer."

"If she's awake. She probably sleeps in a coffin during the day."

Sidney humored him. "Do you want to wait in the SUV, where it's safe?"

He released his seat belt and reached for the door handle. "Hey, I'm just saying, don't be surprised if we encounter Stevana's ghost, looking for vengeance."

The vehicles of officers Amanda Cruz and Darnell Wood pulled up behind them and they all met on the sidewalk. Gripping her crime kit in one hand, Amanda frowned as she took in the house. "You sure this is the right place, Chief? Most of the house is shuttered against the light of day. Looks more like a vampire's lair."

"That's what I told her," Granger said, grinning.

A smile tugged up one corner of Sidney's mouth. "You're watching too many horror movies."

"You better start carrying a vile of holy water in your kit, Amanda," Darnell said, eyebrows wriggling in jest.

"I do. Next to the cross."

"Better get out that cross," he said. "When we get inside, you're taking the lead."

They trampled through the leaves, then climbed the stairs of the front porch and crossed a deep veranda. The windows on the double front doors were stained glass and the matching knockers were brass lion heads. "This house must have been incredibly elegant in its day," Sidney said.

"Yeah, before Dracula moved in," Granger said under his breath. The others laughed.

They heard heavy steps approaching, then the door creaked open about a foot to reveal a figure silhouetted against the dim light. "What do you want?" a deep, husky voice asked.

"I'm Police Chief Becker. We're from the Garnerville Police Department. Are you Bonnie Lingheimer?"

"Yes."

"Ms. Lingheimer, we have a warrant to search the premises. Could you please step aside and let us enter?"

"What on earth?" The woman stood frozen for a long moment, then she opened the door just wide enough for them to squeeze through one at a time. "Come in quickly so the cats don't get out."

When they all stood in the dimly lit hall, Sidney got a good look at Bonnie. She was a tall woman with broad shoulders, a long, hollow face, prominent cheekbones, and a no-nonsense demeanor. Sidney thought she looked like the female version of Lurch. Her raven black hair was drawn back into a chignon that highlighted the severity of her sharp features. A fitted black dress revealed a well-muscled figure that indicated her devotion to weightlifting.

They were all distracted by a herd of meowing cats trotting down the hall to greet them.

Granger whistled. "That's a lot of cats."

Varying in size and color, the dozen or so cats grouped around their legs, some twining in and out, eyes large and luminous.

"Stevana loved cats," Bonnie said in a tone that was barely polite.

"I see that." Darnell gently extracted a calico kitten that was climbing up his pants leg.

"They won't hurt you. Just ignore them and they'll leave you alone."

As though to contradict her, a Bengal kitten that was an expert climber scrambled up Granger's body from behind and perched on his shoulder. He rubbed it under its chin. "Cute little guy."

"That's Blinky. Always climbing to greater heights. He thinks he's a goat." Bonnie's voice had momentarily softened, then she caught Sidney's eyes and her tone sharpened. "A warrant, huh? What could you possibly hope to find? Stevana and I lived a quiet life. You won't find any illegal drugs, counterfeit money, weapons, or exotic animals."

Sidney handed her the warrant. "That's not what we're looking for. I understand you're now the executor of this property?"

"Yes ...." Her eyes narrowed with suspicion as she read the warrant.

"We need to see Stevana's will and trust documents."

Bonnie sniffed indignantly. "So that's what this is about. You're afraid I'm taking more than my due. That's laughable, as you will soon see."

"You can start with the kitchen, Amanda," Sidney said. If the poisonous needles of the yew plant were to be found, the kitchen was the likeliest place.

"It's down the hall through the dining room on the left," Bonnie said crisply. "Try not to mess anything up. I've seen on TV what you people do. You'll ransack the place."

"We'll be careful," Sidney assured her.

Amanda left with two shorthair tomcats padding purposefully behind her.

"Want me to start upstairs, Chief?" Granger asked.

Sidney nodded, and he headed for the grand staircase directly in front of them, the kitten still attached to his shoulder.

"He won't be up there for more than a minute," Bonnie said with a smirk.

Sidney ignored her remark. "We need to look at those documents."

"They're in the office." She nodded at an open door on the left.

"Darnell, go with Bonnie and start reviewing the will." *In other words, don't let her out of your sight.* Suspects were only too eager to destroy evidence when cops weren't looking.

"Where's Stevana's bedroom?" Sidney asked.

"Last door on the right." Bonnie smirked, then she and Darnell disappeared into the office. The cats ambled down the hall, scattering to destinations unknown. Sidney followed several into a spacious room that was once an elegant ballroom. High, arched windows lined one wall, crystal chandeliers hung from the ceiling, and a gilded mirror hung above a carved marble fireplace. The ballroom now served as a haven for cats. A community of cat condos commanded the center of the room. Each unit had a circular window and was lined with faux fur. Graceful, sleek, sinuous cats traversed bridges that connected one unit to the other. A blue-eyed Siamese and her kittens stared out from a third story penthouse. A domestic shorthair emerged from a tube tunnel and trotted over to inspect the hem of Sidney's pants. Wooden steps climbed the walls to reach lofty hammocks and perches, now occupied by several cats who looked down at her with challenging stares.

"A cat paradise," Granger said, coming in behind her. The Bengal kitten had taken up permanent residence on his shoulder. It looked perfectly at home.

"You're done with the upstairs already?" Sidney asked, surprised.

"Bonnie was right. There's nothing to see up there. Just a bunch of shuttered, dark empty rooms. Not a stitch of furniture. The doors are kept shut to keep out the cats."

"That's strange."

"Everything's strange about this place."

"Let's check out Stevana's bedroom. We need that DNA sample." Sidney opened the door to the last room in the hallway and immediately felt a sharp pang of disappointment. The room was stripped bare of everything, even the curtains, and the wood floors gleamed from a recent polishing. They crossed the room to the bathroom. It had also been stripped and cleaned.

"What the hell?" Granger asked. "I was expecting expensive furnishings. Antiques. Signs of life."

"At the very least, a toothbrush. Bonnie's been busy ...."

"No shit. My bet, she poisoned Stevana. You have to admit, Chief, she looks like a psycho killer incarnate. Those unseeing eyes. The size of her shoulders. Like a lineman. Remember Refrigerator? I wouldn't want to arm wrestle her." He was scratching Blinky's head, and she could hear the kitten purring. "Bonnie could easily have carried the old lady's body out of the mortuary, and then into the Colby's yard."

"She has some explaining to do," Sidney said calmly, amused by Granger's stream of consciousness ramblings.

"She has motive," he said.

"Motive without evidence is as useful as fairy dust."

They backtracked to the office and found Darnell diligently poring over papers on the desk. Bonnie stood over him, arms crossed, face inscrutable. In the dim light, her cheeks looked even more hollow, her eyes dark shadows, her face skull-like. Her ability to be so still, so expressionless, gave Sidney a chill.

Darnell looked up. "Everything here is in order and authentic, Chief. Stevana was in debt up to her nose. The house has been sold and the income will pay off her creditors. What's left, around $50,000, goes to Bonnie, as long as she upholds her duty and oversees the sale of everything."

"That's why the rooms are empty?" Sidney asked.

Bonnie responded with a shallow, empty kind of smile. "I need to be out of here in two weeks."

"Where are all the furnishings?"

"Gone. Stevana sold them off incrementally over the last six months. You think it's cheap keeping up this huge drafty barn? It's over a hundred years old. Everything needs repairs. She sunk her fortune into this money pit. What a waste."

"What about her bedroom furnishings?"

"The auctioneer came last week."

"Her personal effects? Clothes, shoes, beauty items?"

"Clothes went to Goodwill. Everything else is in boxes in the garage. Ready to throw out."

"I need something with her DNA on it."

"Look in those boxes."

"Granger, go out and gather a few items."

"I'm on it." He detached Blinky from his perch and set him on the floor. The kitten mewed piteously and tried to follow. "You are a wailer, aren't you?" Granger faked annoyance, but let the Bengal climb back up to his shoulder, then he took his leave.

"Did Stevana have kids, or any other relatives?" Sidney asked.

"No kids. She may have some distant relatives, but none she ever mentioned. No one ever visited in twenty years. Except for the pastor."

"So, no one who might swoop in and contest the will?"

"No. I'm the closest thing to family, or a friend." Bonnie gave Sidney a penetrating stare, then narrowed her eyes questioningly. "What's going on? Why do you need DNA? What's this Taxus brevifolia you're looking for?"

"Bonnie, why don't you take a seat? We need to talk."

They sat on two office chairs facing each other. "Are you the one who found Stevana's body?"

She nodded.

"Tell me about her last days. What were her symptoms?"

"She didn't really have any. Stevana was as frail as a bird, anyway, confined to a wheelchair. Always tired. Slept a lot." Bonnie recited the facts mechanically, devoid of emotion. "More than usual the last two weeks, though, and she barely ate. Then she was gone. Her heart finally gave out. Doctor Farrow said she went fast, in her sleep."

"You don't seem to be too broken up about her death."

Bonnie sat perfectly still, her mouth pinched, as though weighing what she should say. "She died in her sleep. She didn't suffer. That's the most any of us can hope for. And she was spared this." She made a sweeping gesture with her hand. "Watching the house close down."

"After twenty years together, you must have been close." Sidney studied her, keeping her expression neutral. She was an ace at reading people, catching the slightest nuance of emotion, finding the tiniest fractures in their composure that spoke of guilt.

Bonnie clenched and unclenched her jaw. "I did my job. I did it well. I didn't have to like her."

"Was she difficult?"

Her mouth turned downward into a scowl. She shifted her gaze away from Sidney's momentarily, then gave a subtle nod.

"I take that as a yes."

Bonnie shrugged one shoulder. "She was an old, sick, frail woman with nothing to live for, except the cats. She sat in that ballroom for hours every day, watching them. Talking to them. Petting them. Giving them treats. It's the only time I ever saw her smile."

Sidney heard a hint of resentment, Bonnie's first reveal of underlying emotion. She wanted to widen that crack. "Stevana spent all her time with her cats. Gave them all of her attention. Adored them."

"She loved her four-legged creatures. The two-legged kind, not so much."

"You included?"

Bonnie rubbed the back of her neck. "There was no love lost between us. I kept my head down. Did my job."

"Stevana had a temper?"

Bonnie shifted uncomfortably in her chair, then blurted, "Hell yeah, she had a temper. The slightest thing could trigger it. Her words could eviscerate you."

"So, you were walking on eggshells …."

"Oh, yeah. Watch out if her eggs weren't poached just right—not too hard, not too runny. Or if her bath water wasn't the exact temperature."

"Not too hot, not too cold," Sidney said in a sympathetic tone.

Bonnie met her gaze and her hard expression softened. "I think you get the picture."

"I do."

"So, you still haven't told me why you're here," Bonnie said, her tone noticeably more civil.

"I have some disturbing news, Bonnie." Sidney watched her closely. "We found a dead body hidden on someone's private property this morning. We have reason to believe it's Stevana."

The caretaker's eyes widened with surprise and her mouth fell open. "It wasn't Stevana. I went to her funeral. I saw her casket go into the ground."

Was she genuinely surprised, or just acting? "We think someone took her body from the mortuary after the cocktail party." Sidney pulled out her phone and scrolled to the picture of the silver locket. "Do you recognize this?"

Bonnie froze, then she blinked. "Does it say, 'Love forever, Forest,' inside?"

"Yes."

"Dear god …."

"Who was Forest?"

"Her husband, and the love of her life. The only person she ever showed a hint of affection toward. Forest was a lawyer; brilliant, charming, warm. Stevana was his opposite. I don't know what tied him to her. She was gorgeous when she was young. Guess that's it. He died two years after they moved here to Garnerville." She swallowed. "So, the body you found … is Stevana."

"We want to exhume the casket to be certain, but first we need to be sure it's her."

Understanding momentarily lit up in her eyes. "That's why you need the DNA."

"Yes."

Bonnie exhaled slowly. "This is incomprehensible. Why would someone steal an old woman's body? It's devilish."

"We think they were motivated by the jewelry she wore. The diamonds and the emerald."

"Diamonds? That paste? The emerald was colored glass. The real stuff was sold months ago. Do you think we're stupid enough to bury her in expensive gems?"

"So, the jewelry was fake." Sidney pondered this for a moment.

"Unfortunately, it appears someone thought it was real." *Morticia for one, and Gordon, and everyone else at the cocktail party.*

"Do you know anyone who stood out at the party? Anyone particularly interested in the jewelry?"

Bonnie stared at her hands, then she looked up, her eyes sparking with anger. "Yes, I can think of someone. One of the little bastards! One of those misfits …."

"Who are you talking about?"

"A bunch of motherless brats from Wellspring Community. I told Pastor John not to let them anywhere near her funeral."

"Please explain."

"A bunch of homeless boys, orphans, are sheltered in the basement of the church. They have nothing better to do than crash funerals. One of them snuck into Stevana's cocktail party. Gordon escorted him out, but not before he stuffed his face with hors d'oeuvres. And of course, he saw the jewels."

"What's this boy's name?"

"Don't know. You'll have to ask the pastor. But he's the oldest boy, and obviously their leader."

"Hmm. We'll talk to the pastor next."

Granger walked in carrying a small box of Stevana's personal items. "Got more than enough DNA in here. Hairbrush, toothbrush, old shoes."

Amanda walked in right behind him holding something in her gloved hand. "I think I found what we came for, Chief. I went through the whole kitchen, which is pretty much empty. Just a few things left in the pantry. This included." She removed the top and handed a small canister to Sidney.

Inside on the bottom were a few dried rounded needles. The label was decorated with flowers and hummingbirds and the product was named Winter Mix. Under ingredients, nothing was listed. "This container can be bought at any gift store. The label is homemade, printed from someone's computer."

"That's Stevana's special tea," Bonnie volunteered. "I made it for her every night."

The room went dead silent. Bonnie had just confessed to poisoning Stevana.

"Where did you get this?" Sidney asked.

"Stevana ordered it. It came in the mail a couple of weeks before she died."

Another long silence.

"What's all the fuss about?" Bonnie's brow creased into deep furrows. "Is that the Taxus brevifolia mentioned in the warrant?"

"Yes."

"Do you think it had something to do with Stevana's death?" She looked at the tight faces around her and her eyes opened wide. "Oh heavens, you do …. You don't think her death was natural." There was suddenly a slight manic quality to her. "You think I had something to do with it?"

"Who sent it?" Sidney asked sternly, ignoring her question.

"I don't know. It was in the mailbox with her regular mail. Stevana opened it."

"Where's the packaging it came in?"

Bonnie thought for a moment. "Stevana wheeled herself over to the trash bin and stuffed the packaging in there. I thought it odd that she wasted no time trashing it. She told me it was a special medicinal tea sent by an old friend, and she wanted a cup every night before bedtime." Bonnie paused and nervously rubbed the back of her neck, then her voice quickened. "It went into the recycling bin, which hasn't been collected yet. The bin is in the garage. It's bright yellow."

Sidney looked at Granger. He took the hint and headed back to the garage, pulling nitrile gloves from his duty belt. *If there were any prints or other trace evidence from the sender, it might be preserved. There might be DNA under the stamp from the sender's saliva.*

"Did Stevana say anything else about the tea, or the person who sent it?"

"No. Never said a word when I brought it to her room each night. The cup was always empty the next morning."

"You didn't notice anything different about her behavior?"

"Like I said, she just slept more. Didn't eat much."

"How did you know how much to use?"

"There was a tiny handwritten card inside with directions. Two teaspoons for every 6 ounces of hot water."

"Did you keep it?" Sidney asked.

"Yes. It's in the drawer with the silverware."

"I'll get it, Chief." Amanda quickly left the room. She returned moments later with the card placed in a plastic evidence bag and handed it to Sidney. It was the size of a business card, blank on one side, handwriting scrawled on the other.

Granger swept back into the room holding a larger evidence bag. Folded brown wrapping paper was inside with the address facing out. "No return address, Chief."

Sidney compared the handwriting to that on the card. They matched. "We need to have Stewart examine all this stuff. Darnell, run everything over to the lab. Tell him we need a DNA match ASAP." The station was five minutes away. They should have an answer within the hour.

"I'll tell him to get right on it." He left with the tea canister, the two evidence bags, and the box of Stevana's personal possessions.

Bonnie had been sitting very still, as though trying to be invisible, probably fearing arrest. She had motive to kill Stevana. She obviously felt intense animosity toward her employer. Fifty thousand dollars didn't go far these days, but folks killed for less. On the other hand, a guilty person would have gotten rid of the poisonous tea after it served its purpose. You don't leave a murder weapon lying around in plain view. The old lady was clearly on her way out and Bonnie didn't need to speed up the process. Plus, she lived here and wouldn't be in a rush to go out and find new housing and employment. At this point, the caretaker had moved to the very bottom of Sidney's suspect list. "We're done here, Bonnie, for now. But we may have more questions for you."

She released a sigh of relief. "I'll be here for two more weeks."

"Then where are you going?" Sidney asked.

She shrugged. "To Mexico, maybe. It's cheaper to live there on social security."

"Where are all the cats going?" Granger asked with a note of concern. Blinky looked relaxed crouching on his shoulder, his pink tongue partially out, his eyes at half-mast.

"To shelters. Except for the ones that are handicapped. The Wellspring Animal Rescue is taking them."

"I can take Blinky off your hands, if you want."

"Take him. He's yours."

Sidney and her two officers left the residence and conferred on the sidewalk.

"I think the old lady knocked herself off," Granger said, putting the kitten on the ground. They all watched as it found a place to do its business, then he scooped it up again.

"I agree. Stevana ordered the tea. She planned her own death," Amanda said.

"Unless someone with nefarious intentions deceived her into thinking it was medicinal," Sidney said evenly. "We're investigating all possibilities. Every angle. We still have many people we need to talk to before we draw conclusions. Hopefully Stewart can help us find the person who sent that tea. Right now, let's concentrate on who snatched Stevana's body." She pulled out the list of suspects that had attended Stevana's funeral party and handed it to Amanda. "You two can start interviewing these performers. And Granger, make sure you get Blinky some cat food."

"I'm dropping him off at your place. Selena is going to cat sit until I get off work."

"Just don't forget to take him home. Four cats are plenty in our house." Most nights, at least two of the cats took up real estate on her bed, which she didn't mind until they pinned down a limb and cut off her circulation, or laid across her face, cutting off her oxygen.

CHAPTER SIX

GRANGER CONTACTED ED HORTON, the manager of the entertainment company, and was told all four performers on Morticia's list were currently at work, though one of them, Max Biggs, was just finishing up a gig at a birthday party. They couldn't interrupt the other three performers and would have to catch them during a break. With Granger riding shotgun, Amanda wove through blocks of suburban streets to reach the address on Maple Leaf Drive. A brightly painted van with Mr. Biggley the clown pictured on the side was parked in the driveway. The house sat on wooded property and a crowd of people were gathered under the trees, all eyes focused on the clown. Not wanting to disrupt the party, Amanda and Granger left the patrol car and stood in the driveway by the van, watching the entertainment.

"Who likes balloons?" The clown asked, his baritone voice loud and spirited. All the kids eagerly responded.

"I do!"

"I do."

The clown skillfully twisted balloons for each child—a dog, a flower, a hat, a horse, and two swords, which two of the boys used to poke the giggling girls. Parents sat behind them in a semicircle of lawn chairs, sipping drinks and laughing.

"Just one last magic trick," the clown said, pushing up one sleeve. "As you can see, there's nothing up my sleeve." He pushed up his other sleeve, and a corner of a bright red scarf peeked out. "And nothing up this sleeve."

"There is too!" said a toothless girl with chestnut pigtails.

"Really? Come show everyone."

She ran up and grabbed the scarf and pulled. Only it kept coming out, getting longer and longer, and changing colors from red to green to blue to orange. To uproarious laughter, she kept pulling until the fabric was a big pile at her feet, then she gave up.

"Okay, boys and girls." The clown bowed to the kids and the parents. "I must depart, for other children await my awesome talent and magical tricks."

"Come get some birthday cake," a woman called out cheerily, and the kids crowded together around a picnic table. The clown quickly packed his gear and walked to the driveway carrying a trunk. He wore a colorful suit, a shaggy orange wig, and a big red nose. His face was painted white with a painted smile taking up half of his face. Within the smile, he wore a scowl that deepened when he spotted them. "To what do I owe this displeasure? The ex-wife complaining again?"

"No, sir," Amanda said. "We're here on another matter." She introduced herself and Granger, but he brushed past them, sliding open the door to his van and shoving in the trunk. The interior was stuffed beyond capacity with props and outfits and trinkets to give out as prizes.

He seemed very agitated.

"You okay, Mr. Biggs?"

"Now I am. Glad that's over with. Luckily, this one went down without a hitch. Kids are evil. The devil incarnate. Screaming toddlers are the worst. Ever have cake slung in your eye? An ice cream cone put down your pants? Not fun." He gestured to the contents of the van and exclaimed loudly, "Welcome to the weird and wacky world of Mr. Biggley, clown, mime, and magician. At your service." Then he continued in a normal tone, "I also do respectable theater. Shakespeare. But those gigs are rare and far between these days."

Amanda had a hard time seeing past the huge red nose to picture him doing King Lear.

"But I think the birthday party went well, don't you?" His eyes seemed to bore into her, as though commanding a good response.

"Sure. The kids loved it."

His eyes darted to her nametag. "So, what is it you need, Officer Cruz?"

"You were hired by Morticia Solace to attend a funeral party two weeks ago. Stevana Thornburg."

"Yes, that's right. Morticia's affairs are some of my better gigs. Lots of Champagne. Good food. But Mrs. Thornburg as a hostess? Not so much. She was rather stiff." He laughed at his own joke.

"What did you think of her appearance?" Amanda asked. "The dress … and …." She waited to see if he'd fill in the blanks.

"And …?" he said.

"The jewels."

"Didn't really pay much attention. It was a costume. Everyone was in costume. I wore a tux. I was F. Scott Fitzgerald." Then he proceeded to quote the writer in a stilted, dignified tone, *"I hope she'll be a fool—that's the best thing a girl can be in this world, a beautiful little fool. Nothing is as obnoxious as other people's luck."*

"That's very impressive," Amanda said, unimpressed. "Did you notice anyone else paying undue attention to Mrs. Thornburg?"

"Everyone ignored her after they realized she wasn't good at repartee. Oh, with the exception of one young man. He was quite dashing and exuberant, and he carried on a rather lengthy conversation with her. He obviously found her witty, because he laughed out loud a few times."

"Who was he?"

"We all went by theatrical names. It was odd that he wasn't wearing a suit. I believe he called himself the Masked Marauder. He wore a mask and a scarf over his hair. Like Zorro. Dressed all in black."

"Can you describe him?"

"He wore a mask, was all dressed in black," he said with a smirk.

"Anything else?" Granger asked with an edge.

Mr. Biggs face sobered. "He seemed very young. Late teens, maybe. Tall. Good build."

"What time did you leave?"

"Morticia and Gordon literally chased us all out at 10:00 p.m. Guess they didn't want to open up any more Champagne. We went through quite a few bottles."

"Then where did you go?"

"Home. Where else on a Sunday night? Everything shuts down around here by 9:00. Except Barney's. I sure wasn't going to Barney's Bar and Grill dressed in a tux. That would really be slumming it."

Amanda silently agreed. Barney's was definitely a bar for the rough and tumble crowd who drank too much, secreted in drugs, and got into brawls. "Can anyone confirm you were home?"

"Yeah. My dog and my parrot." He reached into his van and pulled out a brochure. "My number's on there. My parrot answers the phone. You can ask him."

"That's very funny, Mr. Biggs," Granger said curtly. "Can anyone who's human vouch for you?"

"No." His scowl was back. "Why do I need an alibi?"

"Mrs. Thornburg's body was stolen from the mortuary the night of the party."

"What?" His penciled eyebrows lifted into his wig. "And you suspect me?" He looked shocked for a moment, but then he laughed. "That's funny.

Why anyone would steal that old bag's body is beyond me. I prefer my women younger, and not dead."

"This is a serious matter, Mr. Biggs," Granger said. "It's a felony to tamper with a dead body. Right now, you're a prime suspect."

"In all seriousness, I was too far gone to steal the old bag's body. You can ask anyone at the party. It wasn't my finest moment, okay? I got carried away. My girlfriend and I had a big fight earlier and I was nursing a bruised ego." He recited another Fitzgerald quote. *"First you take a drink, then the drink takes a drink, then the drink takes you.* Morticia called me a cab. You can ask her."

"We'll check out your story," Amanda said.

"So, can I go? I have another party I need to get to."

"That's all for now. Stay out of trouble."

Amanda and Granger got into her vehicle and watched him for a moment. He reached into his pocket and pulled out a handful of clown paraphernalia—balloons, confetti, fake dollar bills, a kazoo. Then he tried the other pocket and located his keys.

"He's sure a barrel of laughs," she said drily.

"Yeah, I can't stop laughing."

"Tell your face that."

"I'm laughing on the inside."

"This Zorro character needs a closer look," she said. "He called himself the Masked Marauder. Marauder means pillager, plunderer, bandit."

"Wonder if he was taking his character too seriously. He's probably the kid Bonnie was telling us about."

Amanda made a quick call to Morticia and confirmed that Mr. Biggs was indeed "three sheets to the wind" when he left the funeral party, and yes, she did call him a cab. "Who was the guy dressed as Zorro?"

Amanda heard her exhale sharply. "Some orphan kid from the church. By the time I realized he wasn't one of the actors, he'd already downed a plate of appetizers and a half a bottle of Champagne. Gordon threw him out. His name's Rafe."

"Mr. Biggs said Rafe showed Stevana a lot of interest."

"I didn't really notice. I was trying to keep everyone fed and entertained. But he's probably a delinquent if he's living at the church. No foster homes want those kids. They're all misfits. You think he may be the guilty party?"

"We'll talk to him. Thanks, Morticia. We'll be in touch."

"So do you think Mr. Biggs is still a suspect?" Granger asked.

"He's an actor. He could've easily faked being drunk."

"Yeah, that's what I thought. And he has no alibi, I don't care what his parrot says. He needs a closer look." Granger's thumbs tapped out a text to Sidney. He gave her the gist of their interaction with Biggs, and that a kid from the church, named Rafe, was the one who crashed the party.

Amanda took out the suspect list and scanned the remaining three names. "Let's see who's next to interview." She chuckled. "This should be good. Valentino, exotic male dancer. He's performing at a private birthday party tonight."

"I hope it's for adults."

"I hope we get there before his act is done. I wouldn't mind catching an eyeful."

CHAPTER SEVEN

BUILT IN 1875, Wellspring Community was a beautiful white church with three steeples and rows of stained-glass windows. Creekside Cemetery, dotted with tombstones, stretched out behind it like wings. Stewart called as Sidney pulled into the parking lot. "Good news, I hope."

"The DNA is a match, Chief. The compost corpse is definitely Stevana."

"Good work, Stewart. That gives me cause to dig up that casket."

Sidney entered the church and crossed the vestibule into the nave. It had been years since she attended a wedding here. Nothing had changed in the long rectangular interior. The rows of wooden pews, worn with age, were still divided by three aisles and no iconography decorated the clean white walls. In the sanctuary, the only ornamentation was the light slanting through a stained-glass window that cast a rainbow across the altar and lectern. It was a nondenominational church that welcomed people of all faiths and all walks of life. Pastor John entered from a door in the sanctuary. He was a robust, middle-aged man with unflagging energy who had changed very little over the last few years, though his hair had gone from brown to gray and he was fuller around the middle.

"Hello, Pastor John."

"Chief Becker, it's a pleasure to see you," he said amiably.

They made friendly small talk, then Sidney got to the point. As she related the details of her investigation, the pastor's eyebrows lifted several times and he looked genuinely shocked. "Heavens! Stevana's body was stolen from the mortuary? And found in a yard across the lake? Oh, heavens. What a fright to that poor family."

"Yes, it was. We need to exhume the casket as soon as possible. Something was buried in there. We need to find out what it is. It might help us identify the thief. Stevana had no relatives to give us permission, so we need yours, as the overseer of the cemetery."

"I understand," he said gravely. "It's profane to have something foreign buried in a sacred spot meant for Stevana. Her remains need to be returned, and of course, we'll do another service. Let me contact my custodian. Hold on, and I'll send him a text. Hopefully we can get this matter taken care of today." He pulled his phone from a pocket and tapped out a message, then met her gaze with a frown. "Why would someone do such a thing?"

"There was jewelry on her body. We found out that it was fake, but the people at her send-off party thought it was real, and very valuable. The jewelry was stitched to her body."

"Oh dear." He released a troubled sigh. "Well, that explains it, doesn't it? Do you have any suspects?"

"Not at this time. We're in the initial phase of our investigation, making inquiries, trying to establish a timeline." Sidney cleared her throat. "Bonnie told us no one ever visited Stevana, except you."

"I was one of the few."

"How often did you see her?"

"Once a week. She had become very withdrawn these last two months. I think seeing her home and her security dissolve around her was very distressing. I saw her the night of her death. She looked unwell. She was as frail as a bird. I instinctively knew she was nearing the end. She knew it, too. That's why she planned her funeral. But I attributed her death to general poor health. Her body finally gave out."

"Could she have been suicidal?"

He frowned. "Hmm. She never alluded to taking her life. I would have done everything in my power to prevent it." He arched an eyebrow. "Why, did the M.E. find something?"

"Yes. Please keep this in confidence. She had a poisonous substance in her body. It was in the form of tea that came in the mail from a private party. Did she ever mention anything about a medicinal tea she was drinking?"

He shook his head. "Not that I can recall."

They were both silent for a moment.

"I was told you have several orphaned boys living here."

"Yes, we do. We foster five boys ranging in age from six to sixteen. They're good boys. A social worker meets with them monthly. She's very pleased with the arrangement."

"I'm certain everything is in perfect order. I'm not here to check on their welfare. I heard that they habitually attend funerals."

"Yes, that's true. It's not as morbid as you may think." He gave her a questioning smile. "What does that have to do with Stevana?"

"Maybe they noticed something unusual at one of the funerals, or around the cemetery in general. Maybe someone creeping around at night. Kids see things others don't. And one of them attended Stevana's send-off party. The oldest boy."

"That would be Rafe McEnery." His brow furrowed. "Is he a suspect?"

"No." Sidney did not want to point an incriminating finger at one of the pastor's boys. She needed his cooperation and didn't want to put him off. "But he may have witnessed something at the party that may be of help."

"I wasn't aware that he was invited."

"Apparently, he wasn't."

"Hmm." He rubbed his chin. "Rafe is adventurous, I'll give him that. He's at that age, you know. Experimenting with boundaries. He came to us late, you see, with a lot of set behavioral patterns that don't work in his favor. His father's in prison."

"I'm sorry to hear that. And his mother?"

"She abandoned him at eight. No one knows what happened to her. Rafe has been in a half dozen foster homes since then. Was never able to adjust."

"That's tragic." She felt genuine sympathy.

"All the boys are troubled in one way or another. We take the ones that can't be placed elsewhere and do our best to set them on a good course."

"You have a big heart, Pastor John. These boys are indebted to you, and so is the community."

He smiled at her kindly. "It's a team effort. We have many caring volunteers. We do God's work." His phone pinged and he read the text, then looked up at her. "The casket will be dug up today. My custodian is heading over there as we speak."

"Great."

"Shouldn't take long with a backhoe. Well, let's go down and see who's here. All the boys have jobs, you know, some here at the church, some at the animal rescue. Strictly on a volunteer basis." He continued to talk as he led her across the sanctuary and into the hallway, then to a stairwell leading downstairs. "Watch your step. I'm very proud of the boys. They perform needed public services. Taking care of rescue animals. Attending the funerals of those who have no family. We've buried several homeless folks. The church picks up the tab, of course. The needy come to our soup kitchen. The boys help serve the food and get to know them. It's heartbreaking to see folks down on their luck, but it builds compassion."

They went down another hall and he paused outside a door. "This is the cafeteria. We serve meals to whoever walks in. All the food is donated." He glanced at his watch. "We open the kitchen door in twenty minutes. The dining hall will fill up quickly, but you can talk to the boys beforehand." He opened the door, and they entered a big hall with tables and chairs scattered about. At one end, a kitchen was separated by a food bar where covered stainless steel food containers were being set in place by two men. Behind the bar was the kitchen, where several women and men were busy preparing food.

A tall, lanky Asian boy, about fourteen, was busy stacking trays and dishes at one end of the bar. His Goth look was a study in ebony, from his jet-black shirt and pants to the black tattoos on his neck, to his raven hair that fell across his shoulders like a veil.

"That's Foley Macada," Pastor John said.

At one of the tables, a small boy seated himself with a tray of food. He wore an oversized gray sweatshirt with the hood pulled over his head, hiding his face.

"Let's start with Joey Nolan," the pastor said, nodding toward the boy. "He's ten, but small for his age, and very sensitive. He eats by himself before everyone else comes in and crowds the tables."

They approached, but the boy did not acknowledge them.

"Hi, Joey," Pastor John said. "We have a visitor today. Chief Becker from the Garnerville police department. She wants to talk to you for a minute."

The boy didn't look up, but concentrated on a bottle of ketchup, shaking it out in huge dollops, covering the scrambled eggs and sliced sausage on his plate.

"You like ketchup," Sidney said, friendly.

Joey ignored her.

"He douses everything with ketchup." The Goth teen had wandered over and was wiping down the next table. Two small silver rings pierced his bottom lip, one pierced his left eyebrow, and several shimmered on the outer rims of his ears. The black pencil lining his eyes gave him an exotic look. "Ketchup is his favorite vegetable. That, and pickles."

Joey pulled a baggie from a pocket, opened it, and sprinkled some of its contents over his food, then he speared a slice of sausage and shoved it into his mouth. Immediately, he spit it out. "Ick! Those are the worst potatoes I've ever eaten."

"Those aren't potatoes, genius," Goth boy said. "That's sausage."

Joey pushed his plate away. "Gross. I don't eat animals."

"No, just bugs."

"You don't know anything, Foley," Joey said. "Insects are good for you. Protein."

"If you say so." Foley stood watching, no doubt curious as to why the pastor brought a cop down here.

Sidney couldn't see Joey clearly. Half his face was in shadow from the hoodie. "So, you like to eat insects?" she asked, following his train of thought, wanting to gain his trust.

He kept his head bowed. "Yeah. Insects can save the planet. Feed poor people around the world. Billions of insects can be raised in a small factory, instead of taking up millions of acres of land to raise livestock. They've been eating insects in other countries forever."

"I've heard that. But I've never tried eating any myself."

"They're pretty tasty. They're crunchy like chips if you roast them just right." He held up the baggie. "These are roasted cockroaches. Try some."

"Thank you, Joey." Hoping it wasn't too gross, Sidney took something small from the baggie and popped it into her mouth." It was crispy and tasted like barbeque. "You're right. It is tasty. Do you mind if we sit with you for just a moment?"

He nodded.

"Foley, too?"

He shrugged. They took up the other three seats at the table.

"Pastor John tells me that you boys do a lot of good work for the town. You help feed people here in the cafeteria. And you go to funerals."

"Yeah," Joey said. "We help dead people who don't have anyone who loves them. It's sad. But somewhere they're looking down at us, thanking us."

"Yes, they are," Pastor John said warmly.

"That's really nice of you. Did you go to Stevana Thornburg's funeral?"

"The old rich lady?" Joey shook his head. "She had a fancy party. I wasn't invited."

Sidney gave Goth boy a direct stare. "What about you, Foley?"

The teen averted his eyes. He studied a hangnail on his thumb.

"Did you go to the party?"

He licked his lips but wouldn't look at her.

Sidney sat quietly waiting. It was one of her best skills. People with something to hide often felt uncomfortable with dead silence. Their guilty thoughts rose in volume in their heads, compelling them to speak.

"Do I look like someone who'd be invited to a fancy party?" he blurted.

He had a point. Foley would have stood out like a mutt at a poodle convention. "But you know someone who snuck into the party …."

"Yeah, I know someone."

"Don't be a snitch!" Joey said.

Foley looked at Joey with contempt, and said, "Joey's lord and master was there."

Sidney ignored the sarcasm. "And who would that be?"

"Rafe McEnery. That's all I know. I heard Rafe mention it to Garret. They stopped talking when I walked in. He and Rafe are as thick as thieves. Garret's at the animal rescue today. That's all I know."

"Snitch!" Joey jerked up his head and his hoodie fell back. He had a sensitive face, shaggy blond hair, and a shiner that nearly closed one of his sky-blue eyes. Half of his upper lip was also swollen.

"Holy Jesus, Joey. What happened to your face?" Pastor John asked.

The boy pulled his hoodie back over his head, crossed his arms and sat back in defiance.

"Joey, who did this to you?" The pastor asked gently.

Silence.

"Foley, would you get Joey an ice pack?" Sidney asked.

"Yeah, sure." He left the table.

"Joey, you aren't in trouble," Sidney said. "But the boy who hit you needs to be dealt with. Identifying a bully can keep other boys from being injured. You don't want another boy to be hurt, do you?"

He shook his head.

"This bully scares you, doesn't he?"

He nodded.

"You're afraid that if you tell on him, he'll hurt you even worse next time."

He shifted uncomfortably in his seat.

"Was it someone at your school?"

He shook his head.

Foley returned with a bag of frozen peas and handed it to the younger boy.

"Foley, can you give us some space?" Pastor John asked.

He nodded and went into the kitchen.

Joey pushed back his hoodie and pressed the peas to his eye.

"Did the bully hit you anywhere else?" Sidney asked.

"No." Tears escaped his eyes and ran down his cheeks. He knuckled them away, then said in a choked voice, "But he held me upside down by my ankles and shook me. He wanted my money. His two friends just stood there watching, like it was funny."

Sidney heard the shame beneath his words. She and the Pastor exchanged a glance, trying to hide their alarm. *Poor kid.* It must have been both terrifying and humiliating to be held hostage at the whim of a cruel and violent person, not knowing what he might do next, while witnesses laughed. This bully had to be tall and strong to hold Joey up by his ankles.

"That must have been very scary," she said gently. "I'm so sorry that happened to you."

He sniffed.

"What's the name of the boy who hurt you?"

Silence. Joey stuck out his bottom lip in determination.

"We're going to find out who he is, one way or another. You can save us a lot of time and trouble if you just tell us now. He's going to keep on bullying if you let him get away with it."

The boy lowered the ice pack and met her gaze with a frightened expression. His fingers gripped the edge of the table. "Everyone calls him Wacko Jacko."

"What's his last name?"

"Jacko Krall. He's a senior at the high school."

A high school student picking on a little kid! Sidney saw red for a moment, but forced herself to appear calm. "You were very brave to tell us about Jacko."

Joey swallowed. Then he gave her a wobbly smile. "Thank you, Chief Becker."

"Do you have any idea why Jacko singled you out? Why he thought you had money?"

"Because I do. I have a business. I sell my roasted insects at a vegetable stand owned by Mrs. Ferris. She's really nice. She sells corn and eggs and apples and stuff. I asked if she wanted to sell my insects. She tried them and really liked them, and she said I could sell them myself on weekends. I have a little table on the end of her stand."

What an industrious little kid! Only ten years old! Sidney beamed him a smile, marveling at his ambition. Everyone in town knew Mrs. Ferris. Her colorful stand was a landmark on Twisted Oak Road on the east side of town where the suburbs turned into farmland. Sidney had bought produce from her many times and knew her to be a responsible business owner. Fruit and vegetable stands located on a farmer's property were exempt from requiring a license. Homemade foods such as granola, chips, popcorn, and baked goods could also be sold. Joey's roasted bugs, if prepared in a sterile environment, fell within acceptable parameters.

"We let him use our ovens," Pastor John said. "Everything he uses is meticulously clean."

"Do you sell a lot of insects?" she asked the boy.

"Yep. About eight or nine bags every weekend." There was a hint of a smile at the corner of his mouth. "The chocolate covered ants and the crispy garlic and chili crickets sell the best. People are coming back for more."

"Sounds delicious. It also sounds like a lot of work."

"Rafe and Garret help me cook and bag them. I make about fifteen or twenty dollars every weekend. I'm saving for college."

"That's impressive. Did Jacko see you at the stand today?"

"Yeah. Then he and his creepy friends stopped me when I was riding my bike home."

"And he attacked you."

He nodded. "He would have hurt me more if not for Rafe."

"Rafe came to your rescue?"

"Yeah. He was walking to the animal sanctuary down the road from the stand. He had a stray dog with him that looked like it really needed help."

Rafe again. Rafe the "big brother" who helps Joey in the kitchen. Rafe who protects him from bullies. Rafe who takes stray dogs to the sanctuary. Rafe was sounding more and more like a shining example of kindness, not someone who would steal an old lady's body and hide it in a compost heap. "Where is Rafe now? I'd like to talk to him."

"Probably at the rescue place. He said the dog needed a flea bath, bad."

"Joey, think very carefully. I want you to tell me everything that happened today between you and Jacko."

Joey sucked in a deep breath, his mind flicking over the events of the day.

CHAPTER EIGHT

Earlier That Day

MRS. FERRIS, a stout, red-faced woman who wore corduroy and flannel and no-nonsense rubber boots, started closing down the produce stand at 4:00. As Joey carefully placed the leftover bags of roasted insects into his backpack, she placed a chafed hand on his shoulder and beamed him a smile. "You did good today, son. I'm proud of you."

A hesitant smile played on his lips. "Thanks, Mrs. Ferris."

She had strutted around the stand all day like a lovable mother hen, selling her wares, and also directing customers to try his free samples. With looks of surprise, most passed on the offer, but the ones who didn't were pleasantly surprised. It was Joey's best day yet—ten bags of garlic and red chili crickets and six bags of chocolate coated ants—sold! Joey put on his helmet, mounted his bike, and waved as he peddled out of the lot toward the road.

Mrs. Ferris waved back with a big grin. "See you next week."

It was late Saturday afternoon and gray clouds hung low in the autumn sky. Here in the farming region of Garnerville the air smelled of rich moist earth and burning leaves. It would be dark in an hour, but it would only take twenty minutes to ride back to the church.

He felt a strange twinge of elation when he thought of Mrs. Ferris, an emotion that had been pushed so far back into his memories that he had forgotten it existed. He also felt a pang of sadness. She had called him son, just like his mother used to. That sent his thoughts cascading back in time.

Joey had grown up in a foggy little logging town on the Umpqua River on the Pacific coast of Oregon. It was a damp, dusky world of towering trees, big trucks, and big men. He remembered his father being a giant of a man, strong as an ox, invincible, but he died in a lumber accident when Joey was five. His world turned upside down and he was swept out to sea, but his anchor was his mother, whose fierce love was a compass in the storm.

She moved them to Garnerville and worked as a waitress at Barney's Bar and Grill, and she came home at night smelling of grilled food and beer. A brain tumor killed her six months ago, just five weeks after her first doctor's appointment for headaches and exhaustion.

Joey went into a freefall, but there were no other relatives to catch him. Overcome with grief and a sense of hopelessness, he retreated from the world. Social services placed him with a foster family, but it didn't work out. He overheard his foster mom telling his social worker that he was emotionally unresponsive. He wouldn't interact with her family, he wouldn't eat unless everything on his plate was covered in ketchup, and he woke the family at night, moaning from nightmares. She was returning him like a useless piece of luggage.

His social worker brought Joey to Pastor John, whom she said had an uncanny ability to help kids like him. Joey found the pastor to be gentle and kind and always available if Joey needed one-on-one time with a substitute dad. But being tossed into a din of rowdy, noisy, abrasive boys, two others sharing his bedroom, was another matter. Suddenly having no privacy and no place to hide his tears was a shock to his nervous system, like being thrown into an icy lake with no way to get out. The boys somehow intuited what he needed and left him alone to figure it out for himself—sink or swim. They didn't pressure him to act "normal," or join in their games and boyish antics when he sulked in a corner and refused to talk. In time, he learned that each of the boys had suffered unimaginable loss just as he had, yet somehow each found the will to go on, to find meaning in existence, to carve out his own role in the order of the pack. Slowly, Joey constructed his own role to play, his own quiet, unobtrusive way to coexist. His battered soul began to respond to the raucous stimulation around him. His emotions started to come back to life. The pain he held in his chest, weighing him down, loosened its hold. Sometimes he even forgot about it and for a moment felt like himself again.

Joey had only gone a half mile down the narrow country road when his thoughts were abruptly pulled from the past to the immediate present. Three teenage boys stepped onto the street from behind a thicket of bushes, forcing him to make a screeching halt just five feet in front of them. He recognized them instantly; three punks who dressed like badass bikers and hung out in the park downtown, smoking, whistling at girls, looking tough. Joey had been alarmed when the biggest of the three, a tall stocky teen known as Wacko Jacko, appeared at the stand today. Towering over Joey, he had picked up a bag of ants, sniffed it, and snarled, "What kind of freaking nut job eats freaking bugs?"

"If you aren't buying anything, don't touch the merchandise," Mrs. Ferris said sharply, her hands on her broad hips, looking impressively tough herself. Jacko had given her a brazen look, but he clambered to his motorcycle and peeled out of the lot in a cloud of dust.

"Asshole," she had said under her breath.

But Mrs. Ferris wasn't here to protect him now, and Jacko had a nasty look on his face, like he wanted to pulverize someone. Joey felt cold fingers of fear run the length of his spine.

"Hey loser, or should we call you cockroach, like the filthy, disgusting bugs you eat?"

Joey tried to back up his bike, but Wacko grabbed the handlebars and yanked the bike upwards, flinging the boy onto the pavement. Wacko reached down, ripped off Joey's backpack, and emptied the contents on the road; five bags of roasted crickets, three of chocolate ants, and the plastic envelope that held his cash. Wacko unzipped it and pulled out five one-dollar bills. "Where's the rest of the money you made today?"

"Mrs. Ferris keeps it for me," Joey said shakily, scrambling back to his feet. Suddenly it felt like the sky was pressing down on the earth.

"Let's go, Jacko," one of his friends said. "Take the five. Let's get out of here before someone sees us."

But the hulking teen wasn't satisfied. "I know you have more money on you, cockroach. Hand it over."

Joey felt like he couldn't breathe. He stood motionless, frozen with fear.

"You have freaking balls to charge people for this shit." Jacko smashed the bags under his big biker's boot, grinding them into the road. "This is what I'm gonna do to you unless you cough up some money. Now!"

Joey bolted and ran about ten feet before Jacko grabbed him by the hood of his sweatshirt and yanked him around. He grabbed Joey by his collar with both hands and lifted him up until he was on his tippy toes. "Money. Now." The brute's face was so close that specks of spittle flew onto Joey's face.

The small boy didn't see the fist coming at him, just felt it crash into his cheek. Fireworks exploded. Another blow came quickly but Joey jerked his head and it glanced off his upper jaw. He fell backward, his head smacking the asphalt. Pain radiated throughout his scalp. *I'm not here. I'm not here. This isn't really happening*. But the torture wasn't over. Joey felt hands tighten around his ankles, then Wacko lifted him into the air, hung him upside down, and started shaking him.

"Put Joey down, you fucking moron!"

It happened fast. A blizzard of pain screamed inside his head and Joey couldn't be sure if he had heard it right. Then the cold commanding voice sliced through the chaos again like a razor-sharp knife.

"Put Joey down!"

Joey was abruptly up-righted and set on his feet. He made out a tall, athletic figure approaching them. It was Rafe! A scrawny, downtrodden dog trotted at his side.

Matching Wacko in height, but leaner, Rafe approached with such an intensity that it scared Joey a little bit. He'd never seen this side of the older boy. Before Rafe had the chance to strike first, Wacko swung a massive arm at him. Rafe caught his fist in midair and held it there, frozen in time. Everyone else froze, too, stunned by the display of strength and control. Rafe started to squeeze the brute's fist and he grunted in pain, then he swung his other arm. Rafe knocked it aside like a twig and walloped the brute's throat with the side of his hand. Wacko's eyes bulged out and he stood weaving for a moment, as though drunk. Rafe then pummeled Wacko hard in the crotch with his knee. The brute released a strangled cry and his eyes rolled back into his head.

Wacko's two partners watched wide-eyed, unsure what to do. A dark shadow passed over their heads, and a large black bird descended from the sky. It swooped low over their heads, screeching, then came back and swooped again, so close his wing touched one boy's ear. A big blob of bird muck landed on his shoulder. Waving their hands over their heads in a panic, they made a dash for cover, disappearing into the thicket.

Wacko's knees had buckled, and he lay on the road groaning like a dying animal.

"If I ever hear that you've hurt another kid," Rafe growled. "I'm going to come after you. Next time, you won't get off so easy. Now get the hell out of here."

The brute struggled to his feet, grunting and groaning, and limped off into the bushes.

Wow. Wow. Wow. Joey's mind was spinning. He gazed at the older boy as though he was a superhero who came down from the sky on a beam of light.

Rafe turned his full attention to the boy, tilting up his chin and examining his face. "You're going to have a nice shiner, Joey." He pulled a handkerchief from his back pocket. "This is going to sting a little, but I'm going to wipe away the blood from your lip."

It stung. Joey winced and struggled not to cry. He wanted to be brave, like Rafe. He realized the salty taste in his mouth was blood.

Rafe smiled. "There, good as new. No one gets through boyhood without a couple of shiners, right?"

Joey nodded.

"That shithead won't bother you again. Guys who pick on smaller guys have undeveloped brains. They try to feel superior by flexing their outer muscles, making up for what's missing between their ears."

Despite himself, Joey smiled.

"That's the spirit." The older boy picked up the backpack and slipped the straps over Joey's shoulders, then he gestured with his chin toward the smashed bags of insects on the road. "Don't worry about that stuff. I'll help you make more. Okay?"

"Okay."

"Caw. Caw. Caw."

"What's with the raven?" Rafe asked, squinting at the huge bird with a look of awe.

Joey shrugged, equally amazed.

The raven picked something off the road then hopped toward them with a dollar bill in its beak and dropped it at their feet.

"That's my money. Wacko took the other four dollars." He smiled at the raven. "Thanks, buddy."

"Nevermore," the raven croaked. It took flight and disappeared above the trees.

"I'll be darned," Rafe said, scratching his head in wonder. "Now I've seen everything. He left you something." He picked a sleek ebony feather off the road and handed it to Joey. "Looks like you now have a spirit animal. Keep this with you. It's good luck."

"What's a spirit animal?" Joey asked, running his fingers over the silky feather.

"A messenger and protector that comes in the form of an animal."

"Do you have one?"

"Yeah."

"What is it?"

"A beautiful horse." Rafe grinned. "Come to the sanctuary sometime and I'll show you."

"I'd like that." He carefully tucked the feather into the outer pocket of his backpack.

"You're going to be okay, Joey. Go on home before it gets dark. Put some ice on your face. I'll be there soon. I need to take care of this poor old dog. He needs a good meal and a flea bath, bad." Rafe set the bike upright and Joey took the handlebars.

"Thank you for saving me."

Rafe ruffled the smaller boy's hair. "Hey, that's what big brothers do, right?"

A laugh actually came out of Joey's mouth, foreign but wonderful. He rode back to the church feeling like the luckiest boy in the world. *What a day!* He sold lots of bags of insects, Mrs. Ferris called him son, he had a spirit animal that spoke and chased off bad guys, and he had a big brother who was a superhero. The beating from Wacko had fallen to the shadows of his mind.

***

"Wow, Joey, that's quite a story." Chief Becker said gently. "You had an incredible afternoon."

"Yeah, I did."

"I'm sorry Jacko roughed you up. We're going to talk to him, and his parents. Make sure this doesn't happen again."

"But now I have a spirit animal." He looked at her, then at Pastor John. "Do you believe me? Do you believe that a raven can talk?"

"I believe you," Pastor John said sincerely. "I believe in miracles."

"I believe you, Joey, because I know the raven you're speaking of. He spends a lot of time with a lady I know. Ann Howard. She has an organic farm on the lake. She taught him to talk. He knows about a hundred words. His name is Arthur."

Joey's mouth fell open. So did Pastor John's.

"I agree with Pastor John. It was a miracle that Arthur happened to be just where you needed him to be today."

"And Rafe."

"Yes, and Rafe."

They were quiet for a moment, reflecting on Joey's remarkable story, then Sidney asked, "Who taught you about eating insects?"

"My mom. She was a nature lover. She was always reading me stuff about how we're polluting the earth and the oceans and rivers. What's really sad is that thousands of animals, birds, and insects are dying. We keep taking away their homes, their food, by using pesticides and cutting down forests to make room for more cattle. If people cut back and just ate beef once or twice a week, it would make a huge difference. We wouldn't have to kill so many cows."

Joey's words were so earnest, so heartfelt, that Sidney's heart went out to him. Poor kid, left alone in the world, and still caring about something much larger than himself. Children shouldn't be burdened with something as calamitous as climate change. There was a much larger picture when it came to the causes of climate change, and Sidney shared the boy's fear and frustration. Oregon and other western states were suffering from severe drought due to climate change, and sources of water that had been reliable for centuries were drying up. Forests were parched, and fires now erupted by the thousands each year, burning millions of acres, and sometimes wiping out entire communities overnight. "I understand and I agree with you, Joey. Climate change is scary. But we have to hold on to hope about the future. Lots of people care, and they're working very hard all over the world to save the planet. To save animals."

"I know. That's what my mom said. I'm showing people that eating insects, instead of so much meat, isn't gross. I use all of Mom's recipes. She used to grind them up and use them as flour in cakes and bread. You can't tell the difference, and they're full of protein."

"So, in your own way, you're helping the earth, and paying tribute to your mom."

He nodded.

Feeling a wave of tenderness for the sensitive boy, Sidney reached out and covered his hand with hers for a moment. "Your mother would be very proud of you."

Joey smiled shyly.

The cafeteria was starting to fill up with folks needing a meal. The line at the food counter was growing and a third of the tables were taken. "I just have a couple more questions for you. You told Foley not to snitch on Rafe. We already know that he was at Mrs. Thornburg's funeral party. Why didn't you want Foley to tell us?"

"I don't want Rafe to get into trouble."

"He isn't in trouble, Joey. We just want to talk to him about who was there that night. Do you know something about that?"

His bottom lip came out again and he sat back in his chair with his arms tightly crossed.

Sidney wouldn't press the boy further. His loyalty to Rafe was unshakable, and he'd already had a really rough day. He was carrying a lot on his slender shoulders. "Thank you for talking with me. And thank you for the delicious snack."

He picked up the baggie. "These are for you, Chief Becker. Texas barbeque cockroaches. They're addictive. Spread the word."

"You can count on it, Joey."

Sidney heard her phone ping and read a text from Granger. They had interviewed a clown and confirmed that Rafe was the party crasher. Now they were off to question a male stripper. *Police work was never dull.*

She and the pastor went back upstairs and headed out to the cemetery to watch the exhumation of Stevana's coffin. The sun was sinking, and deep shadows filled the spaces between the barren trees.

"Thank you for being so sensitive with Joey," the pastor said. "He had a very distressing day. On top of the other trauma he's had in his short life."

Sidney was struck by the gentle tone of his voice and his empathy for the boy. It was obvious he cared deeply for his charges. "Thankfully, the intervention by Rafe and the raven saved the day," she said.

"Rafe has adopted the role of protector for all the boys. He does many good deeds very quietly. And that raven. I know they're highly intelligent but this one seems rather exceptional."

"Arthur is exceptional."

"Tell me about him."

"He started visiting Ann Howard a few years ago. Ann's the business partner of my sister, Selena."

"Of course. They call their business 'Selena's Kitchen.' They make organic products at Ann's farm. I buy their lavender honey."

She smiled. "Arthur's been bringing Ann little gifts for months; buttons, shiny paper, beads, polished rocks, in exchange for treats. He hopped from bush to bush, following her around the garden, and she started teaching him words. He even started joining her at the outdoor table, sitting on the back of her chair. Two years ago, he helped us solve a murder. Samantha Ferguson."

"Ah, yes. Tragic. She was a lovely young woman. How did Arthur help?"

"He found a crucial piece of evidence near the crime scene and brought it to Ann while Selena was there. It had blood on it. Selena called me immediately. That was a break in the case."

"Astonishing." He shook his head. "The Lord works in mysterious ways."

They reached the gravesite. The caretaker had already excavated a foot of earth.

Sidney contacted Dr. Linthrope and Stewart and told them to head on over.

CHAPTER NINE

IT WAS ALMOST 6:00 P.M.. and darkness had settled around them when they reached the address of the birthday party. Amanda heard the music as soon as she and Granger left her vehicle. It increased in volume as they mounted the porch and rang the bell. No one responded.

"They can't hear the bell," Granger said.

They knocked loudly. Still no answer.

He opened the door and they stepped into the foyer. The source of the loud music, as well as pulsing colored light, was coming from a large living room at the end of the hall. They caught a young woman's attention who was standing in the back, and she waved them in. They stood behind her, their eyes sweeping the room, taking in the mania. About twenty college-age women were hooting and hollering and rocking out in their seats while watching the male dancer, Valentino. It was pretty wild. On the table was a half-eaten cake and food platters, and there was a streamer going across the room that read HAPPY BIRTHDAY DANA. Obviously, from the many empty wine and Champagne bottles, some pretty serious drinking had been going down.

Amanda saw that Granger was suppressing a grin. Pretty coeds cutting loose was immensely entertaining, but Amanda was more impressed with the dark, sultry good looks of Valentino. He was one of the best dancers she'd ever seen, agile and limber, and unabashedly seductive. The song was "I'm Too Sexy" and he was certainly embodying the lyrics. Wearing a flirtatious smile, Valentino ripped off his shirt in one fluid motion without missing a beat, revealing a hunky physique, every muscle sculpted and defined. The women whistled and shouted their approval.

Valentino had been making his moves around a pretty redhead seated alone up front, no doubt the birthday girl, Dana. He looped his shirt behind her head and used it to pull her face closer to his gyrating hips. Though blushing, she wore a grin from ear to ear. Valentino paused dramatically and ripped off his pants. His fitted underwear showed off his manhood and his glutes to maximum advantage. He took the young woman's hand and slowly pulled her arm between his legs from the front to the back while moving his hips sensually. The screams in the room rose a decibel.

It was time to spread the charm. The dancer moved to the front row of women, straddled the legs of each and slowly gyrated his hips close to her face before moving on to the next. As he made the rounds, several spanked him on the ass or stroked his thighs and back. They were laughing like drunken nymphs seeing an unclothed man for the first time, going a little out of their minds. Valentino had spread the love throughout the room by the time the music stopped, and he was bombarded by crumpled bills. After collecting his tips, he made his exit to a back room and the flashing lights gave way to soft overhead lighting. The sudden silence was deafening, the music still throbbing in Amanda's ears.

The young woman who had waved them inside turned, and said, "I'm Cary." Her eyes sparkled devilishly as she appraised Granger from head to toe. "Wow, you guys just get cuter and cuter. That is one authentic costume."

"It's not a costume," he said with a smile.

She grinned back. "If you say so."

Before he could reply, she turned to the crowd and announced in a loud, enthused voice, "Our next entertainers have arrived, girls. Cop strippers!"

Whistles and hoots rose from the women.

"What a hottie!"

"Smoking hot!"

"Whoooa, a twosome!"

"Come on up front, gorgeous!"

Another song with a pulsating tempo blared from the speakers as two more cops appeared on the scene, a male and female. Looking confused, Cary cried, "I didn't hire four cops."

Amanda and Granger quickly sized up the newcomers. They were both good-looking, and their skin-tight uniforms revealed toned and muscled bodies. Clearly, they were the entertainers Cary had hired. "We're not real cops," the guy told Cary. "But they are."

Her eyes widened. All of her guests were watching with quizzical expressions. Cary snapped into action, giving the entertainers a little nudge. "Go do your thing." The two wasted no time turning heads back to the front of the room. They immediately started performing hip hop dance moves that were energetic, synchronized, and sexy.

"I'm so sorry," Cary yelled at Granger. "Did someone complain about the noise?"

"No. We're here to talk to Valentino."

"He didn't touch any of the women inappropriately."

"He's not in trouble. Could you tell him to step outside for a minute?"

"Sure. I'll go get him."

Amanda and Granger went out on the porch and shut the door behind them, relieved to put a barrier between themselves and the music.

"Wipe that look off your face," Granger teased Amanda. "You look enthralled."

"I am. Valentino can sure move his body. He was oozing testosterone. He had every woman in there hot and bothered."

"Yeah, and apparently you hated every minute of it."

"Like you hated watching those women melting in their seats."

He grinned. "The job does have its perks."

Loud music momentarily poured into the night as Valentino opened and shut the door and joined them on the sidewalk. "I can't stay long. I've got another performance coming up here. What can I help you with, officers?" He directed the question right at Amanda. Fully dressed in jeans and a t-shirt, he looked lithe, fit, and sexy. Here was a man who was confident in his masculinity and was accustomed to having sway over women.

Amanda snapped into her professional demeanor and introduced herself and Granger.

"I'm Greg Taylor," he said. "Valentino is one of my working names."

"Greg, we understand that you were hired by Morticia Solace to attend a funeral party for Mrs. Stevana Thornburg."

"That's right." He thought for a moment. "About two weeks ago. One of the weirder gigs I do, but Morticia pays well, and a guy has to pay the rent. I prefer that to stripping, honestly. At least there's no screaming music, and I don't have to worry about being mauled."

"Mauled?"

"Drunken women." He rolled his eyes. "I've been scratched, groped, yanked, jumped on, you name it. At least with the funeral gigs, I leave with all my body parts intact."

"Didn't realize it was so rough."

"Don't get me wrong. What guy doesn't want beautiful women screaming their name and offering sex? At the same time, there's a double standard. As a man, I get more freedom but not as much empathy if something goes wrong."

This glimpse into the pros and cons of being a male stripper was enlightening.

"Why are you asking about Morticia?" Greg asked. "Did she do something illegal?"

"No one is being accused of any wrongdoing," Granger said. "We're just gathering information. What did you think of Mrs. Thornburg's costume?"

He laughed. "I thought she looked pretty good for a corpse. Though I thought it was bonkers that they were burying her in all that bling. I heard the old lady was loaded, so I guess burying a few grand didn't faze her."

"Did your fellow actors feel the same?" Amanda asked.

"Yeah. We all thought it was nuts. Any one of us could live for a couple of years off that emerald ring alone. You'd think she could have donated it to charity or something."

"Anyone particularly interested?"

"Yeah, all of us."

"Even Mr. Biggs?" Amanda regarded him carefully, looking for any nuance, any giveaway that he was lying or deflecting blame.

"Max Biggs? Oh, yeah. He's the one who told us the jewels were valuable. I wouldn't have known. He looked up the old lady before he arrived. Said she lived in Montford. The neighborhood of millionaires, right?"

"Was Max wasted?"

He shrugged. "No more than usual. That guy can hold his liquor."

"He said Morticia had to call him a cab."

Greg laughed. "I think that was his way of getting a free ride home. He's a cheap bastard."

"How'd he get there?"

"I picked him up."

"Anyone else show interest in the old lady's jewelry? Morticia or Gordon?"

"They were pretty busy with food and drink, taking photos, chatting us up." He paused a moment. "Wait, there was this young guy. Dressed like Zorro. I forgot about him because he was only there for a short time. I've worked with Max, Liz, and Sheila before, but no one knew who he was. Kept to himself except for when he was talking to the dead lady. I saw him toasting her, but I didn't hear what he was saying. When Gordon found out he was a crasher, he very quickly escorted him out the door."

Cary appeared on the porch with a sudden blast of music. "Better get ready for your next set, Valentino."

"I gotta go. I'm a cowboy next. Gotta get my duds on."

"One last question. Where did you go after the funeral party?"

"Me and the two girls went to Barney's. We were there until it closed at

1:00."

"In cocktail clothes?"

He shrugged. "Why not? We lent some class to the place."

"Just so you know, Mrs. Thornburg's jewelry was fake. Just colored glass. And she wasn't loaded. She was broke when she died."

He looked genuinely surprised. "Hmm. Well, at least she had a great send off."

Yeah, until someone tossed her into a compost heap, Amanda thought.

It began to drizzle. They thanked Greg for his time, scrambled back into Amanda's Jeep, and compared notes.

"Greg sure put a different spin on Stevana's party," Granger said. "Mr. Biggs said he didn't notice Stevana's jewelry, but he's the one who told everyone it was valuable. He looked her up before the party. Thought she was loaded because she lived in Montford."

"Then he probably faked being drunk," she said. "And he doesn't have an alibi. He definitely looks suspicious."

"What's your take on Greg?"

"He seemed pretty open, down to earth. On the other hand, he thought it was crazy to bury valuable jewelry."

"Let's go to Barney's, see if his story checks out. Morticia said there was a three-hour window when the body could have been stolen. If he and the two girls were there until it closed, their alibis are airtight."

CHAPTER TEN

DARKNESS HAD DESCENDED and a light rain was falling when the coffin was completely pulled from the earth. The caretaker used a broom to sweep off the dirt, then the casket was lifted onto a gurney and pushed into the coroner's van. Sidney followed the van out of the cemetery and through the downtown area to the small community hospital on the edge of town. The van backed down a sloping driveway and parked outside a back door, used for moving dead bodies in and out of the morgue. After parking in the lot, she followed them into the basement and down the hall. Filled with a mix of dread and anticipation, Sidney stood watching as Stewart unlocked the coffin and carefully lifted the lid. A familiar stench was immediately released, a dire forewarning. The two men peered inside with professional interest. Sidney stayed a few feet back, but she saw enough to confirm that it was a body in decomp, bloated from gas, and deep red in color.

"Another decomposing corpse," Stewart said matter-of-factly. "A woman. Two in one day. You better come take a closer look, Chief. You need to see this."

Viewing decomposing bodies was not her favorite part of the job, but a necessary one. Sidney stepped closer, looked inside, and felt an immediate adrenaline spike. The woman's face was disfigured and unidentifiable, but what was clearly identifiable was the diamond necklace she wore. "That looks like Stevana's necklace." She fished out her phone, scrolled through her photos, and found one of Stevana at her funeral party. She enlarged it to see the details of the necklace, then compared the two. "It's a match. Is this some kind of sick joke?" She thought of frat boys who had been known to steal cadavers from the science department, dress them up in costumes and plant them in public places—in her opinion, a grotesque and misguided attempt at humor. "Someone was very clever. Getting Stevana out of her casket, putting in this woman, and adorning her with Stevana's necklace. Did they dump her body in that compost heap knowing it would lead us to this?

What are they trying to prove?"

"There's dickery afoot," Stewart mused in a British accent, obviously intrigued by the deviousness of the perpetrator. "Someone's playing musical corpses."

"One thing I can tell you, Chief," Dr. Linthrope said, ignoring Stewart's theatrics. "This body is in a natural state of decomp. No formaldehyde. It never saw a mortician."

"Where did it come from? What happened to her face?" Sidney's mind raced through possible scenarios.

"Can't tell you that, or give you cause of death until I do a full autopsy. Looks like she's been dead approximately two weeks."

"She died about the same time as Stevana," Sidney said.

"Can't be a coincidence," Stewart said.

"Not even close." Sidney didn't believe in coincidences. "A lot of planning went into this body exchange. Let's see if we can find out this woman's identity and cause of death. Hopefully, you'll find something that will lead us to the perp."

Stewart started snapping photos. "I'll take tissue samples and see if she's in the system."

"Can you forward photos to Winnie, ASAP?"

"Yes, ma'am."

"It's too late to do anything else tonight," Dr. Linthrope said. "We'll get Jane Doe out of this casket and into cold storage. Then I'll start on the autopsy first thing tomorrow. We should have something for you by 10:00."

"Great. Thanks, guys." Sidney was only too happy to get away from the smell and the casket's occupant. But when she turned away, the woman's grotesque face still stared up at her.

***

Sidney sat in her vehicle in the parking lot with thoughts ricocheting through her mind, trying to make order out of chaos. They had made progress today, identifying Stevana's body and her cause of death—poisoning by the common yew plant. But was it suicide, or murder? Now she had the baffling mystery of another anonymous woman to unravel. How did Jane Doe die?

Sidney and her team had been going at it all day. She glanced at the clock. It was after seven and fatigue was setting in, plus her stomach was rumbling with hunger. When investigating time-sensitive cases like this, Sidney often plowed through the day without eating, a habit she was trying to break. It was time to refuel, get everyone up to date and on the same page. She called the department's administrator, Winnie, who could multi-task like a circus juggler, and Sidney relied on her to keep all the loose ends together.

"Pizza for the whole department? Coming right up," Winnie said.

"I'll call in the troops for a briefing."

The wipers pushed water off the windshield as she drove back through the center of town. Soft light glowed from the shops and restaurants and folks under umbrellas rushed to and fro on the streets. All the pumpkins and autumn displays in the windows reminded Sidney that Thanksgiving was just a week away. Serious crime did not bode well for a town that depended on tourist dollars. Folks going into the holiday didn't need to be worrying about some nutcase who was tampering with dead bodies and might very well be a killer. The pressure to quickly wrap up these cases weighed heavily on her shoulders.

Lights glowed from inside the Art Studio and Sidney caught a glimpse of her fiancé standing in front of an easel, paint brush in hand. She had expected to spend the day relaxing at his house on the lake, making love, watching movies, listening to the rain drumming the roof. She felt a stab of disappointment that their day had been upended. David didn't teach classes on Sunday, but he often came into the studio to paint. As a business, the Art Studio just broke even, but David didn't need to make a profit. He was financially independent. His objective was to provide a space where artists could congregate and share their passion, and that gave him an opportunity to teach, which he thrived on.

A feeling of tenderness warmed her as she thought of the sturdiness of his character. David was an all-around decent guy, willing to take a back seat when emergencies kept her busy for days on end. And he was inherently trusting. Sidney, on the other hand, kept trust on reserve. Her profession had taught her to always be on guard and never trust appearances. Danger could erupt at any second from behind the guise of innocence.

On a whim, Sidney pulled over to the curb and entered the studio. It smelled faintly of oil paint and turpentine and art of every kind hung on the walls; charcoals, pastels, watercolors, oils.

David stood in front of an easel with his back to her. He was in the zone, oblivious to the world around him, applying bold brush strokes to a landscape of Lake Kalapuya and the mountains. His work was masterful and commanded high prices from clients and art dealers. She watched him for a moment. From the back, he looked like a young man, lean build, broad shoulders, light on his feet. He wore jeans and a blue shirt with the tail out, and boat shoes with no socks. His dark hair curled around his collar, lightly salted with gray.

She tapped him on the shoulder. He turned, startled, and then his handsome face broke into a grin. "Hey, beautiful." He gave her a hug and pressed his lips warmly to hers. "I didn't think I'd see you today. From your text, it sounded like you had a pressing case."

"Mystifying, more like it."

His warm brown eyes held hers. "You look stressed. Whatever you're working on has you in knots."

"Pretty much."

"Have time for a cappuccino?"

She nodded, smiling into his eyes. "I can only stay a few minutes, but I could definitely use a java jolt."

With his hand on the small of her back, he walked her to the updated kitchen in the back. Modern-style chairs were arranged around a rustic wood table and tasteful art crowded the red brick walls. David pulled two white porcelain cups from a cupboard and turned to a commercial coffee machine that took up half a counter. The smell of strong coffee quickly filled the room. The machine hissed as he crowned each cup with a cloud of steamed milk, then they settled at the table.

She sipped her cappuccino. "You make a mean cup of java."

"I know." He smiled. "Anything you want to talk about?"

She released a sigh of frustration. "Two dead women were found today. The body of one was stolen from a mortuary two weeks ago and found across the lake on private property. We exhumed her coffin today and found the other woman inside. A Jane Doe."

His eyes widened in surprise.

"We identified the stolen body as Stevana Thornburg."

"Ah, the elusive Mrs. Thornburg. Strange. Why would someone steal an old lady's body?"

"You knew her?"

He shook his head. "No one did. She never left her mansion. She had a reputation, though, as being difficult. And an unwilling philanthropist."

"What do you mean?"

"Some of my well-heeled clients have tried for years to squeeze money out of her for their respective charities. But she barely parted with a penny."

Sidney wasn't surprised that David knew of Stevana. He migrated with ease into the higher social stratosphere of Linnly County. He had routinely hobnobbed with the rich and famous when he was a real estate developer in

San Francisco. After his wife died and his two daughters left for college, he moved to Garnerville and opened the studio. Some of his students were quite wealthy, and on occasion he and Sidney were invited to ritzy fundraisers.

"But what folks don't know about Mrs. Thornburg," David continued. "Is that she quietly donated to animal causes. She made regular donations to Wellspring Rescue Sanctuary."

"How do you know this?"

"I made it my business to know, because Dillon volunteers there. I go out there myself sometimes to help out. I wanted to make sure everything is above board. It is."

"You volunteer there?" This surprised her. Dillon was David's sixteen-year-old son. She had grown very attached to the personable teenager and enjoyed the "family" time the three spent together. "How come you never mentioned that to me? You didn't want me to join you?"

"Hey, it's not like that. It's just something that Dillon and I do together. The girls grew up and were gone too fast. Living their own lives. I look back and wish I had spent more time with them. Now I want to create lasting memories with Dillon. Doing something meaningful."

"I get it. Father and son time." Still, Sidney felt a little left out. David knew she loved animals, and she would have been happy to help. On the other hand, she had a time-consuming, high-pressure job. Being on call, even on her day off, made it hard for her to commit to anything. "Some of the orphan boys from Wellspring church volunteer there."

"Yeah, they do. Troubled kids." He shook his head. "Tough life, losing parents, being on their own. They lean on each other, and they work really hard to care for needy animals."

"You've met Rafe?"

"Of course. He's out there a lot. He and Dillon share classes at school. They're friends. He's been to the house a few times." His brow creased. "Why are you asking?"

She shifted uncomfortably in her chair. This case had just gotten very close to home. She wouldn't share with David that Rafe was on her suspect list.

"You don't think he had something to do with the body snatching, do you?"

"I'm not pointing a finger at anyone at this point. But he's someone I'd like to talk to. He may have witnessed something."

"He's a complicated kid, Sidney. He has trust issues, but who wouldn't after what he's been through. I can't imagine him being involved in a crime."

Sidney could mask her feelings from everyone while on the job, but not from David. He could pick up her emotional vibrations as though her thoughts were a tuning fork. He now sat studying her, trying to read her motives.

She drained her cup and rose from the table. "I've got to run. Got a briefing at the station. Thanks for the java."

He walked her to the door. "When do you get off tonight?

She shrugged. "Not sure. It may be late."

He pulled her close and she inhaled his wonderful scent of sandalwood soap. It felt good to be in David's arms, protected from the travails of the world. She knew this man intimately, every contour, every line radiating from his eyes. She knew him in bed. She loved his intelligence, his humor, his lack of ego, the ease she felt in his company.

"Come over when you get off," he said softly. "Crawl into bed with me."

She definitely wanted to crawl into bed with him. "I'll try."

He planted a soft kiss on her mouth. Fleeting, but thrilling. Then she was out the door.

CHAPTER ELEVEN

SIDNEY PULLED INTO THE DRIVEWAY of the old Garnerville Bank building, circa 1910. It still featured elegant Doric columns on each side of the brass-plated door and the original red brick exterior. The interior had been gutted and renovated in 1960 into a functional police department—three cells, a bullpen, a couple of small offices, and a conference room—offshoots from the spacious central lobby. In many cases, the old vault was used for secure storage of evidence. The population of the town had doubled since then, and so had crime. They had outgrown the space, and manpower, but because of budget restraints, they made do. New vehicles and an additional officer were promised by the end of the year.

Sidney parked behind the station and used her code card to access the back door. She bypassed her office and entered the conference room, dominated by a rectangular oak table that seated eight if you didn't mind rubbing elbows. A buzzing refrigerator and sideboard stocked with snacks and coffee paraphernalia stood against one wall. Historical photos of the town and former police chiefs, including her dad, crowded the walls.

Three large takeout boxes were spread across the counter, and the tantalizing aroma of pizza filled the room, making Sidney's stomach growl. Jesse, the dispatcher, was distributing drinks and napkins around the table. Stewart had forwarded photos of both corpses and Winnie had printed them out. She and Darnell were taping them to the white board at the far end of the room, starting a crime board.

"What's with the Jane Doe?" Darnell asked. "Where'd she come from?"

"Hold on to your questions. Everything will be answered shortly."

Granger and Amanda walked into the room from the bullpen.

"Finally, you're all here," Winnie said.

"Being forced to smell pizza for ten minutes while starving is its own kind of hell," Jesse said.

"Sorry. You should have started without us," Sidney said.

"You can believe we will, next time." Winnie was an exotic beauty of mixed race who wore clothes that accentuated her voluptuous figure, a style she called 'classy but sassy.' Jesse was a retired science teacher, as skinny as a rail. They were the first to step up to the counter and the rest of the crew crowded around them. Pizza boxes opened and hot gooey slices slapped paper plates. Everyone arranged themselves around the table. Caps twisted off drinks. Granger had shoveled five huge slices onto his plate, piled high with ham, sausage, veggies, and melted cheese.

"You know, it's okay to get seconds," Sidney mused.

He gave her a little nod but was too busy stuffing his mouth to comment.

Sidney ate standing in front of the white board, jotting notes on the sides of photos.

After fifteen minutes of companionable small talk, Jesse and Winnie returned to their stations in the lobby.

While eating, Amanda and Granger studied the white board, eyes darting from one photo to the next. Granger mumbled something barely coherent, his mouth full.

Amanda translated for him. "Who's the rotting corpse in the coffin?"

Before Sidney could answer, a spark of realization lit up Granger's eyes. With one cheek bulging, he asked, "Is that Stevana's coffin?"

"Yep," Sidney said. "We exhumed it this evening."

"Who's that inside?" Darnell asked.

"A Jane Doe. Hopefully, Stewart can get us an identity."

"How'd she die?" Amanda asked.

"We won't know until we get the autopsy and lab reports."

"Judging from her face, she could be the victim of violence," Amanda said. "Domestic abuse or murder."

"Or she may have suffered an accident, like falling down the stairs," Darnell said.

"The only thing we know for sure is that this woman never went to a mortuary," Sidney said.

Everyone at the table sat silently digesting that information.

"So it's a homicide." Granger wiped his mouth with a napkin, crumpled it, and threw it across the room into the trash can. "You don't just find a random dead body lying around. "Where did she die? And why would someone put her in Stevana's coffin?"

"Good questions. No answers."

"Is that Stevana's necklace she's wearing?"

"Yes."

"Very odd," Amanda asked. "Right necklace. Wrong corpse. Where's the emerald ring?"

"Don't know. What we do know is that someone took Stevana's body, planted her in the compost heap. Took her jewelry. The necklace ended up on this Jane Doe. The emerald ring has not turned up yet. Whoever took Stevana's body, planned beforehand to put Jane Doe in her place."

"What would possess someone to do that?"

"That's the million-dollar question. Our case just doubled in size. We have work to do. People to talk to. Let's start from the beginning."

The three officers got out notepads and pens.

"Stevana Thornburg was poisoned, and possibly murdered. Her body was stolen from her casket and dumped into a compost heap, and Jane Doe was put in her place." Sidney pointed to various photos as she talked. "We have a three-hour window of opportunity between 10:00 p.m. and 1:00 a.m. after her funeral party. During that time, Morticia claims to have left the key to the casket on her desk in plain sight. Likely suspects include Morticia, her assistant, Gordon, the four entertainers, and a teen boy from the church named Rafe. Apparently, they all thought the jewelry was valuable." Sidney paused to sip her soft drink through the straw. "The emerald ring is still missing. We're still looking at jewelry theft as a possible motive. Of all the suspects, we've ruled out Bonnie, the caretaker, for now." She turned to Amanda. "Bring us up to date on your interviews."

She looked up from her notes. "We questioned Max Biggs first, aka Mr. Biggley the clown, who was one of the guests at Stevana's party. He had shown a lot of interest in the jewelry. He falsely believed that Stevana was loaded. And he doesn't have an alibi."

"He stays on the list." Sidney wrote his name under the heading, "Suspects."

"Then we interviewed the stripper, Greg Tayler. He said he and the two female performers, Sasha and Ruby, went to Barney's after Stevana's party. We talked to the bartender and waitresses. The three of them were definitely there, but the place was crazy busy. People were moving around between tables, the bar, and the dance floor. They couldn't confirm that they were there for the entire evening."

"So, we can't rule them out either." Sidney added their names as suspects. She also added Gordon, Morticia, and Rafe, then turned back to them. "Hopefully, we'll have more to go on when we get the autopsy and lab results in the morning. Granger and Amanda, you need to talk to Sasha and Ruby tomorrow to see if their stories align with Greg's."

"Will do," Granger said.

Amanda nodded.

"I'll speak to Gordon," Sidney continued. "He distracted Morticia when she was in her office, that's why she allegedly left the key to the casket out. And he had the easiest access to it. Then there's Rafe, the teenager who crashed the party. I'll talk to him as well. Darnell, go talk to the auctioneer who sold all of Stevana's belongings. Make sure everything was above board. See if the actual jewelry in question was in fact sold."

"Copy that."

"We'll meet back here at noon to confer. That wraps it up. Get your reports done. Then go home."

They scraped back chairs and headed out to the bullpen. Sidney headed to her office to attend to a pile of paperwork.

CHAPTER TWELVE

SIDNEY AND DAVID lay in bed in the cabin of the sailboat, limbs intertwined, lulled by the gentle rhythm of the lake. They had walked down to the dock to get some privacy from Dillon, who was watching *Star Trek Beyond* in the living room in stereophonic sound. While chowing down on pepperoni pizza, they had all watched *Star Trek into Darkness* together, but neither was up for a sequel of blasting phasers and extraterrestrial villains. Dillon barely noticed when they slipped out of the room.

They had caught up on the lovemaking they had missed earlier in the day due to her emergency homicide investigation. David's touch, his scent, his closeness, helped her forget the responsibilities that went along with the uniform, and rotting corpses had been pushed to the furthest realms of her mind. It was delicious to be loved by a man who wasn't in a hurry, who knew how to please her, who let her take the lead when she wanted and encouraged her to be uninhibited. Now she lay naked in his arms, damp and satisfied, while he ran his fingers gently over her back.

"We'd better head back to the house," he said. "I have to make sure Dillon gets to bed at a decent hour. And you. You'll be putting in long hours this week."

She sighed. "I wish we could lay here for days."

"Me, too." He pulled her closer and she lingered in his arms, enjoying the feel of his body close to hers. Their lips met and they softly kissed. "Let's continue this in the bedroom," he murmured.

"It's a deal."

They both dressed and went out on deck. Lightning shimmered in the distance and a soft rain was falling, stippling the surface of the water. David took her hand, and they hurried back to the house. Explosions boomed in the living room; an interplanetary war was in progress on the big screen TV. Dillon was stretched out on a recliner in his sweats, his face intently focused on the action. He looked up when they walked in, and his finger pressed a button on the remote. The screen turned black, and silence filled the room.

"I was just about to turn in. I wanted to make sure you two got in okay," he said with a mocking smile. "Danger lurks in the night."

"We managed to make it back alive," David said. "Though Sidney had to fight off a few Klingons. I watched, cheering her on."

Dillon got up from the chair and gave them both a hug. He was as tall and handsome as his father. He disappeared down the hall, saying over his shoulder, "See you for breakfast. I want waffles."

"Waffles it is," David said. He loved cooking in general, but he especially enjoyed his quiet mornings cooking for his son, and Sidney when she stayed over. "Waffles okay, or should I scramble eggs just for you?"

"Let's worry about that in the morning."

They padded down the hall to his bedroom and he turned on a soft light. His beautiful brown eyes held her gaze and his mouth tipped into a sensuous smile. "Now, where were we before we left the boat?"

"Naked."

They undressed and he pulled her down on the bed on top of him. His hands followed the curve of her spine and came to rest on the swell of her hips. They kissed, sweet and slow. She felt a warm current of pleasure spreading to her belly and thighs. Her mouth traveled down his body, gently kissing his exposed skin, her hair falling around her face. She felt his sudden intake of breath when she performed an act that he found exquisitely pleasurable.

After lovemaking, they lay in each other's arms and spoke of nothing of consequence. She just liked listening to David talk, feeling the vibration of his words in his chest, soothing her until she drifted into dreamland. Her dreams took her to another world where dark figures hid in forests of dead trees, watching, waiting … for what? She awoke in the night, thankful to find David's reassuring presence, his body pressed against hers.

CHAPTER THIRTEEN

IT WAS 2:00 A.M. and the house was dead quiet. Dillon left his bedroom, crept past his dad's room, and made it to the front door without making a sound. He stepped out on the porch, then walked past Sidney's Yukon that was parked in the driveway. When he thought about what lay ahead tonight, he felt a little spasm of guilt. It was ironic that while his father was sleeping with the Chief of Police, he was going to be out committing a crime.

A half-moon hung in the sky, and in the shimmering darkness, he saw the profile of the massive Douglas firs and cedars on the hills surrounding the lake. His dad's sailboat bobbed next to the floating dock, and the night was silent except for the water lapping the shore.

Overhead, the stars twinkled in the vast network of the solar system. He was momentarily awestruck. It was unfathomable that all the stars were orbiting in a nearly circular path around the center of the galaxy, and none of them collided. Dillon believed that something supernatural controlled the universe, something that was one with nature, from cosmic dust to the planets to the human race. Science revealed parts of this mysterious connection, but the deeper secrets were unknown to mankind, whose brains were too simple, too unevolved to understand more than a glimmer of its own existence. Different cultures around the world called it God and worshiped it, maintaining a lifelong relationship of fear, hope, and uncertainty. Dillon thought that was like fearing the weather—feeling punished when there were floods and earthquakes, and feeling rewarded when the sun shone bright and their crops did well. Better to just accept what nature doled out as best one could. His dad tried to convince him that he had influence over his own life, over his future. But since his mother died a slow agonizing death from cancer when he was twelve, and he witnessed the grief his family suffered, Dillon had lost faith. Why put trust in something so feckless, so capable of that kind of cruelty? Now he believed that what happened day to day was just a random roll of the cosmic dice.

The night was chilly, and he saw his breath turn into white vapor. He had dressed all in black, and he was warm in his fleece jacket, knit cap and gloves. He walked to the end of the driveway until he reached the highway, and then he saw the old truck from Wellspring Community waiting, coughing out plumes of smelly exhaust. He hopped inside and greeted the teenager behind the wheel. "Hey, man, how's it going?"

"It's going." Rafe's smile flashed in the darkness, then he revved up the engine and they took off down the highway.

Dillon's life had changed dramatically since he started volunteering at the animal sanctuary and he met the motley group of orphan boys. He and Rafe bonded like brothers almost from the start. They were the same age, shared classes at school, and were both independent thinkers who challenged authority. But their backgrounds couldn't have been more different. "I was raised by a pack of ferocious wolves," Rafe had told him with a mocking laugh. "My dad was a tough old bastard to my mom and me, but he'd rip your heart out if you tried to hurt us. He and mom were both drunks. Neither could keep a job. We just moved from one subsidized apartment to the next. Mom abandoned us when I was eight. Can't blame her, I guess. Soon after that, dad went to prison. Killed someone. DUI." Rafe had grown a hard shell during his childhood, impenetrable armor that allowed him to seal off his emotions. He only revealed what he wanted you to see. But Dillon detected a sadness in his voice when he spoke of his parents, a subtle slip in his expression. Maybe that's what connected them so strongly. Dillon had also suffered the loss of a parent. Both teens lived with a wound at the core of their beings that never healed, that was hypersensitive to outside triggers, that could instantly bring a stab of pain to the surface.

Like Dillon, Rafe was tall and athletic, and he exuded quiet strength and confidence. But he had a fearlessness that veered into recklessness, and Dillon worried it would get him into serious trouble one day. Especially now that they were doing these midnight escapades—which were thrilling and heart-thumping, if not goddamned insane. During these nocturnal missions, Rafe issued commands with absolute authority, and Dillon let him take the lead. Rafe had street smarts drilled into his character that Dillon couldn't begin to understand, and it had gotten them out of more than one slippery situation.

After driving about five miles, Rafe turned onto a narrow dirt road, drove a few hundred feet through a tunnel of barren trees, then pulled over and parked. A coyote slunk out of the bushes and loped across the road in front of the truck with a small animal caught in its jaws. To their right, Dillon saw a tufted field dusted with moonlight. A thin corridor of silvered water meandered through it and disappeared into the forest. On the far side of the field sat a squat house camouflaged by evergreens.

"That's where we're going," Rafe said, gesturing with his chin. He reached behind him and threw off an old tarp to get his tools.

A figure popped up from under the tarp like a jackrabbit.

Dillon's heart jumped in his chest. Adrenaline shot through his fingertips.

"What the hell!" Rafe cried in shock.

Then they both saw that it was Joey.

"You scared the crap out of me, Joey!" Rafe said. "What the hell are you doing here?"

In the dim light the boy's eyes looked enormous, and his thin face was milky white under his crown of shaggy hair. "Don't be mad. I just wanted to come and help."

"I am mad," Rafe said, his tone one note under furious.

The three sat in silence and the tension in the cab was taut as wire. Rafe's jaws were clenched tight, and Dillon imagined the wheels turning in his head, trying to decide what to do next, trying to tamp down his anger.

"You should be in bed," Rafe said, his voice somewhat calmer. "You have school tomorrow."

"So do you and Dillon."

"We're older. We don't need as much sleep."

"Let me come with you," Joey pleaded.

"That's not even an option. I'm trying to decide whether to just abort the mission tonight or not. Take you home."

"I'm sorry, Rafe. I didn't mean to screw things up," Joey said. "I'll just wait here in the truck."

"What we're doing is dangerous. I don't know that you'll be any safer in the truck."

Joey pulled something from his pocket and held it out to Rafe. "I have a spirit guide now. Here's my lucky feather. You have a spirit guide, too. We're protected."

Miraculously, after a long tense moment, Rafe's face broke into a grin. He reached out and ruffled the smaller boy's hair. "All right, you can wait here. But if anything happens, if you see men coming toward the truck, jump out and hide."

The boy nodded.

"You promise?"

"I promise, Rafe."

"Okay. Hand me my bag of tools."

Rafe opened his canvas bag and pulled out two ski masks which he and Dillon pulled over their heads. A couple of minutes later, they were clambering over a split-rail fence that surrounded the meadow. They carved a path through the wet shrubs, the tools clinking softly in Rafe's shoulder bag. They followed the fast-flowing creek, rich with the smell of minerals and moist earth. From time to time, a frog croaked and plopped into the water. When they reached the trees on the east side of the house, they crouched low, listening to the stirrings of the night. No lights shone in the windows, and no human sound reached their ears. The vicious men who lived there had turned in. The boys crept to the front of the house and Rafe separated the bushes, giving them a clear view of a padlocked shed. "We need to get inside that shed," he whispered, handing Dillon the bolt cutters. "We need to get in and out in under a minute."

"Got it." Dillon's heart thudded against his ribs and despite the cold, he broke out in a sweat. He tensed his muscles and waited for the command that would propel him forward into the treacherous darkness.

***

Joey sat rigid in the back seat of the cab, his eyes straining to make out moving shapes in the meadow. He rolled down the window a few inches and listened. He heard the noise of trees, the wind sighing across the sky, water cascading over rocks in the creek. It seemed the older boys had been gone a very long time. He desperately wanted to see them heading back to the truck. The familiar fear threatened to surface—the fear that people he loved were tragically ripped from his life—and he struggled to push it back down. After another long while, he heard a dog barking shrilly, then it was quiet again. A beam of light appeared near the house, darting from left to right, and angry voices cut through the night. The deep, hollow, concussive sound of an explosion boomed and blossomed across the meadow. Joey started trembling. He knew the sound was a gunshot. Tears filled his eyes. A sob escaped his throat.

Then through blurry vision, he saw a dark figure hiking toward the cab. He tensed, until he saw that he was wearing a ski mask. He nearly fainted with relief. He carried something heavy in his arms. It looked like a body.

***

Sidney showered, pulled her auburn hair into a ponytail, then dressed in the spare uniform she kept at David's house. She joined him in the kitchen, lured by the rich aroma of fresh ground coffee. Dressed in jeans and a t-shirt, David stood at the stove making an egg scramble with mushrooms, zucchini, and fresh herbs.

"I thought we were having waffles. Where's Dillon?"

"He's not feeling well. Said he has a sore throat and he's not hungry. He's staying home today."

"For a teenage boy to miss a meal, he's gotta be sick," Sidney said. "Did you recommend gargling with salt and warm water? And herbal tea with lemon with honey?"

"Yes, and yes. Couldn't get him to budge out of bed. He doesn't have a fever. He was still dead to the world when I left him a few minutes ago."

"No fever? Bed rest should do it." She poured coffee into a mug at the counter and peered out the window. A fine mist had settled over the lake and hung like bridal veils from the cedar branches. She put sugar and cream in her coffee and took a sip. *Nothing beat that first cup of coffee in the morning.*

David put the finishing touch on his masterpiece, shredding aged Parmesan over the top. He divided the scramble onto two plates with sliced fruit and buttered sourdough toast on the side. "Voila."

"Merci very much."

They ate at the island, making small talk until her phone buzzed. "Duty calls," she said. "It's from Dr. Linthrope. Autopsy results. And so my day begins, in the morgue." Sidney felt an immediate psychological shift take place. A steely reserve surfaced and fit into place like a second skin.

"Uh oh. Someone just morphed into cop before my eyes."

"Crime never sleeps."

David leaned over and planted a kiss on her mouth. "Call me when you can spare a minute, Chief Becker."

CHAPTER FOURTEEN

SIDNEY HAD NO DESIRE to confront Jane Doe's remains again, but duty prevailed, and she braced herself as she entered the morgue.

Wearing scrubs and gloves, Dr. Linthrope was standing over Jane Doe's remains weighing her liver on a scale.

"Morning," she said.

"Good morning," he replied, his demeanor unusually subdued.

She approached the stainless-steel slab and inadvertently wrinkled her nose as she viewed the corpse and caught the foul odor.

"Sorry, there's not much we can do about the smell. But this will help." He stripped off his bloody gloves and handed her an open jar of ointment, made of camphor, eucalyptus oil, and menthol.

"Thanks." She smeared some under her nose and the smell was instantly diminished.

"Better?"

"Far better." She smiled her thanks.

He didn't smile back, just gave her a subtle nod.

She saw that he was midway through the autopsy. He had made the Y incision on the torso, peeled back the skin, and cut the ribs to reveal the organs underneath. Water was running, which was washing away blood and fluids released during the procedure. Each organ had to be individually examined and weighed and replaced in the body cavity. The liver was still sitting in the scale.

The corpse of Jane Doe, in Sidney's mind, was repugnant, but she knew that wasn't what was darkening his mood. He'd worked on corpses much worse than this during her tenure. Obviously, he had found something about Jane Doe that was deeply disturbing.

"So, what did you find?"

He stated in a professional tone, "To start with, this woman was not in our data system. No prints or DNA match. We have no way to identify her."

"Dental records?"

"She has no teeth. Most likely, she had dentures, but where they are, who knows?" Behind his wire-rimmed glasses, his hazel eyes narrowed. "She was in her mid-thirties, about five-foot-four in height, with brown hair, and she lived a hard life. She shows signs of malnourishment. Despite her bloated appearance due to putrefaction, she had low body weight, low fat and muscle mass, which suggests chronic starvation. My guess, Jane Doe was homeless and had difficulty getting regular meals. That accounts for her poor dental hygiene and the need to have all of her teeth extracted." An underlying tension crept into his tone. "Starvation is not what killed her. Jane Doe is a homicide victim."

Sidney's worst suspicions were confirmed. She held her breath, waiting for the bomb to drop.

"This woman has missing organs. I believe she was killed for her kidneys. Stewart found chloroform on her clothes, which suggests that she was abducted against her will. She was anesthetized, her kidneys were removed with surgical precision, and then she bled out. She would have died within minutes."

Sidney was speechless. The horror of the crime and its implications reverberated through her mind. She had encountered organ trafficking in the Bay Area of California, which had a population of millions, and every kind of crime flowed in the back channels of illegal activities. The stories were grim. The cases usually involved victims who were poor, destitute, and uneducated. Easy prey for killers with no conscience. Most of these cases were impossible to investigate. It wasn't an act of revenge or jealousy, where witnesses and suspects could be identified. The motive was greed, pure and simple. Kidneys on the black market could sell for a hundred thousand or more. An illicit clinic could crop up in some back alley apartment overnight, conduct business, then disappear without a trace. Sidney sharply exhaled her frustration.

"It's a puzzling case," he said. "Never seen this here before."

"Is there anything else you can tell me, Doc?"

"Not at this time. I'll finish up here. I know Stewart has something for you."

Sidney put a comforting hand on his arm. "Thanks, Doc."

As professionals who dealt with the dark underbelly of society, they had trained themselves not to let emotions cloud their judgment. But in this case, neither could completely hide their feelings.

A sense of dread hung over her as she walked down the hall and entered the forensic lab. A cold-blooded killer had set up a hack clinic in her community. It had been two weeks since Jane Doe's murder. Had they moved on, or were they sticking around, planning to target other vulnerable people?

Sidney found Stewart at his workstation, his head bowed over a microscope. In addition to being a top-notch CSI, he was an expert in lab analysis. His results were reliably accurate which made her job infinitely easier. Staff in bigger labs were routinely overworked, underfunded, and backed up for weeks, even months. Stewart on the other hand, could conduct in-house tests in just days, or hours.

"Hey, Stewart."

He looked up and nodded toward the table in the corner. "Hey, Chief. Grab a seat."

Hoping for a breakthrough, or just a good lead, Sidney removed her jacket and hung it on the back of a chair, then took a seat.

Dressed in a white lab coat over khakis and a striped rugby shirt, Stewart picked up a file folder and some evidence bags, pulled out a chair, and joined her. "I'm sure Dr. Linthrope told you that we believe Jane Doe was abducted."

She nodded. "You found chloroform on her clothes."

"Fortunately for us, the airtight casket kept it from degrading." He leafed through a few printouts and pushed a page across the table. "After two weeks of putrefaction, I didn't expect much from the toxicology report. And I was right. Any drugs or medication in Jane Doe's system have deteriorated. She has a high blood alcohol concentration, but I can't give you an accurate read on whether she ingested it, or it was produced by putrefaction." Stewart pushed his glasses higher on his nose and handed her another page. "No defensive wounds. No surprise. She was no doubt sedated during her abduction and surgery so she couldn't fight back. In terms of trace evidence, there could be something of consequence on her body or under her nails. All the samples I collected still have to be analyzed, but I'll have results over the next couple of days."

"Anything on her clothes besides chloroform?"

"They're still being processed. There's a lot of blood, but I expect it's all her own. She was sloppily stitched up after she bled out, no doubt to keep the rest of her organs from falling out. But that didn't prevent blood seepage." He pulled two plastic evidence bags out from under his folder and pushed the larger one across the table. "We also have this."

Inside was Stevana's fake diamond necklace. *Had he found DNA on it? A hair from the killer?* "Oh, her fake diamonds."

He gave her a sly grin. "With a 1200x magnification on a power microscope, you are able to see inclusions and small differences that real diamonds have, while man-made diamonds are perfect and have no flaws. I also examined them with an x-ray machine to tell if the stones had a radiolucent molecular structure or a radiopaque molecular structure. Diamonds are radiolucent while fakes like cubic zirconium and crystals have more radiopaque features."

"What does all that mean in English?" Sidney asked.

"These diamonds aren't fake. They're brilliant white diamonds set in 18 karat white gold. Their total weight is 21.42 karat. You'll have to have the necklace appraised by a reputable jeweler, but my guess, it's worth at least $75,000."

"Holy hell." Sidney sat processing this new information. "That means the emerald ring is probably real, too."

"That's a reasonable deduction," he said. "An emerald that size would be extremely valuable. Upwards of $70,000."

"Whew. And it's still missing." Sidney released a frustrated sigh. "Any way to ID Jane Doe, or her killer?"

"Possibly." He pushed the smaller evidence bag towards her. Inside was a turquoise and silver St. Christopher medal on a chain. "She was wearing that under the diamond necklace. It has her DNA on it, and someone else's, who isn't in the system."

"Hmm. A St. Christopher medal is believed to provide protection for travelers. Someone who cared about her may have given it to her." Sidney picked up the bag and felt a mild surge of optimism. Here was something she could use—a small link in the chain of evidence that could move the investigation forward. "Folks in the homeless community may have seen Jane Doe wearing this." Sidney took a few photos of the medal with her phone, then stood and grabbed her jacket. "Great work, Stewart. Right now, I could kiss you."

His face reddened, and he grinned shyly. "A hug will do."

Sidney gave him a warm hug and was out the door, unanswered questions spinning through her mind. This case was full of contradictions. It felt like she was investigating distinctly different crimes that had somehow collided. It was time to stir things up in the community and see what crawled out from under the rocks. First course of action was to put out a press release that warned the public of possible danger. She headed for the station.

***

Sidney immediately got to work hashing out a press release. In a briefing to the mayor's office, she wrote:

Please advise townsfolk:

Be on the alert for any unusual activity or suspicious persons that might be part of an organ trafficking gang. Do not put yourself in harm's way by wandering alone in an isolated part of town. Make sure you know where your family members are at all times, and that they are safe.

If you know of a homeless woman in her mid-thirties, five foot four with brown hair, who went missing two weeks ago, contact the police immediately.

Sidney added the number of the Police Tip Line at the bottom and then emailed it to Mayor Burke's office. One of his PR experts would massage the wording so that the danger was clearly communicated, and then the press release would be sent to local newspapers. The story would break first thing in the morning along with a photo of the turquoise and silver St. Christopher medal. Hopefully, it would heighten the town's awareness without setting off a wave of panic—and give her department some much needed leads.

***

As her three junior officers filed into the conference room at noon, Sidney went to the sideboard and filled her mug with coffee. She gathered her thoughts while stirring in sugar and cream. When everyone was seated around the table, she filled them in on Jane Doe's autopsy and lab reports. Pausing to give them time to process the shocking news that she'd been killed for her kidneys, she sent a photo of the St. Christopher medal to their phones, then she faced their grim expressions. A sense of growing unease had filled the room.

"Damn," Granger said under his breath, scowling.

"That's monstrous. Jane Doe was easy prey because she was homeless," Amanda said, anger coloring her cheeks. "Killed for her kidneys. What kind of people do that?"

"People who can make easy money," Sidney said. "Most likely, more than one person was involved because of the logistics; the surgery, the sale, the packaging, and transport of the organs. Someone who has surgical skills.

Perhaps a doctor who killed a patient on the operating table and lost his license because he was a drunk or an addict, a med student who knows just enough to extract organs."

"That's a scary proposition," Amanda said.

"Just like water finds a crack, these trafficking rings flow to vulnerable communities, set up shop, do their grisly business, and move on."

"If they're still around, other people are in immediate danger."

"Time is of the essence," Sidney said. "An article will be coming out in the morning paper tomorrow warning folks to take precautions. In the meantime, we need to do everything we can to find these killers."

Sidney then told them that Stevana's jewelry was real, and worth a small fortune.

"I can confirm that it was never sold at auction like Bonnie said," Darnell added. "I spoke with the auctioneer, William Turner, this morning. William told me that several pieces of jewelry had been given to him by Stevana a month before she died. He picked them up at her house. Bonnie didn't witness the meeting, but when William was leaving, Stevana told Bonnie in front of him that everything of any value was going to auction. The auctioneer showed me the list, signed and dated by Stevana, and the receipts of each item sold. The diamond necklace and emerald ring were not among them."

"Why did Stevana want to be buried with them?" Amanda asked, scratching her chin. "Was she delusional at the end? Making irrational decisions?"

"And how did Jane Doe end up at the mortuary at the same time Stevana's body was snatched?" Granger asked. "She could've been dumped in the forest. No one would've missed her. Why put a diamond necklace on her? Why put her in the casket?"

They spent the next few minutes rehashing what they knew, looking at it from different angles, but more questions were raised than answered.

Sidney sensed the tension and anger beneath their words. Nothing fit together. She cast her glance around the table. "These crimes are linked, but we haven't yet discovered how and why. We're going to keep scratching in the dirt until something tangible crops up." She turned to Granger. "On another note, did you interview either of the two female entertainers that were at Stevana's party?"

"We spoke to Sasha this morning. She works as a barista at Lava Java in between entertainment gigs. She pretty much told us the same story as Greg. Everyone thought it was freaking nuts that the old lady was going to be buried with expensive jewelry. She said that there was no opportunity for any of the entertainers to steal the jewelry even if they wanted to. Morticia and Gordon never left the room. They were all chased out at 10:00 p.m. After that, the three of them were at Barney's until it closed. But we have no way to verify that. The other woman, Ruby, hasn't responded to our phone calls and she wasn't home. There was no car in the driveway. So, as of yet, we haven't talked to her."

"Okay, let's get back out in the field and talk to more people," Sidney said. "Granger and I will go to Wellspring Community, and we'll also talk to Gordon. Darnell and Amanda, team up. Make the rounds of all the shelters in the area, and any churches, parks, or camps where homeless folks congregate. Let's see if we can get a hit off that St. Christopher medal. Show the photo to anyone and everyone."

"Copy that."

"We're on it."

They left with a sense of urgency.

CHAPTER FIFTEEN

DAYS OF MISTY RAIN and dark skies had finally let up, and Sidney drove under a translucent blue sky with Granger riding shotgun. Across the road, she caught a glimpse of the sparkling lake between the trees.

Granger picked up the baggie of roasted insects lying on the console that Joey had given her. "Do you mind, Chief?"

"Go ahead." Suppressing a smile, she heard him crunching as she turned off the main drag and drove to the Montford neighborhood, passing the Thornburg mansion. By the time she parked in the driveway of Beyond the Grave Funeral Home, the baggie was empty.

"Those chips were good."

"They weren't chips. They're Texas barbeque cockroaches."

He laughed. "Funny."

"What's funny is that you just ate a whole bag of bugs."

His expression sobered. "Seriously?"

She grinned. "Seriously. One of the orphan boys gave them to me. He sells them. They're a clean source of protein."

There was a long silence and Sidney started feeling guilty. Maybe she should have told him up front.

"I'd buy them. They're probably healthier than the crap I usually eat."

"That they are. He sells a variety of roasted bugs at Mrs. Ferris' produce stand on weekends."

"Good to know. I'll have to stop by. Support the kid's efforts."

"Good man. Buy a few for the department. My treat."

They climbed the stairs, crossed the veranda and entered the foyer. Immediately, they were blasted with loud music coming from the closed room on the right where the casket selection lined the walls.

"That's "Cuff It," by Beyonce," Granger said. A music buff, he could spout out performers in every genre, a talent largely unappreciated by Sidney. She listened to a select repertoire of musicians, mostly soul and blues bands.

Hoping they weren't interrupting a customized funeral, Sidney opened the door a foot and they peered inside. A very good Beyonce impersonator was dancing and lip-syncing to her lyrics with three excellent dancers working up a sweat behind her, two men and a woman.

"Those are some of the entertainers that were at Stevana's cocktail party," Granger said above the music. "That's Sasha doing Beyonce, and Greg is one of the backup dancers. Oh, and the other guy is Max Biggs, the clown. Didn't recognize him without his big red nose. The other woman could be Ruby."

Sidney continued to watch them. They were riveting. "We'll talk to them when we're done with Gordon."

"Did I hear you mention my name?" a male voice said behind them.

Sidney turned and hid her surprise. "Are you Gordon Ortega?"

"That, I am."

Does anyone in this mortuary not wear a costume? Just as Morticia was a double for the matriarch of the Addams Family, Gordon Ortega captured the essence of Gomez Addams to a tee. Lithe and suave, with Latin good looks, he bore a resemblance to Raul Julia, who played Gomez in two of the movies. He had a pencil thin mustache and wore a dark necktie and chalk-stripe suit.

"Morticia said you'd be back to talk to me. What can I do for you, Chief Becker?"

"This is Officer Wyatt. We have a few questions about the night of Stevana's party."

"Of course. Let's go in here where it's quiet." He ushered them into the office, and they seated themselves on the velvet chairs in front of the gas fireplace. Granger pulled out his notepad and pen.

"We understand that you're Morticia's assistant. What is it exactly that you do?"

"I help coordinate the funeral events," he said with a hint of a Spanish accent. "Stage the settings and bodies of the deceased, book entertainers, caterers, and the like."

"So, you were present the entire evening for Mrs. Thornburg's event?"

"Yes."

"After the entertainers left at 10:00 p.m. that night," Sidney said. "You and Morticia locked Stevana's body in her casket, then she came into the office to lock the key in her desk drawer, but you interrupted her. She was distracted and left the key on top of her desk. Between the hours of 10:00 p.m. and 1:00 a.m., someone took that key, unlocked the casket, and removed

Stevana's body. We found her yesterday across the lake. Her jewelry was missing."

He listened attentively, then responded. "Yes, Morticia filled me in. It's all very shocking. I've worked with her for over two years, and nothing like this has ever happened. If you look at the photos in our album, you'll see that several clients have been buried with valuables. Nothing ever taken. We've been very distressed, but we have work to do, so we're carrying on as best we can." He nodded toward the other room. "We have an important funeral tonight. The dancers have to have their choreography down pat."

"What was the interruption that night, Gordon?"

"Morticia's car alarm started blaring. It was parked right out front, but I didn't have the key fob. She had to run out and turn it off before the neighbors complained."

"What caused the alarm to go off?"

"I have no idea. I also didn't know the coffin key was left out. I would have brought it to her attention. I left right after that without going back into the office."

"Where'd you go?"

"Home. My girlfriend can verify that. She's in the other room, dancing. Her name's Ruby Bryant."

"And she was home when you got there ... at what time?"

"About 10:30."

Sidney mulled this over in silence and glanced at Granger who shook his head slightly, acknowledging that his alibi had some big holes in it. Greg told Granger in his statement last night that Ruby and Sasha were at Barney's until it closed. Sasha confirmed that in her statement earlier this morning. *Who was lying?* They would have to question the dancers one by one. "Do you or Morticia have any idea how much that jewelry was worth?"

"No. Bonnie said it was fake, but Morticia wasn't sure. Stevana told her that Forest had given it to her as a wedding present. But who knows what an old lady might say? Morticia said that at their last meeting, a week before the funeral, she seemed looney. Kind of demented."

She was being poisoned. Of course, she was loony. "The night of the party, did anyone show an unusual amount of interest in Stevana's jewelry?"

"Yeah. Max Biggs told everyone it must be worth a fortune. They all examined it up close and made comments about how nuts it was to bury it."

Shaky alibis, avid interest in the jewelry. The entertainers were still suspects.

"There was a young man there, named Rafe. You kicked him out for crashing the party. What can you tell me about him?"

Gordon was quiet for a long moment and then one corner of his mouth tilted upwards. "Rafe is a good kid. He didn't crash the party. I let him in through the kitchen door. He wanted to pay his last respects to Mrs. Thornburg. Rafe works out at the rescue sanctuary, you know, taking care of animals that are really in trouble. That place wouldn't exist if the old lady hadn't put up the initial investment. She bought the property and had the barn, corrals and pens built to house the animals. There's a trust to pay for vet bills. Rafe truly cared about her. Probably the only person who gave a rat's ass whether she lived or died, besides the pastor."

"Rafe knew her?"

"Yeah. He went to visit her a few times. I would go so far as to say she was a surrogate parent in some way. He took her little gifts."

"What kind of gifts?"

"I think he said he took her supplements and herbs. To help her."

Sidney's antennae shot straight up. "Herbs? Like tea?"

"Not sure."

"Where'd he get them?"

"I imagine from the health food store. Maybe the farmer's market."

Granger was furiously scribbling on his pad.

"How do you know so much about Rafe?"

"I volunteer out at the sanctuary myself on occasion. I got to know some of the boys." Gordon's chocolate-colored eyes locked on Sidney's with an intensity she found both disturbing and curious. "I know a little something about growing up in a parentless home, the endless yearning to be part of a real family, the hole it leaves in a boy's heart."

"You were an orphan?"

"Yeah," he said with a hard, unflinching look in his eyes. "I grew up in a Catholic orphanage in Barcelona. Strict. Cruel. Debasing. That's all I'll say about it. The boys at Wellspring Community are lucky. Pastor John is a really compassionate man." Gordon glanced toward the door and then continued in a lowered voice. "Please keep what I told you about Rafe under your hat, Chief Becker. Morticia wouldn't approve. She thinks the boys at Wellspring are delinquents. Rafe never would have been found out if he had worn a suit to the cocktail party. He could have zipped in and out. But he came as Zorro. Go figure. He has a rebellious streak, but he's not a delinquent."

The more Sidney heard about Wellspring, the more she admired Pastor John's commitment to the community of underprivileged people. And the more she wanted to unravel the enigma of the teen, Rafe, who had a curious relationship with an eccentric old lady, who had a relationship with her fiancé and his son. *Did Rafe know where the tea came from that killed Stevana?*

"How do you think the thieves got into the mortuary? Could you have left the kitchen door unlocked?"

He shrugged. "It's possible. These doors wouldn't be hard to get into. They're old. Anyone who knows how to pick a lock could get in easily. Morticia will be getting an alarm system installed this week."

The music stopped across the hall and Sidney heard footsteps approach the office, then a husky voice called out. "Mon Amour," and Morticia sauntered into the room. Sidney was again taken by her total embodiment of the fictitious character, Morticia Addams—long flowing black hair, black dress, red lips and nails, pale skin—and how she really brought her to life.

"What is it, Cara Mia?" Gordon asked, his expression softening.

"Oh, I didn't know we had visitors. Excuse me, Chief Becker, but Gordon is needed in the kitchen for a moment. The caterer is here."

With their pet names for each other (completely in character), their costumes, and the Victorian house filled with Victorian furnishings, Sidney felt like she was on a movie set, or in an alternate reality.

"Gordon, before you go, we need to bring you both up to date on our investigation. Morticia, you better take a seat."

Wary, Morticia seated herself next to her assistant.

"We exhumed Stevana's coffin yesterday. As you suspected, it had another occupant. The body of an anonymous homeless woman. The worst of it is that her kidneys were missing. She may have been killed by an organ trafficking gang."

They both sat frozen for a long moment, eyes wide, then Morticia's hand flew to her mouth.

"She was wearing Stevana's diamond necklace," Sidney continued. "The ring is still missing. Do either of you have any idea how that could've happened?"

"Oh my God. No," Morticia said, blinking, coming out of her shock. "It all sounds like a nightmare. It's horrific."

Gordon was more composed. Sidney couldn't read him.

"I want you both to think really hard. Was there any kind of clue, any disturbance, that might have precipitated this crime?"

"There was my car alarm going off. But I wasn't focused on what was going on outside. I just wanted to turn the damn thing off." She sat thinking. "A dog was barking next door in the neighbor's yard. When I came back inside, I said goodnight to Gordon. We were both exhausted. He left. I went to bed. Until I got up at 1:00, like I told you." She paused. "Now that I think about it, it was the dog that woke me. He was barking again. Very aggressively. I thought it was probably a deer, or fox, or some other creature." Her eyes opened wide again. "Do you think it was the thieves? Had they put that woman in the coffin by then?"

"We believe so."

"So cold-blooded killers were in my house while I was sleeping." Tears welled in her eyes and she visibly shuddered. Gordon reached out and took her hand. She held onto it like a lifeline. They shared a gaze that was extremely intimate, then she looked back at Sidney. "This is all so frightening. That poor woman! I don't understand any of this."

"Gordon, anything else you want to add?" Sidney asked.

He shook his head. "I'm beyond shocked."

"Just one more thing." Sidney brought up the photo of the turquoise and silver St. Christopher. "Have you seen this before? On a homeless woman perhaps?"

"No. I'm not around homeless people," she said.

"Me, either," he said. "I'd show it around Wellspring Community Church. They feed people every night who are down on their luck."

"We're heading over there next. Go take care of business, Gordon." He nodded and left the room. Sidney turned to Morticia. "What kind of funeral are you doing tonight? Those dancers are really good."

"My favorite four entertainers. They can do anything. Tonight we're fulfilling a young woman's dying wish. She had terminal cancer. She wanted to have a flash mob at her funeral. The dancers are going to be scattered in the audience. It will feel like a somber affair, but then Beyonce's music will play, and the dancers will rise from their seats, dance their way to the front of the church, and do the routine you saw them rehearsing. My client loved music and dancing. She wanted a celebration of her life."

"That sounds great," Granger said. "Everyone will love it."

"I try to walk my clients on that path to get to peace. We're all going to die, but it doesn't have to be ugly. And it can leave friends and family with happy memories."

The music started up again across the hall.

"Now we'd like to talk to the dancers. Granger will go in and watch them and send one in at a time. The others can keep on practicing."

"Have at it. I can't imagine any of them being involved in any kind of shady activity. I'm going to go help Gordon." She left.

"Granger, make sure they don't quiz each other."

"Right. They'll try to rearrange their initial statements and coordinate their alibis."

She smiled. "Send Ruby in first."

CHAPTER SIXTEEN

RUBY WALKED IN a minute later in damp dancewear, holding a water bottle in one hand with a towel draped around her neck. A redhead with freckled skin and sapphire blue eyes, she was as fit as a ballerina without a pinch of extra fat on her. Sidney thought she probably hadn't eaten a carb in years. "Have a seat," Sidney said pleasantly.

Ruby seated herself directly across from her.

"You're a hard woman to reach. You didn't return any of our phone calls."

"Sorry. I had a busy morning. I work at a childcare center, then I raced over here to rehearse."

"I understand you're Gordon's girlfriend?"

Her eyes narrowed for a split second, enough for Sidney to know the question surprised her.

"So, you aren't in an exclusive relationship?"

"I don't know why you're asking about my personal life, Chief Becker. I thought this was about Stevana's stolen corpse."

"It is." Sidney had hit upon a flaw in her composure and wanted to exploit it. "Please answer the question," she said more firmly. "Are you in an exclusive relationship with Gordon?"

Ruby huffed out a breath and stared at her hands, obviously conflicted about what she should say. "Look, I don't want to be dragged into something. You're putting me on the spot."

In other words, she hadn't been briefed on what to say. None of the entertainers knew they'd be blindsided today with another round of questions. "Then tell the truth, Ruby. I know you want to protect your friends but lying to a police officer and purposely obstructing an investigation is a serious crime."

Her face paled, and she mumbled, "Gordon and I hook up sometimes."

"Does he hook up with other women, too?"

"Yes."

Sidney thought of the intimate look Gordon had shared with Morticia. "Is Morticia one of them?"

Ruby shifted uncomfortably in her seat. "You should ask him about that."

"When you left the party, did you notice anything unusual outside the house? Any cars parked out on the street? Any kind of disturbance?"

She looked pensive, deep in thought. The music from next door ended, then started up again. "Hmm. There was a white van. A laborer's van. I thought it was strange because it was parked out on the street late at night, not in someone's driveway. This isn't a blue-collar neighborhood. No one parks in the street."

Sidney felt an adrenaline spike. *A van was perfect for transporting Jane Doe's body.* "Think very carefully. Did it have writing on it?"

"No."

"Did it have windows on the side?"

"No."

"Did it look old or new?"

"New."

"That's a great recollection, Ruby."

She half smiled.

"Where did you go after Stevana's cocktail party?"

"To Barney's, with Greg and Sasha."

"How long were you there?"

"Not even an hour. He and Sasha were getting pretty flirty. I felt like a fifth wheel. I went home."

"And you were there alone?"

"Gordon came over around midnight. He stayed until morning."

"You're sure about the time?"

"Yeah. He woke me from a dead sleep. I looked at the clock."

Gordon had said he left for Ruby's house at 10:30, a ten-minute drive. That left a discrepancy of an hour and twenty minutes unaccounted for. *Plenty of time to take Stevana out of her casket, and guide someone in to replace it with Jane Doe. He had some explaining to do.*

"Thank you, Ruby. Want to send in Sasha?"

"Sure."

***

Sidney spoke with Sasha for about ten minutes. She was a pretty black woman who actually did bear a resemblance to Beyonce, especially in her talent as a dancer. She was young, twenty-one, just starting out in her career. Sidney thought she had the potential to be very successful when she moved to L.A, which was her dream. Sasha stuck to her original statement, that she and Greg were at Barney's until closing. She admitted they didn't really notice when Ruby left, because they were on the dance floor most of the night, and they did a lot of tequila shots. Sasha didn't notice the van on the street.

Greg came in next. They had finished practicing and he was about to head home to shower and eat. He was a remarkably handsome man, very pleasant and down to earth. She imagined he was extremely popular on the male stripper circuit, and probably drove the ladies a little out of their minds. She'd been to a few bachelorette parties and they could get pretty wild. Sidney talked to Greg for the same length of time as Sasha, trying to trip him up, stump him, but he persisted in sticking to the original script. They were at Barney's until it closed. And yes, they did a lot of shots. Too many, he laughed. He felt it when he woke up that morning.

Neither he nor Sasha had an airtight alibi. If Sidney broke up the crimes into separate parts, it was possible to see one or more of the entertainers as suspects. They didn't strike her as people who would be involved with a coldblooded trafficking ring, but removing Stevana's body from a casket was another story. Stealing the emerald ring from an old lady who didn't need it might not seem too terribly criminal to them.

Max Biggs came in last, accompanied by Granger. He was older, fortyish, and he looked fit, but he wasn't in superb condition like the others. This had probably been quite a workout for him.

Right off the bat, he was uncooperative and arrogant and stood over her in an intimidating stance. "Look, I already talked to Officers Wyatt and Cruz yesterday. I have nothing more to say. I've been dancing all afternoon. I'm hot, tired, and hungry. And I'm getting pissed about being harassed by you guys."

"Have a seat Mr. Biggs," Sidney said politely.

The muscles tightened on his face, sharpening his features, but he plopped down on the couch. "Can you make this quick?"

"This won't take long. Please run through the evening of the party for me."

His face pinched with dislike.

"The sooner you start talking, the sooner you'll be on your way."

He recited the facts in a monotone, almost verbatim to what he originally told her officers.

"The other entertainers said you showed quite a bit of interest in Mrs. Thornburg's jewelry."

"Yeah, so what?"

"How did you know they were real?"

He gave her a patronizing stare. "I know my diamonds. I've been in enough jewelry stores in my day, buying gifts for girlfriends, then a ring for my ex. There are ways you can tell. They are more faceted than fakes, and they have tiny imperfections. Fakes are flawless. Then I studied the setting those diamonds were in. Exquisite. It wasn't machine made."

"Some of the other entertainers said you weren't as drunk as you pretended to be. You have no alibi. You could have come back and taken Stevana's body, stolen her jewelry."

"I looked at my calendar for that week. I didn't kill anyone. Are you done with your farcical tale? You have no proof I did anything illegal. I'm leaving." He stood up and started walking to the door.

"Just one last question. Did you see any vehicles parked on the street when you left here?"

He stopped and turned. "Yeah, a white van. I noticed because a guy was standing beside it, smoking. The cab lit him up for a second."

"Can you describe him?"

"He wore a bill cap and he put his head down, so I didn't see his face. He was dressed in black. Average build." He rubbed the back of his neck and looked thoughtful. "That's probably your thief. Waiting for everyone to leave."

"Thank you, Mr. Biggs. You've been very helpful."

He scowled and left.

"Granger, call the sheriff's office. We need to get a BOLO out on that van."

CHAPTER SEVENTEEN

DILLON HEARD his bedroom door open. He knew his dad was standing there, checking on him, and he was racked with guilt. The last thing he ever wanted to do was hurt his dad. He never wanted to see the trust and pride his father felt for him dim in his eyes. His dad's calm, steady presence had always been an anchor, supporting him through the trials life threw at him, holding the family together after his mother died, when it felt like their world was falling apart. That trust stood in glaring contrast to Dillon's recent behavior—sneaking out at night and lying—and now his world had collided with lowlife scumbags who committed savage crimes.

Dillon hadn't slept a wink since Rafe dropped him off at 4:00 a.m. Now he pretended to be asleep until the door quietly closed.

He tossed and turned for another hour, trying to harness his renegade thoughts, but the aftershocks of what happened in the woods still rumbled through his body. The nightmare image of what was in the shed surfaced from a deep black pool in his mind.

He and Rafe had squatted behind the bushes at the house in the meadow for some time, scoping out the night, the shed, the yard—building courage. "Let's do it," Rafe finally said. They crept up to the door and Dillon used bolt cutters to snap open the lock, then Rafe slowly cracked it open. It creaked. Standing in the doorway of the musty shed, they heard the sudden shrill barking of a dog coming from a distant neighbor. They both froze. The inside of the shed was dark as pitch, but they heard ragged, labored breathing. Someone, or something, was very sick. The dog stopped barking and Dillon switched on his flashlight. The beam fell across a pitiful dog lying on the floor, its ribs heaving in and out like bellows, then the beam darted to the back of the shed.

They both gasped. A female pit bull was sprawled in the dirt, head at an odd angle, her eyes locked on them. They remained motionless. Then Dillon saw that her eyes were lifeless, like dull gray stones. She lay in a pool of blood.

"Jesus," Dillon muttered, stunned. "Poor dog."

"Makes me want to hurt the bastards who did this," Rafe said in a chilling tone. He shocked the hell out of Dillon by lifting his jacket and showing a gun tucked into his waistband. They stared at each other with looks like warning flares.

"What the hell?" Dillon whispered.

"Just in case we have to scare someone," Rafe whispered back. He touched the injured dog's ear. Part of it had been ripped off. "Look what they did to Buddy. He's all torn up. Looks like they drugged him. They're gonna pay for this." He lifted the poor rasping creature off the floor. It had to weigh sixty pounds. "Let's get out of here."

They barely made it through the door when the neighbor's dog started barking again, this time sounding like it was flinging itself against a chain link fence. A light came on inside the house.

"Shit," Rafe said. "Run!"

They reached the meadow as footsteps sounded on the porch. Flashlight beams crisscrossed behind them, and angry voices cut through the night. Rafe stumbled a few times, his uneven bundle slowing him down.

"Give Buddy to me." Dillon grabbed the dog from Rafe's arms, and the boys made a beeline for the truck, which meant angling through the creek. They splashed into the icy water and Rafe made it easily to the other side. They were thirty feet from the truck. Dillon slipped and slid, trying to climb up the opposite bank, but his balance was off, and he needed both hands to hang on to the animal. He fell backwards on his ass, the icy water soaking through his jeans and shoes, but he held the poor creature above the water line. Buddy released a soft whimper.

Men were cursing behind them, gaining ground.

Pow-WHOP!

A sharp crack exploded, followed by a guttural boom that rolled over the terrain.

Adrenaline shot through Dillon's system like an electrical shock. *Gunshot!*

"Shit, shit, shit." Rafe waded back into the creek and gave Dillon a hand, pulling him by his jacket out of the water, then pushing him up the bank. "Start the truck! I'll cover for you."

Rafe stood on the bank and pulled out the gun and fired a few rounds towards the house. There was a grunt and a yelp and one of the men hit the ground.

Amped on adrenaline, heart pumping, Dillon stumbled ahead, tripping a few times, but he made it to the truck. Joey sat in the driver's seat and the truck was idling. He had both doors open wide. Dillon pushed Buddy onto the passenger seat, climbed in beside him and pulled him onto his lap.

Watching out the door, Joey released a few frightened gasps. "Hurry up!"

When Rafe was ten feet from the truck, Joey released the brake and the truck started to roll, then he moved to the middle of the seat as Rafe ran alongside the vehicle, then hopped in behind the wheel.

One of the men was so close that a flashlight beam lit up the interior of the cab. He screamed something that sounded like 'you're dead!' Rafe stepped on the gas, and they peeled out, the truck sliding like a sidewinder in the dirt.

No one said a word. Their bodies were rigid. When they reached the highway, they ripped off the ski masks and the tension began to disperse. Dillon glanced across the seat at Rafe. Their gaze met briefly, and he saw at once that his friend's eyes were full of hurt. But his jaw was set, and he stared ahead over the steering wheel rather than turning again to look at him. Dillon held Buddy tightly to his chest as though his life depended on it.

"Who were those men, Rafe?" Joey asked, crowded on the seat between them.

"Better you don't know, Joey."

"What happened to the dog?"

"Those men hurt him."

"Will he be okay?"

"Yeah. I'll take care of him." He glanced down at the smaller boy. "Don't worry. He's sedated. He doesn't feel anything. You did good tonight. I'm proud of you. Everything will be okay."

When they reached the driveway that led to Dillon's house, Rafe parked and got out. He rounded the hood and helped Dillon get out, setting Buddy gently on the seat. The dog moaned a little but didn't open his eyes. When they were both standing outside and out of Joey's hearing range, Dillon asked, "Who the hell were those men? I have a right to know, considering the risk I took tonight."

"It was fucking Jacko and his brother, Dickhead," Rafe said. "I'm sorry things went south, but we did what we set out to do. Look, I gotta go. I have to drop off Joey and take care of this dog."

"How do you know Buddy?"

"He belonged to a friend. She died. I've been looking for him ever since, asking around."

"What happened to him and that other dog?"

"Someone told me Jacko's involved with a dog fighting ring, and he had injured dogs in his shed. One of them looked like Buddy."

"Is he going to be okay?"

"I hope so."

"That guy threatened us. He'll come after us."

"We were wearing masks. He doesn't know who we are."

"We need to report this, Rafe, get help."

"No!" Rafe hissed between clenched his teeth. "We don't need help. You agreed to work with me, no questions asked. You gonna renege now that things got tough?"

"Tough? We fucking got shot at! You shot back. You may have hit someone."

"I didn't. I shot into the air. Don't tell your dad. Or his girlfriend. No cops, okay?"

"Chief Becker isn't like that. She'll help us."

"I don't trust a cop as far as I can spit." Rafe clenched and unclenched his jaw. "Let me take care of those assholes. I have a plan. I just need you to keep your mouth shut. Can I count on you?"

A long silence stretched between them. Dillon weighed his options— betraying a friend who had become like a brother or concealing a crime. There was no right answer. "Promise me you won't go after those men alone. And you won't use that gun again."

"I won't do anything without keeping you in the loop."

"Okay, then." Dillon heaved out a breath. "You can count on me. Tonight never happened."

"Good man." Rafe slapped him on the shoulder. "I'm going to disappear for a few days and take care of this poor animal. I'll be in touch." He hurried back into the truck, then it disappeared down the highway in a billowing cloud of exhaust.

CHAPTER EIGHTEEN

"TELL MORTICIA AND GORDON to come in again," Sidney said, reviewing Granger's notes.

"Copy."

Moments later, Granger ushered the couple into the room.

"Take a seat," Sidney said.

For several minutes, Morticia and Gordon sat silently across from Sidney and Granger on the velvet settee. Sidney flipped through the notes, seemingly engrossed, but she was covertly watching the couple's body language. When people were hiding something, long silences tended to make them uneasy. Morticia shifted her body weight several times, crossing and uncrossing her legs, clasping and unclasping her hands. Sidney cleared her throat, handed the notepad back to Granger, and finally looked at them. Gordon was just sitting there, hardly moving, face expressionless, hands relaxed on his knees. Sidney wondered what was churning behind his dark, mysterious eyes. She cleared her throat, and said, "I've talked to all the dancers one by one. There seems to be some discrepancies in your statements." She leveled her gaze on Gordon. "Why did you say Ruby was your girlfriend?"

"She is my girlfriend ... of sorts."

"What does that mean?"

"It's an open relationship."

"Meaning you both sleep with other people?"

"Why is my sex life coming into question? What does that have to do with anything?"

"A lot, since you're using it as an alibi."

"I did spend the night with Ruby."

"But you didn't get to her place until midnight. You and Morticia both said you left here at 10:30. What were you doing between then and midnight, Gordon?" She watched for an off-key note in his voice or a glint in his eye, but there was no discernible change. Then came a twitch at the corner of his mouth. He and Morticia glanced nervously at each other.

"Maybe you two were working together," Sidney said. "You certainly had plenty of time to take Stevana's body out of her casket, steal the emerald ring, and switch bodies."

"We'd never do something as crass as that," Gordon said indignantly.

"I run a respectable business," Morticia said. "Whoever swapped bodies killed that poor homeless woman. We aren't violent people."

"Maybe you two were working with the killer. Maybe you let him in."

"That's crazy!" she looked quite horrified.

"Where were you both during that time period?"

Gordon's head swiveled toward Morticia, and their eyes locked on each other. Her expression was kind and loving, and his instantly mirrored hers. All pretenses disappeared. The space between their bodies was charged with energy that was unmistakably amorous. Sidney could practically see the pheromones flying.

"We were together," Morticia said softly, turning back to Sidney. "We were upstairs in my apartment the whole time. We didn't have a clue what was happening down here."

Sidney watched them for a long moment. "Can anyone verify that?"

"No." Her voice quivered, and she bit her bottom lip. "We were making love, not committing unspeakable crimes."

Gordon took her hand in his and held it. They shared a gaze that was warm and tender. "We're in love."

"Then why did you leave at 10:30 to sleep with another woman, Gordon?"

He sighed. "I didn't sleep with Ruby. I live there. We're roommates."

"Why didn't you just say that up front? Why all the lying?"

"Why do you think? For the very reason you just mentioned. We were both here when the crimes took place. We look like suspects. But we had nothing to do with any of it," he said earnestly. "Morticia built up this successful business. Why would we jeopardize that? Why would we commit crimes right here where we work? We're not stupid. That's like killing someone and leaving the murder weapon at the crime scene with our fingerprints all over it."

Sidney exchanged a glance with Granger. He looked taken in by their story. She had to admit, they did appear to be telling the truth, finally. That didn't mean they weren't guilty. Just good actors. They wouldn't be crossed off the suspect list at this point. Sidney needed more evidence before anyone was arrested. "I advise you not to lie to the police in the future," she said sternly. "It's a serious crime to impede an investigation."

"Understood," Gordon said.

"Just one last question. When you left at 10:30, did you notice any vehicles parked on the road?"

Gordon stared at the ceiling, deep in thought. "Hmm, funny you should mention that. There was a van parked on the left side of the road. I thought it odd because no one parks out on the street here in Montford."

"Can you describe it?"

"Only that it was a light color."

"Thank you for your time. If you recall anything at all that relates to this case, call us right away."

They both looked relieved when Sidney and Granger stood to take their leave.

CHAPTER NINETEEN

DARNELL KNEW that Chief Becker would be covering Wellspring Community Church to question folks about Jane Doe's identity. He and Amanda spent the morning making the rounds of other churches and shelters. They showed a photo of the St. Christopher medal to anyone who would talk to them, but repeatedly struck out. Some wouldn't even look Darnell or Amanda in the eyes, let alone talk to them, but just lowered their heads and skulked out of their way. To most, their uniforms were a barrier. A barbed fence. Many of these folks who moved from town to town had histories of disturbing interactions with law enforcement. Cops were the ones who forced them out of their encampments, even though they had no other place to go, sometimes trashing their tents and meager belongings in the process.

Last on their list was the county's shelter for abused women, housed in a rambling brick and mortar dwelling that once had been a mental hospital. Respecting the sensitivity of women who had been abused by men, Amanda went in alone. It still had an institutional feeling, but the living room was homey, with couches and armchairs and colorful prints on the wall. Children's laughter came from a playroom, where a woman sat with kids playing with various toys.

The manager walked out of an office and Amanda introduced herself. She was a middle-aged black woman with pleasant features, a gray afro, and thick glasses that enlarged her amber colored eyes. "I'm Annabelle Moore. How can I help you?"

"My partner is waiting outside. Would you mind coming out for a moment?"

"Not at all."

When they joined Darnell out on the sidewalk, Amanda described Jane Doe and showed her the St. Christopher medal. "She disappeared about two weeks ago. Has anyone fitting her description come through here?"

"First and foremost, I have to protect the privacy of our residents, but

I can say with certainty that the woman you're looking for has not been here. Our current residents have been here for a while. Where else have you looked?"

"Other shelters and a few churches," Amanda said.

"Have you been to the tent community near Aspen Falls?"

"Didn't know there was one."

"These folks don't stay in one place too long. As soon as they're discovered trespassing in the parks, forest rangers swoop in and evict them. There're about twelve tents out there."

"We're not interested in harassing anyone, we're just trying to identify this woman," Darnell said. "Can you direct us to the camp?"

"Better than that, I'll go with you. They won't appreciate seeing cops, but they know me. I take goods out to them."

"What do you take? Maybe we can help," Darnell said.

"Ditto that," Amanda said.

"That's very kind, Officers. They have basic needs. Toiletries. Paper towels. Food. Clean socks."

"How about if we stop at Archie's Budget Emporium and stock up?" Amanda said. She and Darnell both had two kids at home and money was tight, but they wanted to help. "And it won't break the bank."

"Almost everything costs a dollar." Annabelle smiled. "That's where I shop."

Forty-five minutes later they had parked a half mile off the highway and were following Annabelle on a path through the woods. Each carried several bags stuffed with supplies. The smell of damp leaves and moss permeated the air, and a babbling creek ran next to the path. A cool wind blew out of the north, making the branches rustle. Up ahead, Darnell saw tents spread out under trees in an area marked "No Trespassing." Two barking dogs shot out from the campground and made a beeline for them, then romped around their legs, tails wagging vigorously. A half dozen full garbage bags lined the edge of the campground.

"My co-workers and I arrange a volunteer work day to come and help clean up this area and carry away the garbage bags," Annabelle said. "It's hard for folks who have no plumbing or utility services to keep things clean. It's easy to be unsympathetic to the homeless when all you see is the mess that's left behind."

The campground was bathed in the brilliant copper light of mid-November and the ground around the tents was hard packed from daily use. But there was no one in sight.

"The camp seems abandoned," Darnell said.

"Many of them leave to get meals in town or find little odd jobs to help them get by."

They set down their bags next to a family-sized tent with a baby stroller tucked away in front. There was an expensive portable propane heater and a cat food dish filled with fresh kibble. People had been there that morning.

An elderly man poked his head out of a tent across the clearing, then quickly withdrew back into his shelter.

"It's me," Annabelle called out. "These officers helped me buy you supplies. They're not here to evict you."

A bedraggled young couple stepped out from behind some trees and sauntered over. The woman balanced a toddler on her hip. They wore good hiking gear, though their clothes needed a good wash.

"Hello, Tom, Mary." Annabelle smiled at the little girl. "Hi, Sunny."

Sunny gave her a toothless grin that touched a deep chord of sympathy in Darnell's heart. He had a daughter about the same age. He couldn't begin to imagine the hardship of living in the woods like this, let alone with a child and a cat.

"This is Officer Woods and Officer Cruz."

The couple said polite hellos, but their attention was focused on the bags at their feet.

"Go ahead, take a few things."

Mary set the girl in the stroller then joined Tom who was squatting over the bags, sorting through them. He set aside a package of toilet paper, shampoo, and dish soap. Mary took a big box of disposable diapers. They each took a pair of the dozens of socks. Sunny started fussing and Mary lifted her up to her hip.

"That's a nice tent you have," Darnell said to get a conversation started.

"We're grateful to have it," Tom said. "Back in the day, we did a lot of camping. Never thought we'd be living in it permanently."

"Tom lost his job five months ago," Mary said. "Our savings didn't last long. We stayed in our apartment until they evicted us last month. We were locked out. Couldn't take anything with us. Thank God we kept all this stuff in the car, just in case."

"I'm sorry to hear that," Darnell said with genuine sympathy. His sentiment was mirrored in Amanda's expression.

"Did you apply for any social services?" she asked.

"We have food stamps," Tom said. "I want to work, but it's hard to go on interviews when you live in a campsite and constantly have to move. I imagine we'll be kicked out of here before long."

"It's hard to look presentable with no washing machine or shower," Mary said. "We sure appreciate these things you brought us."

"Maybe you could help the officers with something," Annabelle said.

"Sure." Mary shifted her daughter to her other hip.

"We're trying to identify a woman who went missing two weeks ago." Amanda described Jane Doe, then showed them the photo of the St. Christopher medal.

Tom and Mary both shook their heads. "Sorry."

The gray-haired man left his tent and ventured over. He was sixtyish and rail thin. Then another man left his tent and joined them. He had a round nose and probing, dark eyes. It was hard to tell his age beneath his full red beard and scraggly hair, but Darnell guessed he was in his thirties. Both men started going through the bags.

"What about you, Chester?" Annabelle asked. "Have you seen anyone wearing this?"

The old man squinted at the photo. "Nope. Never seen it."

"What about you, Buck?"

"Yeah, I seen it. It's the one Delores wears. Ain't seen her for a while. That's her tent I'm living in. It's better'n mine. She warn't here, so why not use it?"

"Makes sense," Amanda said, friendly, encouraging him to continue speaking. "Do you know Delores's last name?"

His heavy-lidded eyes fixed on her with a bland indifference, as though he wasn't completely focused on the here and now. "Naw. We go by first names here."

"Are her belongings still in there?" Darnell asked.

"Uh huh." He stared at his feet while he spoke. "I tried to be respectful. Pushed them all to one side. Figure she'll be back, by n' by."

"Officer Cruz is going to take a look through her tent, okay?"

"Have at it."

Amanda disappeared into the tent.

"Buck, did any of the other folks here have a grudge against Delores?" Darnell asked.

Something in Buck's eyes, a faint glint, made him look just a bit unhinged. "Naw. Don't think so. I warn't here all the time, you know. Most days, I'm picking up litter. Collecting cans and bottles to recycle. Looking in dumpsters."

"You ever see anyone visit her?"

He shrugged. "Naw. She kept to herself."

"What about you, Chester?"

He scratched his grizzled chin. "There was this one guy ...."

"Tell me about him."

"He was standing outside her tent. Then Delores and her dog left with him. Too dark to tell who he was. He wasn't from the camp, though."

"When was that?"

"Don't know. Every day's kinda the same."

"Could it have been two weeks ago?"

"Could've been."

Darnell pulled out his notepad and pen and jotted notes. Annabelle nudged his arm and he noticed that Tom was watching attentively.

"You recall something, Tom?"

"Yeah. Now that Buck pointed out her tent, I know who she is. Like he said, she kept to herself. But I saw her one night in the field where we park our cars. She was with a guy. She and her dog got into his van. Her car hasn't moved since. It's still in the same place, now covered with leaves."

"Can you describe the van?"

"It was white. That's all I know. We were busy getting Sunny into the car seat, so we didn't pay much attention. But our headlights lit him up as we drove by."

"Can you describe him?"

He puffed out a breath. "Let me think. Just saw the bottom of his face. He wore a bill cap and was dressed in dark colors. Normal build. Close cropped beard. He was about a foot taller than Delores."

"Great. That's helpful information, Tom."

He smiled. "Glad I'm useful for something."

"What kind of work do you do?"

"Construction, mostly. But I do everything. Painting, flooring, carpentry, siding, roofing .... You name it."

"Do you have a resume?"

"Yeah, I do. Want one?"

"Please."

Tom emerged with a crisp white envelope. "Resume's inside."

"Very professional." Darnell handed him his card. "Stop by and talk to me when you're in town. I know lots of folks. I'll put out some feelers for you."

Tom grinned. "A referral from you would be great. Thanks, Man. Will do."

Buck looked a little wild-eyed and was shifting from foot to foot. "What happened to Delores? Is she okay? Where is she?"

"She's dead, isn't she?" Chester asked. "That's why you're here?"

"Sorry, we don't have answers at this time," Darnell said gently.

"It's okay, Buck," Chester said. "They don't know anything yet. Don't worry."

The younger man nodded, looking a bit calmer. The two men resumed looking in the bags.

Amanda emerged from the tent with a garbage bag that was half full.

"Wow. Bonanza," Annabelle said.

Amanda lowered her voice so the two men couldn't hear. "Bonanza is right. I got a hairbrush. Should be able to get a DNA match off it. Lots of personal info, too—paperwork, photos. Maybe we can identify her next of kin." She held up a ring of keys. "Apparently Delores had a car."

Tom said, "An old Subaru. It's over in the field."

"We need to take a look at it."

"I'll show you where they park," Annabelle said.

Chester and Buck had each collected some goods from the bags. Tears were running down the old man's face.

"Hey, are you okay?" Amanda asked.

He sniffed and held up two pairs of socks. "I needed socks, bad. They help keep my feet warm. The nights have been pretty cold lately."

"Mine are cold, too," Buck said. "And with no socks, my shoes are giving me blisters."

"This is like Christmas," Chester said.

"We're glad to help." Amanda's eyes moistened. She cleared her throat. "Take a few more pairs. There's plenty. I'll make a point of coming out with new socks in a couple weeks."

Chester beamed.

"You're a nice lady, for being a cop," Buck said.

"Thanks. The cops here in Garnerville are all nice. Don't ever be afraid to talk to one of us, okay?"

"Okay."

"Now, let's go look for that car," Annabelle said.

"This is depressing, isn't it?" Darnell said as they followed Annabelle along another path.

"It's definitely depressing," Amanda said. "I almost lost it when Chester teared up. Poor old guy. Living rough through no fault of his own, except for falling on hard times. It could happen to anyone."

"You're right. A lot of people in this country are one check away from homelessness," Annabelle said. "Being poor puts you in a whole other category. Survival living, day to day. You become invisible. People look right through you. Chester is a veteran. We're trying to get him housing. We're close. Actually, everyone here is on a housing list."

"How come they don't stay in a shelter in the meantime?"

"Some don't think they're safe. One of the women here was sexually assaulted in a shelter. That was in Jackson. The guy was arrested, but it could happen again with the next guy who's got a mental issue. We have a staff shortage. It could take months to get everyone processed."

They reached a clearing where two cars were parked. One, an old Subaru, was covered with brown leaves. Darnell wiped the leaves off the windshield to let in light and Amanda pressed a button on the fob. The lights blinked on and off and they heard the doors unlock. The inside of the car was empty, except for a blanket thrown over the back seat that was covered with white dog hair. Amanda opened the glove compartment and sorted through papers. "Here's her registration. Her name's Delores Wilkins." From the driver's side, Darnell looked through the console. There were a couple of energy bars, a box of tissues, and a baggie filled with what looked like chips. "Let's get all this stuff back to the station and sort through it. We'll drop the hairbrush off to Stewart."

"What happened to her dog?" Amanda asked.

"Good question," Darnell said.

They trudged back to their vehicle with mixed emotions. On the one hand, they solved the mystery of Jane Doe's identity, which would help move the investigation forward. On the other hand, witnessing the lives of those much less fortunate than themselves left a residue of sadness.

CHAPTER TWENTY

DILLON MANAGED to get through most of the day lying in bed, tossing and turning, falling into periods of tortured sleep. Finally, he got up at 3:00. His thoughts bounced around in his brain like a ping pong ball, weighing the consequences of two conflicting choices. Rafe wanted him to trust him. Dillon didn't want to betray him, but there were aspects to his friend's character that he didn't understand. Long dark tunnels of mystery. Why did he bring a gun on their mission last night? Rafe knew beforehand what the scumbags were up to, but he didn't forewarn Dillon. *What kind of friend does that?* After discovering Joey was with them, they should have aborted the mission. They were shot at! That could have ended up so wrong.

Before last night, their missions were always clear cut. They snuck onto someone's property under the cloak of darkness, quickly took care of business, and made their escape without leaving a trace of their identities. But last night was a whole different ball game. They had stumbled upon criminal activity that was savage and cruel. He envisioned the female pitbull with the unseeing eyes, her body lying in a pool of blood—and he was sickened. *That poor animal.* Used and abused by humans. Dillon's parents had imprinted into his character a deep code of morality. They lived by example, choosing the higher path when trouble brewed, even when that choice was extremely difficult. Dillon knew instinctively that Jacko and his brother should have been reported immediately to Sidney. But he listened to Rafe, who said he had a plan on how to deal with them. Now in the light of day, taking measures into his own hands sounded foolhardy and dangerous.

Dillon tried to call Rafe. No answer. He was probably off the grid somewhere with no cell phone service. His head was buzzing. The house was too small to contain the enormity of his thoughts. He hurriedly dressed in jeans, a knit shirt, and sneakers, and left his room. As he walked by the room that had been turned into a home gym, his father called out, "You up?"

"Yeah." Dillon backed up and paused in the doorway. His dad was lying on his back, lifting heavy weights above his head. Muscles rippled beneath his t-shirt. He put down the weights and sat up. "You okay?"

"Much better. Can I borrow the car? I think I'll go work at the animal rescue for a while."

"You haven't eaten all day."

"No worries, Dad. Don't get up. I'll make a peanut butter and jelly sandwich."

"Okay. You know where the keys are. Don't stay out too long."

"That's the plan."

His dad went back to weightlifting.

CHAPTER TWENTY-ONE

LATE AFTERNOON SUNLIGHT was slanting into the valley when Sidney and Granger left the mortuary. Long shadows stretched across the lawn. As soon as they were strapped into the Yukon, Granger's stomach growled, loudly.

"You got a timer on your stomach?" Sidney asked, pulling out of the driveway.

"It speaks for itself." He shrugged. "A man needs food."

"Sorry, I did it again, didn't I? Blew right through the afternoon without stopping for lunch."

"Yes, ma'am." Granger put on his shades. "It wouldn't hurt my feelings if we ate something."

"Let's take a food break. Then I want to talk to the boys at Wellspring Community."

"Big Burger?"

"You know I love their burgers, but I must say no. David wants me to watch my cholesterol. How about Miguel's? They have killer halibut tacos."

"Suits me. Glad you didn't suggest dried lizards, or whatever else those kids are concocting at the church."

She grinned. "I'm pretty sure it's just bugs." Her phone pinged. It was Amanda. She put it on speaker. "What'cha got?"

"A payload. We believe we've identified Jane Doe. Her name's Delores Wilkins. She was living in a camp near Aspen Falls. We ran a background check, came up clean. Got a photo of her license from DMV database. Age, thirty-eight. Last known address, Spokane, Washington. We have a bag full of her stuff. We'll sort through it at the station. We're dropping her hairbrush off to Stewart to get a DNA confirmation. She was last seen getting into a white van at the camp."

"A white van was parked outside the mortuary the night the bodies were swapped. We got a BOLO out on it," Sidney said. "Did your witness see who was driving?"

"We have a partial description."

"Great. Shoot."

Amanda relayed what they had.

"Not much, but it helps. How tall was Delores?"

"Five feet, four inches."

"And the driver was about a foot taller."

"That puts him well over six feet," Granger said.

"Send me the photo on Delores's driver's license," Sidney said. "We can show it around at the church."

"Copy that."

"Good job. Keep us posted."

Sidney parked at Miguel's and the two went in, grabbed a booth, and ordered. A text with a photo attachment came through. Delores was a brunette with hazel eyes and pleasant features. Sidney sighed, at once relieved that Jane Doe had been identified, but saddened that she met such a savage fate. Her photo would make it a hell of a lot easier to track down her movements on the night of her murder.

CHAPTER TWENTY-TWO

JOEY RODE HIS BIKE to the rescue ranch after school, a ten-minute ride. A beautiful oasis of greenery, the sanctuary was located just minutes from the nearest neighborhood, but it had the feeling of being secluded out in the country. The ten acres had fenced pens and corrals for small and large animals, with a big barn at one end and a pond for ducks in the middle. The manager, Mr. Hana Hiroko, lived full time in a small cottage that sat across the clearing from the barn. Douglas fir trees were scattered around the property, their wide branches giving shade in the summer and shelter from wind and snow in the winter.

Joey rode his bike to the mouth of the barn and immediately the four resident dogs ran out to greet him. They were all mutts that had been abandoned by their owners. They were found starving and nearly dead on the side of the road or at the dump trying to live off scraps. Bogie only had three legs, Jasper was old and blind, and one of the smaller dogs had no use of his hind legs. Volunteers had fashioned a little doggie wheelchair that hoisted his rear end and useless legs off the ground. Now he could get around like a little NASCAR driver, playing and barking and doing what dogs were supposed to do.

Joey was petting the dogs when Mr. Hiroko came out of the barn. He lost both hands as a child, but that didn't stop him from getting chores done in record time. He was lean and strong, and he used his arms to grip and hold things —something as big as a bag of feed, or as small as a pen to write with. Joey thought he was like the Terminator, rushing from corral to pen, distributing feed, managing the supplies, and assigning duties to whatever volunteers showed up. He once had told Joey that the sanctuary was a place of healing for both animals and people—healing injuries on the outside and the inside. He was right. Since Joey had started volunteering, he had found a new sense of purpose, something that he could take pride in. Watching people help animals, and watching animals learn to trust people, taught him that there was still lots of love and caring in the world.

"Hi, Mr. Hiroko."

"Howdy, Joey." The manager dressed like a cowboy in Wrangler jeans, denim jacket, and western boots. He tipped back the brim of his big brown Stetson and frowned. "Looks like you got a nice shiner there."

"Yeah." Remembering what Rafe told him after Jacko hit him, he recounted his words. "You can't go through boyhood without getting one or two, right?"

"Wise words, Joey."

"What do you want me to do today?"

"Volunteers were here all day. We're pretty much caught up. Why don't you just visit some animals? They get lonely. Have you met our rabbits yet?"

"No, sir."

"Come with me." Mr. Hiroko made a bee line to a fenced area built around a wooden enclosure. Inside were seven large, fluffy rabbits. "Go on in and say hello, Joey. They love attention."

"Okay." He entered the pen and sat on the floor. Immediately a big black rabbit approached, his nose and whiskers twitching. Joey must have smelled okay because he hopped onto his lap. Joey pet him and his nose kept twitching. "He's so soft. And sweet."

"That's Ebony."

"These rabbits don't look hurt. Why are they here?"

A lot of parents buy baby rabbits at Easter for their kids. "They're ridiculously cute. But then they get big and people decide they don't want them anymore. They think it's okay to abandon them outside. Bunnies raised in captivity can't fend for themselves. They're killed by dogs, cats, big birds, they're hit by cars, they starve to death. These seven, luckily, were rescued and brought here. We once had fifteen. Eight were adopted. Hopefully, these will be, too."

"I'd adopt one, but we can't have pets at the church."

"They're always here when you need a rabbit fix. I'll be around if you need anything."

"Okay." Joey wasn't aware of the time passing until the shadows stretching across the ranch darkened the rabbit pen. The sun had lowered to the tree line and there was a chill to the wind. It was time to head home to the church. They'd be serving dinner soon. He left the rabbit pen and hiked toward the barn, passing the bird sanctuary where a variety of birds; finches, sparrows, towhees, and juncos flitted among the branches. They were twittering their hearts out, filling the ranch with bird song. Deep, hollow croaks drew his attention to the ranch's newest resident, Jezebel, the largest raven he'd ever seen, about two feet tall. Mr. Hiroko was inside her giant cage, feeding her pieces of pears and apples.

"What happened to her?" Joey asked.

"She was shot by a pellet gun. A good Samaritan found her hobbling around a busy parking lot with her wing dragging on the ground. It'll heal, but she'll never fly again."

"That's sad."

"There's a lot of sadness in this business, Joey. Lots of birds don't make it. But Jezebel will. That's a good thing. She's adjusting. She's now chatting with other ravens that fly by. One in particular. A male that seems to be smitten."

As if on cue, a giant raven soared over their heads, then came in for a graceful landing on the top of the cage. He had a dead mouse in his beak.

"Speak of the devil, that's him," Mr. Hiroko said. "He brings Jezebel gifts."

The raven dropped the rodent into the cage and Jezebel hopped over and picked it up. She hid it behind her water bowl.

"They like to hide their food. She'll eat it later."

The raven on top of the cage tilted his silky black head to one side and his onyx eyes fixed on Joey. It was strangely beautiful to be the focus of the bird's attention, and he felt a mutual recognition deep in his soul. "Does he talk?" he asked, though he already knew the answer.

Mr. Hiroko narrowed his eyes. "Yeah. How did you know?"

Awestruck, Joey said in a hushed tone, "Because he's my spirit guide. Hello, Arthur."

"Hello." The raven flapped his huge wings and hopped from foot to foot doing a crazy, funny, ecstatic dance. "Hi. Hi. Hi."

"He's happy to see you."

"I'm happy, too." Joey pulled the long sleek feather from a pocket and waved it at the raven. "I still have your magic feather!"

Arthur cackled like an old lady.

Joey laughed back.

Then Arthur made a low wolf whistle.

Mr. Hiroko was looking at them both with amazement.

"We met yesterday," Joey said. "He chased away some mean guys who were giving me a hard time."

"That how you came by that shiner?"

"Yeah."

"And Arthur helped you." Mr. Hiroko shook his head in wonder. "Animals sometimes pick humans to bond with and protect. Arthur chose you. You're lucky to get this magnificent bird. Ravens and crows are the world's smartest birds. They're very social and they like to perform."

"Meow," Arthur said. "Meow ... meow ... meow."

"See what I mean?"

Joey grinned.

"Evermore," Arthur said.

"Looks like he's going through his whole vocabulary. Who taught him to speak?" Mr. Hiroko asked.

"A lady named Ann Howard."

"Well, I'll be. I know Ann. She sells organic products."

Jezebel starting screeching at top volume and jutting up and down on her perch. She would not be ignored!

"Obviously, she wants Arthur's full attention," Mr. Hiroko said.

"Yeah, I need to get going anyway. It's dinner time at the church. Bye, Mr. Hiroko. Bye, Arthur."

"Adios," Arthur said.

When he reached the barn, Joey saw that his bike was gone. *Mr. Hiroko must have put it in the barn.* He entered the cavernous dwelling, and an icy chill touched the back of his neck. It wasn't from the wind. Joey felt an ominous presence. A scream welled and lodged in his throat as a figure loomed over him. *Wacko Jacko!* One of the older boy's gloved hands covered Joey's mouth and the other dragged him deeper into the darkness of the barn.

"You little shit," he growled, his voice low and dangerous. His hand tightened on Joey's throat. "You think I didn't see you in that truck last night?"

Tears burned in Joey's eyes. He started shaking like a leaf.

"You're going to tell me right now who broke into my shed and stole my goddamned dog!"

CHAPTER TWENTY-THREE

THE DINING HALL was filling up when Sidney and Granger arrived in the basement of Wellspring Community Church. Folks were lined up at the food bar. On the other side, Foley and Pastor John were serving meals from the steaming stainless-steel containers. Behind them, the kitchen was bustling with volunteers preparing food. A tangy smell of Italian seasoning and garlic scented the air. Sidney looked around the room and saw two boys sitting at the table that had been occupied by Joey yesterday. She didn't see Joey or anyone fitting Rafe's description. Wearing a white apron around his waist, Pastor John looked up and spotted them. He signaled to a volunteer to replace him, then he stepped out from behind the bar. After greeting them with a concerned expression, he asked, "Have you made any progress with the case?"

"We're plugging away. Why don't we talk where we have some privacy," Sidney said.

"Certainly."

They followed him out into the hallway.

"We have a photo we'd like to show you," Sidney said. "We believe this is the woman we found in Stevana's casket. You might know something about her." Sidney showed him the photo on her phone.

His face paled and he said in a hushed tone, "That's Delores Wilkins. Are you sure it's her?"

"Pretty sure."

"Oh, dear Jesus. Someone murdered her?"

"Yes, I'm afraid so. You seem to have known her well."

"Delores had been coming here for meals for several weeks. She also volunteered as a greeter at our services on Sunday." He ran a hand over his face and suddenly looked exhausted. "No wonder we haven't seen her around. She attended AA meetings here. I thought she may have fallen off the wagon."

"We don't know if that's the case. What we do know is that she was abducted by force. We found traces of chloroform."

"Oh, dear Lord." He inhaled a deep breath and released it. "How could something like this happen to Delores? She was such a lovely person. Very well-liked. She'd been sober for several months. We were all very proud of her. What a shame. She was on a list to get permanent housing."

"When did you see her last?"

"She hasn't shown up for church or her meetings since the weekend Stevana died."

"So, about two weeks ago. The timing fits. The night she died she got into a white van without windows. Does that ring any bells? Any of your congregants?"

"Hmm, there're are plenty of white vans around. None in particular come to mind. Sorry, I can't help you." His shoulders drooped as if with sudden fatigue. "This will be very upsetting to the congregation. Especially the boys."

"The orphan boys?"

"Yes. Delores took them under her wing. She was tutoring Joey and Cooper in reading. She also helped in the kitchen when they made their insect recipes. Her death will come as a shock. Another tragic loss in their lives."

"Have any of the boys mentioned her?"

"Every day. They miss her. I haven't known what to tell them. I just say she went out of town for a while."

Sidney felt a deep stab of sympathy for the boys. "Don't tell them about her death until we get a definite DNA match. Maybe we can come up with a way to soften the blow."

He nodded.

"We need to speak to them. Maybe they heard or saw something that could help us."

"Yes, of course. Three of the boys are here. Joey went to the animal sanctuary after school. He should be back any time."

"What about Rafe?"

Worry creased his brow, and he sighed. "We don't know where he is. He didn't come home last night."

"Is that something he's done before?"

"Yes. When he first came to us last year, he stayed out all night a couple of times. He told me that he needs to be alone when life gets to be too much for him. He has to take a break, calm down. It's hard to find privacy here. He shares a room with Garret, and then, of course, the church is always full of people."

"Where does he go?"

"He wouldn't say. Only that he has a safe place, and I didn't need to worry." The pastor's kind eyes filled with a subtle but detectable sadness. "All teenagers are testing the boundary of independence, trying to figure out how to turn into adults. But Rafe is particularly troubled and has greater challenges. When children have alcoholic parents who are essentially missing in action, they have to raise themselves. And in many cases, they have to take care of the parents. The parent-child relationship is reversed. These kids have no role models and are searching outside the home for clues on how to develop in a healthy manner. On the path to healing, there are many obstacles. Many detours. I try hard to trust the process. I have to trust that God is watching over Rafe, helping him stay on the right path."

"You can only do so much, Pastor. What you've done already is invaluable. You've provided the boys with a loving home, and they have each other. A ready-made family."

"I do my best. But I still worry."

Sidney felt for the pastor. Not only did he care for the orphan boys, but for his whole congregation. He carried a lot of weight on his shoulders.

He ushered them back into the cafeteria and they joined the two boys at their table. They were finishing up meals of spaghetti, meatballs, and garlic bread. One was a black boy about thirteen years old. He had gold-flecked brown eyes and multiple braids that hung past his shoulders. He glanced up and his eyes widened as he took in their uniforms. Some emotion, maybe apprehension, flickered across his face. He wiped his mouth with a napkin and pushed his plate away.

"This is Garret. He helps Joey and Rafe make the insect recipes."

Whatever had passed across the boy's face was now well-hidden behind a dazzling smile. "Hi."

"Hi, Garret," Sidney said. "We really like your barbeque cockroaches,"

"I ate a whole baggie's worth." Granger shot a mildly accusing glance at Sidney. "I couldn't help myself."

"We're making Thai curry roasted crickets tomorrow," Garret said.

"I love Thai," Granger said. "Save us a dozen bags."

"Okay." He grinned. "Joey will be stoked."

"And this is Cooper." Pastor John gestured to the other boy who was six, the youngest of the five boys. His dark blue eyes watched them from beneath a sheaf of blonde hair that fell across his forehead. He wore a forlorn expression. "Cooper is a marvel on the piano," the pastor continued. "A natural. He just picked it up and started playing by ear. Now a volunteer is giving him lessons."

"That's wonderful." Sidney smiled. "What do you like to play?"

"Mostly funeral music," he said with a somber expression. His blue eyes narrowed. "I play at funerals where people don't have any family."

The melancholy behind his words saddened Sidney. "That's very kind of you, Cooper."

"I don't have a family either," he said. "My dad and mom and sister were killed when our house caught on fire." Cooper pulled up his shirt and showed burn scars that covered a third of his chest. "My bedroom was on the other end of the house where the fire wasn't so bad. The firemen got me out in time."

Sidney was momentarily struck speechless by the immense tragedy the boy had suffered. "I'm so sorry to hear that, Cooper."

"It's very sad to lose your whole family," Granger said very gently.

"Now we have Pastor John," Garret said, throwing a protective arm across the boy's shoulders. "And he has me. Cooper's my little bro. I watch out for him, right Cooper?"

"Yeah. Garret takes me to play with the animals at the sanctuary. I like the turtles best, and Milly, the baby pig. Milly's an orphan, too."

"Cooper's giving a concert here at the church this week," Pastor John said with levity in his tone. "And Garret will be singing in the choir."

"I hope you'll come," Cooper said.

"You can count on it," Granger said.

"I wouldn't miss it," Sidney said.

Cooper half smiled.

Sidney broached the subject of Delores in a friendly tone. "Pastor John says you met a nice lady here named Delores."

"Yeah, she's really nice," Cooper said, "We used to see her all the time. But she left town. We don't know when she's coming back."

"When was the last time you saw her?"

"The day we roasted a batch of chile-lime crickets. She helped us."

"That was Saturday, the day before Stevana was buried," Pastor John said.

"Did she give you any idea where she was going after she helped you in the kitchen?"

"No," Garret said. "Only that she was going back to her tent. She lives in the woods with her dog." He momentarily met Cooper's eyes, just long enough for a subtle communication to pass between them.

"What about you, Cooper? Do you remember anything Delores might have said?"

He shook his head, but his face flushed red.

"I want you to think very carefully, Cooper," Sidney said softly.

He glanced at Garret again, no doubt looking for guidance.

"Don't look at Garret, Cooper, just answer me honestly. This is important. Do you remember Delores saying anything about where she was going?"

"It's okay, Cooper," Pastor John said. "You can trust Chief Becker. She just wants to help."

The boy swallowed. "I heard her tell Rafe something about a new job."

"What kind of job?"

"I don't know. Rafe would know. He and Delores are good friends. She has a car. She drives him into town to buy stuff for the church."

Sidney smiled. "Thank you for telling me. Do you know where Rafe is? We'd like to talk to him."

Cooper shook his head.

"What about you, Garret?"

"He didn't come home last night," Garret said. "He wasn't here for breakfast either."

"We know he has a hideaway where he likes to stay sometimes," Granger said. "Do you know where that is?"

Cooper shook his head.

"I dunno," Garret said.

"What do you know about Delores's dog?"

Cooper smiled. "He's cool. And really smart. He does tricks."

"When did you see him last?"

"He was here with Delores."

"What does he look like?"

"A white wolf. His name's Buddy."

"He's a white Husky mix," Pastor John said.

"He does sound cool. Thanks for your help, boys. Remember, you can always call us if you're worried about anything. Or if you remember anything about Delores." She placed two business cards on the table.

Cooper looked up at them, his face wistful and expectant. "Are you going to find Delores and Buddy? We really want them to come back home."

***

"Whew, that was tough. Those poor kids," Granger said when they were back in the Yukon. "I feel for the pastor, too. He's got a lot on his plate."

"Yeah, he definitely has compassion fatigue." They both strapped themselves in and she pulled out of the driveway. "We need to find Rafe. Again, he seems to be right in the middle of everything that's going on. He was close to Stevana, bringing her gifts. And he was friends with Delores. Both women are dead."

"You think he had something to do with it?"

"I don't know what to think."

"Clearly, the boys are hiding something."

"They may know where he holes up. But they think they're protecting him by not talking. Let's head over to the sanctuary. See if anyone knows anything about Rafe over there."

The fused warm light of dusk was now creeping down the summit and the roads were dappled and muted. Sidney slowed to let a herd of white tail deer bound across the highway. By the time they neared the sanctuary it was nearly dark, and it was getting colder.

CHAPTER TWENTY-FOUR

WHEN DILLON ARRIVED at the rescue ranch, the lot was empty except for the manager's old Dodge Ram and an unfamiliar mud-caked motorcycle. He shut off his dad's BMW, sat with the window open for a moment, and listened to the quiet. He was amped up, wired. Maybe the serenity of the ranch would help quiet his careening thoughts. He got out of the car and was immediately jolted by loud, harsh, piercing cries. It made his skin crawl. Some animal was in deep distress, warding off an attack. He raced toward the clamor coming from the barn. Mr. Hiroko was racing, too, from across the pond.

Dillon couldn't believe his eyes when he entered the barn. A huge black bird was attacking a tall stocky man, its claws digging into a tight knit cap on his head. The man frantically waved an arm, trying to protect his face. Dillon's first thought was to drive off the bird, which he thought was a vulture gone mad. Then he saw the man's other hand was roughly gripping a young boy's jacket collar. *Holy shit! It was Joey!* The bird ripped off the man's hat, and Dillon felt the swish of its wings as it flew like the wind over his head and out the door.

"Help!" Joey cried. He was trembling, and his face was ashen.

Unaware of Dillon's presence, the man put his arm down and immediately tightened his hand on Joey's slender neck. "Shut the fuck up!" He had sharp cheekbones, a wide jaw, and a heavy brow. His eyes were hard, and his lip curled back in a sneer. Dillon recognized him from school. *Wacko Jacko*. All the emotion that had been building inside of him all day was churning in the pit of his stomach, itching for release. His hands clenched into fists.

Jacko's head snapped up as he approached.

Dillon's expression must have been intense, because Jacko let go of Joey and put his hands halfway up in half-hearted surrender. Dillon raised his fist and smashed Jacko in his sneering mouth as hard as he could. The hulking teen stumbled backwards against the rail of a stall, lids fluttering, eyes dazed. But only for a moment. Then he grabbed a shovel leaning against the stall. His face got harder, his jaw tighter. The air between them charged with what felt like an impending lightning strike. Dillon wasn't violent. He'd never struck another human like that before. But his system was flooded with adrenaline. He felt raw. His heart was jackhammering.

Jacko swung the shovel at Dillon's head. He dodged it. Jacko swung again. Dillon dodged but the back of the blade glanced off his shoulder. Searing pain shot down his arm.

"Stop it!" Joey screamed, trying to grab the shovel handle. Jacko smacked him aside like an insect.

"What the hell is going on?" Mr. Hiroko stood a few feet away, his body rigid with tension, his eyes wide and darting from one to the other.

"This creep was beating on Joey," Dillon said between clenched teeth, clutching his shoulder.

"He was choking me," Joey said.

"You hurt this boy?" Mr. Hiroko eyes sparked with fury. Dillon had never before seen the mild-mannered ranch manager show anger. He was rather terrifying. "A man that hurts a child is a coward."

Jacko threw the shovel into the stall and it clanged against the wall. His mouth twisted into a cruel smile. "Says who, old man?"

"Get the hell off this property. Now!"

"Or what? You gonna run me off, grandpa? You talk pretty big for a man who's got no hands." A half foot taller, and thirty pounds huskier, Jacko tried to push his way past Mr. Hiroko, ramming him hard with his shoulder.

The manager's response was so fast it was a blur. His leg snaked out and caught the teen around the knee. Jacko was sprawled on his back instantly and Mr. Hiroko's elbow was pressed against his neck. Jacko's eyes bulged with shock and pain.

"Don't come back here," the manager hissed. "Ever."

Jacko grunted his compliance.

The manager released his arm.

The teen got to his feet and was out the door in a flash. Seconds later, they heard the angry screech of his motorcycle as he peeled out of the lot.

"You both okay?" Mr. Hiroko asked with grave concern.

Joey nodded.

"I think so." Dillon swung his arm. His shoulder wasn't dislocated, but it hurt like hell.

"I needed to get him away from here, but now we must call the police. That young man is extremely dangerous."

You don't know the half of it. "I'm calling right now," Dillon said. "I have

Chief Becker on speed dial." Now that the adrenaline was dispersing, the reality of what just happened welled large in his mind. Jacko was swinging that shovel with all his strength, and he could easily have bashed in Dillon's skull. He had just come very close to being dead. Quick reflexes, instilled from years of basketball, saved his life. His hands shook a little as he pulled his phone from a pocket and pressed some numbers.

Chief Becker answered immediately, her voice friendly. "What's up, Dillon?"

His mouth was dry, and he swallowed past the lump in his throat. "I'm reporting an assault at the rescue ranch."

"Who was assaulted?" Her tone turned crisp, professional.

"Me and Joey."

"Is the assailant still there?"

"No."

"Are you okay?"

"Pretty much."

"Hang tight. We're about a minute away."

***

It was dark when Sidney pulled into the lot and saw the lights glowing from inside the barn. A cold wind raced down from the mountains carrying the pungent smell of juniper and pine. She and Granger hustled to join the two boys and the manager waiting inside, out of the wind. She quickly assessed the situation—no one critically hurt, no one in immediate danger. Mr. Hiroko looked composed, but his tense stance spoke of his concern. Dillon looked awful, puffy blue rings under his eyes, one hand with red knuckles clutching his shoulder, his other hand was on Joey's shoulder, lending support. There was discoloration around Joey's eye from his altercation with Jacko yesterday. He was trying to look brave but the dried tear tracks on his face told another story. *The poor kid didn't need another ordeal. What happened here today?*

"You're hurt, Dillon," she said, stating her biggest concern.

"It's okay. I'll live."

"Okay, tell me exactly what happened. Who wants to start?"

"Better let the boys tell you," the manager said. "I only saw the tail end of it."

Joey looked up at Dillon. "Go ahead."

"I got here maybe fifteen minutes ago," Dillon began. "I heard very loud screeching and thought an animal was dying. I ran into the barn and saw a huge bird attacking some tall hulking guy. The bird clawed off his hat and flew out of here with it."

Joey's face brightened. "It was Arthur!"

"Really?" Granger said. "Arthur was here at the ranch?"

Joey nodded.

"Then I saw that the guy was holding onto Joey," Dillon said.

Sidney asked, "Who was the guy?"

"Wacko Jacko."

"He attacked me and dragged me over to that stall where no one could see us," Joey said. "Then Arthur flew in. He was protecting me again."

"Jacko started choking him," Dillon said.

"Jacko was choking you?" Sidney felt a jolt of anger.

"I punched him in the mouth as hard as I could," Dillon said. "But then he grabbed a shovel and swung it at my head. I ducked. He swung again and caught my shoulder."

"Jesus," Granger said.

A very keen rage ignited in Sidney's stomach, and it spread rapidly through her system. She had established a bond with Dillon that went deeper than flesh and blood, that breathed in her psyche. He was David's son, and she had been emotionally morphing into the role of his future stepmother for months. The urge to stampede out of the barn, tear across town, and wring Jacko's neck was nearing a combustion point.

"Chief ...." Granger caught her eye and gave her a look that said whatever she was thinking of doing ... don't.

Sidney realized her jaw was clenched tighter than a vise. Anger was crowding out her reason. She took a long moment to compose herself, then forced herself to think rationally. It would be best to send two of her officers over to pick up Jacko, keep her distance. For now. "What happened next, Dillon?"

"Mr. Hiroko rushed in. The asshole rammed into him, trying to knock him out of the way, but Mr. Hiroko got the better of him."

"He was like the karate kid." Joey grinned, his voice animated. "He showed the big ape who was boss."

Granger and Sidney both looked at the manager with appreciation.

"I took self-defense classes," he said modestly, raising his handless arms. "I had to, didn't I? Disabled people are easy targets."

"Smart move, Mr. Hiroko," Granger said.

"Thank God you were here to intervene," Sidney said. "Sounds like you saved the boys from very serious harm. Why was Jacko here?"

"I've never seen him before," Mr. Hiroko said.

"Did he say what he wanted from you, Joey?"

The smile disappeared from the boy's face, and he suddenly looked guarded, just like the boys at the church. He glanced up at Dillon.

"Dillon?"

Dillon shrugged, and he wouldn't meet Sidney's gaze, either. The corners of his mouth twitched slightly.

Both boys were hiding something, and she suspected neither would talk to her in front of the other. She needed to speak to Dillon alone.

"What are you going to do about the nut job who attacked us?" Mr. Hiroko asked.

"I'm going to send two officers to pick him up," Sidney said. "He attacked each of you. We now have three witnesses who can corroborate each other's accounts. Jacko could have killed you, Dillon," she said gravely. "And he tried to choke you, Joey. That's aggravated assault, a second-degree crime. He'll be arrested." Sidney wished she could promise more. But she had no control beyond arresting him. If this was Jacko's first offense, a good lawyer could get a decent plea deal and he might not serve any time, other than the time he spent in holding until making bond.

Still, the two boys and the manager looked greatly relieved.

"He deserves to be behind bars," Dillon said heatedly. "He's much more dangerous than you can imagine."

Sidney gave him a piercing stare. He looked away. *What else did he know about Jacko?* "We'll talk more about that. Right now, we need to get your shoulder looked at."

"Nothing's broken," Dillon said.

"You're going to the ER. We're not taking any chances. Just one last thing. Does anyone know where Rafe is?"

Both boys shook their heads.

"I don't know either," Mr. Hiroko said. "He dropped off a stray dog here yesterday afternoon. Haven't seen him since."

"How's the dog?"

"Rafe gave him a flea bath. Other than that, he just needs to be fattened up. I've been seeing to that. Wherever he is, he's on horseback. He sometimes takes a mare out to ride the trails. Gracie was given to the sanctuary by Stevana Thornburg a few months ago. The horse was just living in a corral at her mansion with no other animal for company. We keep her out in the pasture with our rescued donkey."

"And Rafe just takes Gracie out without telling you?"

"That was Stevana's wish. She and Rafe were close. She financed this place. We're going to honor her wishes."

"Understood. Well, if you hear from him, contact us right away."

"Will do,"

"That's enough excitement for one day," Sidney said. "Granger, will you take the Yukon and drive Joey back to the church? He needs to eat dinner."

"Sure thing."

"I'm going to drive Dillon to the ER in David's BMW."

They all walked back to the parking lot together and Sidney pulled Granger aside. "After you drop off Joey, I want you and Darnell to go pick up Jacko."

"Copy that."

***

They'd been on the road for a couple of minutes, sitting in uncomfortable silence. Something was weighing heavily on Dillon's mind. He was really wound up, his knee bobbing up and down, his hands twisting in his lap. Sidney didn't want to have to squeeze it out of him, word for word—better to let him get his bearings and voluntarily confide in her. Another long minute went by. *Nothing.* He squirmed a little in his seat. Sidney was about to initiate the conversation, but he cleared his throat and blurted, "I have to tell you something, Sidney."

"Sure. What's up?"

He cleared his throat again. "I snuck out of the house last night and met Rafe after you and dad fell asleep."

What?

He had a desperate look on his face that disturbed her even more than his words. There was another long pause as he searched for words. "We went to Jacko's house out in the sticks and broke into his shed. He and his brother came running out of the house with flashlights." He glanced at her, waiting for her reaction.

What the hell? Sidney took a deep breath and released it slowly. "Why did you break into his shed?"

"To rescue a dog. Last night wasn't the first time. We've gone out three other times during the night and rescued dogs from owners who were abusing them."

His confession alarmed her, but she wanted to keep him talking. She answered calmly. "Where are the dogs?"

"They were all injured. We gave the first three to a rescue in another town, so that the owners can't find them."

"And Jacko's dog?"

"Rafe has him."

"Does Jacko know you took his dog?"

"No. No one knows. We wore ski masks. But the thing is … it wasn't his dog. He stole it. Jacko and his brother are involved with a dog fighting ring. The dog is in bad shape. There was another dog in the shed, too. It was dead. Lying in a pool of blood." Dillon's emotions were flitting back and forth between guilt, sadness, and anger. Then his words gushed out in a flood, as though a dam broke. "That's not all, they shot at us last night. We were running for our lives. Joey was waiting in the truck. One of them lit up the cab with his flashlight as we were peeling out. He must have seen Joey. That's why Jacko came to the ranch today. Somehow, he knew Joey volunteered here and he came looking for him."

The words hit Sidney like a hammer. The crimes committed by Jacko and his brother went far beyond the assaults committed at the ranch today.

The tension in the car was taut. What Dillon and Rafe did was wrong on so many levels; ill-conceived and foolish and extremely dangerous. She was aware of her impulse to reprimand him, but she held her tongue. She was on the job, and Dillon needed to be treated in the same manner that she would treat anyone involved in criminal activity.

"I'm so sorry, Sidney," Dillon said. "I know I should have told you, but Rafe said he wanted to take care of them himself. He has a plan." Dillon's voice split, and he looked straight out the windshield and pinched off his tears. "He has a gun."

Shit. This just kept getting worse. Now Rafe was on some vigilante kick. They needed to save the teen from himself before he got himself killed, or he killed someone else. "Where's Rafe?" she asked, her voice no-nonsense.

"I don't know. I swear."

Her hands tight on the wheel, Sidney pulled into the parking lot of the ER. "I'm going to call your dad and have him meet us here."

"Does dad need to know?"

Sidney looked at his troubled face and felt the growing knot of tension tighten in her stomach. This was an exceptionally difficult moment. She said as gently as she could, "Dillon, your dad has to be involved. I'm sorry, but I'm going to have to charge you and Rafe."

Dillon's eyes widened for a moment. "Are we going to jail?"

"Let's not get ahead of ourselves. I just wish you and Rafe had come to me first. I would have helped. There are legal channels to go through to rescue abused dogs. But you two chose to commit crimes. I know you were trying to do the right thing for the right reasons. That doesn't excuse you in the eyes of the law. But it does create extenuating circumstances which a judge will take into consideration." She released a weary sigh. "That being said, I have to appraise you of your Miranda Rights."

He nodded his understanding.

"You have the right to remain silent. Anything you say can and will be used against you in a court of law. You have the right to an attorney. If you cannot afford an attorney, one will be appointed to you. Do you understand?"

"Loud and clear."

Sidney didn't mention that his friend Rafe might not be so lucky. He possessed a gun, no doubt illegally. He was the mastermind behind these escapades. He seemed to have knowledge of criminals involved in a dog fighting ring and didn't report it. In addition, he had close ties to two murdered women. No telling what the facts would reveal by the time she had him in custody.

"I have to get hold of Granger." She called her junior officer on his cell phone.

"Yeah, Chief. I just dropped off Joey."

"We're going to need an arrest warrant and a search warrant for Jacko's house and property. We'll be looking for evidence of illegal dog fighting and cruelty to animals."

Granger whistled.

"I'll call the judge and pick up the warrants. Then I'll meet you at the station and we'll go from there—coordinate a plan of action. Give Darnell and Amanda a heads up. Call the sheriff and see if we can get some backup."

"Copy that."

Sidney then called David and gave him a very brief overview of what was happening—no mention of Dillon's nighttime raids or that she had to charge him. *One shock at a time.*

"Your dad's on his way. Let's go in and have that shoulder looked at."

The ER was located on the eastern end of the small community hospital. They entered a large rectangular room with the waiting room up front and six curtained cubicles in the back. It was quiet, with a single doctor and nurse on duty, both busy behind a curtain, and one other person waiting to be seen. Sidney checked Dillon in with the gray-haired woman seated at the administration desk, then they took seats and waited. Dillon looked dejected, wincing from time to time when he moved his arm a certain way.

David arrived ten minutes later, a frown deepening when he took in his son's appearance. "You okay?"

"Don't know yet," Dillon said. "Don't feel too great."

David met Sidney's penetrating gaze.

"We need to talk," she said. "Let's step outside."

Standing out in the autumn chill, David jammed his hands into his pockets and stared at her expectantly. "You both look like the end of the world is near. What the hell is going on?"

"Where do I start?" Sidney proceeded to relate the series of events in the order she had encountered them, starting with the assault by Jacko at the ranch, then Dillon's confessions of his nighttime raids, and finally, their dangerous skirmish with Jacko and his brother last night. David's expression grew more serious, his eyes widening with shock several times, but he said nothing until the end. Then his tone was incredulous, "You're charging Dillon? For trespassing and saving dogs?"

"Yes. I'm sorry, but I have no choice. My hands are tied. For Dillon's sake, I have to go by the book."

A mix of emotions flickered over his face, including anger. Sidney thought he was going to let her have it, but instead, he walked away and paced back and forth before stopping in front of her again. "You can't be serious, Sidney. We both know Dillon isn't a criminal. He's a good kid. He's never been in trouble before. He isn't the villain here. Those two brothers are. They're violent! They shot at the boys! Jacko assaulted three people at the ranch today!"

"I understand you're upset and angry, David," Sidney said. "Believe me, I am, too. But if this goes to court, Jacko's lawyer will try to find anything that smells like favoritism. They'll pick apart everything I do tonight. Even a whiff of impartiality will work against Dillon."

David listened, his face tight.

"Dillon and Rafe knew they were committing multiple crimes. They wore ski masks to hide their identities. They're going to be charged with any number of things—breaking and entering, trespassing, felony theft, possibly criminal conspiracy. There's no getting around that. They have to be charged for the sake of the cases against Jacko and his brother. They have to admit their own culpability to be convincing witnesses."

"I can't believe this is happening. Dillon has always been so level-headed. How did he let himself be talked into this? I thought more of Rafe. I guess I misjudged him."

"They're teenage boys. They're not stupid, just developing."

"You're right, Sidney. I'm really wound up. I'm not thinking straight."
He blew out a deep breath of frustration. "They're dealing with testosterone
surges, immature brains, a hunger to test themselves."

"They thought they were doing something good. Which led to poor
choices and risky behavior."

He shook his head. "I was quite a wildcard myself at his age. Christ, the
things I did that my parents never knew about …." He met her gaze. "What's
likely to happen to Dillon?"

"With a good lawyer, he could wind up with a deferred verdict, or at least
suspended sentences. Maybe several hundred hours of community service."

"I'll make sure he has a damned good lawyer."

"I'm going to have a detective from Jackson question him. I need to
back away, keep my distance."

David nodded his understanding.

"When will you take him into custody?"

"Not tonight. I have my hands full. I have to plan a strategy with my
team to go and arrest Jacko and his brother. I'll let you know when to come
down to the station to get processed. In the meantime, get a lawyer. Also,
until this gets cleared up, I won't be coming to your house. We don't need
Jacko's lawyer telling the judge I'm sleeping with the defendant's father."

"We'll do whatever it takes." His brown eyes softened, and he pulled her
close. "Thank you, Sidney. I miss you already." Then he turned and walked
back into the ER.

CHAPTER TWENTY-FIVE

"WHOA, GRACIE!" Wincing against an icy wind in his face, Rafe gave a slight tug on the reins and the twenty-year old mare stopped on the shallow bank of Catfish Creek. It was almost dark, the time of day when silent herds of deer moved through the woods and meadows. The tops of the trees seemed to be on fire and the reflection of the sunset turned the cascading water blood red. After Gracie drank her fill, he pressed his heels to her ribs, and she gingerly crossed the creek to the other side. It was calming to have Gracie as his companion when he needed to get away from the pressures of life—from the mental hazards of being around people. Animals could be trusted. Few humans could. A cross between a quarter horse and a thoroughbred, the mare was intuitive and responsive and gorgeous to look at. She had been a lonely prisoner living in the small corral at Stevana's stable. When he brought her to her new home at the sanctuary, she trotted back and forth through the pasture, playfully bucking and neighing, while the donkey joyfully honked and tried to keep up with her. Rafe had laughed, sharing her joy at being liberated and having a new pasture buddy.

Gracie pushed through an opening in a wall of fir trees and followed a winding elk trail for about a hundred yards. The grove of trees provided camouflage for an abandoned bunker used to store ammunition decades ago. Then it was used as a dispatch center; and a bathroom, wood stove, and a few windows were put in. Thick moss blanketed the walls and roof, allowing it to blend into the surrounding forest. It had become Rafe's refuge—the perfect escape when the misery of the world weighed down on him. Over time, he had stocked it with dried food, firewood for the woodstove, kerosene lanterns, and camping gear.

Rafe used all of his strength to wrestle open a groaning rusted steel door, then he turned on his flashlight and led Gracie inside the cavernous space. The door clanged shut behind him and the mare's hoofs were amplified on the concrete floor. He lit a lantern and a balloon of light radiated around him. The air was musty and cold, and there were still patches of the original yellow paint on the heavily reinforced walls. The place had once been lit with industrial neon tubes, but they had long since seen their day. He tied Gracie, quickly removed her tack, then carried the lantern through the darkness to the rear of the bunker. The odor of smoke grew stronger, and he felt heat coming from the stove in the far corner, and he heard the soft whimpering of a dog.

"It's okay, Buddy. It's just me." He cast the lantern light across the white dog lying on a sleeping bag.

Buddy sat up and thumped his tail and he saw that the animal was much improved. Last night, after rescuing him and bringing him here, the dog cowered and trembled when Rafe examined his injuries. Rafe had one of the medical kits from the ranch and he gave Buddy antibiotics and pain medication. The sedative his captors gave him wore off by morning, and as Buddy came out of his haze, he recognized Rafe and realized he was safe. The animal's body relaxed, and his tail started to wag. Rafe teared up when the dog's brown eyes latched onto his and his warm wet tongue licked his hand. The dog showed interest in eating, and he started moving around very carefully, exploring the bunker. The poor animal had been doubly traumatized—first losing his beloved owner, Delores, who treated him like a prince, and then being abducted and forced to savagely fight for his life. The dog looked like a wolf, but he was gentle and friendly. *What had it taken to force him to fight? They probably jacked up all the dogs on amphetamines.*

Squatting next to Buddy, he stroked the dog's beautiful head and back, avoiding the crudely stitched wounds on his ear and neck. *Thank God the bastards knew the basics of vet care.*

Rafe felt a gut punch when he thought of Delores. He had failed her, and he had been living a nightmare ever since. Tears squeezed out of his eyes, and he fought against the self-pity that threatened to engulf him. The least he could do was to make sure Buddy lived out his days in safety and comfort. When Rafe thought of the sick men who murdered Delores and tortured dogs, his anger turned red hot, and his thoughts channeled into acts of fierce revenge. The brothers and their ring of vicious criminals would not get off lightly. Sitting in a jail cell and getting three meals a day was too good for them. No, he had other plans. Refining the details of his upcoming vengeance, Rafe crossed the bunker and returned to Gracie. She was contentedly eating a pile of hay. He spoke to her softly, trying to lose himself in the rhythm of brush strokes as he groomed her from top to bottom.

CHAPTER TWENTY-SIX

AFTER PICKING UP the warrants from Judge Rosenstad, Sidney wasted no time getting back to the station. She came through the back door, bypassed her office, and entered the small conference room where her junior officers were waiting. Granger stood speaking in front of the crime board, and she sensed tension in the air, to be expected when their mission tonight was to apprehend armed and dangerous criminals.

After everyone exchanged a quick greeting, Granger said, "We were combining notes, Chief, getting up to date on our interviews at the mortuary, finding out Delores's identity, and the suspicious white van spotted by witnesses in different locations. I was about to brief them on what happened at the rescue ranch."

"Go ahead, while I get a strong cup of coffee."

Sidney sipped her coffee while Granger continued, making references to the updated crime board. A photo of Delores and Rafe had been added, and photos of the Krall brothers, Jacko and Daggur. "I ran background checks and both Krall brothers have records. Felony DUI and a drug bust for Daggur. Petty theft for Jacko. Daggur has been Jacko's guardian for the last four years. He's seventeen. Daggur is twenty-six." He went on to describe the events at the ranch, how Jacko assaulted three people and could easily have killed Dillon.

Amanda and Darnell looked at Sidney with widened eyes, shocked that Joey and David's son had been victims of assault.

"Joey's back at the church. Dillon's okay," she assured them. "I just left the ER."

"That brings us up to date, Chief," Granger said. "Except for what Dillon told you on the way to the ER."

Sidney took Granger's place in front of the crime board. No one needed to know at this point that Dillon had been involved in midnight raids, she thought. That could come out later. Right now, the focus had to be on tonight's mission. "What I learned from Dillon, is that the Krall brothers are involved in dog fighting. To what degree, we don't know yet. They are also connected to Delores."

That raised eyebrows around the table.

"Holy hell," Darnell said.

"She owned a dog that was rescued from their shed last night. It was injured from a dog fight."

"And we know that the dog was with her when she was last seen alive," Amanda said. "Getting into that white van."

"Correct. Something we want to question the brothers about. What we're going to be looking for tonight are the remains of another dog that was also in their shed, and any evidence of animal cruelty or that dog fighting took place on their property." Sidney paused to sip her coffee and gather her thoughts. "This is the first incident of dog fighting that I've heard about here in the tri-town area. That doesn't mean it doesn't exist. Dog fighting is one of the most callous and brutal pastimes known to man. Despite that, it's popular in many places, and as strong as ever. Unfortunately, there's money in it. In some places, dog fighting bouts can have purses up to $100,000. I'm sure they're considerably less here. But money goes a long way toward showing why people are involved in it. With that much money changing hands, it's not an easy activity to stamp out." Sidney sucked in a breath and continued, recalling a police raid back in California. "Years ago, my unit came across a ring in the Oakland hills. What we found was sickening; injured dogs and dead dogs. Many had to be euthanized."

"Barbaric," Amanda said.

"Barbaric is right." Around the table, her team also looked sickened. They were all pet owners and animal lovers. Granger's family ranch was a virtual zoo with horses, pigs, dogs, cats, and dairy cows.

"I'm telling you this so you can be prepared for whatever we may find tonight. Dog fights are hubs for other crimes as well. People involved in dog fighting rings tend to be involved in drug deals, illegal weapons, and other illicit activity."

"If they knew Delores, they might be involved in the illegal organ trade, too," Darnell said.

"Or they may know who is," Amanda said. "They may know who her killer is."

"That's very possible." Her department was too understaffed to deal with these kinds of complicated cases, but fortunately, other departments could step in to help. Sidney turned to Granger. "Did you call the sheriff?

Can we get some backup tonight?"

"The SWAT team is engaged on the other side of the Cascades. But two deputies will assist us. They should be here momentarily."

"Good. Okay, gear up. We leave as soon as they arrive."

***

Bulked up in their helmets, body armor and cold weather gear, the three officers stood silently in the hallway outside of Sidney's office. She sized them up. Granger had military training and SWAT experience. Amanda and Darnell had only a few experiences in these kinds of armed confrontations, but they operated well in a crisis situation, and she trusted their instincts. She sensed their adrenaline pumping, as was hers.

The voice of one of the deputies came over the radio on the tactical channel. "This is Sergeant Slade with the sheriff's department. We're in the lot. We have the GPS coordinates, but we'll follow you."

"Copy that."

"When we get to the Krall's property, stay alert," Sidney said to her team. "Stick to training. Copy?"

"Copy," Darnell said.

Amanda nodded.

Granger gave her a thumbs up.

"Let's roll."

Granger and Darnell rode in one vehicle, Amanda rode shotgun in Sidney's vehicle, and the two deputies followed behind. Their high beams carved tunnels of light on the highway as they sped through the forest of towering trees. "Our turnoff is coming up on the right, Chief," Amanda said after about twelve miles. Sidney veered onto a narrow road, then wove deeper into the woods along rutted dirt roads.

"It's at the end of this road, last house on the left."

Sidney turned off the headlights and drove slowly for a quarter mile, then parked a hundred feet from the driveway. The other two vehicles did the same. They all climbed out into the cold night air and quietly conferred. The deputies looked formidable in their military-style uniforms, ballistic vests, and helmets. Both carried shotguns in addition to their duty weapons. Sidney had worked with both men before, Gabriel Slade and Tom Jenkowski. The latter had a battering ram slung over one shoulder. "So, we're looking for two brothers, armed and dangerous," Slade said.

"Copy that," Sidney said.

"These bastards are part of a dog fighting ring?" Jenkowski asked.

"Afraid so," Sidney said.

"I've seen what they do," he said with a touch of anger. "Found a ring outside the county a few years back. Most of the animals had to be put down. We saved a few."

"Jesus. Glad they made it," Amanda said.

"They're really dug in back here," Slade said, looking into the woods. "Out of sight. Good thing you caught wind of this."

"Tip of the iceberg," Granger said. "But it's a place to start."

"Copy that."

"Okay. Let's do this," Sidney said.

Moonlight filtered in between the tree branches. The tall pines soughed. A fast-moving creek ran alongside the road. Staying in the deep shadows, they trekked to the border of the property and viewed a ramshackle house from behind a barrier of fir trees. A rusted truck sat in the driveway and discarded junk was strewn around the yard. Lights glowed from the windows and smoke curled from the chimney. Granger and Slade circled the house and returned minutes later. "A man and woman are watching the tube in the living room, drinking," Granger. "It's a small house, with three bedrooms in the back. Don't know if there are other occupants."

A prickling sensation dropped into Sidney's gut. The same unease she used to feel in Oakland when entering a building where suspects were holed up. She didn't know what form it would take, or how bad it would be. Many cops had been ambushed and killed after knocking on the door of a suspect just to serve a warrant. She motioned to her three junior officers. "Stay out here and watch the sides and back of the house. Tom, Gabriel, we're going in through the front door."

Jenkowski gestured toward the battering ram. "Hopefully, they'll be good little criminals and we won't have to use this."

A few chuckles, which eased the tension a bit.

Pushing against the brisk wind, the three officers darted out of sight. Sidney drew her pistol, and the two deputies had their shotguns at the ready. They quietly positioned themselves on either side of the front door. Sidney knocked, then yelled, "Police. We have a warrant. Open the door."

In a heartbeat, the inside lights turned off.

Shit. They're going to make it hard. Sidney tried the door handle. Unlocked. She pushed it open with enough force to slam it against the interior wall. "Police! Search Warrant! Come out with your hands up!"

Long moments passed. Nothing. The only sound came from logs

crackling in the fireplace. Feeling her adrenaline humming, Sidney nodded. With lights mounted on their weapons, they made a fast orbit through the living room. "Clear," Sidney said. They hurried through the small kitchen. "Clear." They inched to the hallway and Sidney panned the opening without exposing her body. It was a long hall with two closed doors on each side.

"Police! Search Warrant! Come out with your hands up!"

No answer.

Slowly and methodically, they advanced down the hall as one unit, the deputies in front with shotguns raised, Sidney bringing up the rear. Slade threw open the first door. An empty bathroom. Jenkowski opened the door on the left, entered briskly, shotgun going from left to right. No movement. A bedroom. Unmade bed, clothes on the floor. Closet door open. Empty.

Two doors left.

Slade threw open the door on the right. Another dirty bedroom. Empty.

They stood on either side of the last door on the left. "Come out peacefully," Slade shouted. "We don't want to hurt you."

"I'm armed," a man's angry voice yelled back. I'll shoot if you open that door."

They could burst into the room, Sidney thought. Spray it with rounds and take him out. Or she could try talking him down.

"I'm Police Chief Becker," she called out. "We have the house surrounded. Why don't you come out and talk to me? No one has to get hurt."

A cough, then the man's angry voice, words slurring. "You can't just bust into a man's house. I got rights. I gotta right to defend myself!"

"We have a warrant. That gives us the right. We just want to talk. We don't want to hurt you."

No answer.

"There's no way out. We have officers inside and out."

"My girlfriend just went out the window," he said, the anger tamped down a bit. "Don't hurt her. She done nothing wrong."

"You have my word. No harm will come to her. Who am I talking to?"

"Daggur."

"Is anyone in there with you, Daggur?"

"No. I done nothing wrong, neither. I'm just defending my house."

"Come out, and maybe we can work something out."

A long silence, then Daggur asked gruffly, "You mean that, about working something out?"

"Yes, I do. Come out peacefully. Let's talk."

"Okay. I'm coming out."

"Put your weapon down. Hands up."

Slade found the light switch and the hallway lit up. A disheveled, stocky man with a full beard and close-cropped hair opened the door and stepped into the hall, hands raised. He wore a plaid flannel shirt, jeans, and workman boots. He smelled of sweat and beer.

Slade stepped behind him and said with steel in his tone, "On your knees. Hands on top of your head." Daggur obeyed. Slade pulled the man's hands down one at a time and cuffed them behind his back. Then he pulled him to his feet and searched him. The man stared at them, his gaze darting from one to the other, blurry-eyed.

Jenkowski's face hardened, and his eyes shot poisoned darts, but he kept his cool. No doubt thinking about the dogs tortured by men like Daggur.

Sidney kept her expression neutral and hid her feelings of animosity. They needed his testimony. She didn't want to intimidate him, which might encourage him to clam up.

They walked Daggur into the living room and sat him down on the couch. A dozen empty beer bottles were on the coffee table.

Granger's voice came over the radio. "Hey, Chief, Amanda and Darnell pursued a woman running from the house. They crossed the creek. They're just getting her back to the house."

"Good work. Bring her in."

Granger came in first. Amanda and Darnell followed, ushering in a cuffed woman wearing jeans and a dark sweatshirt. The bottom of their pant legs were soaked. She was short and round with straggly brown hair. The flesh around her right eye was swollen and discolored. "This is Mindy Baxter," Amanda said. "Apparently, she walked into a door yesterday."

Right. Shiners seemed to be a trademark of the Krall brothers. "Put her in a back room for now. Stay with her, Darnell."

Daggur turned to his girlfriend and snarled. "Keep your trap shut, Mindy, or …."

"Or what?" Granger asked heatedly. "You threatening her?"

Daggur gave him a murderous stare.

"Where's your brother, Daggur?" Sidney asked.

He shrugged. "Hell if I know. I ain't seen him today."

Sidney and Granger seated themselves across from the suspect. "Where's Jacko?" Sidney asked again.

"I don't keep tabs on him. He could be anywhere. Sometimes he stays with friends."

That explained the wildness of the teen's character. No parenting.

"You're supposed to be his guardian," Granger said testily.

"I feed 'im. He's got a roof over his head. I been on my own since I was fourteen. That's more'n I ever had."

"We're going to take a look around the property," Slade said. "Make sure he's not holed up somewhere." The two deputies left.

"We know you're involved with dog fighting, Daggur," Sidney said. "You can help yourself, here. It'll go a long way with the courts if you cooperate. Tell us where to look."

"I don't know what you're talking about."

"You had two dogs in your shed last night. One was dead."

He sawed his jaw back and forth, thinking. "So that's what this is about? A couple of shitheads broke into my shed and robbed me, and you're coming after me? That dead dog got hit by a car. I just didn't have time to bury the poor thing. But I did, today."

"What about the other dog? The big white one that was injured."

"Found him like that. I was just trying to help."

"Where'd you bury the dead dog?"

"I don't like where this is going. I don't know nothing about no dog fighting."

Sidney tried another tactic. "Did you ever meet a woman named Delores Wilkins?"

"I meet a lot of women."

Sidney brought up the photo on her phone and showed it to him.

His eyes widened. He recognized her. "Never seen her before. I ain't saying another word. Except one. Lawyer." To punctuate his statement, he belched loudly.

"Okay, have it your way. Amanda, go get the Yukon and park it in the driveway. Daggur can sit in the cage while we search the place."

CHAPTER TWENTY-SEVEN

TEN MINUTES LATER, Daggur was sitting in the caged back seat of Sidney's SUV. Granger was searching the front of the house. Amanda had retrieved her crime kit and camera and was snapping photos, starting with the back bedroom. Darnell brought Mindy into the living room and removed her cuffs. She rubbed her wrists and shot him an appreciative glance.

Darnell pulled out a notepad and pen and stood ready to take notes. Sidney turned her attention to the woman who sat meekly on the couch. She was sitting stock-still, eyes wide and sad.

"Mindy, that swollen eye looks painful. Does your boyfriend have a temper?"

She shrugged, stared at her hands on her lap.

"Look, I understand that you're afraid to talk. But we can protect you. Daggur will never hurt you again."

"I'm afraid of him," she said, still staring at her hands. "There will be hell to pay if he thinks I talked to you."

"He can't hurt you if he's in jail. We can arrest him for assault and battery. Threatening to shoot the police is also a crime, especially when we repeatedly identified ourselves, and we had a warrant."

"He'll come after me when he gets out."

"There's a really good shelter for women here," Sidney said gently. "They can help you start a new life."

Mindy blew out a shaky breath and her eyes filled with tears. "I've been wanting to clear outta here for a long while now. All I want is a chance to better myself. I wanna climb outta this rat hole I'm in."

Her voice, the rawness in it, went straight to Sidney's heart. "Talk to me. Help me put him away for a long while."

"He's a nasty sonovabitch when he drinks too much," she said, pointing to her face. "He gave me this last night. And this." She lifted her sweatshirt and showed bruises on her abdomen. "Just because I told him to slow down on his drinking."

"I'm sorry for your situation." Sidney took a breath to fight off the tightness in her chest.

At that point, Amanda walked into the room, camera hanging from her neck, evidence bags in both hands. "I got his Glock 19, and a pile of cash. A few thousand dollars in hundred-dollar bills. And this." She held up a bag holding containers of pills. "Looks like opioids."

"This just keeps getting better," Sidney said. "Possession of illegal drugs. That stack of money certainly wasn't obtained legally."

"And he racked up that felony DUI a couple years back," Darnell added. "He's a felon in possession of a handgun. Another felony to add to the list."

"And we're just getting started." With a grin, Amanda set the bags on the table. "That's just the first room. I'll go search the others."

They had the bastard! The search warrant was paying off big time. Sharing Amanda's upbeat feelings, Sidney turned back to Mindy, now viewing her with a skeptical eye. Was it possible that the woman lived with Daggur and hadn't been an accessory? To keep her talking, Sidney would let her believe that she was still being viewed as a victim. "Just between you and me, Mindy, Daggur's going down. He's looking at serious jail time."

A spark of hope lit in her eyes. "How much time?"

"A lot. He won't be able to hurt you again."

"He sold those pills and took them himself," Mindy blurted. "He's strung out."

Sidney nodded approvingly. Darnell was scribbling notes.

"What else do you want to know?" Mindy asked.

"Tell me about the dog fighting."

Mindy nervously rubbed her hands together. "I had nothing to do with that. I swear. I hate it."

"How long has Daggur been involved?"

"We've been together for about a year. That's about the time it started. He got laid off. At first, he just went to watch the fights and bet a little money. But over time, he told me he was doing really well. I don't know what that means. He kept collecting unemployment, but he didn't look for a job. He always had money. Recently, he started getting his own dogs. He doesn't care if they're hurt or killed. He even bets against them. He's so heartless, I know he'd kill me, too, in a heartbeat, and never look back."

If Mindy was being straight with her, she had been living a nightmare. Held prisoner by a violent drunk, back here in the woods, hidden from the world. "Is Jacko involved?"

"No. Daggur took him to a couple of fights. I don't think he likes it."

"Taking an adolescent to a dog fight is a felony." Sidney shook her head. "His crimes are just piling on."

"Good," Mindy said, showing a spark of passion. "I hope he rots in jail."

"Do you know where Jacko is?"

"No. But he's following in Daggur's ways. He's also a brute. He should be locked away, too."

"If you hear from him, contact us immediately. He's now a minor without a guardian."

"You can count on it."

"Do you have anywhere to go? Anyone to stay with?"

"Now that Daggur's gone, I can stay here, for now. Rent's paid up for the month."

"Did Daggur ever hold dog fights here?"

"Yeah. A few times. There's a dog fighting pit out behind the creek. Lots of men attended. I could hear them yelling, whooping." She shivered. "I heard the poor dogs. It was a nightmare."

"That's a major nail in his coffin, Chief," Darnell said.

"Got that right. It'll be hard to claim that he had a sudden humanitarian interest when he was organizing dog fights here. Mindy, you'll have to testify in court."

"Gladly." She smiled for the first time. "We're going to nail his ass."

"Looks that way. One last thing. Do you know anything about a tall, bearded man who drives a white van?"

She thought for a moment. "I don't know. The front of the house is like a parking lot when there's a fight."

"Can you show us where the pit is?"

She nodded.

Granger walked into the room from the kitchen. "Nothing in there, Chief."

"Let's go out and talk to the deputies."

***

The temperature had dropped several degrees when they all stepped outside. The air was heavy with moisture and pockets of mist hovered over the creek. The deputies soon joined them. "What'cha got?" Sidney asked.

"Nothing but a whole bunch of rusted junk out here," Slade said. "But a goddamned gold mine in the shed. There's a virtual pharmacy of medications and bandages in there, and quite a few blood spatters."

"You know anything about that, Mindy?' Sidney asked.

"He's been keeping injured dogs in there for a while," Mindy said. "Three or four the last couple of months."

"Also, his truck has blood in the back, and dog hair," Jenkowski added. "He no doubt used it to transport dogs to and from fights."

"The shed and the truck are crime scenes," Sidney said. "They need to be photographed and processed for hair, fiber, and blood."

"That's a lot to process."

"Yeah, I need a small army."

"I'll call the sheriff," Jenkowski said. "He'll get the county crime scene unit out here to help."

"Mindy says there's a pit behind the creek where they held some fights," Sidney said.

"Lead the way," Slade said.

Jenkowski stayed behind, already on the phone to the department.

Sidney and the other three officers followed Mindy through the woods to a makeshift bridge and crossed the creek, then they wove through the trees to a small clearing. A large square pit had been dug about a foot into the ground. A fence surrounded it to prevent the two fighting dogs from escaping. The earth was packed down hard by the feet of the dozens of men who had stood and watched the atrocities, drinking, betting and conjuring future criminal activity.

"Vile and thoroughly disgusting human beings," Sidney said, her gut rumbling with emotion.

Anger radiated from the eyes of the officers.

"Not fit to be called human," Granger said.

"Some sub-category of prehistoric slime more like it," Slade said.

"That just about covers it," Sidney said, sickened to her core. She steeled herself for the long night that stretched ahead of them.

CHAPTER TWENTY-EIGHT

RAFE SADDLED GRACIE and left the bunker around 11:00 p.m. It was cold and dark. The moon offered faint shafts of light as he directed the mare through the fir trees and across Catfish Creek. He rode through the forest for several miles on an old fire road that was almost a direct route to his destination. The air was still. The night was quiet except for the clopping of hooves and a creak of leather when he shifted in the saddle.

There was nothing to engage his mind other than his mission. It was a simple plan. Easy to execute but it would have devastating results. This would propel him into a whole new category of criminal. But he didn't care. The emotions he felt most of the time these days were rage and pain. His life had once again been turned upside down, destroying what little happiness he had found.

Last year when he moved into the church, he figured it would be another short-term stay. He didn't fit in anywhere. He had always been a loner. Self-reliant. A tough nut to crack, one of his foster parents had said. But the younger boys at the church were as fucked up as he was. They had all been knuckled and bruised by life. For some reason, they came to rely on him, listen to him, look up to him like he was some kind of glorious leader. Their loyalty and affection opened up fissures in his character that he didn't know he had. A new confidence. An ability to care for something beyond himself. A feeling of belonging. It was all unexpected, and startling. He didn't know what to do with those new emotions. It was a role he had to adjust to, and finally accept. In turn, he would do anything for those boys, including taking down the men who ripped Delores from their lives. She had been a bright light, kind and gentle, consistent and dependable. She had taught them to trust again, to have a glimmer of hope for the future. And that hope had been stamped out. Her absence left them struggling in darkness.

Now little else mattered to Rafe except getting revenge. It was the driving force in his life. These backwoods men were less than human. They had no guilt. No conscience. Ice cold blood ran through their veins. He would make them pay for their savage actions. One by one, if necessary.

When his thoughts of vengeance ran out of steam, he tried very hard not to think about Delores. But his mind took one of those wrong turns, and images started flooding in. He squeezed his eyes shut and wished them away. But the image of her lifeless body in the back of the white van loomed large in his mind, as though a movie projector was stuck on repeat, playing the same few seconds over and over. They say it takes a long time to comprehend a tragedy. You're numb. You can't accept the harsh reality, but then it settles into your being, into your bones. And you live every second in immense agony.

Gracie pulled him out of his grim thoughts. The fire road butted a dirt road, and she came to a dead stop, waiting for his direction. He gave a slight tug of the reins and she turned to the right. After they plodded a half mile, he was startled to hear noises in the night. Human-made noises. Voices. *What was going on?*

Up ahead, he saw a number of vehicles parked alongside the road. He dismounted and led Gracie into the woods and tied her to an aspen branch. Staying in the shadows, he trekked closer to the ramshackle house, and saw that the vehicles belonged to law enforcement, and there were others that had the county emblem on the doors. He quietly approached the edge of the property under cover of trees and bushes. The house was completely lit up and he saw people moving around indoors past the windows. He also saw movement and bright light in the shed, and flashlight beams darting in and out of trees behind the creek. Right away, he knew what was going on. Someone had tipped off the cops to all the illegal activity that took place here. And he knew who that informant was. *Dillon.* He should have known he couldn't keep his mouth shut. His dad's girlfriend was the Chief of Police, for god's sake. No doubt, he snitched on Rafe, and they were probably looking for him. Thanks to Dillon, the Krall brothers would live another night. *But heaven help them if they were released on bail.*

A sudden movement across the road caught his eye. A deer? A bear? The form took the shape of a man, dressed in black, moving in and out of the shadows. The way the man was hunched over, the stealthy way he moved, told Rafe he was not part of the law enforcement team. Rafe crept to the edge of the driveway in front of the house to get a better view. The man appeared and disappeared in the shadows, then he crossed the road and made his way to the police SUV parked in the driveway, just fifteen feet from Rafe's hiding place. He peered into the window of the back seat, then tried the door handle.

It didn't open. He circled the vehicle, trying every handle. None opened. When the man came around again, he was holding a huge rock the size of a football. He was quite tall, about three inches taller than Rafe, lean and muscular. He faced the back window of the SUV and raised the rock above his head.

Rafe sprang out of the bushes and flung himself at the man. They both flew along the driveway and skidded in the dirt for several feet. The man took the brunt force of the fall, hitting the ground hard, his body cushioning Rafe's. The air was knocked out of his lungs, and he gasped for breath. Rafe completely miscalculated his brute strength. He was an animal. He twisted beneath Rafe's weight and managed to free his left hand. He corkscrewed his upper body and clubbed his fist against Rafe's temple. Stunned, Rafe went completely limp, blinding pain pulsing through his head.

Lightening quick, the man shoved him aside like dead weight and Rafe found himself sprawled on his back staring up into the barrel of a gun. Above the gun was the man's face, his expression as tight as a fist. Several things struck Rafe at once. He recognized him as the driver of the white van. The man who killed Delores. And he was about to kill Rafe. Closing his eyes tight, he waited for death. Nothing happened. The man had silently vanished. Rafe sat up and spotted him sprinting into the woods, darting through the brush like a deer.

Rafe peeled himself off the ground, his head throbbing. *He had just looked a stone-cold killer in the eyes. Why wasn't he dead? Why was the killer so interested in the SUV?* Rafe lumbered over to the vehicle and peered into the window. Inside, Daggur Krall was slumped against the seat, head back, eyes shut, drool running down his chin. Anger rose like a wave inside Rafe's chest. The killer was attempting to help Daggur escape. The two were working together, just as Rafe had suspected. If he hadn't tackled him, both men would now be on the lam.

Rafe felt for the gun pressed into the back of his belt and pulled it out. He aimed it at Daggur's ugly mug and went through the motions of shooting him right between the eyes. Then he put the gun away and left the premises. Daggur was in custody. But his shithead brother was still out there, loose and free. Rafe had every intention of finding him before the cops did.

***

The gentle mare plodded along with little direction from Rafe, as though guided by an inner GPS, and they arrived back at the bunker sometime after midnight. A deep chill had settled into the woodland and every twig and blade of grass shimmered with frost. It felt good to get out of the wind into the warm interior. Buddy greeted him with ecstatic wriggling and vigorous tail wagging. Rest and medication were working. He was now resembling his old self. "Hey boy, hey Buddy. Sorry to leave you alone for so long."

Rafe let the dog out to do his business, then he took care of Gracie. As he groomed her, he went over the events of the evening minute by minute. Nasty pulses of white-hot rage flared when he thought of the surprise appearance of Delores's killer and how Rafe let him get away. When he leapt from the bushes and tackled him, it all happened so fast. He acted on instinct, not rational thought. The man got the upper hand, and he could have been shot. If Rafe had used better judgment, he could have whacked the man's skull with a branch and knocked him unconscious, or maybe even shot him in the knee, messed him up for life, and left him bleeding for the cops to deal with.

Rafe had been lucky. The man hit him in the temple pretty hard. A little harder and that kind of blow could have damaged his brain or his inner ear, but all he had was a little swelling, and it hurt when he pushed on it or opened his jaw widely.

He cranked open a can of beans with his camp knife and swallowed the beans straight out of the can, then he cleaned up and crawled into his sleeping bag. After a long while he felt himself drifting into sleep, then sliding into the canyon of doom where vivid memories of Delores lived. He slipped in and out of a kind of cruel half-consciousness as the memories replayed relentlessly. The sound of her voice disturbed him, woke him up as though she was leaning over him, speaking in his ear. He opened his eyes, half expecting to see her seated in one of the camp chairs by the stove. They had spent several evenings holed up here, talking about their lives, their hands warmed by mugs of hot chocolate.

He recalled the first time he laid eyes on her at an AA meeting at the church six months ago. He attended the meetings often, not because he was a recovering addict, but because he related to people who had been dealt a bad hand in life. He understood their suffering and their determination to find meaning in their lives, for he was on the same desperate quest.

That night, thirty people sat in rows in a room that was empty except for folding chairs and tables pushed against the wall to hold refreshments. Delores, pale and thin, in a faded dress with faded blonde hair, gave a brutally honest testimonial about her twenty year struggle with alcohol. In a trembling voice, she spoke of how it destroyed her marriage, her attempts to hold down a job, to keep a roof over her head. Now at thirty-five, her only possessions were an old car and a tent. She lived in a homeless camp in the woods with no running water or electricity. That tent and car meant everything to her. They provided shelter and transportation. They enabled her to be part of a community and to come to these meetings. They were her lifeline. She had been sober for a very difficult six months. Without the numbing effects of alcohol, she felt raw, as though her skin had been sheared off and her nerves were exposed. Life without self-medicating was all ragged edges and tilting planes. She was navigating blind, without a manual or guidebook to give her direction. She resisted one day at a time the lure of the devil, the threat of being pitched back into a nauseous, soul-scorching hell.

As she spoke, her eyes sometimes opened wide, taking measure and calibrating the response of the people watching her, and sometimes her eyes blinked or squinted as the enormity of her emotions were reflected back to her, mirrored on their faces.

The pain in her voice haunted him. Rafe was drawn to her, to the jagged beauty of her face, worn and aged well beyond her years. He was drawn to her courage to stand before strangers and bare her soul. He got it. A battle raged inside Delores. Every day, she fought for sobriety with every fiber of her being.

After the meeting, Rafe sought her out and invited her to come to the church for free meals and to meet the boys. She blushed with pleasure. "Yes, I would really like to meet the boys. Warm meals sound really inviting, too." Later, after they became friends, she told him she had been overwhelmed that a handsome, clean-cut young man thought she was fit to be around children. As a homeless person on the streets, when women with kids spotted her, they carved a wide berth around her, or crossed to the other side.

Delores came to the church the next day, and every day thereafter. The boys took to her like abandoned puppies to a stray bitch. When Delores was with the boys, whose psychic wounds were on full display, life became softer, gentler. They became shock absorbers for each other.

Laying in his sleeping bag, Rafe realized he was smiling, remembering the good times that followed. Delores accompanied the boys to Sunday services and to all the funerals. She tutored the younger boys in reading. She helped to roast and package insects, and even ate some. She told Joey they were delicious. Delores became an intrinsic part of their lives, Rafe's life—always ready to say yes to whatever they asked of her.

She routinely drove Rafe to town to pick up supplies for Pastor John. During these short stints of private time in her car, with the world at bay, they shared deeply their layers of anxiety, their challenges, their small accomplishments, their goals for the future. They grew closer and came to feel protective of each other. He placed a hand on her shoulder to guide her through crowds on the sidewalk, and she touched his arm or hand with affection when he shared something heartfelt. She was the only person he ever invited to the bunker.

He recalled her dear face, etched by the calamities of her life, and her perfect smile, afforded by dentures after she lost her teeth to malnutrition. Delores was a woman, but she was also childlike. Rafe had taken care of his father, who was a dysfunctional drunk, until he went to prison. It was familiar to him to swap roles with his dad, moving seamlessly between child and adult, and he and Delores naturally fell into that same pattern.

The last night that she came to the bunker they sat in the camp chairs, warmed by the stove, and she looked comfortable and relaxed. He had been wanting to ask her a question but had waited for the right time, and that seemed to be it. "Why did you start drinking at fifteen?"

It was a difficult question to answer, and he saw the quiver of her pulse in a vein on her forehead. One thing he could rely on from Delores was frank talk. She didn't mince words or spin them to make herself look better. "I was sexually assaulted by my stepdad. I got pregnant," she answered without hesitation. Her voice was a monotone as though she was trying to recite the words without feeling emotion. "When mom found out, she blamed me. Long story short, mom chose the abuser, and I was banished from the house. I was sent to live with my Aunt Freida in Spokane. After I gave birth to a beautiful, healthy baby girl, they took her away in the delivery room and I never saw her again. They didn't let me say goodbye. I couldn't touch her or hold her. I couldn't give her a name." Her green eyes pierced his and seemed to look into his soul. "From that day on, Rafe, I chose to be a victim. I could only see the savageness beneath the veneer of society. The cruelty. I started drinking on the sly, and it increased over the years. Inebriation stunted me. I didn't evolve or develop properly into an adult. I don't remember much of my life. It's just an alcoholic haze." She swallowed. "I have a lot of growing to do."

Listening to her was a shock to Rafe's gut. "What happened with your mom?"

"Nothing. She stayed with the pedophile. She came to visit me once a year on my birthday. When I turned eighteen, I married a guy from high school, just to get away. Really, so I could drink as much as I wanted, in peace. Surprisingly, Lance stuck it out with me for ten years." She shook her head. "Poor Lance. He deserved so much more." She studied Rafe for a long moment and her brow creased into deep furrows. "My story hurt you."

He nodded.

"Don't let it. I wasted too many years drowning in self-pity, focused on the bad side of life. But I've come to see there's just as much good. Despite the hardships in your life, Rafe, you turned out to be a good man. Despite your dad being a drunk, you have character. Kindness. Generosity. Don't lose that. Now you have a new beginning. A new family. Pastor John. The boys. Me. We love you and appreciate you."

She reached out a hand and caressed his face. He put his hand over hers and held it there for several long moments. It felt wonderful to be touched by someone with genuine affection. It was as intimate and tender a gesture as he had ever received from his own mother. What little he remembered of his mom, what stayed with him all these years, was the gentleness of her touch.

"I am grateful, Delores," he confessed with deep emotion. "Especially for you. You're the best friend I've ever had. I feel as comfortable with you as I do with animals. With Buddy and Gracie."

Delores found humor in what he said, and she laughed. It was a beautiful sound.

The corners of Rafe's mouth twitched into a smile, and he blurted, "As awkward as that sounded, it was a compliment."

"I know it was. I'm laughing from happiness. That may be the nicest compliment I've ever gotten."

"Animals live in the here and now. They aren't chasing monsters in their minds. Animals calm me down, and so do you."

"You're the best friend I ever had," she said softly. "You calm me down, too."

Their emotions were raw. Rafe felt immensely vulnerable, but he also felt safe exposing his most deeply hidden feelings to her. Basking in her adoring gaze, a lightness came over him. He felt as if he could float up to the ceiling.

Delores left soon after to go back to her tent community in the woods. That was the last time he saw her alive.

Rafe reached out to the upturned bucket he used as a nightstand and picked up a small cardboard box. Inside was an earring she had dropped in the camp chair. It was all he had left of her. He brought the box to his lips and kissed it, then pressed it close to his heart.

Memories rushed into his mind, and he was transported back to the mortuary the night of Stevana's funeral party. He had become friends with Morticia's assistant, Gordon, from working together at the sanctuary. Two days before the party Gordon informed him, regretfully, that he had been excluded from the guest list. Stevana had told Morticia that she wanted him there as the guest of honor. It was a formal affair, with everyone dressed in cocktail attire. Morticia wanted professional actors only, who could maintain a certain decorum, not the orphans from the church, whom she thought would be disruptive.

It angered Rafe that Morticia was going against Stevana's wishes. She and Gordon lived in a whimsical world, dressed as characters from the "The Addams Family." *Was that decorum?*

Sympathetically, Gordon told Rafe that he would leave the kitchen door unlocked, so he could sneak in for a few minutes.

In defiance of Morticia's tyranny, Rafe dressed as the mysterious masked swordsman known as Zorro, whose true identity was the nobleman, Don Diego de la Vega. The fictional character fought against injustice in favor of people who were poor and disadvantaged. Zorro, in Spanish meant "fox," and Rafe likened himself to that wily creature, infiltrating the party and saying his personal goodbye to Stevana, dressed as the dashing and heroic masked avenger. Stevana would have loved it! If she were looking down on him, she was applauding!

When Gordon spotted Rafe dressed as Zorro, his eyes widened with surprise, and he turned away suppressing a grin, pretending not to see him. Minutes later, Morticia looked shocked when she saw him standing in front of Stevana, raising a glass of champagne in one hand, and a sword in the other. "We will meet again one day in the afterlife, Señora Thornburg," he exclaimed loudly with a Spanish accent. "Tonight I come upon you like a graveyard ghost, and like a ghost I will disappear."

Staying in character as the ethereal Spanish warrior, Rafe proudly swung his cape across his shoulders and marched from the premises, apologetically escorted by Gordon. "Glad you got to say goodbye, Zorro," Gordon said with theatrical gravity and a bow.

Rafe gently tapped Gordon's shoulder with the tip of his sword. "I declare you a brother in arms, Señor Gomez. Your kindness will not be forgotten."

"Stay safe. Buenas noches."

Alone outside, Rafe noticed a suspicious white van parked out on the street. A dark figure stood behind it, smoking and watching the house. Dressed all in black, Rafe easily blended into the shadows. For the next hour, he intently watched the watcher. After everyone left the party, the van quietly drove into the cemetery. Rafe followed on foot, darting from one tombstone to the next.

What he witnessed that night lived and breathed in his being as a horrific nightmare, lying just beneath the surface, no matter where he went, or what he did. Until he avenged Stevana and Delores, his spirit would not rest free.

CHAPTER TWENTY-NINE

AS DAWN CREPT above the tree line, the CSI unit and Sidney and her officers wrapped up their exhaustive forensic work and piled into their respective vehicles. Feeling the fatigue and deep chill from her hours in the woods, Sidney heaved out a weary breath, thankful to be driving away from the place of evil. Amanda rode shotgun, and Darnell sat in the caged back seat. Sometime after midnight, Granger had taken Daggur back to the station to book him and get him settled in the drunk tank. The warm air blowing through the vents was cranked up high—but it still didn't completely diffuse the sour smell Daggur left behind.

Downtown Garnerville looked peaceful in the golden morning light, shops closed, streets empty, the residents just starting to shake themselves awake. Sidney turned into the driveway and parked behind the station. She and her team were dead on their feet and desperately in need of sleep, but first order of business was to check on Daggur and do their reports. Auxiliary officers would already be heading in to man the station and take over their patrols.

***

It was 7:00 a.m. by the time Sidney left the station and got behind the wheel of her SUV. Emotionally and physically wasted, she knew the best therapy was to drive to David's house, crawl into his bed and melt into his arms. But for Dillon's sake they needed to keep their distance for a while, a harsh but necessary separation. Instead, she headed for home to grab a meal and catch a few hours of sleep—if only she could quell the storm spinning through her mind. Scraps of evidence from multiple investigations flitted about like hurricane debris. Nothing was fitting together, and in the meantime, Delores's killer was still out there, a real and dangerous threat to her community.

She turned off Main Street, passed Selena's yoga studio, and drove the short distance to the two-story clapboard home where she was raised. The trees were stripped bare. The vegetable garden and flower beds, lovingly tended by her sister during the growing season, were barren and brown. Nature was in limbo, waiting for winter to come sweeping in.

Feeling tarnished from her exposure to Daggur's depraved world, she pulled into her father's old parking spot and sat for a moment, reflecting. She pictured Chief Clarence Becker sitting behind the wheel of his Crown Victoria cruiser, arriving home from a long days' work. Following his career path, Sidney gained greater appreciation for the difficulties he faced on the job every day. Memories of his fortitude, his calm but forceful manner in times of crisis, his uncompromising integrity, gave her a roadmap to follow, and a source of strength to draw from when she needed it. And, right now, she needed it. She focused on the four principles that guided his life, and now hers—honesty, forgiveness, compassion, and responsibility.

Here's to you, dad. Thanks for giving me a moral compass that always points to true north.

Sidney entered the house through the side door and Selena's four cats ran to greet her with loud meowing. Then they followed her into the dining room. Her sister sat in her chenille bathrobe drinking coffee and reading the morning paper. Her perfectly shaped eyebrows instantly knitted together, and she asked accusingly, "Where were you all night? Granger sent me a text at eight saying you'd be working late. All night is way beyond late. I pictured you lying dead somewhere. And by the way, you look like hell."

"Thanks, I needed to hear that."

"I mean you look exhausted. Your eyes are red and puffy."

"Even better."

"I was worried. You could have called."

"Didn't want to wake you." With Selena on her tail, Sidney made her way to the coffee pot in the kitchen and filled a mug. "I was managing my team, two deputies, and an army of forensic techs out in the cold woods all night. We were a little busy."

Selena's eyes widened. "Holy hell. Another homicide?"

"Multiple homicides. Of dogs. We discovered there's a dog fighting ring hidden in the backwoods. We're just getting started with the investigation."

She heard Selena's sharp intake of breath. "Dog killers? Here? Holy hell!"

"Holy hell is right." She stirred cream and sugar into her coffee and took a sip.

"Wow, you really do have your hands full."

"That's what I've been trying to tell you."

"I bet you haven't eaten." Selena's voice was now conciliatory.

Sidney puffed out a weary breath in answer.

"You must be starving. I'll make you breakfast. Go. Sit."

Sidney obeyed. She put up no defense when her sister's maternal instincts kicked into gear. Sometimes, like now, she just needed to be taken care of. She removed her bulky duty belt and hung it over a chair, then sat at the table and watched Selena move around the sun-drenched kitchen. Purring, Smokey and Chili started rubbing against her legs under the table, which was comforting. Sidney sighed. It was good to be back home where life was normal, and simple acts like this helped rinse away the residue of Daggur's smelly world.

Sidney heard the blender rev up, as loud as a boat motor, then with a bright smile, her sister returned with a tall glass of the "dreaded green smoothie." Each of Selena's concoctions was a new experiment, with the emphasis on health, not flavor. That's where their two worlds diverged. Sidney enjoyed the taste of food, and had a weakness for fast food, which her sister thought was sacrilege. Sidney sometimes poured the experiments down the drain when Selena wasn't looking. "This is what you consider breakfast, after I've been out in the cold all night?" Sidney teased.

"That's just to get something healthy into your system quickly." Selena darted back into the kitchen.

Starving, Sidney sipped the smoothie. *Wow. Delicious.* Selena had hit the mark this time. And, if it had health benefits to boot, all the better. She took a few big gulps and her hunger abated.

Selena re-emerged with a bowl of oatmeal and added some cashew milk. Wary, Sidney studied it. She recognized oats, blueberries, walnuts, bananas. *Good.* Real food. But her sister often snuck in extras that were invisible to the eye—brewer's yeast, strange protein powders, maca root, medicinal mushroom powder …. She tried a spoonful. *Again, surprisingly good.* The day was getting off to a good start.

Selena sat across from her and resumed reading the paper until Sidney was finished, then she said, "I understand if you want to go to bed, but if you want to talk …."

"I'm not ready for bed. My brain is buzzing. I need time to decompress."

"Okay, then tell me about this." Selena's eyes were wide with shock as she pushed the paper across the table. "A homeless woman murdered for her kidneys."

Sidney read the headline, then the article. It pretty much followed the press release she sent to the mayor's office. Short. Bare facts. Still shocking.

Growing up in a law enforcement family, the girls learned early to keep their mouths shut about anything related to an open investigation. Selena could be trusted with sensitive information, but Sidney chose to spare her the more gruesome details. "The article pretty much says it all. I know it's shocking, but people need to take precautions to stay safe. We have a few suspects, but not enough evidence at this point to make an arrest." She pulled up the photo of Delores on her phone. "Ever see her around? Delores Wilkins."

Selena shook her head. "No. Poor woman."

"Yeah, she'll be missed. People at Wellspring Community Church loved her. And she was a surrogate mom to the orphan boys."

"What orphan boys?" Selena asked with a bewildered expression.

"Pastor John took in five troubled boys over the last couple of years. They live in the basement of the church."

"How old are they?"

"Six to sixteen. I met the four youngest ones. Really sweet kids, but hard to place with families due to emotional issues. Cooper, the six-year-old, lost his parents and sister to a house fire."

"Jesus, his whole family? How do you recover from something like that?" Selena looked genuinely stricken. Being no stranger to devastating loss, she had a vast capacity for empathy, especially when it came to mistreated kids and animals. Selena yearned to be a mother, but she missed her chance three years ago. The empty nursery upstairs, beautifully painted and decorated, had waited for the arrival of a baby boy when she was married to her high school sweetheart, Randy. But she miscarried in her fifth month, then Randy left her for another woman. A year of misery and heartache followed, and Sidney suffered right along with her. The nursery door remained shut to this day and the beautiful furnishings sat collecting dust. Sidney took care to avoid triggering those memories. There were some places her sister's mind should never go.

"What exactly did Delores do with the orphan boys?" Selena asked.

Sidney knew she had planted a fertile seed. "Mainly, just spent time with them. Helped them cook bugs. Read them stories."

"What do you mean, cook bugs?"

Sidney told her about their unconventional entrepreneurship, with Joey at the helm.

"Joey's a smart little kid," Selena said, looking impressed. "I completely agree with him. Eating a partial insect diet could definitely help the planet.

I confess, sometimes I use flour made from dried grasshoppers. It's rich in protein and has a pleasant nutty flavor."

"Don't tell me ... you've been feeding it to me?"

"I can neither deny nor confirm." She smiled wickedly.

"Let's keep it that way. On another note, we learned that Stevana Thornburg died from yew tree poisoning."

"She was murdered?"

"Possibly. We don't know if it was intentional suicide, or if someone wanted her dead, and conned her into thinking it was medicinal."

"How was it administered?"

Sidney brought up the photo of the decorative canister found in Stevana's kitchen. "This can of dried needles came by mail. Stevana instructed her caregiver to make her a cup of this "tea" every night. She was dead in two weeks."

Selena frowned at the photo. She and her business partner, Ann, produced and sold organic products, and they were experts on every category of plants and herbs. "It says Winter Mix on the can, which could mean anything. No one should sell it as tea. Yew needles are extremely toxic to people and animals. It can cause heart blockage and respiratory failure."

"That was her cause of death," Sidney said. "Do you have any idea where it may have come from?"

She shrugged. "Depends on what kind it is."

"Taxus brevifolia."

"The Pacific yew tree. You can buy the trees on the internet for landscaping. It grows in people's yards. It grows in the wild. The needles are fatal, but some medicines, including a well-known cancer drug, are made from its bark. But to find only the needles dried and nicely packaged like that?" She looked pensive, her finger on her lips, then she met Sidney's gaze. "It could come from anywhere in the country."

"Hmmm. That doesn't help. The source may remain a mystery." Sidney yawned. "One last thing. Have you seen a tall, bearded man driving a white van around town? It may have writing on the side advertising flowers."

"No. Sorry on the van. And there are lots of tall, bearded men walking around these days."

"He's around six feet four."

"In that case, he would definitely stand out. I'll keep my eyes peeled."

Sidney yawned again. Talking to her sister had dislodged the logjam of errant thoughts crowding her mind. "Suddenly I'm brain dead. Time to hit the hay." She pushed herself away from the table.

"You know, Sid, maybe I'll drive by that church tomorrow and meet those orphan boys. I can certainly spare a few hours a week to spend with needy kids."

Sidney studied her sister for a moment, the stoic tilt of her chin, the steady green eyes, the straight posture. She looked so confident, so strong, but a fragile vulnerability lay close to the surface. "That would be great. It would help soften the blow when they learn Delores is dead. Funny thing, Selena. Arthur seems to have taken an unusual liking to Joey."

Selena arched an eyebrow. "Arthur, the raven?"

"Yeah. Arthur chased away some asshole teenager who was bullying him, two days in a row."

"Bullying a smaller kid? I hope Arthur pooped in his hair."

"Me, too." Sidney chuckled. "Now Joey thinks Arthur is his spirit guide. He carries around one of his feathers."

"That's so sweet. Sounds like they have some kind of mystical connection. I should take him over to Ann's house sometime. Let him meet the woman who taught Arthur to speak."

"He would love that. Call ahead. They might go to the animal sanctuary directly from school," she said over her shoulder as she left the room, "See if they know where Rafe is. He's the oldest boy. He's disappeared and we really need to talk to him. Be discreet."

"Got it. Discretion. Sleep tight."

Sidney headed upstairs with a smile on her lips. If anyone could relate to the trauma the orphan boys had suffered, it was Selena. They would welcome her gentle spirit, and it would be the perfect outlet for putting her maternal instinct to good use.

CHAPTER THIRTY

IT WAS 2:00 by the time Sidney roused herself from sleep, fortified herself with caffeine, and drove to the station. Her officers had been instructed to report to duty at this time, and she saw that their vehicles were already in the lot. She entered through the back door and paused in the doorway of the bullpen. Darnell and Amanda sat at their desks hunched over their computers. Granger's chair was vacant, but his computer was on, as though he had just been interrupted and stepped away.

"Hey, Chief," they both said, looking alert despite their lack of sleep.

"How's our suspect doing?" she asked.

"Granger's dealing with him," Darnell said. "Winnie said she got him lunch a while ago but he's too hungover to eat."

"I'll go take a look. Darnell, make sure the video and audio are ready to go in the interview room."

"Copy that."

"Brace yourself," Amanda said, handing her Daggur's file folder. "He's a hot mess."

"Thanks. I've been warned."

The station had two holding cells and a drunk tank which housed suspects until they were transported to Jackson. The Jackson station had six cells, a police force twice the size of her department, a courthouse, four criminal attorneys, and two public defenders. Her department utilized Jackson's legal apparatus when needed, and the system bumped along with relative efficiency.

The drunk tank had tiled walls and a cement floor with a drain in the middle designed to wash away piss and vomit, which is exactly what Granger was doing. He tossed a bucket of sudsy water across the floor, and it ran down the drain. No more puke, but the smell was far from pleasant. Daggur lay on his back on the tiled bench, mouth gaping, his gurgling snores rumbling off the walls.

Granger spotted her through the bars and grinned. "Hey, Chief. You're lucky you weren't here five minutes ago. I could go into graphic detail."

"Not necessary." She smiled back, appreciating a man who could grin through unpleasant work demands. Mucking manure all his life on the family ranch, sleeping in trenches as a Marine in the Middle East, certainly prepared him for the full spectrum of police work. "Let's see if we can get Brad Pitt over there on his feet and into the interview room," she said, entering the cell.

"Hey gorgeous, time to face reality," Granger said, shaking Daggur's shoulder. The snoring abruptly stopped, and his eyes fluttered open. Granger pulled him into a sitting position, then he and Sidney each grabbed an arm and elevated him to his feet.

A few spots of puke were on his shirt and drool ran down his chin. Sidney thought of his girlfriend, Mindy, who woke up next to this for the better part of a year. Worse than a prison sentence.

"Where the hell am I?" he blubbered, wobbling.

"Four-star hotel," Granger said. "Your massage therapist is waiting in the spa."

"Fucking cops," Daggur muttered under his breath, getting a good look at him and Sidney. He stumbled between them like a sleepwalker into the interview room and slumped heavily into a metal chair. Beneath the hard glare of the fluorescent lights, cuffed hands in his lap, he blinked at his surroundings.

"Video's a go," Darnell said, popping his head into the room momentarily. Beyond the two-way mirror on one wall was a room barely larger than a broom closet that featured controls for the video and audio. They glanced up at the camera mounted in one corner of the ceiling, then scraped back chairs and took seats across from Daggur. Granger clicked his pen and opened his spiral notepad.

"Why the fuck am I here?" Dagger asked.

"Do you remember anything about last night, Daggur?" Sidney asked.

He stared at her, his eyes blank and heavy-lidded. He looked ready to pass out again. "No."

"I made coffee, Chief. I'll get him a cup," Granger volunteered.

"Better bring him a quart. Hope it's strong."

"A spoon can stand in it." He left, reappeared, and parked a sixteen-ounce disposable cup in front of Daggur.

"Drink. It's free," Sidney said.

Daggur picked up the cup and took a big gulp. Then another. When the cup sat empty, he shuddered to life. "Why the hell am I in this fucking jail?"

"You're in serious trouble," Sidney said. "We had a warrant to search your house and property last night. You refused to come out of your bedroom."

His face hardened and hostility glinted in his bloodshot eyes. "I was drunk. In my own house. So what?"

"You threatened to shoot us if we opened the bedroom door. Threatening police officers and impeding an investigation is a felony."

His eyes widened as though he suddenly remembered, and he recognized her. "That's all hazy. I was drunk off my ass. I'm not responsible for my actions."

"Actually, you are." Sidney had recited his Miranda Rights last night, but to have it on record on the video, she refreshed his memory. "In case you don't remember, Daggur, you have the right to remain silent. Anything you say can and will be used against you in a court of law. You have the right to an attorney. If you cannot afford an attorney, one will be provided for you. Do you understand what I just told you?"

"Yeah, I know the riff." His lips twisted into a snarl. "You know damn well this ain't the first time I've been arrested. I remember telling you last night that I won't say shit without a lawyer. I ain't confessing to nothing."

"That's your prerogative. We don't need your confession. We have enough evidence against you to put a half dozen men away."

A look of fear tightened his face for a split second and then was gone. "What am I being charged with?"

She opened his folder and looked at the file. "Hmmm. Where should I begin? Let's start with domestic violence for assaulting Mindy. Then there's your firearm possession. As a felon, you're prohibited from owning a firearm, but we found your Glock 19. We also found your stash of illegal opioids and stacks of hundred-dollar bills." She lifted her head and met his gaze.

"Where does a man living on unemployment checks get that kind of cash?" Granger asked.

Daggur just glared. He licked his dry lips. "Those drugs and money ain't mine."

"We have a witness who will testify that you've been selling drugs," Sidney continued. "If that wasn't enough, we discovered your little side business—the dog fighting pit out behind the creek. Dog fighting is one of the most serious forms of animal abuse, Daggur. Not just for the violence the dogs endure during and after fights, but because they often suffer their entire lives, if they even survive the fight. Don't tell me again that the dead dog in your shed got hit by a car. We found her body in a gully. You couldn't even be bothered to bury her." Sidney paused to let Daggur process everything she told him. Feeling disgust for the despicable man sitting across from her, she watched for any small sign of guilt, repentance, or empathy for the dogs. *None.*

But full understanding of the seriousness of his situation sank in. The hostility seeped out of him, and his defiant expression softened like putty.

"That adds several more counts of felony to the list," Sidney said. "Not to mention you took your brother, a minor, to the fights. Another felony. Quite an impressive list, wouldn't you say, Granger?"

"Very impressive. Should rack up some pretty good time."

Daggur's eyes darted from Sidney to Granger, assessing their mood. Neither looked the least bit sympathetic.

"So, you see where this is going. You're in a heap of trouble, Daggur," Sidney said. "You don't have to talk to us. But I'm going to give you an opportunity to help yourself. Cooperate. Help us with our investigations, and we'll talk to the prosecutor on your behalf. We'll ask him to go easier on you."

"You mean like being an informant? Some of these charges might be dropped?"

"Possibly. Depends on how much you help us."

He licked his lips again. "What do you want to know?"

Sidney wanted to bust the dogfighting ring wide open. Apprehend as many of the heartless bastards as possible. But before she approached that topic, she needed something else; something pressing that was putting her community at immediate risk. Last night, when Daggur looked at the photo of Delores, she saw recognition in his eyes, though he denied knowing her. She again brought up the photo of Delores on her phone and held it out to him. "Tell me what you know about this woman's murder."

He stared at the phone long and hard, and then swallowed. "I had nothing to do with that. I don't go in for killing people."

No, you just beat your girlfriend and kill dogs. "But you know who does."

He sucked in a ragged breath, blew it out. "I don't know who does the actual killing, but I know someone involved with them."

"What's his name?"

"You swear this won't come back to me? I don't want to be the next guy whose insides are carved out."

Sidney had said nothing about Delores's organs being removed, but Daggur knew. He was complicit at some level in her murder. "Help us put him away, Daggur. He won't be able to hurt anyone again."

He huffed out another ragged breath. "The man you're looking for is Taron Seminov. He's the middleman. He delivers the people to the professionals."

"Who are these professionals?"

"All I know is one's a doctor."

"Got a name?"

"Nope."

"To be perfectly clear, what exactly does that mean, Taron delivers the people?"

Daggur stared at the ceiling, then at the table, stalling.

Granger had been scribbling in his pad, but he paused, waiting for Daggur to continue.

"Daggur ... ?" Sidney said.

"You know," he said. "The organ donors."

"Where does he find these organ donors?"

"Well, they don't just show up and knock on his door, do they?"

"This is no time to be a smartass, Daggur," Sidney said sternly. "Where does he find them?"

"You'll have to ask Taron. I ain't his fucking agent." He met Sidney's eyes, and they had a staring contest, and finally, he muttered, "He snatches them, my guess, when no one else is around."

"He snatches people off the street?"

"Yeah, that's my guess."

"How do we find Taron?"

"Beats me. He comes to the fights, that's all I know. He buys drugs, gambles, you name it. He's a man of all trades." He smiled, as though he'd said something funny. Catching Sidney's hard expression, his smile vanished.

"Describe him."

Daggur cleared his throat. "Tall son of a bitch. Trimmed brown beard. Longish brown hair. Dresses all in black. That's his style. Thinks he's Al Pacino in "Scarface" or something."

"What does he drive?"

"A white van."

"Anything you can tell us about the van?"

"It's a Ford Transit. Newish. No windows."

Bingo! Sidney felt a spurt of adrenaline. Finally, she was making some headway in her homicide case. Her eyes locked momentarily on Granger's. He gave a slight nod. Taron and his vehicle matched the descriptions given by all their witnesses. Once they had Taron in custody, they were one step closer to catching the doctor who killed Delores. "How many of these "snatchings" do you know about?"

He looked at her for a long moment, as though wondering if she could really be that ignorant. "For a cop, you don't know too much, do you? There's a hell of a lot of shit going on in this county. Most of it's in the backwoods. Guess they're doing a good job of hiding it away."

"How many snatchings?"

He shrugged. "Don't know for sure. I hear things. Maybe he snatched a couple other people besides the woman on your phone."

Sidney studied Daggur closely. How reliable was he? Was there any merit to anything the man said? She didn't trust him for a minute.

"To do business in the backwoods, we all abide by a code of honor. What you might call a gentleman's agreement," Daggur continued, his tone jovial. "I don't piss in your yard, you don't piss in mine."

Sidney kept from showing her disgust. There was no honor in what these savage criminals were doing. But Daggur was on a roll. She wanted to keep him talking. "So you've known about people being snatched. Why didn't you inform law enforcement?"

Again, he looked at her like she was either incredibly naive, or woefully ignorant. "I ain't no snitch, lady. I value my life too much. You know what happens to snitches?" His face suddenly took on a feral, primitive quality. "They're skinned alive." For effect, he enunciated every word very carefully. "Slowly. Inch by bloody inch. Then they're buried where no one will ever find them."

His words were chilling. They hung in the air like daggers. Sidney found the suspect repellent and as cold-blooded as a reptile, but she kept her tone calm and professional. "Do you know this to be a fact, or is it folklore to keep people in line?"

"I've heard things from a reliable source." His eyes looked a little crazy. "He saw what was left of a snitch."

"Do you have any proof, any scrap of evidence, that your source was telling the truth?"

His lips twisted into a smirk. "Look, I wanna help you people. I really do. But you're putting me in a tough spot here. Taron finds out I ratted him out, I'm a dead man." He paused, glancing from her to Granger and back. "And you cops ain't immune, either. I'm forewarning you, right now. There's folks that ain't gonna like cops sticking their noses into their business. They won't hesitate to put out a warning you won't forget."

"What kind of warning?"

"I dunno. Maybe you'll find one of your officers strung up from a tree.

Missing some organs."

If Daggur was trying to frighten Sidney, he wasn't succeeding. Everything he told her so far was hearsay. She glanced at Granger. His jaw was clenching and unclenching. He wasn't amused by Daggur's threats. These folks who lived by their own savage rules in the backwoods had been operating with impunity for too long. Their sickness was seeping into her community, and it needed to be stamped out before it spread any further. She was going to make it her mission to do just that.

"Taron can't hurt you if he's in a maximum-security prison," Sidney said. "You can help make that happen by testifying against him. You have any evidence that he committed these crimes?"

He shrugged. "I know some things."

"We're listening."

"I hear he's the one that gets rid of the bodies after the work is done."

Again, hearsay. "You have names for any of these victims?"

"Naw. But my source does. You know why they get away with it? Because they're smart. They take the people nobody cares about. Drunks, addicts, lowlifes. The trash of society. People who are gonna die in their own vomit in some back alley, anyway. None of them are ever missed. At least parts of their bodies are put to good use before they croak."

The man's callousness gave Sidney a cold feeling in the pit of her stomach. Delores wasn't a lowlife. Her murder had grievous repercussions throughout the community. She had cleaned up her life, found new meaning in the service of others, and had been a surrogate mom to the orphan boys. But victim-blaming worked for perpetrators. Thinking of them as less than human made it easier to commit violent crimes against them.

Sidney locked eyes with Granger. His neck was flushed red, and the color was crawling up into his cheeks. He had an angry head of steam building up. "Granger, why don't you get Daggur another cup of coffee?"

"You want anything, Chief?" he asked, his voice tight.

"Sure. A bottle of water."

Granger left and returned shortly, looking more composed. He placed the coffee and water on the table and took his seat. Daggur lifted his cup and gulped, wiped his mouth with the back of his hand.

Sidney took a sip of water from her bottle and resumed the interview. "We really appreciate all your help, Daggur."

"You help me, I help you," he said.

"What I need from you now is a list of the people who show up at these dog fights." She slid a pad of paper and a pen across the table.

"I can do you one better, Chief. There's a fight this week. A big one. The champion dogs will be there. Taron will be there. One of the dogs competing is his."

"Competing? You mean fighting for their lives," Granger said tersely.

Daggur gave him a look that said fuck off.

"Where and when?" Sidney asked.

"Friday night."

That was three nights from now. Sidney would have to act fast to round up officers from other departments to do a raid. "Where?"

Defiance crept back into Daggur's face. "Not so fast. I'm giving you the grand prize. A couple dozen people will be at the fight. All you have to do is round them up. I'll keep my end of the bargain. You keep yours. In return, I want a guarantee that some of my charges will go away. In writing. Between lawyers. I want to do my time somewhere far away from Taron."

"Sure. Something can be arranged."

"Just one more thing. By now, people will know I got busted. The first thing they'll do is move the location of the fight, just for insurance. But there's someone who'll know the new location. Jacko."

"Why would he know?"

"He gets around. Hears things."

"Where can we find your brother? He's a minor without a guardian. We need to make sure he's taken care of."

"Yeah, I know what you mean by taking care of him. You think he wants to be put in juvie? That's why he's hiding out. He told me he hit a kid with a shovel at the animal shelter. But it was self-defense. The kid hit him first. I want a deal for Jacko, too."

Jacko could have killed Dillon. It was more than self-defense and he deserved time in juvenile detention, or at least anger management classes. But what Daggur offered was indeed the grand prize: rounding up a couple dozen criminals, including Taron. "Let's bring Jacko in. We'll see what we can work out."

"You got it backwards, Chief. Deal first. Then I tell you where he is."

Sidney weighed her options. They'd play this his way. "Here's what we're going to do, Daggur. You're going to be transported and held at the county jail. I'll meet with the prosecutor today. Tomorrow morning, you'll be arraigned and appointed a lawyer. Then you, your lawyer, the prosecutor, and I will sit down and hash out a deal and sign the documents."

Daggur gave her a shifty grin. "We got a deal."

One last thing. I want a description of Taron.

"He's tall, about six-three. Dark hair and close-cropped beard. Thin, but all muscle. Has a tattoo of a rattle snake that wraps around his neck. Its tail and head are in the front, fangs bared."

Pretty descriptive, Sidney thought. Wouldn't be hard to stand out in a crowd.

CHAPTER THIRTY-ONE

THE NEXT MORNING, Sidney met with Daggur, his public defender, and the prosecutor in an interrogation room at the county jail, and after heated negotiations, some of his lesser charges were dropped in exchange for his cooperation. In addition, his younger brother, who was in hiding, would provide them with critical information regarding the dog fight. After the specifics were agreed upon and the documents were signed, Daggur made a phone call to Jacko. The teen cooperated fully, stating the time and new location of the dog fighting event, and he named three of the bad actors who would be attending; two of which had impressive rap sheets and were known felons on probation. Taron Seminov was the third, but he was not in the system, and was probably operating under a false ID.

When questioned about how many participants were normally armed, Jacko stated that perhaps a third of the men packed handguns. Normally, emotions could run high at a gathering, but thus far, no one had ever been shot. Generally, two armed heavies kept things under control, collecting an entry fee of $100 per person and standing guard on the outside of the ring for the duration of the event.

Sidney was relieved. That meant about eight men would be armed with handguns. Not great, but it could have been much worse.

The teen agreed to turn himself in on the morning after the raid. That would keep him from being suspected of informing, but he'd still need to meet with the prosecutor and his own attorney to work out a deal for himself; possibly not being charged with a crime if he agreed to testify.

Sidney returned to the Garnerville station and immediately called Captain Jack Harrison at the sheriff's department.

"What's up, Chief?" Harrison asked, skipping a greeting, and getting straight to business. A call from Sidney usually meant an emergency.

She quickly explained the urgency of the situation; a couple dozen dangerous men, some armed, would be holed up in the backwoods for a dog fight Friday night.

"That sounds like a powder keg waiting to blow," he said, somewhat alarmed. "A shootout is a very real possibility. We need to act fast. Friday is just two nights away."

She exhaled sharply. "We're talking a major logistical operation. Lots of moving parts, SWAT teams, deputies, and officers from several departments. We could defuse it before it gets out of hand with very detailed planning and sufficient manpower."

"What's the location?"

"McCalahan's old goat farm," she said.

"That property's been deserted for decades. Last time I was out there, it was really run down, and the forest was closing in on it. The house was boarded up and practically caving in on itself. The barn was still standing, though. No doubt that's where they'll be gathered."

"We need eyes on the ground ASAP. I'll send two of my officers out there this afternoon to scout the area. They'll map out all the roads leading in and out of the place. Every possible means of escape."

"I'll have a deputy accompany them with a drone," he said. "Take aerial photos."

"That'd be great. Once we have that intelligence in hand, we can plan tactical maneuvers."

"I'll round up all the troops and we'll meet here in our conference room. I'll have the aerial photos enlarged and a topographical map ready. Noon tomorrow?"

"Yes, sir. See you then."

Thursday

Thirty law enforcement personnel, including Sidney's three officers, sat in rows of seats in the conference room facing Sidney and Captain Harrison. Harrison was a tall, lanky man with thinning gray hair and a weathered face. Today, he wore a grave expression, which matched Sidney's mood exactly. A topographical map and enlarged aerial shots of the farm were pinned to the boards behind them.

Harrison nodded to her, and with an efficient stride and cool demeanor, she stepped forward and started the meeting, explaining the extremely dangerous situation facing them and highlighting spots on the photos with her laser pointer. "The farm's been unoccupied for decades and is in bad repair. But the barn is still in good enough shape to house the event. As you can see, this location is isolated, which makes it perfect for concealing illicit activity, but it's also a detriment for the perps. Basically, there's only one way in, and one way out—an overgrown dirt road. The surrounding fields are fenced and have gone back to nature, limiting the ability of vehicles to escape. Also, its remoteness, and the fact that they've been operating for months in secrecy, will give them a false sense of complacency. There could be a couple dozen people in attendance. Most likely they'll be parked here in this clearing in front of the barn. There are two ways to enter the barn, a front and back door, each of which will no doubt be guarded by an armed lookout. Inside, possibly a half dozen people will be packing handguns.

The night of the raid, officers will arrive en mass with many vehicles. You'll park at least a quarter mile away to avoid being heard, and you'll position your vehicles to block the single road. My three officers will already be in place scoping out where the guards are, any visible means of communication, and what type of weapons they have. They'll establish and hold an eyes-on position through the point of the raid to supply immediate intel. The rest of you will quietly surround the barn, trapping the men inside. SWAT will take the lead, creeping up and taking down the two lookouts. All other officers will follow once SWAT gives the go ahead."

In a serious tone, Captain Harrison added, "Some of these men are heavy hitters. I don't need to tell you to take this mission very, very seriously. Our objective is to take control of the inner circle without bloodshed. An ambulance and firemen will be on standby, along with a skilled animal control team to deal with the dogs."

As he spoke, Sidney scanned the earnest faces of the uniformed men and women sitting before her; officers who devoted their lives to the service of their communities, who put their own lives in harm's way every day. The weight of responsibility for their safety pressed against her chest. She and Harrison had planned this mission carefully, paying attention to minute details, imagining and preparing for every possible scenario. But in every mission, there were unknowns. She hid her concerns beneath a calm exterior. Being Chief of Police required her to be a source of stability for others to draw strength from. She had to trust that everyone would do their part, and, if violence erupted, training would kick in and the threat would be quickly neutralized. She wanted everyone involved to go home to their families at the end of the operation.

CHAPTER THIRTY-TWO

AT 4:00 P.M., Selena pulled her Jeep into the parking lot at the sanctuary, slipped her backpack over one shoulder, and walked to the entrance of the barn. The grounds were more beautiful than she expected, quiet and peaceful, shaded by fir trees and parceled into fenced pens and corrals. The manager's cottage sat across the clearing from the barn, and the mirrored surface of a pond reflected white clouds and blue sky. Two old dogs, sprawled on their sides soaking up sun, eyed her with little interest. Two smaller dogs, one assisted with a little doggie wheelchair, trotted out to greet her.

"Hey little doggies." She stooped to pet them as a golf cart pulled up next to her, driven by Mr. Hiroko. He was dressed like a cowboy and wore a dusty Stetson hat. A bale of hay was stuffed into the back.

"Hey Mr. Hiroko, do you remember me? I'm Selena."

"Sure do." He pushed up the brim of his hat with the stump of his forearm. "We've met at your stall at the farmer's market a few times. Last time, I bought your jalapeño honey. It's got quite a kick. Good on chicken. So, what can I help you with?"

"Pastor John told me he dropped Joey and Cooper off here after school. I wanted to meet them. I told him I'd drive them back for dinner."

"So, you haven't met them before?"

"No."

"Let me give you a lift. They'll trust you more if they see me drop you off. They're out mucking the pasture. Should be finishing up about now. It's just behind the pond on the right."

"Thanks. I appreciate it." When they reached the pasture, she saw the two boys pitching the last of the cow patties into a wheelbarrow. A donkey was grazing nearby. Then the smaller boy carried the shovels while the other pushed the wheelbarrow toward the gate. He seemed to be struggling with the weight of it. They gazed over at the golf cart and waved. Selena got out and Mr. Hiroko drove away. She smiled at them as she opened the gate, let them pass through, then latched it behind them. They were cute kids, both sporting shaggy heads of hair. "You must be Joey and Cooper."

The older boy returned her smile. "I'm Joey, and he's Cooper."

The younger boy presented her with a solemn gaze. "Who are you?"

"I'm Selena. Pastor John told me you'd be out here. I told him I'd give you a ride back to the church when you're done. I've been looking forward to meeting you."

"Why'd you want to meet us?" Cooper asked, blocking the sun with his hand.

"Because I've heard amazing things about you. You taught yourself to play piano, Cooper. And you, Joey, make delicious recipes using insects. And you sell them at the produce stand. And you both volunteer here, helping animals."

"We like animals."

She looked down at the wheelbarrow. It was full. "Wow, that's a lot of manure for one little donkey."

"Gracie was here, too. She's a big horse. But Rafe took her."

"I've heard about Rafe. He looks out for you. Like a big brother, right?"

"Yeah."

"I'd like to meet him. Do you know where he is?"

Both boys glanced at each other, and their expressions tightened. Then Joey's face went blank. They knew something and were trying to hide it. Joey shrugged. Cooper shook his head.

Sidney had asked her to question them cautiously about the older boy. She realized very quickly that they weren't going to open up about him to a stranger. "Let me take that wheelbarrow for you. It looks heavy."

"Thanks. We dump it over there in the manure pile." Joey pointed to a clearing behind the pasture. "Farmers come and get it to fertilize their fields."

After the manure was dumped, they started walking back. "I heard a raven befriended you," Selena said.

"Yeah, he's my spirit guide." Joey brushed his hair back from his forehead and grinned. "He protects me."

"Is he here today?"

"I haven't seen him yet. If he is, he'll be with Jezebel. She's an injured raven. He visits her all the time."

"He's her boyfriend," Cooper said earnestly.

"Is that right? Arthur has a girlfriend? Well, I'll be darned. Let's go see if he's here."

As they approached Jezebel's cage, a shadow passed over their heads.

Arthur croaked loudly and soared above them, then he came in for a soft landing on Selena's shoulder. He tilted his silky black head and his onyx eyes fixed on Joey. He released a loud, excited croak.

Joey's eyes were wide. Cooper's mouth fell open.

"Evermore," Arthur said, tucking in his wings.

"Wow. Is Arthur your spirit guide, too?" Joey asked.

"I don't think he's my spirit guide, but we're old friends." A smile tugged up one corner of her mouth. "Arthur looks out for lots of people, especially young boys." She reached into a pocket and brought out a piece of walnut. As the raven ate it, deep, hollow croaks drew their attention to Jezebel, who was doing a frenzied dance on a branch in her cage. Demanding attention!

Arthur cackled at her like an old lady.

Selena and the boys laughed.

Arthur took another walnut from Selena, flew over to Jezebel's cage and dropped it down to her.

"How come you know Arthur?" Joey asked.

"My business partner, Ann Howard, taught him to speak."

"Wow. Really?"

"Yes. Really."

"What kind of business do you have?"

"Mostly, we grow flowers and herbs. And we have lots of beehives. We use the flowers and herbs to make scented candles from the beeswax. And we make flavored honey and vinegar. Arthur has been visiting Ann's farm for years."

"Wow, her farm must be special," Joey said.

"It's very special. A little piece of paradise right on the lakeshore. I was thinking of inviting you boys over sometime for lunch. We could also go out on the lake in her boat."

"We'd love that," Cooper said.

"Before I forget, I brought you a special treat." Selena opened the backpack, pulled out something wrapped in foil, and unwrapped it.

"Chocolate chip cookies!"

"They aren't just any chocolate chip cookies. They're made with special flour. Want to guess what it is?"

"It's made from bugs!" Cooper said.

She nodded, smiling into his blue eyes. "You are a very smart boy. Cricket flour. Go ahead, try one."

They did.

"So good," Joey said after swallowing a bite.

"The best cookie I ever ate," Cooper said.

"Would you like to learn how to bake them?" Selena asked.

They nodded, grinning, mouths full.

"We'll make them at Ann's farm. Do you want to come over next weekend?"

They nodded with enthusiasm.

"Can Foley and Garret and Rafe come, too?" Cooper asked.

"Yes. All of you are welcome. Of course, Rafe can't be invited unless we can find him. Do you know where he is?" she asked gently.

Cooper's grin vanished and he looked at the ground, shifting from one foot to the other. He met her gaze, frowning. "Yeah, I know where he is. But it's a secret."

Joey's face remained immobile, no hint of emotion. Then his expression softened. He shoved his hands deep into his jacket pockets. "If we tell you, you have to promise not to tell anyone else."

A feeling of tenderness warmed Selena. They were sweet boys, part of a tight-knit group that protected one another from the dangers of the outside world. Now they wanted to include her, they wanted to trust her. There was no way she would betray their trust. "Hmm. I'm not sure I can keep it secret. What if there's an emergency and we have to find him? Is it okay if I tell someone if I think he needs help?"

"I don't know …." Joey said.

"Believe me. I don't want to hurt Rafe. But if he's in trouble, I want to help."

Cooper and Joey looked at each other, and some invisible communication passed between them. "Promise you'll keep it secret unless it's an emergency?"

"I promise," she said with a reassuring smile.

"Then I guess it's okay. No one will ever find him anyway." He swallowed and continued in a low, conspiratorial tone. "He's in the bunker."

"What's the bunker?"

Joey shrugged. "Don't know. I just heard him tell Delores one night to meet him there. It's his secret place."

Selena put a gentle hand on his shoulder. "Thanks for sharing that with me."

Cooper leaned over and whispered something in Joey's ear. Then they both looked at her with shy smiles. "Cooper thinks you're pretty. Me, too."

Selena reached out and ruffled the heads of both boys. "I think you two are pretty cute, too."

Impulsively, Joey stepped forward and wrapped his arms around her hips. A little boy hungry for affection from a mother figure. She squatted down and took both of his hands in hers. "Thanks for the nice hug."

A chilly wind touched her cheek and Selena noticed a shift in the weather. Dark shadows had lengthened across the ranch. "It's getting late, boys. I better get you back to the church for dinner."

"Will you eat with us?" Joey asked.

"Sure. I can do that."

CHAPTER THIRTY-THREE

IT WAS 10:00 P.M. and Selena was cleaning up the kitchen after a marathon of cooking and baking. Chicken stew sat on the stove top. A chocolate sour cream Bundt cake crowned with fresh raspberries sat on the counter, and sourdough bread was about to come out of the oven. When she was feeling anxious, and today she was feeling very anxious, she distracted herself by getting creative in the kitchen. Standing on the sidelines while Sidney's department hunted dangerous criminals was nothing less than nerve-racking. Anything remotely resembling normalcy went out the window.

Selena had heard rather than seen her sister in the last twenty-four hours, when Sidney crept in after midnight last night, and she was gone before Selena went downstairs for breakfast. Sidney's whole team was operating on minimal sleep. Selena had not seen Granger in days, and when she talked to him by phone earlier, she heard the edge in his tone, though he tried to hide it. He let it slip that a mission involving several departments was going down tomorrow night, but when she pressed him for details, he made light of it. "More of an exercise than anything else." Clearly, he said that for her benefit, but she wasn't soothed. She called Winnie at the front desk and pretended to be informed about the matter, tricking her into revealing details. *A dog fighting ring! Dangerous criminals! Holy hell!*

As she pulled the bread out of the oven, Selena heard the side door open and close. Moments later Sidney appeared in the kitchen with four cats meowing and twining through her legs. Dressed in her uniform with her hair knotted at the back of her neck, she possessed an aura of authority and toughness, and Selena was momentarily struck by how much she resembled their father. Tall and athletic, she had his strong features, softened by her expressive hazel eyes and full mouth. Though not pretty in a traditional sense, Sidney had an indefinable appeal that attracted men, and more importantly, commanded respect.

"Don't say it," Sidney said. "I know I look like hell." Still in police mode, her tone and manner were commanding.

"Actually, I was thinking you're holding up pretty well, considering."

"Thanks, I think. It smells amazing in here." She scanned the kitchen. "What's that on the stove?"

"Chicken stew."

"Suddenly I realize I'm starving." Sidney tugged the tie from her ponytail and her wavy, auburn hair tumbled around her shoulders. The aura of toughness all but vanished.

"Let me get you a bowl." Selena opened a cupboard.

"A huge bowl, if you're asking. Please and thank you."

"Go sit. I'll bring it to you."

"Not before I eat some of this." She sliced the cake and placed it on a saucer. Then shoved half of it into her mouth as she walked into the dining room.

Minutes later, Selena set down a bowl of stew and a plate of warm bread cut in thick slices. Pats of butter melted on top.

"Did I just die and go to heaven?" Sidney tore off a piece of bread, dipped it into the stew, and stuffed it into her mouth. Then she crammed in a piece of chicken. "Hmmmmmmm."

"My, you are hungry. Slow down, you'll choke." Granger ate the same way. "You cops eat as though every meal is your last."

Sidney didn't pause between bites to comment, but her jaws slowed down a little.

Selena sat and watched her eat, ruminating on the irony of their current circumstances. It was strangely odd and beautiful that she and her sister had become roommates in their childhood home after years of separation. Especially meaningful now, with their dad dead and their mom in a memory care center. She and Sidney had completed a cycle of marriage, boyfriends, and career pivots, and made their way back to each other. Seven years her senior, Sidney had been her protector when she was small, patching scraped knees and warding off bullies. That fierce instinct still burned strong. Two years ago, Sidney saved her from a serial killer who had been stalking her. If she wasn't a highly skilled detective, Selena would be dead. There was no way she could ever repay that debt—but she could certainly make sure Sidney had healthy meals.

When her bowl was empty, Sidney rubbed the muscles in the back of her neck and looked exhausted. "Did you make it over to the church to see the boys?"

"I met Cooper and Joey at the sanctuary today. Then I met the other two boys, Foley and Garret, at the church. We had dinner in the cafeteria. Afterwards, we played cards. Go Fish. It was wonderful. I fell in love with all of them."

Sidney gave her a weary smile. "Good. I'm glad."

Silence stretched between them for a long moment as the unasked question hung in the air. Selena was hesitant to bring up something work-related when her sister was operating on fumes. "Yes, they know where Rafe is."

Sidney sat up straighter in her chair and her expression, miraculously, became alert.

"He's in some old bunker. That's it. That's all they said. And that no one could find it."

"I'll be damned. Rafe is one smart kid. It's true. No one would ever find him if I didn't already know about the bunker. It was used to store ammunition decades ago. Then it was used as a dispatch center. It's been abandoned for years."

"You know where it is?"

"Yeah. Granger pointed it out on a map a couple of years back. He said he used it once when he was out riding and got caught in a lightning storm." Sidney looked at Selena with appreciation. "You just gave me an excellent lead. We've been trying to find this kid. He's central to our investigations. Rafe could answer a lot of questions."

"Happy to do my part." Selena could practically see the puzzle pieces moving around in her sister's head. "Rafe's on horseback, by the way."

"Yeah. Makes sense. Probably no other way to get back in there. I'll get Granger to meet me at the station first thing in the morning with a trailer and a couple of horses. We'll drive up there until we run out of road. Then we'll ride in the rest of the way."

Selena felt a pang of envy that her sister spent so much time with Granger. She and her boyfriend often rode his horses on trails behind his ranch, one of their favorite outings. She wished she could join them tomorrow. "You better hit the sack, Sidney. With the big mission tomorrow night, you need a good night's sleep."

Sidney appraised her sister. "I should've known you'd find out about that. How much do you know?"

"Oh, just that you're going up against a group of armed and dangerous men at a secret location in the woods." Selena tried not to let her anxiety show, but she heard it creep into her tone. "Bastards who exploit and kill dogs."

"I'm sorry you found out about that. A little bit of information is a dangerous thing. This is why I don't tell you about police operations. Better you don't know."

"Too late for that. I'm worried sick."

"Look, we're prepared. We're not going in with guns blazing against a hail of bullets. We'll have the bad guys outnumbered. SWAT will go in first. They're highly trained. We'll follow. Remember, Granger survived a tour of combat duty in Afghanistan. This will be a cinch compared to that."

Selena searched her sister's face for any sign of unease. None. If she was feeling angst, she hid it well. "Okay, I feel better now, knowing you won't be going in first."

"We may not have to fire a shot."

"Hopefully." Selena sighed. "Go to bed. Sleep. I'll clean up."

"Bed. Sleep. Magic words." Sidney pushed herself away from the table and left the room. Chili and Smokey, who slept on her bed most nights, quickly padded after her.

CHAPTER THIRTY-FOUR

AT 8:00 A.M., Rafe dragged himself off his cot after a fitful night of little sleep. He haltered Gracie and led her outside. He followed the contours of the creek to a small clearing where she could get some sun on her back. He'd heard the hard patter of rain early this morning and found everything outside gleaming with moisture. Raindrops hung like crystal beads on every twig and branch. The pungent smell of pine seasoned the air. He dropped a pile of hay at Gracie's feet and went back into the bunker to shovel manure off the concrete floor.

As he worked, his mind drifted. He was getting a little stir-crazy living alone in the bunker, but he needed to make good on his promise to Stevana. He needed to do something useful before returning to his life at the church. It was unexpected and surprising that he and the stern old lady became friends. Four months ago, her stable hand retired. She asked Pastor John if one of the boys could muck out her barn and corral a couple of times a week. Rafe volunteered. She offered to pay minimum wage and he needed the money. Stevana didn't ask him to ride Gracie, but he did so out of his own initiative. The beautiful mare was lonely, and she needed exercise. It was his pleasure.

He saw the old lady's ghost-like face watching from the window, then she came out on the veranda and watched him ride Gracie bareback around the grounds. Stevana waved him over. Expecting a reprimand, he rode up to the porch where she sat in her wheelchair wearing a disapproving expression. "That's a valuable horse you're riding, young man."

"Yes, ma'am. I know it. She's a beauty."

"Where'd you learn to ride like that?"

"My dad worked on a ranch for a while when I was little. Then one of my foster families were ranchers. I picked up where I left off. Riding always came natural to me. Guess horses pick up that I just want to be their friend."

She studied him for a long moment.

He held her gaze.

"There's a good saddle in the tack room. Make sure you use it from now on." With that, she wheeled herself back into the house. From then on, she always watched him from the window. Riding the gorgeous mare was a pleasure, not a task, and Rafe spent extra time every visit to ride and groom her. It was reflected in his paycheck. The old lady wasn't as miserly as folks claimed.

Two weeks went by, then one afternoon Stevana's caretaker came out on the porch. "Mrs. Thornburg wants you to join her for lunch." The tall, broad-shouldered woman looked spooky, grim-faced, and business-like. The house was spookier. Dark, with heavy Victorian furnishings and tapestries.

But the room full of cats was sunlit and cheerful. Stevana sat with two kittens on her lap, watching the other cats frolic and scamper in and out of the cat condos. The old lady was pale with skin like wrinkled paper, and he could see blue veins beneath her skin. Her white hair was pulled into a braid that hung over one shoulder.

"Hello, Mrs. Thornburg."

"Ah, there you are."

A Siamese bounded over to him, and he gathered it in his arms and scratched its head affectionately. "Pretty kitty."

Stevana watched him intently. When he met her gaze, she surprised him by smiling. "Come wheel me into the kitchen, young man."

"My name is Rafe," he said, friendly, as he took the handles.

"Call me Stevana. Do you like chicken salad, Rafe?"

"I'm not fussy. I eat just about anything."

"Good boy." She directed him down a dark hall and they emerged into a spacious kitchen, also bright and sunny. The table was set for two. Chicken salad sandwiches made with thick slices of brioche bread sat on plates, accompanied by sliced fruit and glasses of iced tea. The caretaker stood hovering, viewing him with suspicion, but after a nod from her employer, she left them alone.

"You're probably wondering why I invited you in," Stevana said.

"Yes, ma'am." He waited politely for her to give the signal to eat.

"You've probably heard that I'm old, mean, and eccentric."

He hesitated for only a moment. "Yes, ma'am. That's what folks say."

She laughed. "I was right about you. You're not afraid to say what you're thinking. I could tell by the way you were with Gracie. You didn't seek permission to do something right. You just did it. You think for yourself."

"I'm glad you think that's a good thing. None of my foster parents did."

"People judge others for all the wrong reasons." She smiled. "Go ahead.

Eat."

He returned her smile and chomped into his sandwich.

That was the first of many lunches and dinners. Stevana was nothing like what people said about her. She was talkative, friendly, and interested in him. She didn't pity him for his tough life but praised him for his strength and resiliency. She talked about her life, too, one that he had trouble visualizing. He had a hard time seeing her as a young, beautiful woman who had a long, passionate marriage with the man of her dreams. Forest Thornburg's wealth allowed them to live lavishly, to hobnob with politicians and celebrities, to go to theater and opera and ballet. A world as foreign to Rafe as the dark side of the moon. What he could relate to was that they were both animal lovers, and they gave generously to animal causes. After her husband's death, she funded the animal sanctuary in his honor. A sanctuary for Rafe and other troubled souls, too. A place of healing.

During their brief friendship, Rafe became very attached to the old lady, as with Delores, and he felt protective of her. He brought her little gifts; a bracelet he wove out of wild grass, a robin's nest that had fallen from a tree, an abandoned wasp hive showing the perfect geometry of nature's tiny architects. Stevana displayed them on a tabletop as though they were priceless treasures. As fate would have it, he met her when illness and age were taking their toll, and he had to witness the steady decline of her mental and physical abilities. He wished she hadn't made him her confidante, but she did. Stevana told him she was taking measures to ensure that she exited the world on her own terms, on her own schedule. He didn't know what that meant. But it pained him when she invited Morticia to the house and they began to plan her funeral ceremony. Stevana told Morticia right in front of him that she wanted Rafe to be her special guest of honor at her last "cocktail party."

"Yes, certainly," Morticia had responded, very convincingly. But when the event took place, Morticia reneged on her word. Rafe had to sneak in. To his credit, he put on a show that Stevana would have found both entertaining and humorous, until Morticia had him escorted off the property like a common criminal. The timing was momentous, considering he was the only witness to what happened later in the cemetery.

In her final days, Stevana was too weak to get out of bed. If ever tears were warranted, that was it, but Rafe hid his emotions. When sitting at her bedside, he kept the tears at bay. She was the one showing bravery, no complaints, though she was about to enter the tunnel of death, not knowing what was on the other side. Her last night, she fought to settle her mind, to reach a shaky hand out for his, to form words. He grasped her hand and leaned over to hear her whisper, "I'm proud of the man you've become."

Those words meant more to him than she could ever know.

Pastor John also sat with her, a pillar of strength and faith. She heaved out a long, deep breath from her bony chest and the light in her eyes went out. Rafe took comfort in knowing that at the end, Stevana was bolstered by two sturdy men. They escorted her as far as humanly possible into that great unknown.

As Rafe grappled with this new grief, the pastor was a rock. Watching Rafe struggle for composure, he put a hand on his shoulder and whispered, "You don't have to be tough. It's okay to cry."

Not in front of the pastor ....

Rafe made his way out of the house and cried from the depths of his soul in the quiet of the barn. Only Gracie witnessed his grief, nibbling affectionately on his jacket, blowing into his hair. Deep down in Rafe's gut, something surged—he wasn't sure what, but it was old and familiar and painful. But mixed with his misery was his admiration for the old woman. Stevana made her own choice. She did what she wanted to do. "We all come into this world alone, Rafe," she had told him. "And we leave alone. It's something we will all face in our own time. I made my time in between worthwhile. You make sure you do the same."

He'd make his time here count for something—avenging the theft of the old lady's body and the murder of Delores. That was how Rafe would honor the two women. But he had no idea where to find the killer. He knew the man in the white van was in cahoots with the Krall brothers, and he would no doubt make an appearance at the next dog fight. Rafe had traveled back to the Krall property last night, hoping to catch Jacko sneaking back in, but Daggur's girlfriend was the only one in the house. Rafe had one other connection to Jacko—an old goat farm where he heard dog fights were sometimes held. It might be where he was hiding out, and where the next dog fight would take place. He aimed to go there today and do some surveillance.

CHAPTER THIRTY-FIVE

PULLING THE HORSE TRAILER behind his Ram truck, Granger turned off the highway that hugged the lakeshore. He headed into the higher elevation through a forest of towering ponderosa pine and Douglas fir. A storm had swept through during the night and washed the forest clean, and it gleamed in the morning light. After a few miles the paved road turned into a rutted dirt road, then the dirt road began to disappear beneath weeds and grass. After bouncing over the ruts for a few minutes, he parked and turned off the engine.
"Time to mount up, Chief. Before these ruts eat my tires."

"My stomach agrees."

He opened the back of the trailer, lowered the ramp, and led the saddled horses out. Though Sidney rode often as a kid, and on occasion since she'd moved back to town, it had been a while, and she knew her backside would feel it. Granger had used good judgment in selecting a gentle chestnut bay, who stood patiently as Sidney hoisted herself into the saddle.

"Amigo's pretty much spook proof," he said.

"Good. Because I'm feeling rusty."

"He'll be content to just follow Cisco."

"My kind of horse."

Raised on a cattle ranch just a few miles away, Granger grew up on horseback. He mounted smoothly, pressed his heels into the sides of his Appaloosa, and got into lead position. With little instruction from Sidney, Amigo got in line behind Cisco and matched his ambling gait. Riding single file on a narrow trail, the horses threaded their way through a maze of trees. Sidney inhaled the fresh scent of juniper in the rain-washed air. She was calmed by the gentle rhythm of her mount and the early morning twilling of birds. A cascading stream babbled next to the path, harmonizing with the birdsong. She found the dose of nature an antidote to the stress she'd been carting around, a needed pause before gearing up for the big mission that night. *Now, if we can just bring in the rogue teenager without a fuss ....*

Granger stopped where the trail opened to a field and glanced back, waiting for her to catch up. She took in the wide, sprawling grassland that provided a sweeping view of snowcapped Hopper's Peak. *Postcard beautiful.* A fire road cut through the meadow and both horses snorted and flicked their ears forward and backward. They had caught the scent of another horse. The shod horse tracks of a lone rider were clearly impressed in the damp earth.

"These tracks are fresh," Granger said. "My guess, Rafe rode through here several times in the last few days. The bunker is up ahead, across the meadow and a hundred yards into the woods."

They crossed a stream that also had a maze of horse tracks on both banks. The tracks led to a thin opening in the trees.

"Let's leave the horses here," Granger said. "We don't want to forewarn him as we get up close. If he hears a horse, he'll know someone is sneaking up on him."

"Right. No telling what a frightened boy with a gun will do."

They tethered the horses to a fallen tree and continued through the opening on foot until the bunker materialized up ahead, camouflaged by moss and trees. Horse tracks led right up to the rusted metal door. It was 9:00 a.m., and a thin tendril of smoke curled out of the chimney pipe on the roof. It looked like the teen was up and about. The place looked like a fortress, with thick reinforced concrete walls. There was one window, high up off the ground, which was cracked in some places, and a few panes of glass were missing.

"I'll circle around the back to make sure there's no way to escape," Granger said. "There's another door back there but it was bolted shut last time I was here. Want to make sure it still is."

He returned a minute later. "We're good."

They quietly made their way to the area below the paned window. Before Sidney could yell out to the boy inside, a dog started barking.

"Quiet, Buddy," a male voice inside said. It sounded like Rafe was right under the window.

"Rafe, this is Chief Becker and Officer Wyatt," Sidney yelled. "We'd like to talk to you. Can you please come out peacefully?"

No answer.

"Rafe. Come on out and talk to us."

"Are you going to arrest me?" he yelled back.

"No. We just want to make sure you're okay. Pastor John is worried about you. So are the boys."

A long silence, then, "Okay. I'm coming out. Give me a minute. I'm not dressed."

Silence stretched into a couple of minutes.

"You're sure there's no other way to get out?" Sidney asked Granger, getting nervous.

"Not that I know of." He frowned. "Let's go in."

"Rafe, we're going to come in, okay?"

No answer.

Granger yanked the heavy door, and it groaned open. They entered the pitch-black interior and thumbed on their flashlights. In the light of their crisscrossing beams, they scanned the cavernous space. The entire front portion was empty of everything but a bunch of hay. Sidney got a bad feeling. *Where was the horse?*

She and Granger followed their beams to the far back recess where the teen's camping gear was scattered around the woodburning stove—a couple of folding chairs, a cot, a sleeping bag, a box of food, clothes, other personal items. There was a closed door in the far-right corner. "The bathroom," Granger said. "He's gotta be in there with the dog."

"Rafe, I'm going to open the bathroom door," Granger called out. He heard the low growling of a dog as he turned the handle and pushed the door inward a crack. A white dog stood wagging its tail, its posture friendly. It had a bandage wrapped around its head. "Hold on to your dog," Granger said. No response. He opened the door all the way. The room was empty except for the dog, his leash tied to a towel rack. "What the hell? Rafe's gone! He found another way out."

Sidney cursed under her breath. "Shit. Shit. Shit."

"Shit," Granger echoed. "Stay here, dog."

They rushed outside, each circling the bunker from a different direction until they met up again. There was no sign of the boy or horse. The ground was too thick with fallen leaves to detect any prints. *All this way, the morning spent, only to lose a single boy.*

"The kid outsmarted us," Granger said, his tone apologetic. "He's putting more distance between us by the second." His drawn face showed signs of fatigue and lack of sleep.

Sidney held her anger in check. She pushed her officers hard all week. Granger was doing his best to keep up. "The kid getting away isn't your fault."

"It doesn't inspire confidence, either."

She tried not to make this small failure a premonition of what was to come. The big bust was rearing up this evening and they'd attempt to take down a gang of men. Sidney tried to shake off her nervous tension. She couldn't let anxiety creep into her mind and muddy her thinking. Tonight, she needed to be clearheaded. She needed to don her professional armor and operate at the top of her game. "Let's go back inside and figure out how the hell the kid got out. And get that dog to animal control."

***

Hidden behind a mesh of pine branches, Rafe watched Chief Becker and the other cop circle the entire bunker. They didn't have a clue how he'd gotten out. His narrow escape left his heart thumping, and he was shaky with adrenaline. He was sleep-deprived from his midnight travels, and he felt totally unprepared to deal with a crisis of any kind, especially from cops. He thought this hideaway was his safe place, but someone ratted him out, and now it had been invaded. This surprise ambush left him with a terrible uncertainty about the future. His most frightening memories were of cops coming to the house and arresting his father, then delivering Rafe to the foster care institution called child services. The bad feeling inside his gut was growing bigger by the minute. He had to leave Buddy behind. But the dog was still recovering and needed rest.

No doubt, the cops wanted to drag Rafe back to town and into the station for questioning. Cooperating with them was out of the question. His entire life, he had doggedly made his own way in the world, priding himself on his self-reliance. Nothing was more frightening than allowing himself to depend on others. People let him down. People left him behind.

It was a stroke of luck that he took Gracie out to the clearing a half hour ago, or he would've had to leave her behind, too. But now he still had transportation. He watched the two cops go back inside the bunker. They would soon discover the trap door and the escape tunnel hidden under the floor behind the stove. The cement walls of the tunnel were still sturdy, though they were cracked and crumbling in many places. It opened like the mouth of a cave in the rocky gully behind him.

He waited. Listened. *Time to get the hell out of here.* He took a deep breath, then turned and quickly moved through the underbrush to the clearing. Squinting in the sunlight, he took Gracie's reins in hand, mounted her, and rode bareback into the woods. The old goat farm was a good fifteen-mile ride from there. He hadn't planned on getting there this early, but now he had no choice. Nothing was going to waylay his plans for the day.

CHAPTER THIRTY-SIX

NIGHT HAD FALLEN and the old goat farm was thrust into darkness as black as pitch. Overhead, low hanging clouds blocked out the moon. The smell of ozone in the air warned of an approaching storm. Well hidden behind trees, Granger had maintained an eyes-on position on the front of the barn for the last two hours. Darnell was posted at the rear. So far, not even a hair of man-made activity had been sighted.

At 6:00 p.m., headlights emerged from the black depths of the forest and three vehicles pulled up in front of the barn. Several men entered the dwelling carrying portable lights. Minutes later, lights flickered on inside, then the men trudged back and forth carrying equipment, setting up the place for the event.

Granger and Darnell supplied intel to the center of operations, a mobile command vehicle. Inside, a technician, Captain Harrison, and Sidney were on the receiving end. They were parked in a secluded clearing a quarter mile from the road leading to the farm. Also parked in the clearing were two dozen officers waiting in assorted police vehicles. An ambulance and an animal control truck were also in position in a separate location. Civilians were kept far away from any dangerous law enforcement activity until it was over. The SWAT team was well trained in first aid, as were most of the other officers. If someone was injured, they would provide immediate care until the paramedics arrived.

Between 6:45 and 7:15, Granger reported more people arriving—mostly pickup trucks and vans, a few with dog crates in the back. People were milling around outside, getting their dogs ready, smoking, conversing.

Darnell reported that the back door of the barn opened and a man with a holstered pistol stepped out to smoke, then he tossed his smoke and took up a guard position in the doorway. The folks outside drifted into the barn. Another guard stood in the front entryway, also with a holstered gun. Granger crept closer to the entrance, staying in the shadows of the parked vehicles, and peered into the interior. Behind the guard, people were starting to form a circle around the pit, and a din of voices disturbed the stillness of the night. The place was revving up, right on schedule for a 7:30 starting time. "I counted eighteen men, aside from the two guards, Chief," Granger said into his mic.

"Ditto, that," Darnell's voice came in.

Harrison met Sidney's gaze. "Time to get this show on the road."

"We're on our way," she said to her two reconnaissance officers. "Don't act on your own. Wait for backup." She and Harrison stepped out into the heavy moist air. Everyone drove out of the clearing and parked along the dirt road that led to the farm, effectively blocking the only way out. About a dozen officers grouped together with "SWAT" on the backs of their vests. They looked formidable in their black military-style uniforms, helmets with face shields, modular body armor, elbow and knee pads, and gloves—no skin visible. Several carried ballistic shields.

Like the SWAT unit, all other officers wore tactical vests, and, in addition to their duty pistols, most were armed with assault rifles. Several had shotguns. In situations where there was no time to aim, a shotgun sprayed a wide cone of lead. As long as it was pointed in the right direction, an armed suspect would be brought down.

Everyone did a last-minute check of their equipment. The mood of the group changed minutely, but palpably; a kind of nervous tension fueled by adrenaline. Then they huddled together around Sidney and Harrison. It was deadly quiet. A coyote howled in the distance.

"I want everyone to be safe out there," Sidney spoke calmly in a low tone. "You know what to do. Watch each other's back."

Nods of understanding.

"Okay, let's roll."

Everyone stepped into formation with the SWAT team taking the lead, low mode flashlight beams pointed at the ground. Soundlessly, they made their way along the overgrown dirt road in the direction of the farm. They were diligent about the placement of their feet. Sounds were amplified in the forest and noises out of the ordinary could alert the suspects. The tall pines soughed. A cold breeze slipped through the branches of trees, carrying the first drops of moisture. By the time they reached the outskirts of the farm, the rain increased to a light downpour. Sidney heard the brittle spatter as drops hit their uniforms.

***

Crouched behind the back of a black SUV, Granger felt random drops hit his jacket. Within a minute, a light shower moved in, softly pattering the earth and vehicles. Surmising that all the participants were inside the barn, he was caught by surprise when a truck door opened and shut behind him. Adrenaline shot through his system. A tall man, skinny as a rail, stood about ten feet behind him. Granger froze, hoping to hell he blended into the darkness in his black uniform. An army of cops was about to descend on the farm. If this guy spotted them and warned the others, it would shatter the element of surprise. All hell would break loose. Granger needed to keep the man quiet. He silently pulled his duty weapon from his holster.

The man had a bottle in his hand, which he raised to his lips. He swallowed and then, just slightly, swayed on his feet. He chugged the contents, then tossed the bottle under the pickup. Granger was about to lurch at him, press his gun to the man's head and tell him not to make a sound, but abruptly, the rain increased to a heavy downpour. Granger heard the metallic clang as drops bounced off the trucks.

The man cursed. He was hopelessly off balance. He took off at a run for the barn, slipping like a man on ice, missing Granger by inches. With a sigh of relief, he holstered his gun.

There was a sudden excited uproar coming from the barn, shrill whoops, and hollers. They must have put the first two dogs in the ring.

***

Harrison and Sidney were with the SWAT unit when they reached the perimeter of the farm. Through the pouring rain, the barn faintly materialized out of the darkness, outlined by the dim interior lights. Everyone was drenched. Water ran down Sidney's face and dripped off her nose. Harrison's eyes were blinking against the rain.

"We see the barn," she said to Granger and Darnell. "Are we good to go?"

"Everyone's inside," Granger said. "Focused on the dog fight. The guard in front is facing the pit."

"Ditto with the guard in back," Darnell added. "He's stepped inside out of the rain."

Good. That works well for us.

They needed to know where Granger and Darnell were, so they didn't get shot by mistake. "Both of you, come in."

They waited until both men emerged and joined them, then Sidney signaled to the SWAT team. They divided into two sections and headed towards opposite ends of the barn, blending in with the rain. All other units followed, splitting into groups behind them. Sidney fell in with the unit navigating to the front entrance. The structure grew larger, then loomed above them. A clatter of voices came from inside. Luckily, the roar of the rain on the roof and on the gravel put up a mask of white noise over everything outside.

Some of the SWAT team stacked up to the right side of the entryway while the others positioned themselves to the left. One man rushed in behind the guard, who was tall and beefy, and held a gun to his back. The guard's hands shot up. The rest of the SWAT team rushed into the premises, yelling, "Police! On the floor! On the floor! Face down!"

Shocked silence for a moment. Then shouts and a rapid series of gunshots split the stillness. Sidney rushed in with the other backup officers and squinted down the length of the room through pot and cigarette smoke. SWAT and backup officers had poured in from the back entrance, as well. Most participants were flat on their stomachs. Then she saw that a cop was down, hugging his chest.

Two suspects in shooting stances were pointing pistols at the cops. A shooter was firing from behind a stall. SWAT fired back. Rounds from numerous assault rifles ripped the wood to shreds. The shooter fell forward. Stains of dark red bloomed on his thermal shirt. With a mixture of both surprise and anger, the two armed suspects stood their ground, both now staring dumbly at the dozens of black muzzles aimed at them.

"Drop your weapons!"

One lowered his weapon to the ground.

One was stupid enough to shoot.

"Shit," Sidney murmured. "Shit." She didn't see where the round landed. A dozen shots riddled his body. He flew backwards, hit the ground hard, and didn't move.

"Get that ambulance over here!" Harrison yelled into his mic.

Two SWAT officers bent over the downed cop who was grimacing, obviously in a great deal of pain. His vest stopped the bullet, thank God. But Sidney knew from experience that he probably felt like he'd been kicked by a mule. He'd be taken to the hospital immediately and examined for broken bones or internal bleeding. Other officers checked the wounded suspects on the ground. Both dead.

The dogs in the ring cowered on opposite sides in a standoff position, stunned by the gunshots, both bleeding in spots, but overall in good shape.

The next twenty minutes were highly animated, controlled chaos;

multiple officers rushing around taking care of business. Sidney joined officers who were cuffing men on the ground and searching them for drugs and weapons. Two officers were looping the dogs in the ring and crating them.

Several officers left to move vehicles closer to the barn to load up prisoners and clear the road for the ambulance and animal control.

***

In the aftermath of the storming of the barn, a measure of order descended on the grounds. As the rain slowed to a soft drizzle, the maddening clatter on the roof abruptly stopped. They were all in that quiet zone that follows an intense blast of danger; operating on automatic, following protocol, but Sidney could practically smell the adrenaline coming off them. Paramedics were wheeling the wounded cop to an ambulance. The two wounded dogs were on their way to a veterinary ER. Five other crated dogs were in the parking lot being loaded into the animal control vehicles. There was a palpable exuberance in the air, a feeling of achievement. Twenty suspects lay cuffed and face down on the ground under armed guard—several had been in possession of illegal drugs. If illegal weapons or significant amounts of drugs were found in any of their vehicles, some would be facing serious jail time.

Sidney and Granger walked the length of the barn, looking over each man one-by-one. Astonishingly, no one met Daggur's description of Taron—tall, thin, muscular, dark hair and close-cropped beard. Not a single suspect had the unmistakable tattoo of a rattler wrapped around his neck. A hollow feeling gnawed at Sidney's stomach. The man linked to the cold-blooded traffickers who killed Delores wasn't here. Some of these suspects most likely knew where he was, but who would be willing to talk? They would be questioned over the next few days, which might or might not provide answers. In the meantime, Taron and his cohorts were on the loose, possibly planning to kill again. And Sidney was back at square one, with no leads.

Darnell and Amanda were among the officers lifting men to their feet, walking them outside, and loading them into vehicles. They would be transported to the county jail for processing. Sidney and Granger pulled the two suspects aside who had been guarding the rear and front doors. They smelled of cigarettes and whiskey.

"Did either of you see Taron Seminov?" Sidney asked crisply. "Tall, thin, dark. He's got a rattler tattoo around his neck."

They both stared at her with hostile expressions.

Sidney's gaze sharpened on their faces, no-nonsense, the question hanging in the air.

The guard who was posted at the front entrance spoke up first. He was a burly middle-aged man with a thick beard and bald head. "The Russian asshole? No, I didn't see him. But he would've come in through the back. He always parks off grounds and hikes in."

"Why is that?"

He scowled, and said with a steel edge, "Look, if it was anyone else, I wouldn't tell you shit. But Taron's a dick. Thinks he's tough. Walks around like he's the Terminator. Afraid someone's gonna steal the shit he keeps in his van."

"What would that be?"

"Hell if I know. He's secretive. Paranoid."

Sidney turned to the second guard, a younger version of the first, but with thick glasses, and a red beard. "Did you see him come in?"

He shook his head. "Never made it in tonight. But like Waylen says, he comes late. His dog always fights last. Most likely, he saw you guys storm the place, and he split like the wind." A faint smile teased the edges of his lips. "I hope to hell you find him. Nail his ass. No one here would give a crap."

"You have any idea what he keeps in his van?"

He shrugged. "Who knows. I hear tell he deals in human parts. Wouldn't be surprised. He looks like a vampire."

"What do you mean, human parts?"

"What do you think?"

"Answer the question," Granger said in a commanding tone.

He smirked, said nothing.

"Do you have any idea where he lives?" Sidney asked. "Hides out?"

"In a dark cave," he said with a malicious grin. "In a coffin."

"Okay, smart ass, time to pack you into your Rolls," Granger said gruffly.

Sidney nodded to a couple of deputies. They each took one of the suspects by the arm and led them outside.

As the realization sank in that they had missed Taron by minutes, Sidney and Granger exchanged a look. His face got harder, his jaw tighter. She took a breath to fight off the tightness in her chest.

"He can be anywhere by now," Granger said.

"Yep. No way to hunt a man in a dark, wet forest. Rain washed out his scent. The K-9 unit wouldn't pick up a thing." Now that the adrenaline was wearing off, she felt the exhaustion at the base of her neck, along the backs of her eyes.

"Maybe one of these numbskulls will give him up." He nodded toward the transport vehicles out front.

"We're looking at a lot of interrogations. One by one. With no guarantees." She gazed outside. The driving rain had destroyed the grounds, leaving nothing but shallow pools of muddy water. The rain had ceased, the cloud cover had broken apart, and a partial moon glowed bright in the sky. For now, the pressure to find Delores's killer would remain a heavy weight on her shoulders.

CHAPTER THIRTY-SEVEN

EARLIER IN THE DAY

WAKING UP TO BIRD CHATTER, Rafe blinked open his eyes and wondered where the hell he was. Tree branches formed a canopy overhead, with patches of gray sky showing through. He lay on his back, arms crossed, backpack under his head. Then he remembered. He was sheltered in a thicket of evergreen trees on the outskirts of the old goat farm. Glancing at his watch, he saw he'd been in a dead sleep for several hours. He hadn't meant to doze off, but his sleep-deprived mind and body had other plans. Sitting up, he got his bearings.

He had arrived mid-afternoon after being surprised by cops at the bunker and fleeing on Gracie. They took their time ambling over the fifteen miles of back wood trails to get here. Staying in the cover of the woods, Rafe rode around the entire periphery of the seventy-five-acre farm. Seeing no sign of life, he placed Gracie in an overgrown fenced pasture on the far edge of the farm and he did a walk-through of the property. There was no sign of Jacko in the broken-down utility sheds or the barn, so he investigated the area surrounding the dilapidated house. All the windows were boarded up except for one in the back, and it cast dim light into the dark interior. He opened the window and climbed inside. The place smelled musty and the moist scent of decay was suffocating. Along with thick layers of dust, spider webs, and mouse droppings, Rafe discovered a sleeping bag, bottles of water, and an ice chest holding bread, peanut butter, jam, and a few dozen protein bars. Jacko was definitely hiding out here, but for now, he was somewhere off site. Rafe made two peanut butter sandwiches, helped himself to a few bottles of water and some protein bars, and left, closing the window behind him.

He retreated to this hiding place where he had a good view of the house and barn. With good intentions, Rafe diligently kept watch into the afternoon, but boredom and stillness were not good companions. He struggled to stay awake but lost the battle. Now, hours later, something other than birds woke him. *But what?* He peered through fir branches in every direction but saw nothing out of the ordinary. Then he heard it. Two muffled voices, both male, coming from a hundred feet or so to his left.

Rafe crept stealthily toward the sound. Two uniformed cops stood talking on the fringe of the woods. One was the cop who had been with Chief Becker at the bunker. The other was a black cop, younger, around twenty-five. Rafe crept closer and listened.

"Can you hear us, Chief?" the white cop said into his mic.

Both men had earbuds in their ears, and they paused to listen to a response.

"Yeah, I hear you loud and clear," the white cop said.

"Copy that," the black cop said. "I'm concealed at the rear of the barn. I have a clear view of the back entrance."

"I'm going to find a place where I can surveil the front," the white cop said. Then again, he paused to listen. "Yeah, Chief, I'll keep you updated on any activity. Right now, it's dead as a graveyard." He bade his cop buddy goodbye and disappeared into the trees.

A charge of adrenaline rushed Rafe's system. He couldn't believe his luck. The decision to come to the old farm was a stab in the dark, but it hit the mark, and it was going to pay off, big time. Obviously, the cops got word that a dog fight would take place here tonight. Not only was Jacko holed up here, but the psycho in the white van was bound to show up. Rafe only had to wait and listen. His pistol was in his backpack. Heaven help the bastard if Rafe got to him before the cops did.

***

Rafe entertained himself by occasionally leaving his hideout and spying on the lone cop surveilling the back of the barn. The cop stayed alert by intermittently walking in circles around his small square of real estate. He stretched, ran in place, did a few pushups, then hunkered down talking into his mic to his cop buddy. Rafe returned to his hideout and emulated the cop's surveillance tactics; exercising and breathing deeply, which sharpened his mind, worked the kinks out of his muscles. He ate one of the sandwiches and two protein bars and emptied two bottles of water.

After an eternity, dusk crept in, and gusts of rain-scented wind blew through the trees. Thankful he was wearing a water-proof jacket, Rafe pulled a knit cap from a pocket and yanked it down over his ears. The clouds congealed and the farm was thrust into pitch black. Finally, the first trucks navigated the narrow dirt road and pulled up in front of the barn. Men walked back and forth, carrying stuff inside. Lights came on and he had better visibility. Over the next hour, more trucks and a few vans rolled in. Men stood around outside for a while, smoking and drinking, then a soft drizzle sailed in. The air smelled of rain hitting the earth. The men drifted inside, and a guard posted himself at the door.

Then several things happened in rapid succession. The brunt of the storm moved in and walloped the grounds. Treetops swayed, branches dipped and creaked. Rafe was drenched in minutes. Inside the barn, whoops and hollers indicated the first dog fight had begun.

Then an army of darkly clad, well-armed figures swept onto the property, moving to the front and rear of the barn. The calvary had arrived!

Cops stormed the place, yelling, "Police! On the floor! On the floor! Face down!"

Gunshots!

Panicked yelling!

More gunshots!

A clamor of voices,

The rain abruptly stopped.

Mania persisted; cops rushing in and out, high beams tunneling through the forest, an ambulance and other vehicles arriving, a multitude of flashing lights turning the night red and blue. It was exciting to watch. Rafe was riveted. After a while, the cops started marching cuffed men out of the barn and into vehicles. His heart sang. All the bastards who sold drugs and killed dogs were going to the slammer!

But his elation wore off quickly. The big damper on the evening was that the man in the white van never turned up. The man who killed Delores. He was still out there, enjoying his freedom, after leaving misery and suffering in his wake. The woods suddenly felt foreign and hostile. Water dripped everywhere, branches dipped and waved. A sharp wind whistled through the trees. Rafe's hooded jacket kept his head and torso dry, but his jeans and sneakers were soaked through. He was cold and needed shelter. He stared up at the hard white stars and wondered where to go from here. The bunker was no longer an option. Maybe he could sneak into someone's barn for the night.

Then something caught his eye. Rafe narrowed his eyes, gazed through the darkness, and detected a darting flashlight beam deep in the woods. Someone was there. Every cell in his body yearned for it to be the driver of the white van. He needed to get eyes on the guy before he caught wind of the police raid and ran off. The beam steadily moved toward the farm. With his gun tucked into his pocket, Rafe moved steadily toward the beam.

He crept closer, dodging between tree and bush, crushing wet leaves, an arm protecting his head from the errant branch. Several times Rafe lost sight of the beam and paused, trying to delineate shapes in the darkness until he picked it up again. Angling from the side, he got close enough to make out a man's shadowy figure and that of a dog traveling at his side. Rafe's whole body tensed. The beating of his heart rivaled the sounds of the forest. Why didn't the dog bark? The beam passed over the animal's head and Rafe saw that its mouth was clamped shut with a muzzle. A choke collar kept him glued to the man's side. The cruel treatment of the dog pushed Rafe's anger up a notch.

The man stepped into a pocket of moonlight for only an instant, but it was long enough for Rafe to recognize the thin body and bone-hard face. It was the man who killed Delores and stole Stevana's body, the man he tackled in the driveway of Daggur's house, who then got the upper hand and held a gun a foot from Rafe's face. The man's eyes had burned with a kind of cruel energy, but for some reason he didn't kill him. Now the tables were turned. Rafe had the upper hand, but he felt no mercy in his heart. "Stop right there!" he said, his voice betraying his rage. "Or I'll put a bullet in your head."

The man didn't move. He was absolutely still. His face and body betrayed nothing. One side of his mouth lifted in a half-smile. "You again," he said with a Russian accent. "What is it with you? You keep getting in my way. Why are you hunting me?"

"You killed Delores! I saw her in your truck at the cemetery."

"So that was you." He appraised Rafe for a long moment, his thoughts hidden behind his feral eyes. "For the record, I did not kill her. I am just a driver. I did not know this woman."

"I don't believe you!"

"Then go ahead. Shoot me."

They locked eyes. Rafe's finger froze on the trigger.

"As I thought," the man said. "You are no killer."

"I'll shoot if you make me. I'm taking you in." Nervous sweat dampened his back, but Rafe was surprised at how calm he sounded. "The cops are all over the farm."

The man's eyes widened in alarm. Then he thumbed off the flashlight and stepped deeper into the shadows.

The forest went black and deathly still.

Soft rustling.

Silence.

Rustling again.

A feeling on the back of Rafe's neck like the lick of a ghost told him the man was right behind him. He spun around. Nothing was there. A chill snaked down his spine. He jerked to the left just as a blow glanced off his skull. Light exploded behind his eyes. He staggered, his hand darting to the left and right, shooting off two rounds. He heard a grunt, then the sound of a body hit the ground. The dog made muffled growling noises.

The man tossed his flashlight at Rafe's feet and hissed through chattering teeth, "Get help! Before I bleed to death!"

Rafe captured the man in the sphere of the beam. He lay on the ground grimacing, clutching his side, blood seeping through his fingers. The dog crouched next to him, the choke collar biting into his neck. The shock of what he'd done hit Rafe like a physical force. He stood frozen. Pain reverberated from his temple to the back of his skull. Blood dripped down the side of his face.

"Go!" the man hissed.

Rafe turned and ran, sometimes crashing through bushes, shoes springing off the deep mulch of the forest floor, heading toward the farm.

CHAPTER THIRTY-EIGHT

SIDNEY STOOD in the entryway of the barn, talking with Captain Harrison and her three junior officers. All the suspects had been packed into transport vehicles and were on their way to Jackson County Jail. The ambulance and animal control vehicles were also gone. A few cops remained in the empty dwelling, searching for guns or drugs that might have been hastily hidden when they stormed in. The evening's mission was at its tail end and a sense of relative calm had settled in. Sidney was about to dismiss her officers for the night. Then two sharp cracks came from the woods to the north and all heads pivoted in that direction. Silhouetted against the moonlit sky, the towering trees looked like steeples and spires in some foreign land.

"What the hell?" Harrison said. "That sounded like gunshots."

"Shit," Sidney said. They were exhausted and about to wrap things up for the night, but this had to be investigated. "We'll go take a look."

"Keep me posted."

Sidney and her three officers moved swiftly into the woods, their beams cutting a swath in the darkness, steering them around trees and puddles, an occasional bush clawing their uniforms. The moon faded in and out of the trees, the forest darkened and reappeared, bathed in a metallic sheen. Everywhere the trees gleamed.

***

Before he'd gone a hundred yards, Rafe saw several flashlight beams splintering between trees, rushing towards him. He stepped into a clearing and stood waiting with his hands in the air, heart pounding, trying to catch his breath. The moon glowed bright in the sky.

In an instant, two cops stepped out of the woods, guns drawn, pinning him in their cones of light. Two more were standing in the shadows of the trees holding rifles. "Are you armed?" a female voice asked sharply. It was

Chief Becker.

"I have a gun in my right pocket," he panted. "I'm Rafe McEnery. You've been looking for me. There's a man back in the woods. I shot him. He killed Delores!"

Moving with deliberate urgency, Chief Becker removed his gun and took his flashlight. A male officer patted down his body, then cuffed his hands behind his back. A cop veneer hardened their expressions, and they operated quickly and efficiently.

"What happened to your head?" Chief Becker aimed her beam at a spot above Rafe's ear.

"The man hit me."

"It's barely bleeding now. Are you dizzy? Is your vision blurred?"

"No, I'm okay." Rafe recognized the male cops as the two doing surveillance earlier. Another female cop stood in the back.

"Rafe, you're going to take us to the guy you shot, okay?" Chief Becker said. "If you start to feel dizzy, let us know."

"Yes, ma'am."

She took his arm. "Let's go."

***

Rafe directed Sidney and her officers deeper into the woods. They were moving fast, breathing heavily, trying to shorten the distance between themselves and the gunshot victim. The trees shuddered and rustled in the wind.

Finding the teenager in the woods in the middle of the night was astonishing to Sidney. Seeing him bleeding with his clothes soaked through elicited both sympathy and alarm. This young man had inserted himself into her investigations at every turn, and continually slipped through her fingers like a puff of smoke. Now, here he was in the flesh, inserting himself again, and this time in the vicinity of an extremely dangerous mission. He claimed to have shot the man who murdered Delores. *Taron Seminov?* No kid should be subjected to what he'd been through in the last two weeks. Sidney had a multitude of questions for him, but right now, her priority was finding the victim.

Over the sound of their labored breathing, they heard something. A strange sound, like an animal whimpering or moaning, off to the right.

"He's got a fighter dog with him," Rafe panted.

They picked up the pace and reached a small clearing where a man lay sprawled on his back in the throes of shock. His breathing was ragged, and the bloody hand pressed into his side was shaking. The muzzled dog stood over him in a protective manner, making growling noises. The spiked collar on the poor animal was pulled so tightly it was a wonder he was still conscious. Sidney saw the tattoo of a rattler's bared fangs and tail on the man's neck. "It's Taron."

"Holy hell," Granger said.

Rafe had managed to subdue the vicious man they'd all been looking for.

"Contact Captain Harrison. Tell him to get an ambulance crew back to the farm," Sidney told Amanda.

"Copy that."

"Don't kill my dog." Taron's voice was low and hoarse. "Sergei won't hurt you unless I tell him to." He let go of the leash. The dog started coughing when Darnell loosened his collar. It stood its ground, refusing to leave Taron. Darnell had to drag him away. He tied the leash to a tree.

"The ambulance is about ten minutes out," Amanda said.

"Darnell, hike back to the farm. You'll need to guide the medics in."

"On my way." He wasted no time jogging out of the clearing.

With the dog out of the way, Granger quickly searched Taron. He found a gun, a wallet and car keys, and handed them to Sidney. Then he bent over the man while Sidney and Amanda shone their lights on the wound. The man hissed through his teeth as Granger examined him. Blood was seeping out under his back as well as from the front. "It looks like a through and through," Granger said. "No arteries or bones are affected." He removed two Israeli bandages from a vest pocket and tore off the packaging, then placed the sterile sides of the absorption pads against both the entry and exit wounds. The man gritted his teeth as Granger wrapped the bandage tightly around his waist. There was nothing more he could do for the victim. The paramedics would take over.

They heard the distant wail of the ambulance reaching the barn.

Sidney turned her attention to the teen. He had stood watching, his face tight with concern. "I don't know how you came across this guy, but you're lucky he didn't hurt you. His name's Taron Seminov. He's extremely dangerous. We need to find his van. Where was he coming from?"

"Due north," Rafe said without hesitation. "I have a compass in my pocket. When you spend a lot of time in the woods, you can't be without one." He nodded toward an opening in the woods. "He came through there."

They turned as Darnell and two paramedics rushed into the clearing.

One carried a medical kit, the other a folded stretcher. As the medics attended to Taron, Sidney spoke to her three officers. "Amanda, Darnell, you two can escort Rafe and the two medics back to the farm. Granger, you and I are going to go look for that van."

"It can't be too far," Granger said.

They slipped into the forest and immediately found an old elk trail that wound through the woods. About a hundred yards from the clearing, Sidney caught a sliver of something reflecting moonlight through the burrows of trees. As they crept closer, a white van became partially visible, well concealed behind dense shrubbery. Granger circled around the front. Sidney crept up to the double doors at the rear. The windows were jeweled by rain and partially fogged. She aimed her beam into the interior and her light skimmed over what looked like a body on the floor. Her pulse raced and she stepped away from the doors. "Granger, someone's in there!"

They pulled their weapons and stood on each side of the rear doors.

"Police! Open the door and come out."

No answer.

"Police! Open the door and come out."

No response.

Sidney unlocked the rear door and yanked it open. They both aimed their guns and beams into the interior. A large, muscular man lay on his side, gagged and bound.

"Holy shit." Granger crawled into the van, pulled off the gag and did a rudimentary check. "He's breathing and his heartbeat's regular. I think he's drugged."

The man groaned several times as Granger untied his hands and feet and helped him into a sitting position.

Sidney got a good look at him. He was young, maybe seventeen.

He groaned again.

"Can you hear me?" Sidney asked.

He nodded, and one eye squinted open.

"What's your name?"

"Jacko ... Jacko Krall."

Sidney and Granger shared a sharp glance.

"Thank God you found me." He started sobbing, his body heaving, pushing out words in choking gulps. "Taron was going to ... to give me to ... to the body snatchers. To carve ... out my insides." He wiped his dripping nose with his sleeve. "I was ... so ... fucking ... scared."

"Why did he abduct you?" Sidney asked.

"He called my brother a snitch." He spoke slowly, as though pulling his words together as he thought of them. "He wanted to know what Daggur told you guys. I told him Daggur didn't know shit and he would never talk to the cops. Neither would I. I told him I was hiding out from the cops, too." He paused to exhale a tense breath and tears escaped down his cheeks. "Taron said he was taking me as insurance. He wanted me to call Daggur tomorrow. Tell him he'd kill me if he snitched. He stuck a needle in my neck that made me sleepy. Next thing I knew, you woke me up in here."

"Did Taron say he was giving you to the body snatchers?"

"No. But that's what he does, right?"

"Did he say who the body snatchers were?"

"No … yeah … maybe." He swallowed, wiped his nose again. "I don't know. I heard things. He was talking on the phone. But I might have been dreaming."

"What do you think you heard?"

"He said something like … you owe me … and I'm going to get what I'm owed."

Granger pulled his notepad out of a pocket and jotted down notes.

"Do you remember anything else from his conversation?"

He thought for a long moment, scratching his chin. "He said something about a funeral home … the guy he was talking to … he called him Doc …."

"That's good info, Jacko. Very good. Did you hear him mention Doc by any other name?"

Again, he scratched his chin, thinking. "No, but he mentioned someone else, someone named … Bugs … or something. It was hard to tell with his accent."

Granger scribbled.

Jacko shrugged again. "It's all a jumble in my head."

"You did great, Jacko. If you remember anything else, anything at all, let me know right away, okay?"

He nodded. "Did you raid the place tonight?"

"Yes. Thanks to you."

"Did you get Taron?"

"Yeah. He's in custody. He won't be hurting anyone again."

He heaved out a ragged breath. "I hope he's in a small box for the rest of his life."

"Let's get you on your feet," Sidney said. "You need to clear your head."

He walked around for a few minutes with Sidney holding one arm.

In the meantime, Granger did a basic search of the van, then locked it.

"No drugs or weapons readily apparent, but they could be concealed within the van. It'll have to be towed to a secure area. The county CSI will go over it with a fine-tooth comb."

"Do you think you can make it to the barn?" Sidney asked Jacko.

"Yeah, sure. I feel better now. Not so dizzy."

"Then one of my officers will drive you to the ER to be checked out."

"And then where do I go?" he asked, his shoulders drooping. "With Daggur in jail, I don't have a home anymore."

Sidney needed him to be calm and cooperative right now, which meant avoiding this conversation. Social services would take on that unpleasant discussion. That's what they were trained to do. Jacko was going to have to face some cold, hard facts. He wouldn't be placed in foster care. He was an undisciplined kid with violent tendencies. He was a bully, who beat up little Joey. And he assaulted Dillon with a shovel at the sanctuary, which could have killed him if he had hit his head. There were few options for kids like him who were treading a dangerous path to prison, or worse. He would probably be put in a secured facility for troubled youth. "Let's get you looked at first, okay?" she said. "Finding you a home will be next on the list."

They started walking back through the woods. The moon shone brightly, lighting up the path back to the barn. Sidney's muscles were tight with fatigue while her mind was a beehive of activity. Many loose ends had come together tonight in her homicide investigation. The elusive teenager, Rafe, had been found and taken into custody. He had a mountain of secrets to unlock. The mysterious man in the white van had been identified as Taron Seminov and was also in custody. Sidney suspected that the forensic techs would find evidence in his vehicle linking him to Delores's murder. *DNA, hair, blood, or other body fluids*. Taron would be questioned as soon as he was medically stable. Which meant Sidney could be one conversation away from identifying the organ traffickers he worked with. Jacko overheard him mention a funeral home and a man he called Doc. What funeral home was operating an illicit doner business behind the façade of respectability in Linnly County? A lot of puzzle pieces had fallen into place, but some were floating around not making any sense yet, and some were missing entirely. She could not control the order or pace of an investigation any more than she could control the weather. But she was getting closer to the finale.

CHAPTER THIRTY-NINE

IT WAS 3:00 A.M. and Sidney was practically sleepwalking by the time she peeled off her uniform and did a faceplant in bed. In minutes, she was bogged down in a swampy dreamland; not awake, not fully asleep. Visions of dark figures in a murky landscape emerged between tunnels of trees and then melted back into the blackness.

The next thing she became conscious of was a distant chiming ... church bells ... a doorbell? Submerged in a marsh that had a thick, sticky consistency, somewhere between solid and liquid, she could neither swim nor climb out of it. She peeled open an eye and her bedroom materialized in soft geometric shapes, then hardened into physical objects. The chiming came from her cellphone on the nightstand. She reached for it and answered hoarsely without reading the name on the screen, "Chief Becker here."

There was a chuckle, then her fiancé's voice poured into her ear like warm honey. "Morning, beautiful."

Sidney didn't feel beautiful. She had collapsed into bed without showering or brushing her teeth. After hiking through the woods last night and oozing nervous sweat from multiple adrenaline surges, she felt, and smelled, like one of the swamp creatures in her dream. And her mouth was bone dry. She swallowed, and said, "Not so beautiful this morning."

"Are you in bed?"

"Yeah."

"Naked?"

"Yeah."

"Then you're at your most beautiful."

She smiled.

"It's ten o'clock, by the way. I thought you'd be up and at 'em."

Sidney could not stifle a yawn. "I hit the sack at three."

"Poor baby," he said softly. "Sorry I woke you."

"My alarm is set to go off in ten minutes. It's much nicer waking up to your voice." As always, she felt a warm stirring of affection for him. "I miss you."

"Me, too, baby."

Most afternoons, while Dillon was at school, and before her evening shift began, they met at David's house on the lake. Lunch, sex, nature walks, more sex, just lying in bed talking about nothing in particular—and the weight of her responsibilities vanished into the ether. It was the perfect counter to her highly stressful job. Sidney could use a big dose of David right now, but that wasn't going to happen until after Dillon's arraignment.

"I'll let you go. Just wanted to hear your voice. Can't wait until ...." his voice trailed off. A little sexy tingle raced through her body as she filled in the blanks. "I love you."

"I love you, too."

***

Sidney entered the station through the back door, walked down the hall to the bullpen, and observed her three officers sitting in front of their computers. They looked surprisingly alert. Last night's raid was dangerous, hair-raising, and exhausting, but extremely productive. Several departments worked together seamlessly and brought in twenty suspects. Then in a lucky twist of fate, she and her team brought in Taron and Rafe. That, and the sense that they were closing in on the end of these investigations had given them a much-needed emotional boost.

"Morning, Chief," Darnell said, upbeat.

The other two echoed his greeting.

"How's Officer Reese doing?" she asked, referring to the officer who was shot last night.

"At home. On leave," Amanda said. "Deep bruising. No fractured ribs."

"He was lucky," she said, relieved.

"The force was with him," Darnell said, adding a lighter note.

"How's Rafe doing?" she asked.

"He ate like a truck driver when Winnie brought him breakfast," Amanda said. "Three egg and bacon muffins, a quart of milk, and a couple of donuts."

"Taking advantage of free food." Granger grinned. "That's what teenage boys do."

"He's waiting for you," Darnell said.

Sidney had called ahead and told him to put Rafe in the interview room. She wanted to hit the ground running today. Rafe had been told his Miranda

Rights last night upon his arrest, and he was charged with attempted murder with a deadly weapon and other lesser charges. He would absolutely stay in jail. Bond would be determined by a magistrate or judge based on whether he was a flight risk, and he was the ultimate flight risk. He'd already run from the police, he was very capable of hiding in the woods and living off the land, and he could easily disappear into the mountains and never be seen again. "Let's go talk to him."

She and Darnell walked down the hall and entered the audio room. Sidney studied Rafe through the glass; a good-looking young man, athletic build, a scruff of dark hair, a few days' growth of patchy beard, sitting in an uncomfortable metal chair under glaring lights. When he was booked last night, his clothes were wet and muddy. He was given a clean orange jumpsuit and disposable slippers to change into. He sat at the scarred metal table, cuffed hands in his lap, expression inscrutable. The windowless room had a concrete floor and dull white cinderblock walls. It was not designed to let suspects relax, but to urge them to confess so they could get the hell out of there.

"Did he say anything when you took him in?"

"Nope. His distrust of cops was oozing out of every pore. If looks could burn, my hair would be smoking."

She chuckled. "Let's see if we can tamp down the heat."

Darnell pulled a notepad and pen from his breast pocket and followed her in. They pulled out metal chairs and seated themselves, with Sidney directly across from Rafe. "How are you doing, Rafe?"

He sat up straighter in his chair and gestured to his jumpsuit. "Love the outfit. Love the digs. Gives me a warm fuzzy feeling all over." His tone was sarcastic but then it grew more serious. "Are Gracie and Buddy okay?"

"Yeah, Gracie is back at the rescue ranch. Buddy will be moving in with a foster family soon." Sidney kept her voice pleasant. She always started out gently, putting a suspect at ease, gaining trust. In this case, she had to be careful not to let her guard down, to let her empathy get in the way of her judgment. The boy's hard-scrabble life, his protective manner with animals and the younger boys at the church, the tragic loss of two women that he'd grown very attached to, pulled on her heartstrings, despite his terribly misguided judgment. "He's my dog. I want him back."

"That's up to Pastor John. They'll take good care of him, for now," she said. This was a good place to start the interview, with the dog, where she could make an inroad. "Buddy's a beautiful dog. Looks like a white wolf."

"Yeah, he does. He's as smart as a wolf, too. Wouldn't be alive today if he wasn't."

"I know you've rescued several other abused dogs, as well, to give them better lives."

"People who mistreat dogs should be treated the same way. Tied to trees. Starved. Covered in fleas. Living with injuries. Some forced to fight for their lives like poor Buddy." He sucked in a deep breath, blew it out. "I suppose I broke a million laws rescuing him."

Sidney chose her words carefully. "Your intentions were good, and you thought you were doing the best thing for him, breaking him out of Daggur's shed ... but ...."

"But ...." he said in a guarded tone, his posture stiff. "You don't like my methods."

Trespassing, breaking into someone's shed, carrying an illegal firearm, exposing himself and Dillon to the violence of the Krall brothers, who shot at them! No, she certainly did not approve of his methods. But she wasn't going to admonish him. She wanted Rafe to trust her, to open up. She wanted to crack open his chest of secrets. "I operate under the belief that following the rule of law is a good thing. Without the framework of laws, society would give in to chaos, to violence. The strong would rule. The weak would be victimized."

"Except that cops are corrupt, too. They victimize people and get away with it."

"I'm sorry that your past experiences have led you to believe that, Rafe."

"They beat the crap out of my dad. He was drunk. Couldn't fight back."

But he tried to. Sidney read the police report. Aiden McEnery furiously fought the cops when they tried to arrest him, after he drove his pickup into a Honda carrying a family of four. Killed one of the kids. Put the mother in the ICU. He was still in prison.

"Yes, there are some bad cops, but the vast majority are good people who follow the letter of the law. Who care deeply about people. Who put their lives on the line every day to serve and protect the public. A cop was shot last night, Rafe, taking down the people who hurt dogs."

He regarded her carefully, as though sifting through her words for a particle of deceit. Then he said with sincerity, "I'm sorry to hear that."

"There are legal measures to take to help animals," she continued. "When I learn of an animal being abused, I work with other agencies to rescue them. Trained professionals. Civilians are never put in a dangerous position." *Like Dillon. Like Joey.*

"Yeah, well I've learned you can't trust people to do the right thing. I have to rely on myself. Daggur should never have gotten Buddy in the first place. The one thing I had to do after Delores died, was take care of her dog." He frowned, and Sidney detected a twinge of guilt in the way he clenched and unclenched his jaw. "But I wasn't able to. The least I could do was bust him out of there."

She perceived a sense of failure that accompanied his grief over the loss of Delores.

Rafe opened the door to talk about her, and she wanted to open it wider. "There was no way you could have helped the dog. No one knew Delores was dead."

"I knew something was wrong. I went to her camp and her car was there, but she wasn't. We were supposed to meet up at the church. She didn't show." Rafe spoke in a monotone, betraying no emotion but his hands were tightly clasped in his lap.

Sidney understood. She'd witnessed detachment many times in grieving people. It was needed for them to go on, to function from day to day.

"I talked to a homeless couple who live there," he said. "They said a man in a white van took her and Buddy the night before."

Taron Seminov. "When did you talk to them, Rafe?"

"The morning of Stevana's funeral." He leveled a sober gaze on her, but there was intensity behind his eyes. "Then, of course, you guys discovered her in Stevana's coffin two weeks later."

"We'd like to know how she got into Stevana's coffin. Do you know anything about that?"

No response. His face was expressionless except for his eyes, which darted away from hers.

Sidney thought that not trusting anyone, hiding his feelings, and operating on his own must be exhausting. "You said you shot the guy who killed her. Why did you think Taron Seminov killed her?"

Rafe's face darkened, but he said nothing.

"Talk to me, Rafe. Do you want to see this guy pay for what he did, or not?"

His expression went through several transformations until his shoulders sagged. "Yeah, I want to see him get what he deserves. But why should I trust you?"

"You have two options," she said in a sympathetic tone. "Don't talk. Taron gets off with a light sentence. Talk to me, be a witness, and I'll try to get him the maximum penalty."

He thought for a long moment, then exhaled a tense breath. "Okay. I'll tell you what I know. Starting with Stevana's cocktail party. Stevana wanted me to be the guest of honor, but Morticia didn't want me there. I showed up anyway. Gordon left the kitchen door unlocked so I could sneak in." Rafe went on to talk about his surprise appearance as Zorro, his toast and meaningful goodbye to Stevana, and how Morticia discovered him and had Gordon kick him out.

"Once I was alone outside," he continued. "I noticed a white van parked out on the street. It raised my suspicion immediately. The homeless couple said Delores left the camp in a white van. A dark figure stood behind it, smoking and watching the house. Of course, now I know he was the psycho I saw in the woods last night. Taron Seminov."

The room was dead quiet except for the sound of Darnell scribbling notes.

"I was dressed all in black," Rafe continued. "So I easily blended into the shadows. For the next hour, I watched him. After everyone left the party, he got into the van and drove into the cemetery without headlights. I followed, but the moon was bright, so I darted behind tombstones and trees. He parked behind a mausoleum so he couldn't be seen from the mortuary. Then another guy, all in black, stepped out of the shadows. He'd been waiting. Taron got out of the van, and they stood talking for a minute. Then they walked off, heading for the house. I crept up to the van and tried the back door. It was unlocked, so I opened it." Rafe's voice choked and he looked down at his hands.

Sidney couldn't see his expression. "Rafe, are you okay?"

Silence.

"Darnell, why don't you get him some water."

The young officer quietly left the room.

Rafe sat staring at his hands.

Sidney had listened to the young man intently. She had studied his face, listened to every nuance, every tone in his voice. So far, she was convinced he was telling the truth.

Darnell returned and placed a bottle of water in front of the teen.

"Rafe, take a drink," Sidney said softly.

He lifted his head and drank a third of the water in one gulp. He wiped his mouth with the back of his hand and met her gaze, his eyes brimming with emotion. "A woman was inside the van. She was sprawled on her back, head resting to one side, arms across her chest." He recited the words as though he was seeing the image in front of him. "Her face was no longer recognizable, but I knew it was Delores. She was wearing the necklace I gave her. A turquoise and silver St. Christopher medal on a chain."

That's where Delores got the St. Christopher. Recalling the decomposing victim, her battered face, the necklace, Sidney felt a tightening at the back of her neck. It had been difficult for her, a seasoned homicide detective, to witness. It must have been horrific for Rafe to discover Delores that way; a traumatizing experience that would stay with him for life. Sidney glanced at Darnell. He too looked disturbed.

"I was stunned," Rafe continued, his voice strained. "I couldn't move. I thought I was going to throw up. I put my hands on my knees and took some deep breaths and managed to fight back the nausea. I heard voices. The two men were coming back. Not thinking straight, I just moved into the shadows and watched, horrified. They were carrying Stevana—one had her upper body, one had her legs. They laid her in the van next to Delores. Then they pulled Delores out and carried her back to the mortuary the same way. I knew what they were doing. Exchanging bodies. They wanted to hide Delores. They wanted to get Stevana away from there so they could cut off her jewelry without being interrupted. The ring and necklace were intricately stitched to her skin."

"Stitched to her skin?"

"Yeah. At Stevana's funeral party, Mr. Biggs tried to lift the necklace up to get a closer look. It wouldn't move. When I had the chance, I took a good look. There were tiny stitches around the whole necklace. I guess Morticia does that when people are buried with valuables that can be easily stolen."

He paused to take a sip of water, then continued. "Well, I had news for them. I pulled out my pocket knife and started slicing beneath the diamond necklace, cutting through the stitching. It took an eternity. I probably could've been more careful, but I was nervous that they'd come back before I was done. Hell, it was a corpse. It didn't bleed. Stevana, my dear friend who once occupied that body, was long gone.

The two men returned a few minutes later, this time running. They didn't even open the back and look in. They just took off. They wanted to get the hell away from the scene of their crime. I didn't get to witness their shock when they saw her necklace was missing." His mouth twitched, then one side lifted into a smile. "That necklace was worth a mint, and they didn't get a penny of it."

"What about the ring?"

"I didn't have time to get it off her."

"What happened next?"

"I quietly entered the mortuary and found the viewing room. As I approached the coffin, I stepped on something. It was the key to the coffin. One of them dropped it. They were in such a hurry to get out of there they didn't bother to find it and lock it."

He paused, coughed, cleared his throat, and continued in a softer tone. "I lifted the lid and there she was. Delores. Alone. Murdered. Abandoned. I took her hand, and just held it for a while, saying my farewell in my own way." A spasm of grief passed over his face, and when he continued his voice was husky. "Delores was invisible to most people, but not to me. She was kind, and generous. She had dreams of a better life, but those dreams faded away without a sound. Without anyone really noticing. I put the diamond necklace on her. It looked beautiful around her neck. It made me feel better to see her lying in that elegant coffin, all satin and lace. I knew she was going to have a great funeral, with people attending, and Pastor John giving the last rites. A warm send off, like a rich woman."

A tear ran down his cheek and he roughly knuckled it away. "Then I closed and locked the coffin, put the key on Morticia's desk, and left." He met Sidney's eyes. "I made a promise to Delores and Stevana that I would find the man in the white van. That's what I've been doing while living in the bunker. Finally, I did find him, as you know. Last night in the woods."

"You're sure it was Taron you saw in the cemetery?"

He nodded. "Saw him clear as day."

"What about the other man, Rafe? Could you identify him?"

"No. Never got a good look at him. He had a hoody pulled over his face."

Darnell stopped scribbling and waited. There was a long silence while Sidney mulled over everything Rafe had said. If he had called the police immediately from the cemetery that night, it would've saved them enormous time and effort—trying to figure out what happened to Stevana and how Delores got into her coffin. But on the plus side, Rafe had stitched together some of the loose ends of her investigation. Taron was indeed involved in the murder of Delores, the theft of Stevana's body, and the missing ring. His accomplice may not have been involved with murder, but could be charged with misuse of a corpse, attempted grand larceny, and conspiracy. "Rafe, where did you get the gun that you shot Taron with?"

"It belonged to Delores. I found it in her tent when I went to look for her."

"Something troubles me. You were devastated by the sight of Delores' body, but you had no hesitation slicing up Stevana's body, your dear friend. Why is that?"

"First, I didn't slice up Stevana's body. I may have nicked a small area around her neck to get off the necklace. But it was worth it to keep it out of the hands of greedy thieves. Stevana would have approved. Secondly, I had time to say goodbye to Stevana. I knew for weeks that she was dying. Delores was violently murdered. I had no time to prepare myself for how I found her."

"How much do you know about Stevana's cause of death?"

He shrugged.

"Stevana Thornburg was poisoned and possibly murdered."

His eyebrows lifted. "That's ridiculous."

Sidney gave him a piercing glance.

"Stevana planned her death."

"How?"

"I don't know. She wouldn't say. But she kept getting weaker her last three weeks of life."

"Why didn't you tell someone?"

"Stevana told me not to. What good would it have done, anyway? If someone wants to die, they'll find a way." He shifted uncomfortably in his seat. "Do you think I wanted her to die? I begged her not to go. But she was determined. She said she was ready, that she was tired of living in pain, in a wheelchair, and she wanted to be with Forest. Stevana went on her own terms, with everything tidy and taken care of. Quietly and peacefully slipping away."

"Do you know anything about the herbs that killed her?"

"Herbs?" He looked puzzled. "Like tea?"

"Yes."

"Hmmm. I know she started drinking a strange brew before she went to bed."

"Why strange?"

"It had a pungent, woody smell."

"Where did she get it?"

"Not from me. I bought her healthy teas from the farmer's market as little gifts, to help her. We drank them together. Peppermint. Lavender vanilla. Stuff that smelled good."

"Can you think of anything else that could help our investigation?"

"No. I told you everything."

"Thank you for your cooperation, Rafe."

"What's going to happen to me now?" he asked.

"That's up to your lawyer. He'll argue the shooting was in self-defense."

"It was," he said passionately. "I admit it, I went after Taron to shoot him, but when I had the chance, I couldn't do it. I couldn't pull the trigger. I was going to walk him to the barn. Let you arrest him. But then he hit me with his gun, hard. If I hadn't been moving, it might have knocked me out, fractured my skull. Maybe he would have hit me again. I was in survival mode when I shot him. Him or me."

"You don't have to try to convince me, Rafe. Convince the judge. I'm sure your lawyer will work out some kind of plea bargain. I'll tell your prosecutor that you cooperated fully, and that you agree to testify against Taron Seminov."

His eyes scanned the ceiling while he groped for words, then his gaze locked on hers. "I want to thank you, Chief Becker. You're not so bad, for a cop. Dillon was right. You're easy to talk to."

"It's never too late to have a change of heart about people. About life. About the path you choose to take. You have good people in your life. The pastor. The boys. A safe place to live."

He sighed. "What's done is done. I can't go back and redo things, can I? But I'm going to change my ways."

"With people in the community vouching for you, like Pastor John and Mr. Hiroko at the sanctuary, and with you clearly owning your mistakes, the judge will most likely go with a deal. That doesn't mean you won't serve time. I'll help as much as I can."

He sat silently, pensive. The teen had a lot to think about.

"Darnell, take Rafe back to his cell."

CHAPTER FORTY

GLANCING AT HER WATCH, Sidney walked down the hall to her office, her thoughts turning to the next critical issue on her agenda. A very important conference call was scheduled to take place in thirty minutes. David had hired an excellent lawyer to represent Dillon; Thomas Wright, one of the best in the county. Dillon had been charged with petty larceny and trespassing with the intent to commit a crime. In the best-case scenario, as part of an agreement with the prosecuting attorney, Dillon could plead guilty, the judge could take it under advisement, and basically put Dillon on probation for a year. At the end of the year, if he hadn't gotten into further trouble, the judge could dismiss the case. That's frequently what was done with good kids who screwed up once, but not too badly, and Dillon fit into that category. But she had another idea.

***

David picked up the phone after two rings. She knew he was at the Art Studio. His last morning class would have ended twenty minutes ago. Often, students hung around for a while, asking for his advice on their various projects. By now, they would have all cleared out. Of course, Thomas Wright had informed him of the upcoming conference call with her, the D.A., and Dillon's attorney, and he was no doubt waiting anxiously to hear the outcome.

"Hey, Sidney. Please tell me Dillon got probation," he said crisply, getting right to the heart of the matter.

"As you know, the conference call included the D.A. and Dillon's attorney, but Daggur Krall's attorney also joined the conversation. Long story short, after some negotiation, Daggur's charge for stealing Buddy was dropped. In exchange, Daggur agreed to drop all charges against Dillon. In the end, the D.A. took into consideration Dillon's clean record, his good grades and involvement in sports, and he agreed to the deal."

A moment of silence. Then Sidney heard David exhale a huge sigh of relief. "Wow. That's more than I was expecting. This whole business has been keeping me awake at night. Dillon, too. He's been super stressed. I can't believe it's just going away."

"It's a win-win for everybody," she said.

"I can't thank you enough, Sidney. I know you were fighting for Dillon. Was it your idea to bring in Krall's attorney?"

"I may have suggested it."

"I can't wait to tell Dillon. This calls for celebration. I want to take you both out for a great dinner. You name the place."

"Sounds wonderful. Let me get this homicide case wrapped up first."

"I can't see you until then?" he asked, disappointment shading his tone.

"Sorry," she said softly. "We're getting close. Then you're on."

"Can't wait. Love you, babe."

CHAPTER FORTY-ONE

SIDNEY ENTERED the community hospital in Jackson at 3:00 p.m., strode down the hall and greeted Officer Rick Dunbar, who was stationed outside Taron Seminov's room. Dunbar was middle-aged, portly, and near retirement. She gestured toward the room. "How's our prisoner doing?"

"Hasn't said zip since lunch. Got riled that I wouldn't get him a cigarette. Doesn't think the 'no smoking' rule applies to him."

"What about before lunch?"

"This one's hard to read. Picks his words carefully. Gives nothing away. His eyes look at you like they want to suck out your soul."

Sidney recalled how one of the suspects from the raid had described him. "Like a vampire?"

He laughed. "Yeah. Count Dracula. He even has the accent."

Sidney smiled back, appreciating the moment of levity before she confronted Taron. "Go ahead and take a break, Rick. I'll be here for a while."

"Good. I'm getting stiff just sitting here. Can I bring you back a coffee?"

"You read my mind. I'm wilting around the edges. Cream and sugar, please."

"One mega dose of caffeine, coming up."

After he left, Sidney paused in the doorway and took in the dark, sparse room. The Russian lay against the pillows in the elevated hospital bed with his eyes closed, his face all sharp edges and straight lines. *Very Dracula like.*

An IV tube snaked from the back of his right hand, his left wrist was cuffed to the bed, and his slim body was hidden beneath the covers. Here was the man who worked with organ traffickers, who tortured dogs, and who committed a host of other egregious crimes. A man without a conscience. Hiding her revulsion, Sidney let her face slide into a blank, professional mask and entered the room.

The prisoner's eyes opened and slowly roamed over her uniform, read her name tag, then he gave her a subtle nod. His eyes were dark and intelligent in a feral way, like a predator, evaluating whether she was friend or foe. Then a faint smile teased the edges of his lips. "Police Chief Becker. The boss lady in the woods last night."

"Hello, Mr. Seminov," she said cordially. "How're you doing?"

"I am not dead. For that, I thank you and your comrades."

"Just doing our jobs. The doctor says you'll make a full recovery." *Tomorrow, he'd be transferred to the medical facility in the county jail, then put in a cell. Hopefully for years.* "Do you mind if we chat for a few minutes?"

He pulled at his cuffed wrist. "As you see, I have not much else to do." He nodded at the only chair in the room, next to the bed. "Sit."

Sidney sat in silence for a moment, gathering her thoughts, preparing herself.

"You want to know about man who shoot me, yes?" he asked.

"That, and other things. If you don't mind, I'd like to record our conversation."

He shrugged. "If you must."

Sidney set her phone to record and placed it on the stand between them. "Before we begin, Mr. Seminov, I must advise you that you have the right to remain silent. Anything you say can and will be used against you in a court of law. You have a right to an attorney. If you cannot afford an attorney, one will be appointed for you. Do you understand?"

"Why you tell me this? I am victim here."

"You do understand that you were arrested last night, right?"

"Yes. It is mistake."

"Do you understand your Miranda Rights, Mr. Seminov?"

He met her gaze, didn't flinch, just stared with a calm stillness. "I understand very well. I do not need to confess anything. I do not need to incriminate myself."

"That's correct."

"What is it you like to speak of, Chief Becker?"

"Let's talk about why you're under arrest, the charges brought against you."

He just lay there, hardly moving, his face expressionless. "I am listening."

"Let's start with the dog fight last night …."

"Dog fight? I know nothing of this. I am only walking my dog in woods. Is that crime?"

After midnight, on a deserted goat farm, the same night as a big dog fighting event? A preposterous statement, but Sidney ignored it and continued. "We have several witnesses who will testify that you routinely participated in dog fights, which are felony offenses. The code of silence you were counting on from the other men in the barn is broken. Almost two dozen men were arrested last night. Two made the mistake of shooting at officers. They're dead. We found illegal drugs and weapons on a few of them. Already, several have talked, and they were very willing to implicate you."

"All lies. I am not criminal."

"I'm just getting started, Mr. Seminov. We also have you on kidnapping charges. You kidnapped Jacko Krall, a minor, which is a class two felony."

His eyebrows lifted in mock surprise. "I did not do this thing you say."

"He was found gagged and bound in your van."

"I do not know this person … this Jacko. How he got there, I do not know."

"Jacko remembers quite a lot, despite the fact that you drugged him. He's willing to testify against you in court."

Taron stared at her, his dark eyes impenetrable. "He was drugged? Then it is drugs that are speaking. He does not know what he say."

Taron was toying with her, trying to stir up a little drama, get an emotional reaction. They both knew he didn't have a leg to stand on, and that he was in trouble up to his eyeballs. She didn't oblige him but kept her voice carefully polite. "You've been operating with organ traffickers, Mr. Seminov, disposing of bodies for them."

"What is this … traffickers? I never hear of this. I am innocent man." His eyes looked shrewd, openly calculating. "Someone … how you say … is framing me up."

"You broke into a mortuary and stole the body of Stevana Thornburg. You stole the emerald ring Ms. Thornburg was wearing, then hid her body in a compost pile. You transported the body of Delores Wilkins and concealed it in Stevana Thornburg's coffin. We exhumed her body from the cemetery a few days ago. Her kidneys had been removed, and she bled to death. A vicious, cold-blooded murder."

Taron did not respond. A long silence stretched between them. His eyes were opaque. Unreadable. Sounds filtered in from the corridor; the soft voices of nurses navigating their mobile workstations in and out of neighboring rooms.

Abruptly, a sharp alertness tightened his features. "You speak of dead women. I know nothing of this. I confess to nothing."

Sidney knew when she walked in that she wouldn't get much out of him, which suited her fine. That's not what she was here for. "We don't need your confessions, Mr. Seminov. We have ironclad evidence that you committed these crimes. We have a witness who saw everything you did in the cemetery. We have forensic evidence that puts Delores and Stevana in your van. You seem like a savvy guy. I think you know that you can't squirm out of these charges. No lawyer can make them go away." She paused to let her words sink in. "You've racked up quite a few years behind bars."

Another long silence passed. Sidney waited patiently while Seminov revisited all the blunt points she had driven home. His freedom was being snatched away. Perhaps the reality of sitting in a small cell for years was finally sinking in.

Abruptly, his veneer cracked. His eyes sneered at her out of his bone-hard face. She sensed a strange power emanating from them. Something sociopathic. It was meant to intimidate. He wanted to see fear in her eyes or stoke her anger. Sidney was unmoved. During her fifteen years as a homicide detective in Oakland, she dealt with dozens of psychopaths and sociopaths—people who generally lacked the ability to feel shame or remorse. They either experienced only shallow emotions or feigned emotions altogether. She had learned to put up a wall of defense that deflected their sick manipulations like sun rays off a mirror. "Do you understand these charges, Mr. Seminov?"

He gave her a cryptic, yet borderline predatory look. "What is it you want, boss lady? You do not come here to speak of these crimes. It is information you want, no? I talk. I give you something. Then you give me something. We make deal. Yes?"

"Work with me and I'll see what I can do to help you, Mr. Seminov."

"I am just taxi driver. I do not kill anybody."

"I understand. I'll speak to the prosecuting attorney. Tell him you cooperated fully. That may soften some of these charges against you."

He became calm and still, calculation in his eyes, and she endured another long silence, until finally, he nodded. "I help you. What is it you want?"

"We want to know who you work for. Jacko overheard you talking to someone on the phone. You called him Doc. We believe he works at a funeral home."

"Yes. This is true. It is Gateway Funerals, in Jackson."

Sidney was not familiar with it. "And the name of the man who hired you?"

"Mr. Edgar Hoffman. The owner."

Her adrenaline hummed. Taron was talking, giving names. "This is the man you call Doc?"

"Yes."

"Did he kill Delores?"

"I am just taxi driver. I do not know how she die."

"How many bodies have you transported for him?"

"One only. This lady. Delores."

"Why was Delores chosen?"

He shrugged.

"You were seen picking her up at the campsite where she lived."

"Ask Doc. I am just driver. He say go get this lady. I do as he say."

"How did you get her to go with you?"

"Doc say he want to talk with her. He has job for her. Cleaning funeral home. He pay one hundred dollars each time. She was happy to come with me. She want big white dog to come. I say okay. I take her there. Then I leave. The next night, Doc call me. Say come pick her up. I go. I see she is dead. It was accident, Doc say. I do not want to do this. But Doc give me much money to bury her in woods. I am poor man. I can not say no. I need to eat. Pay bills. I say okay. He tell me take her dog, too.

"He asked you to bury her. How is it that you put her in Stevana's coffin instead?"

"I have Delores in van. I am driving. My friend call. He say old dead lady with jewelry is at funeral home. Worth much money. He has plan. He pay me to help. As I say, I need money. So I say okay. I go to funeral home. Wait outside. He call. I drive into cemetery. We meet. We go in home and take old lady out of coffin. Put her in van. We put Delores in coffin. Then we go. Now we must bury old lady in woods. We go to woods. Then we open van, the diamonds not there. My friend is mad. He is scared. Someone saw us, stole necklace. Maybe this person call police. They look for white van. He is in big hurry. He cuts ring from old lady. Then he say to leave old lady by road. I do not like this. I see house. Big hill of leaves in yard. I put dead lady under leaves. End of story."

"Who is this friend that helped you?"

Taron subjected her to another long silence.

"Don't protect him, Taron. This man isn't a good friend. He was careless. He was in a hurry. If you had buried Stevana, we never would have found her. We would never have dug up her coffin and found Delores." *They would have gotten away with it.*

The corners of his mouth twitched reluctantly.

"Help yourself here, Taron. Tell me his name."

"Max Biggs."

Sidney was only partly surprised. It made sense. Max Biggs was already on her suspect list. He was one of the actors at Stevana's funeral party, the one who assessed the value of the jewelry. But how did he hook up with a man like Taron? They operated in different worlds. "How is it that you and Mr. Biggs became friends?"

He shrugged. "It does not matter where we meet."

"Was it at a dog fight?"

"I do not do this dog fighting." He said unconvincingly.

She took that to be a yes. "What happened to Delores's white dog?"

"I do not know. Max take him that night." After a few beats, he asked, "Where is my dog? Sergei."

"He's in good hands. Animal control."

"Good." He exhaled a long breath. "That is all. I do not know anything more. Now I am tired. I must sleep." He closed his eyes and turned his face to the wall.

Clearly, she had been dismissed.

Sidney was smiling when she encountered Officer Dunbar in the hallway carrying a take-out cup. "Here's your coffee, Chief. You look upbeat."

Her smile widened into a grin. "We just broke the case, Rick. Taron gave us names. Now we just need to round up the bastards."

CHAPTER FORTY-TWO

IT WAS 7:00 P.M. when they reached their destination and their headlights lit up the front of Gateway Funeral Home. From the outside, the mortuary looked respectable and unassuming, an attractive one-story stucco building set back from a manicured lawn. A shiny black hearse was parked in the semi-circular driveway.

Sidney parked behind the hearse. Right behind them, Captain Harrison and two of his officers exited their patrol vehicles, their strobes pulsing blue and red in the night. A white van from county pulled up and four forensic technicians climbed out wearing field clothes and carrying crime kits.

The funeral home was in Jackson, the jurisdiction of Harrison's department, but because most of the investigative work had been done by the Garnerville department, Sidney was taking the lead. The pressure to find Delores's killer had been steadily mounting, but now he was just beyond the front door. Her shoulders tightened as she entered the softly lit lobby with her three officers. Captain Harrison followed with one of his officers.

A red-faced, balding man wearing a dark suit, who appeared to be well past retirement age, stepped in quietly from another room. His eyes widened in surprise when he saw their uniforms, then he spotted the pulsing lights and the others waiting outside. His expression grew intense, and he said in a hushed tone, "What is the meaning of this? We have a bereaved couple in the viewing room. He lost his mother. You need to leave, right now, before they see you!"

"That's not going to happen," Sidney said crisply. "Are you Mr. Edgar Hoffman, owner of Gateway Funeral Home?"

"Yes, I'm the owner."

Hoffman looked as ordinary, as nondescript as someone's granddad, and would never stand out in a crowd—but that was often the case with cold-blooded killers. Their best strategy was blending in, operating under the radar. Other than Taron's testimony, Sidney had no hard evidence to justify an arrest, but hopefully she would very soon. She handed him a warrant. "Mr. Hoffman, this warrant says we can search your entire property, inside and out, which is what we intend to do. Now."

Sidney had never seen a man's face drain of color as fast as Hoffman's as he read the warrant. "This is preposterous!"

"Do you have other employees working here tonight?" she asked.

"We run a respectable business here."

"Please answer her question," Harrison said.

"Yes, two."

"Where are they?" she asked.

"My wife, Marie, is with the couple. My son, Danny, is out back."

The door to the viewing room opened and a fleshy, gray-haired woman poked her head out. With a look of alarm, she stepped quietly into the lobby and shut the door behind her. "What's going on?"

"We're searching your premises, Mrs. Hoffman."

"You can't just run amok over our property!" Mr. Hoffman blustered, his face reddening again.

"I need you both to wait in the viewing room and let us go about our business. I'd advise you to send the grieving family home."

"Kelly, wait with them," Harrison said to one of his officers. "Make sure they touch nothing and don't speak to one another."

Officer Kelly escorted the Hoffmans into the viewing room, leaving the door wide open. Sidney saw a young man and woman standing in front of a closed coffin that was unusually small, maybe three feet long. Kelly spoke softly to them, then they hastily exited the room and left the building, looking bewildered.

Sidney motioned for the rest of the crew to enter, and they quickly got to work, spreading out to various parts of the home.

"Darnell, you and I are going to talk to Hoffman's son out back," Sidney said. They walked down a hallway, catching glimpses of their crew at work in two offices and a morgue.

Outside, bright lights lit up the covered patio that was screened on all sides by evergreen bushes. Hoffman's son, Danny, dressed in medical scrubs was busily hosing something down with his back to them. The business of death always affected Sidney, personally and professionally, but she had learned to portray calm for the sake of her subordinates. Now a burst of adrenaline shot through her veins. What looked like bits of tissue and blood were washing into the gutter and then vanishing into a storm drain. She and Darnell stepped around Danny to get a clearer view. Sidney felt the hair ris on her arms.

"Holy shit …." Darnell said under his breath.

Danny was using the water to thaw a man's frozen corpse, which was headless and lay on a gurney.

"Stop!" Sidney commanded.

Danny froze, then aimed the hose away from the body and switched off the water.

"What the hell are you doing?" Sidney asked.

"I could ask the same question," he said indignantly. "What the hell are you doing? This is a restricted area."

"We have a warrant to search this entire property."

"What?"

"Answer the question, Danny. What's with the headless corpse?"

He glared at her for a long moment. "I'm getting this body ready to dismember."

"Dismember?" Darnell said. "What, so you can fit it in a smaller casket, like the one in the viewing room?"

He ignored Darnell's question. "Obviously, you don't know that Gateway started selling body parts as a secondary business six months ago. It's perfectly legal. The head went to a buyer last week."

"You're a body broker?" Sidney asked.

"Yes, it's clearly mentioned on our website. Is that why you're here? Did someone complain about our practices?"

"I'd like to continue this conversation, Mr. Hoffman, but first, let me inform you of your Miranda Rights."

"Why? Are you arresting me?"

"It's just routine, for your protection."

She recited and he listened impatiently. "Now please explain exactly what it is you do." Sidney knew full well what a body broker did. There was a big market for dead bodies, and it could be an extremely lucrative business. There were no federal laws governing the sale of cadavers for use in research or education. Few state laws provided any oversight whatsoever, and almost anyone could set up a facility and dissect and sell body parts. In most states, anyone could legally purchase body parts. In Oakland, while investigating fraud, her team was sold a cervical spine and two human heads after just a few emails to a broker. It was like the Wild West. Anybody could have ordered those parts and had them delivered to their home for whatever purpose they wanted.

"It's pretty straight forward," Danny said in a condescending tone. "We get dead bodies from donors. We dissect them and sell the parts for medica training and research."

"Why is it frozen?" Darnell asked.

"We store human parts in freezers until the entire body is sold." Noting Darnell's look of disgust, he added, "Look, body parts are essential for training doctors, nurses, and dentists. Paramedics need human heads and torsos to learn how to insert breathing tubes. And we're helping poor people who can't afford a funeral. The donors get part of their bodies buried for free We offer a funeral service and a casket. Which helps grieving families ge closure. Everyone benefits."

"Yeah, especially the broker," Sidney said. "You get a body for free, and then you can sell it for what? Five thousand? Ten?"

"We sell at market prices," he said gruffly.

"But you can't sell live organs."

"Of course not. We only deal with dead bodies."

Time to turn up the heat. "Tell us about the homeless woman who came here two weeks ago," Sidney said, watching him carefully. "Delores Wilkins."

Danny didn't answer for a long moment, then shrugged. "Lots of people come through here. I can't remember everyone."

"According to a witness, Delores was alive when dropped off here. She was dead when picked up the next night."

"That's outrageous! Just what are you accusing me of?"

"Organ trafficking. Her kidneys had been removed."

"That's a horrible accusation. Is that why you're searching our mortuary? His tone rose several decibels and his face tightened with anger. "You hope t find something that incriminates us in a murder? In organ trafficking?"

Sidney said nothing, just let his heated words hang in the air.

"We know Delores was murdered here, Danny. As you know, it's nea impossible to get rid of every minute trace of blood, no matter how much yo sterilize. It leaks everywhere. Is that what happened when you put Delores o the table and cut her kidneys out?"

"This is nonsense." His left eyebrow twitched, and he rubbed it with hi hand. "You aren't going to find anything."

"We're going to tear your embalming room apart. We will fin something." She lowered her gaze to the blood and tissue that had bee spread across the patio. "Do you routinely flush human remains into th public sewer system?"

"Little shop of horrors," Darnell said under his breath.

Danny heaved out a deep breath. "Okay, you caught me. I'm guilty. Bu this is the first and only time. That's little more than a minor pollution issue. Give me a citation."

"When we examine the storm system on this street, are we going to find evidence that you've been doing it for months? Are we going to find DNA evidence that links you to the murder of Delores Wilkins?"

"No, of course not." His eyebrow twitched again. "Who's this witness that says this woman was here?"

"Taron Seminov. You asked him to dispose of the body."

Danny's face went blank, but not before Sidney saw a glint of another emotion. Fear. And he was trying to hide it.

"We'll find DNA evidence, Danny, and we have a witness. That incriminates your whole family."

Danny blanched. "It was my idea to start selling body parts. Funerals weren't paying the bills. My folks need money to retire on."

"Any way you look at it, you and your parents are going down. Who killed Delores, Danny? Your dad?"

"Leave my mom and dad out of this."

"Was it your idea to harvest her kidneys?"

He swallowed. "Look, that wasn't planned. Yeah, the homeless woman was here, okay? But her death was an accident. A horrible, tragic accident."

And then her kidneys jumped out of her body? "Please explain."

Danny started pacing, his expression anxious, one hand rubbing his brow. "It all started so simply, so innocently. Dad was looking for someone to clean the mortuary. They're too old to be working so hard. Dad and mom are very charitable, and they thought we should give a homeless person a job opportunity. Someone at the church highly recommended Delores. Taron did odd jobs for us. We asked him to pick her up. We liked her right away. And Delores was excited to work for us. Mom gave her a tour of the place, showed her all the rooms on this level. Then they headed downstairs where we keep the laundry facility and the cleaning materials. The stairs are very steep. We're used to them and we're very careful." He stopped pacing and locked eyes with Sidney. "That's when it happened. Delores missed a step and lost her balance. She took a horrible, violent tumble down the stairs. Her head hit several stairs then slammed the floor at the bottom. Her face was battered and covered in blood. Blood was streaming from a head wound. She was unconscious. I carried her to the embalming room and tried to stop the bleeding, but she died within minutes. We all stood there, stunned, covered in blood."

He hesitated, heaved out a deep breath, then continued. "My dad said he'd go call the police. But I said not to. I got the idea then and there to harvest her kidneys. Surely you can understand my position. There are many very sick people on the kidney donor list. Many will die before they get a kidney. I thought we could save two lives. I talked dad into doing it. He's a retired doctor."

The fact that Danny offered up this story immediately, without hedging, strongly suggested to Sidney that he was telling the truth. And he appeared genuinely affected by Delores's death and concerned about his aging parents. Sidney remembered when Stewart opened Stevana's coffin at the morgue, and they found Delores inside. Her face was unrecognizable, the injuries consistent with falling down the stairs. This could just be a series of very bad choices made by Danny and his family. In which case, they had committed a multitude of crimes, but it didn't point to an organized organ-trafficking ring in Linnly County. "Harvested organs are time-sensitive," Sidney said. "You don't just pop them out, go to the yellow pages, and call up a buyer."

"Of course not," he said wearily. "I've been approached before to sell organs. To ask a donor's family to notify me as soon as their loved one is dead. I've always declined. But yeah, I knew who would buy them immediately."

"Black market, of course."

He nodded. "That's why I declined."

"But not this time. What did you sell them for?"

"Seventy-five thousand each. That gives my parents money for retirement."

"Except now it'll be used for legal fees," Darnell said.

"We're going to need the name of your buyer."

He crossed his arms and said with a determined look. "Look, I'm not saying another word. Not until I consult a lawyer."

"Darnell, place Mr. and Mrs. Hoffman under arrest. You and Granger can transport them to the county jail."

"Please, don't arrest my mom," Danny pleaded. "She had nothing to do with it. She tried to persuade us not to do it."

"Too bad you didn't listen," Darnell said.

"I'll give you my buyer's name if you go easy on my parents," he said.

"I'll talk to the prosecutor," Sidney said. "See what we can do."

"I'm not talking until we have a deal."

"I'll try to arrange a meeting this week. Darnell, just arrest Mr. Hoffman."

"Thank you."

"Danny Hoffman, I'm placing you under arrest for the abuse of a corpse. Please put your hands behind your back."

Sidney would leave the charges generalized until she talked with the prosecutor. Danny's defense attorney could successfully argue that Delores's death was accidental. The charges would basically be the abuse of a corpse, stealing and selling her kidneys, and conspiracy with his father and Taron. No homicide, but he and his father were still neck deep in serious trouble.

CHAPTER FORTY-THREE

GRANGER CONTACTED ED HORTON, the manager of the entertainment company, and was told Max Biggs was doing a gig at a birthday party in Garnerville. The address was just two miles from the station. With Amanda riding shotgun, he pulled in front of the house and immediately spotted the actor's brightly painted van. They rang the doorbell. No answer. But they heard the laughter of children coming from the rear of the house. They walked to the back yard where a dozen young children sat in front of a clown. Four women sat amongst them acting as chaperones. One, looking distressed, immediately rushed over to them. "Thank goodness you're here. One of the other parents called you?"

Granger's antennae shot straight up. *No, they had not been called.* "You are the property owner?"

"Yes. Louise Bernardo."

"What can we help you with?"

She gestured to Biggs. "He's drunk, or high on something. We want him out of here before he scares the kids."

They turned their attention to Biggs, who was dressed in an ill-fitting pink tuxedo with an orange top hat over a yellow wig. His face was painted white with a huge red grin, and he wore his big red plastic nose. He was just starting a magic trick.

"Let's wait for him to finish this trick," Amanda said. "Then you can announce it's time to eat cake and we'll escort him off the property."

"A clown's job is to act stupid," Biggs said loudly, slurring his words. "Because you kids find stupid adults hilarious."

The kids didn't know what to make of him. They just stared with big eyes.

Biggs whipped off his hat, dislodging the yellow wig which now sat lopsided on his head. "Abracadabra!" He pulled out an obviously fake stuffed rabbit from the hat. The kids stared in confusion, then responded with groans and disappointed expressions.

"Really?" Amanda said. "That's all he's got? What a flop."

"Let's get him out of here," Granger said.

The mother took her cue. "Does everyone want cake and ice cream?"

Whoops of excitement accompanied a stampede to the porch. The other three women herded the kids into the house, and they crowded through the door.

"Little bastards," Biggs said, clearly agitated. "Ingrates." Then he saw Granger and Amanda striding towards him. "You two, again? To what do I owe this displeasure this time?"

"Gather up your things, Mr. Biggs. Time to go."

Mumbling expletives under his breath, the clown stuffed his hat and wig into a small trunk and they escorted him to the driveway. Right off the bat, he was uncooperative and arrogant. "I'm getting pissed about being harassed by you guys." He reeked of alcohol and stumbled over his giant clown shoes several times.

After he placed his trunk in the van and locked it, he stood facing them in an intimidating stance, which looked ridiculous with his big red nose. As an afterthought, he ripped it off and stuffed it in a pocket.

"Max Biggs, I'm arresting you for being drunk and disorderly in public," Amanda said firmly. "Please place your hands behind your back."

Biggs would face far more serious charges once they got him to the station, but right now, they needed to get him into their vehicle with as little trouble as possible.

"Get away from me. I'm not drunk." He tried to twist past Amanda, but she grabbed him from behind, pressed him against the side of the van and cuffed his hands behind his back.

Granger winked and shot her a grin. Amanda fooled many suspects with her delicate Latin features and lean build, but she was all muscle, and her character was imbued with toughness and grit. Granger never had to worry about his back when they partnered together.

With a firm hand on each arm, they walked him to their vehicle. Biggs tugged and pulled and kept tripping over his huge shoes, but they finally got him into the cage of Granger's truck and drove to the station.

***

Sidney entered the video control room with Amanda and looked at Max Biggs through the two-way mirror. He had slept all afternoon, awakened with a bad hangover, had refused lunch, and had been plied with three cups of strong coffee. He looked like something from a freak show. His hair and pink tuxedo were disheveled, his red makeup had smeared into his white makeup, and his red clown shoes made his feet look like they belonged to a giant.

"Jeeze, he's either the funniest or scariest looking suspect I've ever seen," Sidney said.

"He'd scare the hell out of me if I came across him in a dark alley. Looks can deceive. He's a thief, not a serial killer."

"Right. The serial killers are the ones that look like the sweet guy next door. Let's go in. If we can get a confession out of him, our job is done, and we can put these cases to rest."

"Amen and hallelujah. I'd love to go back to a normal schedule. My kids forgot what I looked like this past week. Darnell's, too."

It had been a long challenging week, and Sidney had put her team through the grinder. Sacrifices had to be made when part of a small, overworked police department. But the reward was living in a beautiful rural area, much quieter than communities in congested urban areas. Less crime by far. Her team always came out of these homicide cases tougher, more seasoned, their instincts more reliable.

With pad and pen in hand, Amanda followed her into the interview room. They scraped back the metal chairs and seated themselves. Sidney picked up the stench of alcohol wafting off the entertainer's body. The sooner this interview was over, the better. "How are you doing, Mr. Biggs?" she asked, friendly.

He gave her a patronizing stare. "How do you think I'm doing? I woke up in cell, I'm dressed in my clown clothes, I have a godawful hangover, and I feel like shit."

He'd be transferred to the county jail soon, where he could shower and swap his pink tuxedo for an orange jumpsuit. "Before we continue, let me recite your Miranda Rights." She did. "Also, we're recording this interview."

His eyes darted across the ceiling and located the video camera. "Let's get this over with. I want outta here. I know my rights." His lip curled up in a sneer. "Okay, so I was drunk. I have no prior convictions. I didn't assault anyone. This is no more than a misdemeanor and a fine."

"You're getting ahead of yourself, Mr. Biggs. And you're minimizing your charges. You resisted arrest, punishable by up to a year in jail. But let's put this morning's incident aside for a moment. We want to talk to you about something quite a bit more serious; the night of Stevana's funeral party." She locked eyes with him. "You didn't tell us the whole truth, did you?"

His shoulders stiffened noticeably.

"The other entertainers said you showed quite a bit of interest in Mrs. Thornburg's jewelry."

"Yeah, so what? We already talked about this."

Sidney opened the file folder and continued to use honey in her tone. "Let me refresh your memory. Unlike the others, you knew Mrs. Thornburg's diamonds were real. I quote from your statement 'There are ways you can tell. They are more faceted than fakes, and they have tiny imperfections. Fakes are flawless. Then I studied the setting those diamonds were in. Exquisite. It wasn't machine made.'"

"Yeah, so?" He licked his dry lips. The arrogance had gone out of his tone.

"Some of the other entertainers said you weren't as drunk as you pretended to be. You have no alibi. We believe you came back and took Stevana's body out of her coffin, replaced it with the body of Delores Wilkins, and stole her jewelry."

"Look, I don't know why you're rehashing all this stuff. You have no proof I did anything illegal."

"Are you sure you want to stick with that story? Why not help yourself? Admit your guilt. It will look better for you when the prosecutor looks over your case."

The muscles tightened on his face, sharpening his features. He studied her face as though trying to read it, then he looked at Amanda who stared back with a steely gaze. He called her bluff. "You have no evidence."

"We have a very reliable witness. Your partner in crime. Taron Seminov. He confessed to everything."

Sweat broke out on his upper lip. But he said nothing, just glared.

"Would you like to comment?"

Silence.

"Why was he waiting outside the mortuary that night?"

Silence.

"How did he know about the jewelry, Mr. Biggs?"

Silence.

Sidney needed to break the logjam before he asked for a lawyer. "Look, I want to help you, Mr. Biggs. But you need to talk to me. Taron said you came up with the whole plan all on your own. Right now, the charges against you are stacking up. Abuse of two dead bodies and grand larceny will be added. Are you going to take the whole rap?"

Suddenly, his face screwed up with anger, and he hissed, "Fucking

Taron. I should have known I couldn't trust him. He's the one who let the whole thing get out of hand."

That certainly sounded like an admission of guilt. "Tell us how the whole thing came about."

"Look, the plan was simple; just sneak into the mortuary, grab the old lady, cut off the jewelry in the van, return her to the coffin. A simple, foolproof operation. No one would ever have been the wiser. I didn't know he'd have that dead woman in the van!" His eyes widened so that the whites showed all around. "You can imagine my shock."

"Did you ask why he had a dead body?"

"Taron is a scary guy. To be honest, I didn't want to know. I got caught up in something twisted that I never saw coming. It was his idea to swap the bodies. We put the younger woman in the old lady's coffin, then we were stuck with the old lady. Taron said we should bury her in the forest. We drove into the woods and opened the back of the van. Then we found out her diamond necklace was gone. The whole thing went from bad to worse to a total nightmare. Someone had seen us. Had taken the necklace. May have alerted the cops."

"So, at that point, you wanted to leave Mrs. Thornburg by the side of the road."

"Yeah, I wasn't thinking straight. I was freaked. I just wanted to end the whole thing. But Taron remained cool and calm. He wanted the emerald ring. He sliced it off her finger, then he threw her body over his shoulder and disappeared. I don't know what he did with it ...." His voice trailed off and he stared at her with a look of desperation. "I got dragged into the whole thing by Taron. He's the real criminal here, not me."

"But it was your idea to steal the jewelry in the first place."

Bigg's face flushed crimson from his collar to his hairline. "Yeah, bad mistake. But the old lady was dead, for god's sake. She sure didn't need to be buried with all that jewelry."

"Where's the emerald ring?"

"Taron's holding on to it. He said it's too hot to sell right now. He was going to wait, sell it in another state."

"Anything you want to add to your statement?"

He shook his head.

"Thank you, Mr. Biggs. We appreciate your cooperation."

"You'll talk to the prosecutor, right, and tell him I was only involved with the theft?"

"Your story is very compelling. I'm sure the prosecutor will consider all the facts. A lawyer will be assigned at your arraignment tomorrow morning Today you'll be transferred to the county jail. You'll be able to get cleaned up."

He nodded.

Sidney released a long slow breath. She caught Amanda's eye and nodded slightly. They got their confession. Their part was done. The final outcome for these criminals would be hashed out in plea deals or in court The lives of everyone in the department could return to normal.

"Amanda, please take Mr. Biggs to a holding cell."

CHAPTER FORTY-FOUR

IT WAS 4:30 P.M. and the late afternoon shadows were lengthening across the landscape when Sidney pulled up at David's house. She opened the front door, and feeling playful, walked toward the living room calling out, "Honey, I'm home …."

A male voice responded, singing:

> *"The car won't start, it's falling apart*
> *I was late for work and the boss got smart."*

It was Dillon, singing Shania Twain's hit single "Honey, I'm home." He came out of the kitchen laughing, wearing sweats, carrying a backpack over one shoulder, and then he continued,

> *"My panty line shows, got a run in my hose*
> *My hair went flat, man I hate that."*

Sidney laughed with him. "Very funny."

"Dad's waiting on the boat. I got basketball practice." His grin disappeared and he looked solemn for a moment. "I never thanked you for everything you did for me. Getting me out of that tight jam with the Krall brothers."

"I think you learned your lesson, Dillon. You didn't need more punishment. How's the shoulder, by the way?"

"It's much better. Don't worry, I won't play as aggressively tonight as I usually do." He pecked her on the cheek and shot her a wicked grin as he brushed past her. "You two behave now."

"Yeah, we'll be sure to do that." She followed him outside as he ran down the steps and hopped into David's BMW, then revved up the engine and disappeared down the driveway. It was good to see that Dillon had recovered from his traumatic skirmish with the law and was back to his good-natured self.

The sleek white sailboat was at the end of the dock, standing out against the deepening blue twilight. She spotted David on deck, rigging the lines.

Tiny white lights accentuated the masts and cabin, setting a romantic tone. *Perfect, they were going out on the water.* They loved to anchor in the middle of the lake, bobbing on the currents, watching the sun go down. It was its own special kind of therapy.

She walked to the end of the dock and David smiled at her from across the bow. "Hop on board." He wore jeans and a denim work shirt and his dark hair was tousled from the wind. His eyes were bright in his tanned face. She felt a little tingle in her stomach. *It should be illegal for a man to look so attractive without any effort.*

"Hey, beautiful," he said softly, pulling her close. His eyes crinkled at the corners and a smile flickered on his mouth. "Finally, I've got you all to myself. I was beginning to think I was going to have to abduct you to get you alone." They kissed, long and sweet, and she felt the pleasurable stirrings of desire. She stroked his back, feeling the lean muscles under his shirt.

"Let's get out on the water," he said. "Then we can relax. I brought dinner."

Of course, he did. David took care of everything when they were together, took care of her every little need. She knew what he meant by relaxing. A lot of sexual yearning had built up during their long absence from each other. Out on the water they had quiet, privacy, and the gentle rhythm of the boat moving with the currents. The perfect setting for making love in the cozy confines of the cabin.

***

They lay quietly together, saying nothing for quite some time. He liked to hold her in his arms after lovemaking, so that her back curled neatly into his chest. His fingertips moved lightly over her forearms and hands, and she could feel his chest rise and fall with each breath. She was lying in a blissful state between sleep and consciousness when his voice infiltrated and pulled her to the surface. "Hungry?"

"I could eat."

Sunset was at its peak when they went up on deck, and a chill lay over the water. They were now bundled in down jackets. Sidney felt they were suspended in time in a world of crimson and gold where water blended into sky. They ate roasted chicken, asparagus, and scalloped potatoes, complimented by a delicious dry Riesling. A sense of peace ebbed around her and through her. *Ah, this was heaven.* She met the brown eyes she'd lost herself in so many times, and said gently, "Thank you."

"For what? This picnic?"

"For everything you do. For giving me an escape from the madness of policing."

"You navigate policing like a hound with a sixth sense." He shook his head and smiled. "What you did this last week, Sidney, for this community, is nothing short of miraculous. Two dozen drug dealers and dog abusers arrested. The Russian, the clown, and the morticians, arrested. Solved a mysterious death and the theft of a body. You got Dillon's charges dropped." He lifted his hand and his thumb brushed her cheek. "You do all the gymnastics. All I do is give you a soft place to land."

"Well, I had a lot of help. Several departments. But when you lump it all together like that, I guess I am pretty amazing."

They both laughed.

He lifted his glass and they toasted. "Yes, you are."

CHAPTER FORTY-FIVE

ONE WEEK LATER

RAFE GAVE UP his long-held belief that all cops were corrupt. Chief Becker had been right about the justice system being fair, at least in his case. He had entered the courtroom weighed down by an ominous feeling of dread, but to his astonishment, the Wellspring Community Church rallied around him in his time of need. One after the other, members stepped forward at his court hearing and vouched for him, with Pastor John and Mr. Hiroko being his most ardent supporters. Stories of his compassionate work with the homeless at the church and with animals at the sanctuary were related to the judge. In addition, he had kept up his grades and he'd been a good role model for the younger boys. His public defender persuasively argued that his recent behavior was wildly out of the norm, and he had acted out of extreme emotional duress due to the violent death of a dear friend. Rafe was sentenced to a year in jail, but his sentence was suspended, with a five-year probation period and 500 hours of community service. If he reoffended during that time, the sentence would be reimposed, plus the additional sentence he got for the new offense. Rafe was released into the custody of Pastor John. He would do community service at the church and sanctuary, so basically his life would go on as it had before his arrest, only with regular visits to his probation officer.

Rafe drew in a deep breath, his mind flicking over the events of the day. A bit overwhelmed, he realized that he had a vast network of friends and a "chosen family" that cared about him. He expressed his feelings to Pastor John while the two were driving back to the church. "I can't believe how good everyone here has been to me, even though I've caused so much trouble. I'm going to show everyone I've changed, that they can trust me."

"No one ever doubted you, Rafe. We never lost faith in you." Then the pastor asked how he was faring emotionally now that the facts surrounding Delores's death had surfaced.

While he thought about how to answer that, Rafe pulled on the cuffs of his navy-blue suit. It had come from the storeroom of donated clothes at the church, and it was too snug in many places. He couldn't wait to get back into his jeans and t-shirt. "In all honesty, Pastor John, for a while all I felt was anger. It was a relief to find out that Delores wasn't murdered after all, but I'm still dealing with how the Hoffmans treated her. Not reporting her death. Stealing her kidneys. Then wanting to bury her in the woods like a piece of trash." A surge of anger threatened to rear up, but he managed to suppress it. "Lately though, feelings of gratitude are seeping into my feelings of grief. I'm grateful for so many things. Not going to jail. Having a safe place to live. Having the other boys as family …." He cleared his throat. He'd never expressed his gratitude to the pastor in words before. "And it's all because of you. When I first came to the church, I felt like the whole world was against me. I didn't trust anyone. But you took me in when no foster family would have me." Feeling a little choked up, he cleared his throat again. "You're the best man I've ever known."

The pastor glanced at him and the warmth in his brown eyes said everything. "You've been a blessing to me, too, son. All of you boys have been a beautiful blessing."

They sat in silence for a while, then the pastor asked about his nightmares.

"The nightmares about Delores don't come as often as they used to."

"Trauma was taking up all of the space inside you," Pastor John said gently. "Now you're letting it go."

"I still dream about her. But when I wake up, I feel other things, too. I remember the good times we spent together. Then I feel guilty, like I'm moving on, forgetting her."

"Rafe, it's okay to feel something other than sadness. Delores wouldn't want you to forget her, but she wouldn't want you to suffer, either. She'd want you to live your life to the fullest. In time, you'll learn to store memories of her in a safe place, instead of them constantly free-floating in your mind. Try something for me. Every time you laugh, picture Delores laughing with you."

"Will do." He was grateful that the pastor never judged. He listened. He empathized. He always said the right thing. "I did picture her looking down at her funeral and laughing. I'm glad they let her keep Stevana's expensive coffin. She deserved that." Rafe smiled, remembering. The funeral had been a celebration. An event. The congregation had filled the church. Pastor John gave a beautiful eulogy. Cooper played a piano solo. Garret sang with the choir. Many people, including Rafe, got up and told stories of how Delores touched their lives. The officers from the Garnerville Police Department, wearing their dress blues, helped carry the coffin to and from the hearse.

Chief Becker's sister, Selena, was there, too, sitting in the front pew with the boys. Somehow, Selena filled the void left behind by Delores. Cooper and Joey sat nestled on each side of her, like a pair of bookends. At the graveyard, everyone tossed roses onto the casket, except Joey, who pulled a baggie from a pocket, and sprinkled roasted crickets over it. Rafe came to understand that Delores had not been invisible after all. Her acts of kindness had spread to every corner of the community.

"Selena invited you boys over for an afternoon at Ann's farm tomorrow," the pastor said, pulling into the lot behind the church. "Garret said you weren't planning on going. Why is that?"

"Because Dillon and his dad will be there. I don't think either of them wants to see me. Dillon got arrested because of me." Rafe felt his face warm with shame. His reckless behavior had put a good friend through hell and pushed him out of his life.

"You live in the same town. You go to the same school as Dillon. You can't dodge them forever. They're reasonable people, Rafe. Maybe use it as a time to express your regrets."

Rafe blew out a breath. *Why did life have to be so hard?* "I'll think about it, Pastor John."

CHAPTER FORTY-SIX

THE WHOOPS AND LAUGHTER of the boys, who were playing Cornhole, drifted across the lawn to the adults sitting at the table on Ann's patio—Selena and Granger, David and Sidney, and Ann and Miko. To Selena, there was no purer sound than a child's laughter, carefree, unburdened by the difficulties of life — especially these kids who had experienced debilitating trauma. It was a sunny autumn day here at Ann's farm, which was a little piece of paradise. The boys felt safe, all their needs provided for by caring adults.

The only glitch happened earlier when Rafe arrived at the same time as Dillon and David. From a window, Selena watched them standing together in the driveway. She saw Rafe's posture tense and his face turn red. There was an exchange of words, back and forth, then David affectionately slapped the boy on the back. Dillon and Rafe shook hands, smiling warily, followed by a few moments of awkwardness, then they walked together to the patio. Selena breathed a sigh of relief. Now, three hours later, the two teens were supervising the younger boys as though there had never been any ill-will between them.

It had been an active afternoon. The boys were intensely curious and wanted to know everything about Ann's farm. They had run through the fields that stretched down to the lakeshore and brought in the last of the pumpkins, which now decorated the patio. Ann and Selena conducted a tour of the beehives and the gabled red barn where their organic products were made. There was the laboratory kitchen where they experimented with recipes, the four-gallon stainless steel vats used to melt beeswax for candles, the distillery equipment that reduced hundreds of pounds of flowers into essential oils, and the rows of herbs and flowers suspended on drying racks. Their beautifully packaged products, flavored vinegars and honeys, essential oils, and scented candles lined the shelves.

Then the mouthwatering smell of chicken lured everyone back to the patio where Granger stood over the smoking grill. In addition to chicken, there were biscuits, corn, sweet potatoes, salad, and homemade pumpkin pie for dessert. The mood was festive and light-hearted, and everyone ate heartily.

"So, how's work at the rescue ranch these days?" Selena asked the boys.

"It's fun," Cooper said. "I like to hug the bunnies."

"We have a blind pony and a pig that are best friends," Garrett said. "The pig guides her around the ranch. A goat and a dog are best friends, too. Mr. Hiroko said they have to be adopted together."

"That's really sweet," Selena said.

"The funniest story is about the eagle they rescued a few months ago. He thinks he's a mom," Rafe said. "He built a nest and sat on a rock for a few days, trying to hatch it. He was very protective of it. He wouldn't leave, even to eat."

Everyone laughed.

"Did it hatch?' Granger asked.

Again, everyone laughed, and Rafe continued. "Then an eaglet was rescued and put into his pen. He turned into mother of the year, feeding it the bits of fish we put into his cage."

"Another sweet story," Selena said.

"'Hope is the thing with feathers,' Emily Dickenson wrote," David said.

"The ranch is a great place to learn about animals," Ann said. "I heard you and Arthur have a special relationship, Joey."

"Yeah. He's my spirit animal. I was hoping he'd be here today. But I guess he's with Jezebel."

"She's his girlfriend," Cooper said. "He spends a lot of time hanging around her cage. Mr. Hiroko said he'll let Jezebel out to hop around the ranch once her wing is mended. But she'll never fly again."

After lunch, the boys moved out on the lawn to play Cornhole, and the adults watched from a distance, drinking wine and relaxing. After a while, the laughter quieted, and the boys marched back to the patio. "Ann," Dillon said. "When are we going out on the lake? It's starting to get dark."

"Now is a good time." Ann was a pretty woman with a slender build, blue eyes, and dark hair streaked with grey.

"I'll go with you," Miko said, rising from his chair. He was Ann's boyfriend, and his fragrant apple orchard bordered her farm.

The four remaining adults watched the boat glide out into the gold-colored water that was as smooth as glass. The chattering and laughter faded as they chugged deeper onto the lake.

David and Sidney left to walk along the lakeshore, his arm draped across her shoulder. Selena remained at the table with Granger, sipping wine. His strong body relaxed next to hers, his knee grazing her thigh. His face looked tan and his blue eyes caught a ray of golden light. A nice layer of stubble accentuated his strong jaw. Selena was flushed with warm affection. He ran a hand down her arm from her shoulder to her wrist. Her heart stuttered a little. It was a small, sweet gesture, and his touch felt good.

"What do you say we head back to your place?" he said softly.

Sidney was staying at David's. They'd have the house to themselves. "I was just waiting for you to ask."

Also By Linda Berry:

THE DEAD CHILL

Book Two of the Sidney Becker Mysteries

CHAPTER ONE

HE ALWAYS CAME at night. A soft, creeping terror surfaced in that realm between sleep and consciousness, startling Selena awake. She sensed the man's presence in the room like a force field, standing in the deep shadows, watching. In one smooth, practiced movement, her fingers gripped the hilt of the Beretta M9 under her spare pillow and aimed. She switched on the light. The shadows disappeared. The room was empty. The only sound was her labored breathing. Wide-eyed, she sat trembling until her pulse quieted, then she lowered the gun.

This behavior was irrational. The man who viciously attacked her four weeks ago was locked in a cage in Jackson County Jail. Yet his presence never faded. His shadow lurked on the fringe of her vision. His smell lingered. She felt his sour breath on her face, even when she was surrounded by students in her yoga class or barricaded here at home. The new state-of-the-art security system didn't vanquish ghosts.

Hearing footsteps scuff the hardwood floor outside her bedroom, Selena slid the pistol back under the pillow. The door opened and her sister appeared. Sidney's evening shift as Garnerville's police chief had just ended at midnight.

"You okay?" Dressed in her uniform with her hair tightly knotted at the back of her neck, Sidney possessed an aura of authority and toughness. She was born to be a cop. Duty and service were encoded in her DNA—passed down from their dad—Garnerville's Police Chief for twenty years while they were growing up. "I saw your light come on."

Selena swallowed and found her voice, which sounded calmer than she felt. "Just the usual mind-bending nightmare."

Sidney's expression softened. "Bad dreams fade with time." She was the voice of experience. A former homicide detective in Oakland, California, she had a decade's worth of grisly crime scenes embedded in her psyche. "Want some company?"

"Only if you need to talk about work."

"Nope. Uneventful. All the criminals took the day off."

"It's the snow," Selena said soberly. "Everyone's hibernating. Dad used to say a crime lull was the quiet before the storm."

"Yeah, he did." Sidney smiled. "No doubt the bad guys are gearing up for Armageddon." She glanced toward the window. "More of the fluffy white stuff is coming down as we speak. We'll have another four inches by morning."

Selena followed her gaze. The wind-driven flakes slanting past the glass were on a mission to create more havoc on the roads. "Yippie. More shoveling."

"Good exercise. I won't have to go to the gym."

Selena was momentarily struck by how much Sidney resembled their father. Tall and athletic, she had his strong nose and chin and hazel eyes. Her full mouth softened her features. Though not pretty in a traditional sense, Sidney had an indefinable appeal that attracted men, and, more importantly, commanded respect.

Sidney tugged the tie from her ponytail and her wavy, auburn hair tumbled around her shoulders. The aura of toughness all but vanished. "Want a cup of chamomile tea?"

"Don't worry about me, Sid. I'm okay." Selena settled back under her covers and turned off the light. "Get some rest. You'll need it for the crime spree tomorrow."

Her sister laughed as she backed out of the room.

Feeling safer with her sister home, Selena ruminated on the irony of their current circumstances. After years of separation, she and Sidney had completed a cycle of marriage and boyfriends and career pivots and made their way back to each other. With their father dead and their mother in a memory care center—early onset Alzheimer's—she and Sidney now lived as roommates in their childhood home. When they were kids, Sidney had been Selena's protector, patching scraped knees and warding off bullies. That fierce instinct still burned strong. If Sidney wasn't a highly skilled detective, and if she hadn't arrived in the woods at the precise moment she did, Selena would be dead. There was no way she could ever repay that debt.

CHAPTER TWO

SELENA'S SHOULDER MUSCLES burned with tension as her mare groped for solid footing on the icy trail. Granger Wyatt rode a horse length ahead, the collar of his sheepskin jacket flipped up, western hat pulled low, his strong body swaying with the rhythm of his gelding. The horses trod on a narrow trail snaking through the Sacamoosh Forest, their breath steaming in the crisp mountain air. The interior world was blanketed in white, and hillocks and snowdrifts sparkled in the filtered light. But the serene beauty didn't ease Selena's anxiety. The pungent smell of juniper was suffocating.

Granger headed into the higher elevation through towering ponderosa pine and Douglas fir. The mare snorted, her ears flicking forward and backward, listening. Picking up signals of danger? Selena took comfort in the holstered handgun under her down jacket within easy reach. Granger carried his own sidearm, adding another layer of security. At her request, he'd also shoved a shotgun into the scabbard on his saddle. A former Marine with combat experience, and now one of four officers in her sister's small police department, he was a formidable bodyguard.

A wedge of ice fell from a branch and startled her horse into a sidestep off the trail. Selena gasped. The familiar terror threatened to surface. With a shiver of revulsion, she fought it back down and firmly guided her mare back on course.

Granger stopped where the trail opened to a wide meadow and glanced back, waiting for her dapple-gray mare to catch up to his chestnut bay. He was all-American handsome with an angular face, square chin, and contagious smile. Raised on a cattle ranch just a few miles away, he had a country boy's down-to-earth sensibility and a cop's mental toughness. His brow furrowed as her horse pulled alongside his. "You okay?"

Selena realized her face had tightened into a mask. She cracked a smile. "Yes. Fine."

She wasn't fine. Since her attack, she felt disembodied, as though she had lost her bearings, and she was living a life that belonged to someone else. Out here in the forest, she felt even more adrift. "I'm a little nervous, that's all. Being back in the woods …."

Granger's eyes were on her, reading her emotions with his cop's sixth sense. He frowned, and she detected a twinge of guilt in the way he clenched and unclenched his jaw.

"I shouldn't have brought you out here. It's too soon."

"I made the decision to come, Granger. Garnerville is surrounded by forest. I can't hide in town forever. I need to face my demons."

His frown deepened.

"Really. This is good for me." She took a deep breath, trying to reassure herself, as well as him. A month had passed. Selena should be moving on, putting the trauma behind her, but she rarely left home except to work. Lounging on the couch in sweats, watching Hallmark movies with her four cats, she had lost all sense of time, and her connection to a social life.

Granger routinely stopped by to check on her. It never took much persuasion for him to settle next to her and share a bowl of popcorn. Though he hid it well, watching fluffy movies with happy endings must have been stupefying. Last night, he gently encouraged her to step out of her safety zone, come out to the family ranch, and partake in a big country brunch with his parents and brother. After stuffing herself and enjoying the feeling of being insulated within a close-knit family, she felt a bit like her old self. On a whim, she and Granger saddled two quarter horses and set out to explore this forest wonderland. And now, here she was, quaking in her saddle.

Selena took in the wide, sprawling meadow, open in every direction, and sighed her relief. Here, no one could sneak up on her. Cyclists, hikers, and equestrians used this trail in the summer, and cross-country skiers in the winter, but today no one was in sight. Cascading water drew her attention to the creek winding through the snow. Beneath the partially frozen surface the current moved with force and purpose. In some areas, the water was so still she could see the fine grains of sand at the bottom. "This is Whilamut Creek," she said, to lighten the mood. "Whilamut is Kalapuyan. It means 'where the water ripples and runs fast'. Kalapuya people once occupied this entire territory between the Cascades and the Calapooya Mountains."

"Some still live here. There's a small Native American community down the road a couple miles."

She nodded. "On the shore of Nenámooks Lake. One of my friends from high school lived there." The sun spilled out from behind a cloud and she raised a hand to block the glare. "She moved a decade ago. I haven't been out there since."

"I know some of the villagers," Granger said. "Visit regularly."

"To keep the peace?"

"Mostly to visit a friend. Tommy Chetwoot."

"The healer."

He tipped up the brim of his hat. His eyes, reflecting the sun, were exceptionally clear, like blue glass washed up on the beach. "Guess just about everyone in town knows of Tommy."

"And his grandmother, the medicine woman. I've never seen her, but my friend told me she's scary, and has strange powers. Supposedly, she's raised people from the dead."

"Not sure about the scary part." Granger smiled. "Paramedics raise people from the dead every day. But she's definitely not sociable. I caught a glimpse of her once. She's small, bent over, eyes black as obsidian, white hair streaming down her back. Could be eighty, or a hundred. Hard to say. I've never seen anyone so withered. Tommy learned everything about healing from her."

"Do you see Tommy to get help for your dad?" she asked gently. Granger's father suffered from Parkinson's disease. Once a stalwart pillar of the community, he'd gradually retreated from his involvement in the town's civic affairs.

"Yeah." Granger's mouth tightened for a moment. "He makes Dad an herbal concoction that eases the pain."

"Your dad looked fine this morning."

"He has good days and bad. Tommy's potion isn't a cure-all. Dad's still getting worse every year."

"I'm so sorry." A tremor of sadness passed through her as she thought of her mother, now living among strangers in the memory care center. "I'd love to talk to Tommy."

Granger gave her a long, steady stare, seeming to assess her motives.

"I know the villagers don't like outsiders rambling in without an invitation, but maybe he can help my mom."

He nodded, understanding. "I'll talk to him. See if I can bring you next time."

She smiled her thanks.

He gestured with a jut of his chin. "There's a nice view from that bridge up ahead."

They tethered the horses to a timbered post and crunched through the snow to the middle of the bridge. To the west, the corridor of water meandered through the meadow and disappeared into the forest. Far below to the east, bloated gray clouds hung over their small town, nestled in the forested hills.

"A snowstorm's sweeping in," Granger said, staring straight up the mountain. He stood close, his arm brushing hers. "It's already snowing up on top."

Though barricaded in thick jackets, she felt the warmth of his presence, his instinct to protect her. "It feels good to be back on a horse," she said. "I used to ride all the time. It's been a while, though. A couple years."

"We'll have to remedy that." He turned, his face close to hers. Close enough to kiss. Despite the cold, Selena's cheeks warmed. She and Granger had been spending a fair amount of time together and his romantic intentions were clear. He made her knees go weak a little, but she had kept him at arm's length. After the poor choice she'd made in her husband of ten years, and still feeling the aftershocks of their divorce, falling into a new relationship was a frightening proposition. She needed to take her time and make sure this was a good move, not another dead-end street. Before she lost her resolve and kissed him, Selena crossed the bridge to the opposite rail.

In just a few minutes the gauzy white clouds had taken on a harder, darker sheen. As if fleeing the scene, a flock of geese cut a lopsided wedge through the sky.

"The storm's moving in pretty fast," Ganger said, joining her. "We better head back."

Nodding, Selena lowered her gaze to the creek. The wind had cleared patches of snow from the frozen surface, revealing fast-moving water underneath. A stain of scarlet about the size of a maple leaf appeared near the bank. "Hmmm," she asked. "Wonder what that is."

They moved to the end of the bridge to get a better look. The wind excavated more snow and the leaf turned into a knitted scarf, partially frozen beneath the surface. Under the scarf, a human hand was exposed. A hand. Fingers spread wide.

Selena stood paralyzed; her eyes fixed to the spot. The wind continued its work, revealing the cuff of a blue jacket.

Granger lurched into motion and eased down the slippery bank, ice crackling beneath his boots. He squatted at the edge of the frozen water and his gloved hand brushed away more snow, unveiling an arm and shoulder. Then a woman's face appeared, her glazed eyes wide open. Beneath her body, long black hair swirled with the movement of the water. The red marks on her throat told a grim story. Someone had killed this woman, placed her body in this frozen creek, and abandoned her.

The realization struck Selena with physical force. Her eyes fluttered, then closed. When she looked again, the woman's blank face still stared up at her.

Granger climbed up the bank to his horse, pulled a satellite phone from a saddle pocket, and punched in some numbers. His urgent voice enunciated clearly, relaying the details of the gruesome discovery. He ended the call and made another. This was a man who knew how to handle an emergency, who knew how to react and stay calm. Selena stood motionless, mirroring the dead woman entombed in ice, unable to pull her gaze from the unseeing stare.

Buy THE DEAD CHILL at:

https://www.amazon.com/gp/product/B07R7XT411

ABOUT THE AUTHOR

Linda was one of five children raised in a military family that traveled the U.S. and Europe. Raised around military personnel, she has great appreciation for the men and women in uniform who protect our freedom, including first responders, who run toward danger while others run away. Linda had a twenty-five-year career as an award-winning copywriter and art director in Los Angeles and the San Francisco Bay Area. She now devotes her time to writing fast-paced mysteries, most notably the Sidney Becker series. An avid gardener, nature and animal lover, she currently lives in Virginia with her husband and a very spoiled and adorable miniature poodle.

To learn of new releases and discounts,
add your name to Linda's mailing list at:

https://www.lindaberry.net

Made in the USA
Middletown, DE
28 December 2024

68332565R00163